THE
PARAGON
JUNK

∾

BLAIR MacKENZIE BLAKE

THE PARAGON JUNK
Copyright © 2020 by Blair MacKenzie Blake

Cover layout by Joseph Nagy. Typesetting and editing by Greg Taylor.

ISBN: 978-0-6452094-0-2

TREASURIA PUBLISHING

CONTENTS

"You are guardian of a treasure,
Oh, just like a sleeping serpent
And you shall see, I shall make you
Spin around like that sleeping snake.
Listen to me."

- RUMI

CHAPTER I
ABANDONDERO

That was no way to begin my new life. But at least I knew why it was called the Sandman Inn. Obviously, the chain's namesake crept into my room sometime during the night and sprinkled magical sand into my eyes as my head lay cradled on a lumpy pillow. Dried rheum was the telltale sign. When I woke up to the distorted crowing of the motel's novelty rooster alarm clock, my lids were practically glued shut with the gritty stuff. I was still picking the gunk out an hour later while opening a dinky box of Fruit Loops cereal.

Taking advantage of the complimentary grab-and-go breakfast, I passed on the strawberry yogurt that probably tasted like flavored spackle and grabbed a gas station pastry with none of the advertised free Krispy Kremes left in the basket. Glancing about the lobby, I pocketed a S'mores Pop-Tart for my Christmas dessert.

Actually, the budget lodging in the jewel of Nye County was the most comfortable digs that I had slept in for quite a while. Sure, it smelled like greasy hair, cheap cologne and some funk that I couldn't identify (sweaty bowling shoes?), but no cockroaches scurried across the mildewed linoleum and the person next door wasn't an ambitious meth dealer. Having spent several nights cramped in a Greyhound without earplugs, I was perfectly content to stare at the vinyl wallpapers' shades of salmon, turquoise and marigold until the incessant hum of the mini-fridge lulled me to sleep. The worst part was cheap-o toilet paper and, yes, the Sandman's Technicolor mischief.

How did the lyrics to that song go? Something about turning on a magic beam and bringing a dream… Dream? If it wasn't the antics of the mythological sneak, what involuntary neurobiology was responsible for the green madness that unfolded in my brain with startling clarity? And why had the dramatic flourishing of a horticulturist's paradise turned into a full-blown nightmare that caused me to shriek like a three-year-old girl?

Despite the fact that my past was a blank canvas, I could recall the more disturbing elements of the dream that began innocently enough with my walking down the aisle of a retail nursery similar to any Wal-Mart Garden Center where one buys the obligatory potted plant as a housewarming gift. While looking for an orchid or something, at some point I must have taken one hell of a wrong turn. Even though no one cued the *Twilight Zone* motif, in the incongruity of the dreamshift, I suddenly found myself floating through a labyrinth of botanical curiosities being cultivated inside large spherical terrariums within an ultramodern hydroponics chamber. Beneath eerily diffused golden beams, stunning clusters of leaves sprouted from dangling root systems suspended in the globes' prismatic shimmer.

Moving through the profusion of constantly morphing greenery, my senses were further overwhelmed by the chimerical nature of growth cascading from towering planter trellises. Choked by heady vegetative perfumes, I continued through the disorienting maze of burgeoning enigmas until I detected a flash of movement that was at variance with the synchronized activity of variegated flora glimmering behind translucent panes on sizable domed enclosures.

What at first appeared to be the faint pink mosaic of scales on a large albino snake uncoiling swiftly amid the of bioluminescent foliage, I was shocked to realize was actually the tapered face of a vaguely humanoid figure wearing a cryptic bodysuit that absorbed the fractaling inflorescence. Floating out from the fiery blossoms in the sterilized module, the spindly oddity set down a complex garden tool and glided towards me with the graceful fluidity of a phantasmic ballet. As I stood there paralyzed by the serpentine nature of its pallid, delicate features, the glistening fixity of lidless golden eyes focused upon my growing alarm.

"Watch the dream."

The subvocal impression had a pleasing tonality, but that still didn't keep me from fighting to wake up. As bizarre as the nursery technician looked (wearing a protective suit with amber-tinted goggles, I tried to rationalize), the dream became even more fantastic.

A pale slender finger pointed to an espaliered tree that stood out from the fantastic proliferation of energetic growth. Placed against its trellised branches was an intricately detailed ladder whose twisted golden rungs of metallic glass sparkled with a peculiar quality that reflected the garden's synthetic light source. What appeared next I seemed to view with exceptional clarity, as if the result of some invisible magnifying circle that positioned itself on the tree. This was an unrecognizable species of fruit whose general shape was like an apple, but which had a glossy bluish-purple skin. While slowly approaching the lustrous spiral steps, I looked down at my feet and saw that I was suspended in an unmarked cerulean void. My vertiginous levitation caused me to reach for the ladder, which was beyond my grasp. When the floating blueness beneath me began to darken enough that I could discern the aqueous globe of the earth in the distance, I started flailing my arms until the expected free-fall jolted me awake.

Did the freaky imagery offer a clue to the event that had erased my past? Or was the enlarged piece of fruit just trying to tell me to toss some blueberries into adult bran flakes instead of pouring Toucan Sam's tropical colored marshmallows down my throat? Nope, it was just day residue. The waking mind's leftover garbage. A cleansing process for firing neurons that temporarily shook up its owner, thank you. Not some fortune cookie for the weak minded or symbolic message to be analyzed. I finished my black coffee and brushed some sugar ants off what remained of the stale Tastykake.

Stepping into the bright sunlight with my duffle bag, the first thing I saw after rubbing the last sleep from my eyes was 'Jesus' walking around in patches of desert scrub near the parking lot. Wearing a dingy yellow robe, his bronzed features, epic beard and shoulder-length dark brown hair might have caused some of the more devout Pahrumpites to do a double take had his Jerusalem cruisers not been Birkenstocks.

Watching him pick up a discarded Styrofoam cup, I debated whether he was an eco-warrior or religious nut job doing public penance. Both of these notions were quickly put to an end when he tossed the cup back onto the ground and continued to search for something in stretches of sand that were speckled with litter.

"When I find it I'll tell the world!" he shouted to the unclouded sky. "So, you better hope I don't," his voice trailed off while bending over an empty Funyuns bag snagged on a mesquite bush.

"You looking for the Devil's Hole?" a strident voice uttered.

The elderly fellow who shouted this was seated in a lawn chair placed in front of a rusty gold Econovan. Wearing glinting aviator's sunglasses beneath a Terrible's Roadhouse Casino cap, he gestured to an old matte black dune buggy that was angled in the prickly chaparral.

"Excuse me?" I responded after being surprised to see that 'Jesus' was no longer anywhere to be seen. Perhaps he had chased after the crumpled aluminum wrapper that a gust of wind sent tumbling across the dusty asphalt.

"You the one that called about my dune buggy?"

"No sir."

While stroking a neatly trimmed silver beard on a face that was ruddy from exposure, he rose from his chair in a Calbela's hunting jacket. After finding another plastic cup, he offered me some of the cloudy liquid in a large bottle of Sprite Zero.

"Well, have some Nascar lemonade anyway. Merry Christmas, if that's all right with you. It was Charlie's. Part of the Family's Helter Skelter battalion. Check out the machine gun mount. It's an air-cooled Porsche and it's priced to sell before I stick her on eBay."

"A little early for me, but Season's Greetings to you as well. You said it was Charlie's?"

I noticed that the buggy had been murdered out. Not just the shortened frame and roll bar tubing, but even the furs on the seats had been painted black. Most likely, it belonged to the younger guy seated next to him with the stringy-haired mullet and "Abducted Cattle Jerky" tee that was too big for his gaunt frame. He might have been a meth head, I thought, because of his unsteady bloodshot eyes, bad skin and constant fidgeting with a broken pair of pruning shears. If he was a tweaker, at least he was in scrapper heaven.

"Manson used a fleet like this – though most were VW skeletons, not chopped 356s – while looking for a bottomless portal in the Amargosa Valley. He was gonna slide down into hell's mouth on a special golden rope."

"Why?" I asked.

"Chocolate syrup river, I reckon," he said without smirking.

His friend lit a cigarette even though he already had one going and fixed his unhealthy gaze on me.

"It was the mind stalkers that were fucking with Charlie," twisty face rasped after taking a drag from one of his smokes. "Psychotic gnomes that live under us in networks of caverns. They're degenerate robots called deros that were abandoned thousands of years ago by the elder gods who left the sun's poisoned rays in their giant space-liners. They cause constant mayhem to us surface dwellers with their thought augmenters. Ever ask yourself why Hitler gassed oodles of Jews or Lee Harvey Oswald shot that guy in the Beatles? What about the Challenger smashup... Bin Laden... and Subway's freakin' Fogleby?"

As he started talking faster, the tone of his voice changed.

"They can even mess with you when you're asleep by invading dreams with their ray-science. They're always tampering with shit, the abandondero are, like when someone slips on a banana peel and breaks their neck. Little tykes pulling wings off flies or cooking ants under a magnifying glass – these urges come from the dero. They even sabotaged the Bible a while back. You ever heard of King James Sinner's Bible where it says thou shalt commit adultery?"

With the end of one of the cigarettes about to burn his fingers, he began looking for a place to crush it out, not realizing that he was standing in the world's largest ashtray.

"And what's that other part in the Sinner's Bible, Gabe?"

"I know the verse, but I ain't gonna say it. Not today, anyway," the man with the well-groomed beard chuckled while pouring himself another drink. "Okay, blah blah blah. Relax for a minute before they get you to cut your fingers off and start chewing on them like those jerky strips on that smelly rag," he said while stirring the fumy concoction, careful not to let any of the ice fall out. After taking a gulp, he glanced at me and rolled his eyes.

"If brains were gas, his ass wouldn't have enough to get a mini-bike around a Cheerio."

"Dude-bro, that's the other part! Deuteronomy," the wigger nodded. "Behold, the LORD our God hath shewed his glory and great-asse."

Grinding his teeth, the methster continued.

"All I'm saying is the brainsick trogs want to kill us meat people with their star mech. So watch out for invisible telaug rays beamed from the caverns around here. They even abduct janitors from Denny's and Mexican cleaning ladies from the hotels because they're too fuckin' stupid to know how to swing a mop in their squalid lairs."

The elderly fellow made a dismissive hand gesture while hobbling over to the dune buggy. As he kicked one of the tires, I noticed that a message had been scrawled in white paint on the rear window of the Econovan.

EXEMPT: SOVEREIGN NEUTRAL NON-COMBATANT

Beneath this a faded bumper sticker that was barely readable proclaimed:

JESUS IS COMING SOON

"You interested in the buggy?"

"I don't have a driver's license."

"Neither do I, buddy, and I ain't part of the Posse Comitatus.

Ask the sheriff lady. But as a free person that travels in conveyances, if detained, I have the right to provide UCC paperwork after I'm shown a proper Oath of Office."

Listening to the crank freak's hokum was one thing. The sovereign citizen lingo was different. I didn't want to get into a political brouhaha, especially with all the gun-toters in these parts.

"Well, I better not let the grass grow under me. I mean… well, you know what I mean."

"Don't let the sand plug your ears," he said with a fake smile. "Should you change your mind, it'll be here. Remember what the sign says… The magic of Christmas is not in his presence, but in presents."

"Shouldn't that be the other way around?" I asked with a quizzical smile.

"You didn't see the sign?" he winked. "Well, have a nice visit and don't worry about any alien dwidgets unless they're spinning a roulette wheel."

Before heading across the parking lot I wiped the smudges from my glasses and looked around for Jesus, still thinking it was odd how he had suddenly vanished.

On a street whose traffic signs were freckled with bullet holes, a couple of little girls on identical pink "Flower Princess" bicycles with lavender tires had stopped to admire the seductive blonde in a black satin babydoll on the billboard for a local brothel. In a strategy of ecclesiastical cock blocking, the Desert Bible Church had erected their own billboard directly across from it with a list of the Ten Commandments. From the expression on the face of one of the licorice whip- chewing sweeties, I imaged it was going to be hard to dissuade her when the time came to choose between cathouse greenbacks and the tips from less lucrative "Pardon my reach" jobs in the casinos, even with the fire and brimstone tactics of the ministry. Who knows, though, with the tumbling of the dice, instead of donning the fishnet and feathers of a bordello madam, she might button the power suit of a corporate executive that oversaw the knocking-shop's daily operations.

"That's their mom," a guy on a skateboard said as he tail scraped and jumped off.

When I read the church's message board, I realized why the old fellow had winked.

THE MAGIC OF CHRISTMAS IS NOT IN HIS PRESENCE BUT IN PRESENTS

It didn't seem possible that the pastor or his helper could make such a mistake. Some prankster must have switched some of letters during the night.

Though I was very much awake, it still seemed like I was negotiating the maze of a disturbing dream. With no sidewalks, a Pahrumping I went across stretches of dirt and spread out gravel as the basso thumping of distant hip-hop and screeching of a flock of grackles filled the air. Graffiti-covered storage sheds and a boarded up donut shop weren't the only eyesores. Mobile homes with cinderblock aprons dotted the harsh terrain, where ragamuffins played in a buff-tinged wasteland filled with broken appliances. Separated by dusty horse corrals and pens of ostriches, the facades of deserted stucco houses glittered in the low winter sun - all unlandscaped unless greasewood, yucca, and disemboweled vehicles counted.

"Mister, want to help us find a stork delivering a baby?" a teenage girl wearing a reindeer antlers hair loop asked me as I was about to walk by a prefab trailer onto which a series of oxidized camper shells had been cobbled together. "It's on the list for our church scavenger hunt."

"Leave the man alone," a chubby-faced guy said while seated in a dingy beige recliner.

Leaning forward, he was roasting a dozen or more charred weenies impaled on the teeth of a metal garden rake that he held over the flames of a makeshift fire pit. Behind him, on a patio of sorts, a Christmas tree had been fashioned out of various sizes of recycled tires sprayed with green Rust-Oleum.

For ornaments, the rubber evergreen was festooned with gleaming hubcaps. A large sparkplug topper would have been a nice touch, I thought, but how much Yuletide ingenuity could one expect in this untamed frontier?

While digging through a cardboard box filled with household junk, the girl grabbed the shoulder of a pregnant woman in a gaudy muumuu who was also searching through the various containers.

"I found one, Amanda!" she shouted excitedly while lifting up a pastel porcelain figurine.

"I told you there'd be one in this Padump,"

A wiry, tatted-up dude in a wide brim sun hat flicked a cigarette butt while setting a hunk of Velveeta down on a picnic table placed under a cottonwood tree with mostly dead limbs.

"That's what you needed, Tyler? You little dumbass, I could have given you a jar of Vlasics from the fridge that has a stork Groucho smoking a pickle cigar on it. Knocked up Amandas like to eat pickles with their Dairy Queen."

"Shut up, Dillon," the prego laughed while playfully tugging the back of his long flex shorts.

As I continued along the street, I amused myself by thinking that the scavenger hunt might have been part of some City Council de-cluttering program.

Now, if only I could figure out what had de-cluttered my memory? According to a battery of tests there was no structural brain damage – observable lesions or evidence of epileptic seizures - meaning that my inability to recall my past was most likely psychological in nature, the result of overwhelming stress, perhaps, similar to a repressed memory syndrome. The memories still exist, buried deep in my mind, so I was told by the specialists, and would resurface at some point either spontaneously by some trigger or aided by psychotherapy sessions. Although my amnesia was extremely profound, it was atypical in that it was oddly selective.

The information I retained made me functional. As to what got blocked out and what was held onto – that's something not fully understood about a dissociative fugue. My personal identity and life history – that's what I was hunting for, not the specific, though useless, objects in a party game.

A possible clue was in my duffle bag. This was an address in Sunnyvale, California that was written on a piece of notebook paper. So, like some person in a Hollywood cliché, that's where I was headed. The only other items placed in the bag - by who, I didn't know - was a shaving kit, a spare change of clothes and a small amount of cash that was nearly depleted from my travel expenses.

Besides not knowing my name, I didn't know how old I was. I guessed that I was in my late fifties or early sixties, but I might have been older. I had no idea if I had any children and zero recollection of any family or friends. The strangest thing about my disorder was that I wasn't really sure that I wanted to know who I was. At times I was actually excited about adopting a new identity – a puzzling reaction that I could only attribute to my uncommon condition.

Finally, I was in a more desirable area – one with a zoning ordinance. Instead of dust devils twisting across unnamed dirt roads with "No Trespassing" signs, there were paved driveways with un-dented cars shaded by purple smoke trees that divided manicured lawns in the suburban sprawl. Gone were the 4 wheelin' trails and love ranch bungalows. Animal carcasses, tattoo parlors and Lib-ertarian slogans gave way to fast food restaurants, 7-Elevens and auto parts stores whose fronts didn't look like salvage yards. There was also a place where no influencing rays of the dero were need-ed to get droves of people through the revolving glass door.

The aesthetic torture began the moment I stepped inside.

The décor inside the casino was anything but opulent. Hence, the dirt-cheap shrimp cocktails and dollar domestic drafts adver-tised on the marquee. Although the place was in need of refurbish-ment, its boldly patterned carpet was filled with clusters of modern gaming machinery. Scantily clad waitresses called for drinks to perma-tanned locals playing table games, most of them being grey-haired retirees, cowboy-hatted ranchers and trailer park alkies.

I stopped to check out some framed old photos hanging on a wall near the entrance. While looking at the sepia-toned image-ry of historic Nevada casinos, I overheard two men discussing one of the faded prints on display. They seemed to be particu-larly interested in a man that was wearing an old timers' fedora while seated with other gamblers at a smoky Faro table.

"That's our man of mystery playing Faro at the Pair-O-Dice club in Vegas in the thirties," one man told the other guy, who was busy clicking photos with his smartphone. "There's only one other known photo of Kidd."

"What's that he has in his hand?" the man taking photos asked. Leaning closer, he identified the object. "He's looking at his pocket watch – see, there's the chain."

Thirsty from my walk with the tumbleweeds, I headed to-wards a small deli, passing by carousels of flashing lights where slot zombies 'barely' missed large payouts in the jubilant cacophony of themed touchscreens.

After ordering pastrami on marbled rye and iced-tea, I looked for an empty table. With nothing available, a robust female voice caused me to turn around.

"Why don't you have a seat – if you're not a sexual predator."

Seated alone at a table was a plump middle-aged woman with a raven bob that showed tints of blue. Both of her arms were covered with colorful ink that stood out against a studded black tank top whose wide straps fit tightly against her broad shoulders.

"We can share the table?" I asked.

"Affirmative."

She smiled while picking her teeth to make sure a sliver of romaine wasn't stuck there.

"To tell the truth, I wouldn't know if I was a sexual predator… or a serial killer for that matter… as I'm dealing with amnesia."

"Well, if you are a serial killer, you're in the right city," she said with a throaty cackle.

When I set my duffel bag down and took a seat, she introduced herself as Zonnie, emphasizing the Z. It seemed like this sparked something in my brain, but when I tried to recall where I might have heard the unusual name before nothing came to mind. It was just another dead-end.

"Have we met before?" I asked.

"Not if you were wearing those fancy boots," she croaked.

"Don't know how I got them," I said while squeezing my temple.

When my sandwich arrived, Zonnie told me that she was a long-haul truck driver on her way to a freight terminal in Santa Clara, California. She preferred to drive at night, listening to a "spooky" radio program while crossing desert vistas and the eastern Sierras. She was also a blogger that wrote about her struggles trying to earn a living as a female gear-jammer in a profession dominated by "Rooster Cruisers." She grew up as a tomboy, so the grime of the job didn't bother her. The worst part was sexual harassment from male truckers in the rest areas -- those who said she ought to be at home cooking for her hubby and having kids. For any unwelcome sexual attention, she kept a Louisville Slugger in the cab.

Do you really have amnesia?" she asked.

"Yes, I don't remember who I was... but I knew that I'd like pastrami and not corned beef. Just like I knew that I enjoyed bananas but can't stomach plantains. Weird, huh?"

Before she could respond or ask any further questions, a dramatic brass fanfare with repeated triplets of tympani boomed from the speakers on the small stage in the lounge. This was a taped orchestral version of Strauss's "Also Sprach Zarathustra" that served as the introduction for an Elvis impersonator whose show was about to begin. With the final flourishes of horns, the colored lights switched on a pasty-faced fellow with a greasy jet-black pompadour wig and gold sunglasses with attached mutton chop sideburns. A few old biddies seated in shiny mobility scooters in front whistled as he began gyrating to the entrance song, "C.C. Rider." Despite the elaborate embroidery of the iconic "Patriotic Eagle" jumpsuit, the act seemed to be a clownish parody rather than an actual tribute to the King's Vegas residency, especially with the 'band' consisting of sequencer tracks, a drum machine and recorded backing vocals.

As 'Elvis' swiveled his hips and struck cheesy poses to his biggest hits, Zonnie continued to ask questions about my situation. After feeling me out, she offered to give me a lift to California as long as I didn't mind staying up late and listening to the *Mind-Shift* radio show. Before we would get on the road, she needed to take an afternoon nap in the sleeper cab.

After she left, I wandered into the lounge and ordered one of those dollar drafts to celebrate my good fortune. Noticing the two guys who earlier had been examining the faded pictures were now seated near the back, I walked over and asked if I could have a seat. The one with a 'landing strip' goatee and black circle glasses pulled out a chair and wished me a happy holiday while the other pushed over a paper doily for my beer. As it turned out, they were part of a startup production company called Paragon Makings in the early stage of making a documentary for a pay television network.

The subject was a reclusive prospector named James Kidd, who had vanished without a trace in 1949 after being dropped off to work one of his mining claims in Arizona's Superstition Mountains. Back then people paid little notice to his disappearance. His was just one of many unexplained deaths associated with the place. But that all changed after what was discovered in a safe deposit box that was drilled open fifteen years later as part of the Unclaimed Property Act of Arizona. Somehow, the man who would rather do yard chores to pay his four dollar a week rent, and who said that he couldn't afford the twelve dollar a year membership fee at the YMCA, had managed to amass what today would be worth nearly a half million dollars.

From what his few acquaintances later recounted, Kidd gave a new meaning to the saying, "candle ends and cheese pairings." Even with the amount of money he had in various bank accounts, he would wear the same clothes every day. He ordered the cheapest meal on the menu without tipping. He would save his wad of chewing gum in a candy tin and make a nickel cigar last until bedtime. He even borrowed the mining pick he planned to use the day he was last seen. He was never married and didn't attend church. He didn't have a driver's license, social security number or military record. As he had no known heirs, the state was due to collect his entire fortune until a meticulous public servant chanced upon a slip of paper that contained Kidd's hand-written Last Will and Testament. At first the Estate Tax Commissioner thought it must be a joke. She read the penciled scribbling three times. According to Kidd's wishes, all of the money was to be given to someone that could prove the existence of a soul that leaves the human body at death. Thus began what the newspapers called "The Great Ghost Trial of the Century."

"That's when the circus began," the film's director said. "Relatives crawled out of the woodwork. Alleged heirs, natch. Cartons of mail arrived at the courthouse from claimants ready to meet the stipulations of Kidd's Will. Once the trial started, there was even a letter signed by Kidd, himself, expressing amusement at the proceedings as he watched from the back of the gallery. Another letter sent by someone claimed that Kidd was very much alive in the nineteen fifties, having been spotted in a gambling hall in Las Vegas. Eventually, the estate was awarded to the American Society for Psychical Research... even though, of course, they didn't meet the provisions of the Will."

The Elvis imitator continued to make a mockery of The King's legacy by stomping from foot to foot during a terrible rendition of "Blue Suede Shoes." As he wobbled under the lights with snarling lips and karate chops, the writer of the documentary added further details.

"The questions we're asking are – did Kidd find the lost Dutchman's gold? The legendary hoard responsible for so many deaths by trigger-happy prospectors? Or, did his money come from some other mine in the area – with claims filed by Kidd for some mysterious Spaniard from the Pyrenees that we've learned about? And, why was he so interested in a Kodak of the human soul when he thought that religion was a bunch of baloney?"

"I heard you guys mention the guy was a gambler. Couldn't that explain the estate, at least?" I posed the question even though the whole time they were talking I kept thinking that some eccentric miser who managed to save nearly all the money he earned in his lifetime wasn't that out of the ordinary.

Before one of them had a chance to respond, a cocktail waitress arrived to take drink orders. Her nametag said, "Pollyanna" - apropos in a town that screamed optimism. Both of the Hollywood types ordered Pellegrino with limes as I continued to nurse my flat draft.

"He didn't hit the Wheel of Fortune jackpot," the director was quick to point out. "As a penny-pincher that occasionally played Faro with the boys... it's on the shot list... he carefully budgeted what he could afford to lose. He was also involved in the stock market, having a broker with E.F. Hutton. But with his modest income as a pumpman for a copper mining company, what was the source of his investment money? No, it wasn't his gross earnings... Something else was at play."

"Gold isn't the only thing that does funny things to people."

The voice came from a guy standing at the bar. It was the talkative dude with the straggly mullet that I suspected might be a meth addict. Oh, God, here we go again with a real life version of one of those wiggly advertising balloon figures that danced in front of used car dealers. Suddenly, the garish lights and spinning reels of the pokies seemed more enticing.

"The bloodthirsty lust in the Superstitions comes from the dero. The magical little twerps the Paiute Indians called the Nomorika. Only, it's not trick-store magic they use to drive treasure hunters stark raving mad. The alien gizmos are still in working order… like that rabbit you see on the tube… they keep going and going."

As he babbled on about pulp doodlebugs from the earth's interior, his motions were a bit spastic, but not as bad as before. Even though I hoped he'd go back outside and find a split-open piñata of junk to fiddle with, the filmmakers were all ears to this lunacy. I was just thankful that his breath didn't smell like rotting lobsters when he sat down next to me.

"The stinkin' Apaches believe the place to be the opening to hell," he said with an unfocused gaze, "but it's really a bonanza of ancient star-mech. All the strange shit reported – it's not from gold-fever or heatstroke or Fireball cinnamon whiskey shots, but from midget idiots with stupid minds and pipe-stem arms operating beam-mech that make partners turn on one another. I've seen them around here, too – the serpent people in black-hooded cloaks. I recognize the sick pups… just like I do the plain wrappers in this place… You can bet on that shit."

After ending "All Shook Up" with overstated gyrations, the sparkling caricature wiped the sweat from his brow with his silk scarf before tossing it to one of the motorized blue-hairs in the audience.

"Thank ya. Thank ya, very much. Preeshaydit. How about some hands for my band," he said while gesturing to the drum machine.

Seniors with confused expressions clapped.

"Can I get the deli to whip up some peanut butter, bananas and fried bacon on monkey bread? Not for me, I'm counting calories, but for my pet-turkey, Bowtie, who'd better have left the building on this Christmas day."

"How about a rock-hard muffin chucked at that schnoz job?" a heckler shouted.

"No thank ya. No thank ya, very much. Seeing how Elvis in Norse means all wise, this one's about a little fellow with a buckskin drum... that has no gifts to bring to the newborn king. But, since, I'm also a king, how about a shiny new Cadillac, baby Jesus."

"You're not Jesus," an elderly woman yelled.

"No, darlin', I'm not, but at least I've already returned. Ask those people in Burger King. Okay, are you ready for some Pahrump-pum pum pum from my little machine drum?"

As the rattling snare drum began the beat for his rendition of the Christmas favorite, a bull-necked man in a charcoal plaid shirt set a glass of Chivas down on the table and adjusted his velvety Stetson. "Anybody got a wrench? Damn, that Caveman Keno is irritating. Sounds like a cat's tail stuck in a meat-grinder," he grimaced. "And a dentist using a jack-hammer to perform a root canal. I'd don't know what's worse – that, or Elvis the Pelvis here's caterwauling. I suppose it's debatable."

His brows drew together as he read the tweaker's "Abducted Cattle Jerky" tee shirt.

"Abducted? By who, mudflap?"

His eyes widened as he answered his own question.

"More illegal aliens invading the country? Well, listening to all the liberal moonbattery, I guess passage of the 14th Amendment will also give the little green buggers a pathway to citizenship. Not without a bloody conflict in Casper, Wyoming, though. Sell your cloak and buy an AR-15 like the good book says."

Rather than listen to another sovereign citizen spout nonsense, I grabbed my duffle bag and got up to leave. While doing so, the Elvis impersonator's equipment malfunctioned. First the backing tracks went kerflooey, followed by the drum machine being reduced to a pulsating ghostly hiss.

"Uh-Oh," Elvis said while fiddling with the machine. "This machine drum is a turd. Imagine the King gigging with plastic rubbish. Looks like my beat buddy is toast. Where's Dominic when you need him."

After wiping the sweat off his forehead with another scarf, he returned to the microphone.

"Did you ever wonder why Elvis had alien eyes on his belt buckle? Not like this one – not costume jewelry - but on his actual belt buckle."

There was some grumbling before the audience went silent.

"Hear me out. Did you know that moments after Elvis was born, his father, Vernon, stepped outside, where he witnessed a blue star of Bethlehem-like glowing light in the sky? Gladys, his mother, had been selected by aliens for a cosmic breeding program, which is why she was later so protective… and fearful of boogeymen. Elvis was of cosmic seed… a star child. A product of genetic intervention."

"Why? To walk through those terrible movies?" the same heckler shouted.

Half-amused laughter from those leaning against the bar was followed by the embarrassed shifting of some of the elderly people seated nearby. A couple of blue-hairs in scooters turned away with their mouths agape, as if they were witnessing one of the greatest travesties in all of Elvisdom.

He was gifted with a magical larynx. It had a unique quality. Listen to his flageolet today. Not bad for a wax body in a coffin, eh. Come they told me," he began singing without the backing tracks. "Pahrump-pum pum pum… A newborn king to see… thanks to space people… Shall I play for you… without the machine drum… I see Mary out there nodding… the ox and lamb will keep time… Pahrump-pum pum pum…"

I noticed the film director's perplexed expression as he glanced over at the meth-head, who returned the glance with a "Now, do you fuckin' believe me?" look.

Before the P. A. system crackled with evil chuckles of the dero, I slipped away.

Making my way to the restroom, I paused at the sight of a man standing near a blackjack table. Handsome for his years, he stood out from the locals with a black dress shirt. I had seen him before, wearing the same grey-metal Cartier sunglasses with gold mirror lenses. He had been at the bus terminal, not once during my trip, but twice at two different stations, even though I never saw him on the bus. What made me certain that it was the same person was his unique boots. They were identical to the pair that I was wearing, with high-quality stitching that looked to be very expensive. The hand-painted camo pattern against the laced up oxblood-stained leather was practically a work of art.

With my gaze fixed on the boots, when he took a step sideways, I noticed a gaming chip that he had been standing on. It was black – a $100.00 token. Had he not noticed it against the busy colorful patterns that were allegedly designed to conceal vomit and dropped chips? When he walked away, I went over and nonchalantly picked it up.

After slipping it into my pocket, I tried to follow him, but my steps across the kaleidoscopic swirls were impeded by a cluster-fuck of seniors on mobility scooters. It was like the dero had their grubby paws on a remote-control joystick during some octogenarian bumper car attraction.

After dodging the circling granny-fannies, I was confronted with another obstacle. This was a morbidly obese man wearing a voluminous tent of a canary-yellow tee shirt that said:

I CONQUERED ANOREXIA

"Where's the smart money playing!" he asked no one in particular. "I've got more cash than time."

When I managed to get around him, I noticed the man exiting the casino through the revolving door.

When I reached the parking lot, I saw that it was getting dark and starting to sprinkle. There was no sight of the man with the oxblood boots, only a woman walking in my direction who unfurled a black umbrella. WHOOSH! As it popped open, I felt my heart skip a beat. Paralyzed with fear, my knees buckled, causing the duffle bag to scrape the asphalt. There was tightness in my throat. Feeling dizzy, I clambered to a bench and sat down with rain dropping on my face.

What the goddamn hell just happened? Why had the simple act of a person opening an umbrella caused me to freak out like that? And why was my heart still racing? I also wondered if my strange reaction could be regarded as some kind of breakthrough? Like a certain smell or song or photo that would serve as a trigger enabling me to regain my memory?

But, there were no flashbacks. No repressed memories emerged from my broken hippocampus. Instead, it felt like I was being swallowed further into a void of dark immensity. "The Devil's Hole", like the elderly man wearing the Terrible's cap had mentioned. There was a peculiar ringing in my ears. My hands were trembling and I felt nauseous.

"Enjoying Nevada's Aurora Borealis?"

Looking up, I saw Zonnie pointing to the hazy glow of Las Vegas on the horizon.

"Ready?"

"I just have to cash in a chip," I said while trying to regain my composure.

As we approached the rumble of the idling diesel, Zonnie had donned a pedagogical mask to bring me up to speed for the night's spooky radio program holiday repeat. The subject matter would be the huge geoglyphs in Peru known as the Nazca Lines – one of the landing strips for the star gods, according to ancient astronaut theorists. Among the various images of animals carved on the desert floor by the pre-Inca people was the depiction of the world's rarest spider, the *Ricinulei* of the Amazon basin. Part of the mystery of the glyph is that it was detailed complete with its tiny reproductive organ at the tip of the extended third leg – a copulatory device that is only visible through a microscope.

"It's like the Dogon tribe in Africa who have for hundreds of years known the existence of a star that is totally invisible to the naked eye. It was first seen in the nineteen seventies… only by using the world's largest telescope," she said with eyes like a child full of wonder.

"So, how did they know about it?" I humored her, considering how good of a job she'd done in parroting the bunkola of some fringe undertaking.

"They were told about it by the aquatic Nummo who came from Sirius B", she replied matter-of-factly.

"Do you mean the Nomorika?" I asked, recalling what the tweaker had said about the magical little creatures of the Paiute Indians.

"No, the Nummo."

It was going to be a long ride, but it could have been worse. Paranormal stupidity still beat feel-good sermons by fluff-daisy pastors or, almost as bad, a battering tirade to the ungodly by some hardcore wacko. Plus, if I managed to stay awake in the cab of the Peterbilt, the Sandman couldn't mess with my dreams. But, what about the loathsome dero?

Having just crossed the state line, I noticed that Zonnie kept glancing in the mirror as she sipped coffee from a thermos.

"What is that?" she leaned closer. "The blue light. It's pretty weird."

I shifted position to try and get a look, but all I could see was the reflection of desert scrubland with the silhouettes of hills outlined by patches of brilliant stars.

"There it is again – and it's getting brighter. Whatever it is, it's definitely getting closer," she said with a trace of concern in her voice while keeping her eye on the mirror. "Shit! Is that a cop? Am I getting pulled over for going five miles over the limit?" She banged the steering wheel while shifting gears and braking.

When she pulled over I could see the forlorn glow of a gas station with an attached Burger King up ahead. After rolling down her window and leaning out of the cab, I heard a man's voice with a thick southern accent. Actually, it sounded like...

"You've got to be kidding me," Zonnie's husky voice boomed. "Is this the real Elvis?"

"Pushing it a bit aren't you, ma'am. So, this here is for you."

Instead of issuing her a traffic citation, the man climbed up the rig and scrawled 'Elvis Presley's' autograph on a promotional flyer. For some reason, he then walked around the front of the truck to where I was seated. When I rolled the window down, I saw that it was the same Elvis impersonator from the casino. Although he was now wearing the uniform of a police officer, he still had on the greasy pompadour wig and gold sunglasses with muttonchops attached.

"No need to be in such a hurry... in Death Valley," he said with a drawl as thick as molasses. "You'll get there gradually. Thank you. Thank you very much."

When he walked back to the 'patrol' car, Zonnie looked over at me with a puzzled stare.

"Did that really just happen?"

CHAPTER II
CELLECTECH

"Seek not out things that are too hard for thee, neither search the things that are above thy strength. But what is commanded thee, think thereupon with reverence, for it is not needful for thee to see with thine eyes the things that are in secret. Be not curious in unnecessary matters; for more things are shewed onto thee than men understand."

Sirach/Ecclesiaticus 3:21-23

"Give me the storm and tempest of thought and action, rather than the dead calm of ignorance and faith! Banish me from Eden when you will; but first let me eat of the fruit of the tree of knowledge!"

- Robert Green Ingersoll

When I checked the comments for my most recent blog post, I was expecting to see Zonnie's negative response to the skeptic calling into question certain anomalous features associated with the depiction of the famous Nazca spider – namely that the geoglyph doesn't represent the *Ricinulei* (mite!) with its microscopic ding-a-ling, but, rather, has been identified by professional zoologists as an ant, or, at best, an ant-mimicking spider. Instead, I realized that the site had been hacked again. Despite having installed a new security plugin, for seven days in a row the same message appeared. Due to the nature of the declaration, I assumed that it was from some movement that had recently surfaced (most likely right here in the Bay Area), but after doing a Google search for the name that appeared at the top of the screen nothing involving any kind of cultic activity turned up. Adding to the mystery of that calling itself Ramiel was the striking color fidelity of the caption - vibrant golden letterforms constructed with a custom shadowed effect that was unlike any web aesthetic I had ever seen.

BEHOLD THE BURNING SCROLL OF RAMIEL
THE KEYS TO A HIGHER PERCEPTIONAL LEVEL OF COM-
MUNICATION
ARE ENCODED IN FIRE LETTERS

Beneath this, a message was typed in another unique font that displayed an equally sharp clarity.

WHERE NO FLESH WALKS...
I WALKED...
THE HIDDEN TREE WILL SUPPLY THE FRUIT
AND GIVE RENEWED FERTILITY TO HUMANKIND

As I further examined the intensity of the color components, I had to hand it to the sect's graphic designer. Ditto to the cyber attacker's ability to breach the hosting platform's security features without even as much as an "immediate action required" warning. Before I could delete the announcement, additional text appeared with the same vivid typography:

Concerning the revelatory activity of the rebel Watchers – the forbidden teachings of mining, metallurgy, cosmetics, magic and astrology were worthless mysteries. According to the patriarch, Enoch, the distant generation shall be given the true mystery of the visions imparted to the scribe by an interpreting angel during his tour of the cosmos. As the fulfillment of his commission, Enoch's prophecy was intended for those living in the end-time, when the treasury of souls involved in the EX-PERIMENT shall be analyzed and will no longer have to reside in a special chamber under God's throne. For this reason, the almighty exercised patience and restraint, withholding judg-ment until the pre-determined time, thus allowing the creation to continue in spite of the destructive deeds of humankind. The exact count of the souls of the dead is now COMPLETE, and the sphere of responsibility for the resurrection is RAMIEL's - the angel put in charge of those that rise.

New-Age angelology was a fairly common topic on my blog site. Especially, the ancient apocalyptic tradition ascribed to Enoch – a pre-deluge figure who was said to be the great grandfather of Noah. Supposedly, Enoch was transported into heaven while still alive and given a tour as he quaked and trembled (and prob-ably soiled his garment) at what he was shown. Since much of what he experienced on this cosmic journey was described as being unimaginable to those who are earthbound, the ambigu-ous visions and poetic metaphors have become fodder for ancient astronaut proponents, who assume that the whirlwind blast that lifted him was actually an alien spacecraft described by those lacking a modern vocabulary.

Because the church authorities suppressed Enoch's privileged revelations, decades before advocates of the paleo-contact hypothesis let their imaginations run wild, the fantastic descriptions generated a lot of speculation from occultists when the scrolls were translated into English in the late 19th century.

As always, the skeptic was sorry to have to burst their bubble by informing the Enochites that certain words in the translation from Aramic to Greek or Latin had been corrupted. The fictitious hero was not taken *upward* (by ancient spacefarers or otherwise), but, rather, *within*, as within the recesses of the heavenly sanctuary. Hence, his cosmic tour was in reality a temple tour.

As for the expulsion of the rebel Watchers who figure prominently in the Enochic tradition, when it came to forbidden activity, was it really fallen angels that were of concern, or fallen priests? The myth of fallen angels who engaged in illicit unions with human females was based on ritual impurity in the context of religious law. In particular the corrupt practice of the priesthood defiling the temple after sexual intercourse with menstruating women. While looking for hidden meaning in scriptures it would appear that lady business was even more feared by the authors of Rabbinic Judaism than by modern-day hubbies being sent to Rite Aid to purchase a box of tampons. Entire tractates were devoted to riding the cotton pony.

I had dealt with these crazy notions on the site before. Time and time again I tried to explain Enoch as a literary vehicle for numerous scribes that pronounced judgment against the improper practices of priests. They were the target audience of his testament, rather than the children who were told to assemble around and incline their ears at storytelling that was full of parables and obscure sayings. The message was about polluting the temple - not the angelic origin of technology in antediluvian times.

Looking at the monitor again, there was something about Ramiel's text that was different from other Enochites (and not just the clarity of pixel grids, layered effects and non-standard color schemes). What was meant, I wondered, by the exact count of the souls of the dead involved in an experiment being released after having been analyzed in accordance with a precise timetable? Why the specifics?

And if the experiment had been completed, what was Ramiel's agenda concerning this resurrection mentioned? Although it was probably nothing more than apocalyptic claptrap, the pronouncement was a bit foreboding (especially when combined with the intensity of the graphics). I only hoped there wouldn't be any disastrous consequences as with past doomsday cults.

Without knocking, the hope of tomorrow entered my makeshift office wearing psychedelic Aladdin pants and a black cyberpunk 'BioHacker' tee shirt — the rallying cry of a member of the so-called information age, who desires to become a transhuman. Jag was the nineteen-year-old son of my live-in girlfriend. Other than wanting to become a machine, he was a typical specimen of the millennial demographic cohort (I won't use the term "snowflake", but...). Despite any generational shortcomings, he was a decent enough kid - tolerable at times, though even when argumentative and opinionated (i.e. "woke"), I had to exercise restraint, being that he was part of a package deal. With fair skin like his mother and light brown eyes that were almost hazel, other than wavy jet-black locks, you wouldn't know that he was part Bengali.

"Trying to convince little kiddies that the Easter Bunny isn't real, skeptoid?" he snickered before taking a gulp from a can of Barq's root beer.

"Clearly, no one's convinced you. I heard about your recent hunt - "

"I was geocaching for pathtags and swag — trackables - not basket painted eggs," he replied with an overly defensive tone.

"Well, that's certainly a relief," I patted my chest. "And here I thought you were going to be devastated upon finally learning the truth. Otherwise, I wouldn't have placed those brown jelly beans in the toilet and left telltale tufts of Peter's cottontail on the floor for you to find."

"Ass."

Unable to hold back a smile, he handed me a device that I assumed was the portable digital voice changer that I asked to borrow.

"What are you using it for, Sheldon? Have some of your haters been calling?"

"I've got a new cell phone number and thought I might play a little joke on your mother. I want to sound like a little girl. Is it hard to operate if you're not a digital native?" I asked while handing it back to him so that he could set the thing up.

"Easy freakin' peasy."

Turning the pitch selector knob counterclockwise, he spoke into the gadget's built-in microphone, doing his best impression of a sniveling little girl.

"Mommy, the man inside the thinking box said the Easter Bunny's not real. Remember, you gotta change your speech patterns," he said while still imitating a sobbing child.

"What do you use it for?" I asked as he attached the device to my cell-phone with a Velcro strip.

"Voice warping."

When I shifted position in my office chair, Jag immediately noticed the enigmatic message that was still on my computer screen. For someone as tech-savvy as he was, I was surprised by his excited reaction to the visually stunning text.

"Man, that shit's fire! That's on your site?" he asked with puzzled look."

"I've been hacked. It just popped up in the forum like a malware virus or something. I finally turned off that annoying CAPTCHA and installed a different plugin to filter spam."

"It didn't capture an email address?"

"Nada."

"This must be some new graphics software with a color palette I haven't seen," he said as he leaned closer to the monitor and forked his fingers through his hair.

"Who's this Ramiel dude?"

"Someone in a tizzy over a collection of Woes. My guess would be the trumpeting of the latest doomsday cult. Whatever their game, they've no business trying to recruit my kooks."

"I'm already brainwashed," he joked in a robotic monotone as he continued to gaze questioningly at the futuristic letterforms.

Kidding aside, I could tell that he also noticed something extra unusual about the pronounced text – a subtle rippling or shimmering quality *within* the letters themselves that seemed to draw one into them like a magnet, making it hard to look away.

With the voice changer ready to go, I tapped a number on my smart phone.

"Okay, I'm dialing her Cellectech number."

"Cellectech Biosciences," Aaloka quickly answered in a low matter-of-fact voice that contained only the slightest trace of an Anglo-Indian accent.

"Can you even dye my eyes to match my gown?" I asked while using the slightly distorted little girl's voice setting.

"Uh-huh," she replied. "Before granting you access to the Stork's Nest, is there something else you'd like to tell me?"

"Someone has a new cell number."

There was a short pause on the other end.

36

"Access denied," she said in a clipped tone.

After being hung up on, I glanced over at Jag, who was busy clicking my mouse while searching for that new color table.

"That wasn't weird," I joked. "Access denied?"

"Oh, that reminds me, Sheldon. Mom wanted me to tell you that she's at Punyaaloka. The restaurant's having a private party tonight and she was hoping you might help with some bartending action… or seeing that everyone has papadum."

"But, she just answered her Cellectech line.

"That must have been her gynoid."

He looked away from the computer screen and saw my confused expression.

"She didn't tell you yet? Yeah, a friend gave her an old Telenoid. It has a minimalistic design with a face that doesn't look that much like her… but does have a black wig that looks like her hair…and the voice is pretty good… It's wearing her golden sari – the one that the wine stain didn't come out –"

"Telenoid?"

"Female android."

"Robot? I was just talking to a robot?"

"Yeah, the Telenoid takes her place when she's out of the lab – "

"Why didn't you tell me she wasn't there before I made the call?" I asked with an incredulous stare while disconnecting the voice changer.

"I don't know," he shrugged. "What's the difference?"

I drooped my head, shaking it slowly.

"You truly are the wonder of a miracle – a twenty-first century miracle in pantaloons."

"Fu-sion ware, Shel-don," he said in a deliberate slow manner as he often did when mocking someone. "You should try some... or get a blanket burrito... in case you forgot what it's like to be comfortable, mister scratchy corduroys."

Punyaaloka was a popular eatery serving Bengali cuisine in Silicon Valley. Located in downtown Sunnyvale, the word Punyaloka means paradise, with the extra "a" added as a nod of appreciation to the owner's daughter-in-law. It was here that I met Aaloka over a year ago after Ubering to the address written on a scrap of paper in my duffle bag. As to who placed it there and for what reason I still didn't have a clue. When I told her about this, rather than speculate on any intriguing possibilities, she preferred to think of our meeting that way as the result of pure serendipity. Seeing her for the first time that night, with her striking appearance, jovial demeanor and that delicious concoction she called a Starflower gin & tonic, I was immediately hooked.

In keeping with the restaurant's paradise motif, terrariums of greenery hung from the high ceiling in the main dining area. Along with these mini gardens in glass spires, majolica jardinières of ornamental tropical plants were placed against walls of indigo, madder red and yellow.

Hanging between glimmering sconces were filigreed tapestries of verdant landscapes populated by a stylized menagerie of monkeys, elephants, tigers and peacocks. The larger central wall hanging was a densely embroidered cosmographic frieze entitled "Garden of Paradise" in Bengali calligraphy. With its Edenic imagery, the garden - which Aaloka told me was a talented artist friend's vision of a compendium of mythical flora – was encompassed by the celestial abode of the gods from Hindu epics.

The interwoven silver thread (wire) from which the pantheon of deities in spangled chariots was fashioned reflected the glow of earthen lamps, creating a dazzling luminous effect.

As waiters pushed serving trollies across the glazed ceramic floor, patrons seated in painted Mughal chairs at cluttered tables sampled a variety of traditional dishes. Bottles of regional lagers complemented the ethnic preparations, as did dissonant strains of instrumental music (though, to my ears, at least, that part of the ambiance wasn't suggestive of paradise). The piped stridence was less audible in the opulent coziness of the main bar where I was hanging out while waiting for Aaloka to tell me what kind of help she needed. With my finger, I impatiently stirred my cocktail, trying to figure out how to handle the exchange I was having with the black woman wearing a multicolored headwrap sitting next to me. Besides the awkward conversation, there was something weird about her left eye. Even though it seemed to move in tandem with the other one, I thought it might be a prosthetic and found myself constantly looking away. After setting my third glass of Bombay Sapphire onto the dark green marble, I spooned some spicy red chutney onto a crunchy lentil wafer and dove into it.

"Secrets rarely stay secret, baby," she said over the sound of clinking glasses and people conversing. "What makes you think she'll never divulge the ingredient that gives the chutney its unique tanginess?"

"All she'll say is the acidic kick comes from minced red ants," I smiled. "But if I had to guess, I'd say it's a zippy anchur powder."

"Perhaps with genetically modified green mangos," she glanced at me with raised brows.

I reluctantly nodded my head to that possibility, hoping the conversation wouldn't return to bioethics.

"If it were genetically modified crops or changing mosquitos so they can't transmit malaria, I'd have no problem," she said. "But I do share concerns with the ethics of this whole building the perfect baby thing. Genetic disorders are one thing, but I don't consider not having beautiful blue eyes to be a genetic defect. Same with low SAT scores or if someone's not tall enough to be good at a certain sport. From what I've read, there are few guidelines and regulatory policies in these companies like where your Stanford grad gal works. It's like the Wild West when it comes to the possibilities of gene editing technologies like CRISPR."

"I know the designer baby business is controversial, but it's just an option. Parents call the shots – they don't have to tinker with their child."

Her plump cheeks shrank as she sucked on the dainty straw in a fruit cocktail.

"But those who can afford it will, honey, mostly for superficial purposes. Socially desirable traits… the same eugenic fantasies –"

"The genetic enhancement offered by facilities like Cellectech and Progeny Genomix – eyes now in hazel stuff – aren't exactly monstrous tamperings," I said while looking up at the colonial-period fans. "And please don't say it's wrong because the baby doesn't have a say in it… like any child ever did."

"How does she feel about using prime editing to revive an extinct species from a closely related one?" Maybe resurrect an adorable woolly mammoth."

"That was just a Hollywood thing. The half-life of DNA is a little over 500 years, so I don't foresee eating brontosaurus burgers anytime soon. More likely plant-based muck served at Al's."

Thankfully, I spotted Aaloka approaching the bar. Draped in a gold-brocade sari, even with minimal makeup – a little kohl pencil applied to accentuate her almond eyes and a light carmine shade of lipstick – she drew stares from many of the diners.

"Sheldon might not have any memories of his past, but we can say with certainty that his mother was kept busy when it came to his highchair," she joked while gesturing to all the papadum crumbs next to my empty cocktail glass.

The woman leaned back in her chair and clapped her hands while bursting into fits of laughter.

"I'm pretty sure she didn't serve these brittle things," I blushed while sweeping away the crumbs.

"How did you two meet?"

"Sheldon was the man hidden from himself whose arrival I was told to expect by a fortune-teller that reads shadows… and it's not just the shadow's length that he measures during a specific time… but other parts that are factored in as well."

I had a hard time trying to repress a smile as she continued with this BS.

"Lots of Bollywood stars consult him – the shadow reader – for his unique gift," she glanced at me with a subtle wink before picking up my cocktail glass and rattling the ice cubes. "Dearest, would you mind terribly lending a hand at the bar for our private gathering in the bhoot room?"

When I walked into the private room to help out with things, guests were gathered around antique leather sofas, sipping drinks and chatting almost inaudibly while waiting for an indulgent meal to be served. Over the monotony of voices, devotional hymns of India's wandering minstrels blared from the polished brass horn of a mechanical gramophone. With the themed décor of the bhoot room running the gamut of the various ghosts in Bengali folklore, decorative chandeliers cast light on the tenebrous shades of oil paintings featuring vaporous apparitions. Gilded rosewood cabinetry displaying macabre iconography also added to the numinous quality of the phantasmal taxonomy.

Standing behind a bar of polished teakwood, I combined the ingredients of Punyaaloka's signature drink, the Starflower Cocktail, being a mixture of imported gin, syrup, tonic water, lime and elderflower liqueur that was garnished with ice cubes embedded with bluish-purple borage flowers.

Seated across from me was Aaloka's father-in-law. As the owner of the restaurant, Malcolm was a well-to-do barrister who spoke with a marked British accent. He had a round face with thinning grayish hair and a ruddy complexion from years spent in the sub-tropical sun. As usual, he was impeccably dressed in a slim-fitting dark business suit with lapis dress studs that he constantly fidgeted with. As I prepared some more syrup, he turned around and summoned the Bengali sous chef with an expression of placid command.

To the annoyance of the staff, Malcolm could be intolerably verbose at times, even when it came to something as simple as ordering a dessert.

"Having skipped my luncheon today, there's still room in the old tum after sampling your dainty comestibles for some compote. Tomato and dates... pitted, of course. Slightly tart and slightly spicy with a sprinkling of red pepper flakes... though not with chilies that sprouted from some infernal region. To be served with a cup of chai... steeped orange pekoe... like that expertly prepared in bong – to use a neologism - households I've visited."

"Doodh cha," the sous chef said before heading to the kitchen.

Malcolm turned back to me and adjusted a cufflink.

"What's with the bum-fluff, chap?" he gestured to my facial stubble. "And is this dress-down Friday?"

"We can't all be as dapper as you, Malcolm. Who are these saturnine masks, anyway? Not exactly lampshade wearers, is this bunch. I only recognize one of them from Cellectech."

"Individuals with a shared interest in socio-cultural beliefs concerning spectral manifestations."

"A ghost club?" I laughed in my head. "Where are their blinking gadgets?"

Malcolm smoothed the grizzled wisps on his balding pate.

"Turn around, dear boy, and have a gander."

Hanging on the wall behind the bar were smaller un-framed oil paintings of menacing spectral visitants. In the feeble glow of Victorian pendant lamps, some were depicted with garish pigments while others were portrayed in cadaverous monochrome.

"You've Kanabhulo... an invoked Danori... and the slack Khokhosh dwarves."

"Malicious little dero buggers responsible for my papadum crumbling," I mumbled under the scratchy tinny sound of plucked ethnic instruments and ringing of anklet cymbals that were a bit more cheerful than the dirge-like Sanskrit chants.

As waiters pushing carts entered, the room quickly became engulfed with aromatic spices.

"And that's Jokkh... Protector of hidden treasure who also bestows fertility."

"Besides the greenish tint to his face, Jokkh here looks like a Sunday school picture of Jesus... though you don't often see Jesus holding a grafting knife," I said while gesturing to the tool the figure was using in a lush garden setting that was contrived with a peculiar quality of light.

"After finding Jesus's tomb in the garden empty," Malcolm said, "the first witness to his resurrection, Mary Magdalene, saw what she took to be a gardener standing nearby... the only time in the Bible the word gardener is mentioned, by the way. Have you ever wondered why someone so close to him didn't recognize him? Perhaps this was meant for us to think about all the others who have failed to cream off the real Jesus... and still do."

"Well, to be fair, she was doing a lot of crying at the time, and I'm told it's hard to see through tears... but it definitely contradicts the idea that his body was horribly mangled during the crucifixion... even if he was in disguise, which maybe he was just to keep all the lookie-loos from trampling on the cabbages."

"Or he took the clothes of a gardener instead of being starkers," Malcolm chuckled. "Or... maybe he really was a gardener, complete with dirt under his fingertips," he said with a cryptic wink. "The agent of a new Eden. Ah yes, the call to adventure, which is really initiation. In the story, we've Jesus transformed from his journey... and quite knackered, I'm sure... so that he's unrecognizable at first. This was a common template of ancient mythic tales... the epic return of a heroic figure after receiving a call that involved undergoing ordeals... the road of trials, which the hero embarks on with their faithful guide or magical helper, who, along the way, presents a talisman or special artifact to be used on the quest before gaining the treasure that benefits others. The stuff of our cultural memory... of the deep past... mythologically encoded in scripture," he said as his pale blue eyes remained fixed in strangely absorbed manner on the ghostly image.

"Wasn't the book Elvis was reading on the thunder mug before he plopped dead on the floor about a scientific search for the face of Jesus? I guess those Sunday school portraits of the Savior weren't good enough. Which reminds me, Aaloka and I went to a biblical flick around Easter and afterwards overheard a woman in the lobby tell her friend that the actor really looked like Jesus. Based on what? I wanted to ask her. The stereotype Hollywood Jesus, I'm sure... with Nordic features.... completely ignoring his supposed Semitic heritage."

"Actors portraying actors," Malcolm nodded while still lost in thought. "Without a clue as to what the plot was... not your movie... but the real-life plot."

Not sure what he meant by this cryptic statement, nor caring for that matter, I checked out the other eerie paintings and gestured to one that depicted a lustrous-haired beauty whose facial features resembled that of a younger Aaloka, only with oddly textured skin that also had a light greenish cast.

"Who's this exotic beauty that also seems to be pruning something in a garden?" I asked while pointing to the grafting knife the woman was holding despite her obvious erotic sentiments. "Hopefully, she's gonna trim whatever it is that's growing near the edge of the canvas that doesn't look like it belongs there."

Malcolm's abstract gaze turned into a look of amused disdain.

"Pishachini. Best to be careful with that one I dare say," he said with a scornful tone before smiling good-naturedly.

"Nothing like a temptress with a pruning knife," I winced jokingly while covering my crotch.

"Pruning the vices and propagating virtues by cuttings."

After most of the private party guests left, I wandered into the courtyard where the affluent Silicon Valley tech-bros usually gravitated to after their dinner. Seated on ornate wooden benches near the bamboo garden, many of these social-media kingpins with well-coiffed hair and Patagonia fleece vests sipped hard seltzers while having off-site meetings in the shadowy-flickering of electric candles placed on wall brackets. Seeing Aaloka mingling with a couple of them, I drained my final G&T and walked up to her.

"Please excuse us for a minute. I need to speak to her in private about a unicorn startup," I said with a serious face to the software geeks, while grasping her hand and leading her towards a eucalyptus tree.

"Are you okay to drive that thing home?" she asked as I jingled the Vespa keys.

"Of course. Easy freakin' peasy."

"How many drinks did you have?"

"Just a couple while muddling for the boss."

"Easy peasy, lime squeezy," she smiled

"Spoke with your mechanical doppelganger today."

"Jag told you about the Telenoid," she said as her smile turned upside down. "I was hoping you'd think it was me the next time you visited."

"So, what's this stork's nest that you – that it denied me access to?"

Her eyes darted, paused and shifted again.

"What?"

"After I jokingly asked if you could even dye my eyes to match my gown – using Jag's voice changer – "

"Why did you say that?"

She had a confused look that bordered on anxious concern.

"The Dorothy thing – you know, the genetics connection of changing the color of one's eyes."

"Oh... yeah, I get it," she said with a tight-lipped smile. "The android's old. One of the actuators is on the fritz. Not synced right. It's just a glorified answering machine, really.

An obsolete conferencing tool at this point. I need to upgrade to a Geminoid someday. Anyway, I'll tell my roboticist friend who gave her to me to see if he can figure out why it malfunctioned."

"So, who was that woman that you were talking to at the bar?" she asked while pacing about with roving pupils in the amber glow.

"I just met her and we struck up a conversation. She seemed interested in your work... actually disturbed by what you do would be more accurate... judging by the interrogation."

"Interrogation?"

"She had some ethical concerns, though not to a torch and pitchfork degree."

"Bummer Jaggy can't keep a secret," she contorted her face in frustration. "The telenoid looks like me from behind."

"Speaking of a certain irritant, he told me you bought him a CRISPR kit."

"Yeah, a DIY Cas9."

"I don't know, Aaloka... genome-editing experiments from a mail-order kit that costs a hundred and fifty bucks. It's not like he has a PhD in molecular biophysics or anything. Not sure he should be creating mini Frankenstein monsters in the garage with a do-it-yourself kit."

"He'll be tweaking bacterial strains, Sheldon. Not knocking out the genes of more exotic organisms. It's an educational tool. Thousands have sold already. Who knows, starting with the materials in the kit, someday he might make a world-changing discovery," she smiled, barely able to contain a laugh.

"Yeah, who knows what he'll cook up?"

"Our Frankenstein won't be tampering with anything more complex than fluorescent yeast. Even if he follows the protocols, you know Jag - he'll probably forget to put on the latex gloves while chomping on those Doritos 3-D that he bids on and taint the plate."

"Please don't let him put any of those critters in the fridge."

"What are you concerned about – virulent pathogens or contaminating a ham sandwich?"

"Both. I'm all for scientific advancement, but the whole thing that you guys hijacked from the bacteria's natural system… Oh, fuck, what could go wrong now that it's available to anyone that reads *Popular Science*," I said with obvious sarcasm.

Don't worry… it's just an old trick, really… the cuts. There are upgrades being tested… advances to the first-gen tools. He's not going to be crossing any species barrier with the Cas9 protein. A blob of glowing goo isn't going to slither off one of the plates at night and attack you while you're asleep. I know you don't remember it, but you probably had a Gilbert chemistry kit as a child and didn't have any safety concerns while performing experiments in the basement. Like cyanide poisoning that was one of the risks of the sets… unlike the pink box little girls got as presents so they could grow up to be lab assistants instead of actual scientists like the boys."

Realizing that my "you guys" remark had touched a nerve to the extent that she was unable to hide her resentment of the academic chauvinism of the time, I now had to proceed with caution.

"I just don't like the idea of him playing God in those silly pants. Don't go all Pishachini on me, but I worry about him trying to modify his body – turning himself into a freakin' machine… not just by extreme dieting, but now by messing around with synthetic biology tools."

"He wants to implant a microchip in his hand so he can wake the Vespa," she rolled her eyes.

"The compass on his chest isn't enough? I cringe to think of the little dongle wearing a custom tailored wardrobe from some startup involving molecular scissors."

"Jag, the gentrifier in cashmere and Cucinelli... Yeah, I can see how that would give you the willies," she laughed. "I'll see if there's enough space in the Blueapple for the plate."

"Blue apple?"

"That's what my produce savers are called – those in the crisper in the fridge. It's like modern Tupperware... that absorbs ethylene gas and keeps fruit fresher for my liquid lunches."

"A probiotic smoothie right now sounds... pretty damn terrible," I laughed. "Yes, better to keep his plates in your blue things."

When I walked out into a light drizzle, I saw that Jag's Vespa was missing from where I had parked it on a patch of ground behind the valet station. At this late hour the crew had left so I couldn't ask anyone if Jag had taken it (because Aaloka was concerned that I had too much to drink). If it turned out to be stolen, I would catch lots of grief from the kid for not using his "smart Bluetooth padlock", which was the latest gadget in his obsession with keyless locking mechanisms.

Examining the wet dirt, I could see shoeprints that had the same unique impression of the rubber inserts in the outsoles of my oxblood leather boots with the camo design (Just like the prints I was currently making.)

As I headed back to the restaurant, a fellow with the style palette of a tech-bro was about to open a black umbrella amidst a fruity smelling vaping cloud.

"Hey, man, please don't open that until I get inside," I said. "Is that a Samsonite drip-free?"

After giving me a weird look, to further distract him before I reached the front entrance, I started making shit up.

"You should check out the one that syncs with your mobile device. Raindrops are converted into electrical energy and using the inside canopy-screen you can watch YouTube videos."

When I checked my blog site, I didn't see any further messages from Ramiel. I did, however, finally get a response in the discussion forum from Zonnie regarding my latest post:

Why Not Utilize Telemetry Even If You're An *Ancient* Astronaut?
By
Sheldon Grane

Zonnie was my first subscriber and most ardent critic. Her opinions were usually less than frothy when it came to me challenging the pseudoscientific ideas from certain maverick–ologists and guerilla scholars, especially those making radical assumptions without empirical evidence.

At times her rationale and naiveté were laughable, though her spirited conversational style generated traffic. And social interaction is what blogging is all about. Despite her feisty nature when it came to defending her and others beliefs (those that I often derided as sheer lunacy), she always maintained the respectful civil discourse per my user requirements.

I was also grateful for her helping me start the blog. She recommended a good content management system, taught me how to perceive and monitor social metrics and offered advice on everything from selecting fonts to how to deal with gravatar spam. She also provided the newbie with useful tips on establishing income streams and developing strategies to get more Google juice.

As to my questioning why ancient visitors chose to use geoglyphs of earth animals as navigation beacons to their space oases instead of utilizing sophisticated on-board telemetry, Zonnie replied in her plucky style that I, once again, missed the point. First of all, Nazca depictions like the *Ricinulei* spider weren't copied from biology textbooks.

Secondly, she stressed that the figures were created by the ancient Peruvians to encourage the star people to return to the planet after having witnessed the ambiguous spectacle of technologically advanced beings during an earlier arrival. This was similar to what we've seen with more recent cargo cults started by the natives of Melanesia. When transport planes stopped dropping government-issued supplies by parachutes at the end of WWII, to persuade the military to return with the manufactured goods (cargo) that they shared with others, the primitive tribesmen fabricated mock landing strips complete with crude renderings of straw airplanes, bamboo radar dishes and radios fashioned from coconuts. After being abandoned, the islanders even held special ceremonies, mimicking the behavior they observed by American soldiers by parading about with rifles made from wooden sticks as they watched the skies, waiting for the wonderful aircraft to return. For similar reasons, a pre-Incan culture like the Paracus carved baffling geometric shapes into the hills so as to be illuminated at night during full moons.

Her final point was to be taken in a more humorous vein (I assumed). She objected to my calling the *Ricinulei* spider's organ of insemination a "ding-a-ling."

Though I appreciated her conviction, her argument was unconvincing as it was predicated on an acceptance that an alien presence had previously visited the place, of which, of course, there was no evidence. We know that servicemen handed out Hershey bars and cigarettes to the indigenous people of Melanesia.

I quickly typed my response, stating that the most logical explanation for the Nazca outlines was that they were part of an open-air temple complex. They were constructed for ritualistic purposes (same reason for the magical rites involving crude imitations carried out by tribal societies in the southwest Pacific).

Sacrificial offerings were given in hope that their deities would supply them with the precious gift of water that was necessary for them to survive during extreme droughts in their harsh eco-system. As for the offensive "ding-a-ling", in the future I would refer to the Ricinulei's minute copulatory organ as it's "shrinky-dink."

Taking a break from my blog site, I ambled into the condo's living room with a G&T on the rocks and plopped into the Mughal-era sofa. Though tastefully decorated by Aaloka to look like a Victorian drawing room, the space was cluttered with family heirlooms, *objets d'art* and brass incense burners. Myriads of crystal prisms in a hanging pendant lantern dimly lit the glinting treasure-trove of odds and ends arranged in lacquered cabinets. In the lingering oriental-spicy aroma of Nag Champa, gilded mirrors reflected pastel pouf ottomans set around a dark-polished tea table on an antique patterned carpet. Potted fern-like creepers drooped beneath wall-mounted tribal bamboo masks and colorful hand-woven textiles.

Lying on the sofa was one of Jag's high-tech toys. I had seen him shuffling around the condo wearing the head-mounted device, waving his arms while absorbed in whatever it was he was experiencing. Though I was told that it projected augmented reality effects, I wasn't really sure what this digital content the processor superimposed over the real world was. Just for the hell of it, I took off my glasses and put on the headset. After adjusting it, I pressed one of the touchpad controls to see what would happen.

In the full-color display, I focused on a rosewood cabinet that contained curios, spice boxes and vases of enamel glaze. The centerpiece was a majolica earthenware bust of a swarthy-faced, bearded Middle-Eastern figure.

Suddenly the lustrous visage began to morph, its fleshy tones becoming more lifelike. Once the facial features became almost indistinguishable from those of an actual human, its green eyes blinked with a look of curious self-awareness.

After experiencing some stuttering and fuzziness, in my field of vision there appeared a full-bodied figure with the same bearded lineaments of the glossy sculptured bust. Seated at the tea table, the overlying image was wearing a heavily patched cloak of rough yellow woolen cloth and a mottled lambskin nightcap. What level of augmentation had I activated to digitally conjure up this uncannily realistic looking figure dressed in medieval Persian garb?

While pouring a ruby-colored liquid from a pottery vessel into a ceramic goblet, I heard somewhat distorted in the headset's built-in audio speakers what I thought might be the virtual image quoting a verse from the *Rubaiyat* of Omar Khayyam ... in English.

"Oh Thou, who Man of baser Earth did make,
And who with Eden didst devise the Snake..."

Feeling a tap on the shoulder, I jumped from the sofa. While doing so, I bumped into the virtual character, causing it to spill the contents of the enameled chalice.

Quickly removing the headset, I turned to see Jag standing there with the widest smile that I'd ever seen on his face.

"Dude, you were so shook!"

I was still a bit unnerved as he handed me a keyless griplock for the new scooter.

"Use this if you need to take the new Vespa. Want to guess the code? And here's a caveman's key that fits your aesthetic - until it gets replaced by a stress-free chip embedded in our hands," he said while handing me a key.

"What's going on with this damn thing?" I held up the AR device. "There was a man in here speaking... in rhymes."

"Are you getting twisted on that stuff, again?" he asked while gesturing to the empty gin and tonic on the tea table. "Its just a gaming device – not nearly as layered as the new ones. I'm surprised you didn't barf on yourself from the wonky-ass spatial perception."

"So, you haven't seen the man with the beard drinking wine at your mom's table?"

"Sounds like a glitch... which doesn't surprise me. Just another glitch... on its slow march to the grave."

Moments later I walked into the den that had been converted into my office. Before turning on the computer, I sat in the swivel chair and tried to figure out how purplish stains got on my tan corduroy pants... and why they were still moist. "Truly immersive -- fucking right," I uttered with a nervous chuckle.

When I finally got around to doing a search, I found out that I was correct about the rhymes that I heard in the headset. It was one of the quatrains from FitzGerald's translation of the *Rubaiyat* attributed to the medieval Persian polymath Omar Khayyam. According to many scholars, Khayyam was a freethinker, with his poetry echoing his pessimistic outlook. As to religion, he was agnostic, if not an atheist. However, the question of his religious views remains an open one. Rather than the drunken verses reflecting agnostic skepticism, others are convinced that the intoxication from imbibing the grape is allegorical of mystical ecstasy... of one that penetrated nature's veil. Whether or not he was an ascetic lyrist or a cynical wino, I didn't really care. What I really wanted to know was... who was messing with my head?

On a Monday night when the restaurant was normally closed, I unlocked the door and entered the dining room reserved for private parties. Even though it had been nearly a week since the last time the bhoot room was booked, an unpleasant smell lingered in the air. It wasn't frizzled onions or smoky mustard oil. It was more like a strange perfume or sickly flowery odor than the enduring pungency associated with curry-laced Indian cookery.

After turning on the high-wrought lights, I checked the bar area for a daily planner that had gone missing. While searching for it, my attention was drawn to a hand-written note on high quality stationery that someone had left on the bar. The ornamental cursive was reminiscent of the penmanship of olden days, but what piqued my curiosity even more was the sheer strangeness of the first sentence. This prompted me to keep reading even though I might be invading someone's privacy.

PHOENIX ORIENTEM

Concerning the partial unfurling of this yellow scroll: revealed were glimpses of virid splendor perceived through veridical interstices in the afflicted mirror (not unlike Jacob's dream-ladder eye-opener while asleep on a special pillow). Suspect a dream-incubator involved in externalizing that locked within via supra-encryption. Understand, the stimulus that widens the aperture of this transliminal portal could be anything... including pareidola, although only a twilight pilgrimage shall generate lucidity (terma epiphany) and liberate our treasure locator from the bewitching paralysis induced by the hypnotic fluids.

Witness my hand (The signature was illegible.)
Nigra in Coronam Christi Resuscitati Phoenix

"Can't wait for the paperback, can you?" Malcolm's voice caused me to flinch.

"Jesus, Malcolm, I didn't hear you come in," I uttered while still a bit shaken. "What are you doing creeping up on me like that?"

"I apologize for giving you the collywobbles, but this is the ghost room," he smiled.

While pulling out a stool, he gestured to the hand-written note.

"Just some notes I jotted down. I'm working on a narrative about the Persian Qareen. It's a fairytale of sorts about one's etheric double... in this case a pre-Islamic Jinn-type entity. We all have one lurking deep inside us, either angel or demon... Speaking of the Jinn, why don't you pour us a couple of drinks. And, remember, only a few ice cubes and splash of quinine in mine."

I went behind the bar and grabbed a bottle of Bombay Sapphire gin.

"You've no doubt seen my spiritual double," he turned and gestured to an antique cabinet set against the far wall.

In a room that featured the spectral irradiance of gruesome apparitions, adding a touch of humor was a ghostly portrait of Malcolm on an acrylic easel in a glazed cabinet that displayed miniature lithographs of stark moonlit cemeteries. Blanched cheeks in contrast to his actual ruddy countenance beamed an ectoplasmic sheen. But it was the lurid glare of his eyes that tipped off the paraodic nature of the print; the comic effect being such that the exaggerated spookiness might as well have been eye-following peepholes like those used in low-budget horror flicks or Three Stooges shorts.

"The Qareen use a form of hypnosis to exert control over people - having the victim do the bidding of its master. This is actually a vestige of our archaic mentality − the bicameral mind − from a time when humans were hardwired to be obedient... to the gods. Are you familiar with the hypothesis? Back when humans lacked self-awareness, a pantheon of gods issued auditory commands... divine guidance that initiated man's behavior. Sensing your usual acrid pessimism, when I speak of these gods, I'm actually referring to the once cognitive functions of the divided brain. One chamber being the speaking god, with the other being the listening man."

When I finished mixing the drinks, I handed one to Malcolm, being careful not to spill anything on his esoteric Jabberwocky, even though I was fairly certain the handwriting wasn't his.

"With the advent of consciousness, the god-man partnership started to breakdown. Consider the oracles of the god-nostalgic Greeks and augury of other cultures in classical antiquity. As a carry-over into modern times, humans still experience vestigial traces of bicameralism.

Examples include the castigating voices of schizophrenics, the religious phenomenon of glossolalia, poetic inspiration and the imaginary companions of one's childhood. And, I dare say – possession by demons when certain regions of the brain are activated."

As usual, I didn't give much credence to Malcolm's psycho-babble. As for the nebulous rambling in the note, although it was characteristic of Malcolm's tedious conversational style, I was dubious that it pertained to some planned narrative of his. It seemed more like the cryptic communiqué of an intelligence operative or coded twilight language of some eccentric fraternal Order. Actually, it was more like the creative madness of a schizoid.

"While on the subject of things that don't exist, here's something that will no doubt be of interest to you... just like that weird dream I had in the motel I told you about."

"Ah, yes, the posterior cortical handiwork of that dastardly sandman chap that left you gobsmacked. Well, I admit, I'm intrigued... so let's have it. Ethical principles won't prevent me from nicking any choice nuggets for my ripping yarn, here," he said while tapping the piece of stationery on the bar.

"When I looked through Jag's augmented reality gadget I found Omar Khayyam talking in my living room."

"Omar Khayyam?" his ears perked up. "I see, and just what did the indulgent rhymester have to say?"

"It was a piece of a verse about a snake... that's all. But, this technology is getting a bit scary."

"Absobloodylutely," he concurred. You might have had a genuine encounter - with an actual visitant and mistook it for the gimmick in an overlaying machine. The other day Jag told me that soon patrons of the restaurant would be greeted by an imitation of me... an avatar, he called it... beamed into our customers' funny spectacles. Not just my spitting image - one tailored to look how I would like to appear to them... without flaws. Can you imagine that – an even more dapper Malcolm!" he chuckled. "People could even feel my firm handshake and smell traces of bergamot in my cologne. When I asked the lad if he thought he'd be happier escaping into some pretend existence, his response was that we are already living in a simulated reality... so what's one more layer. Anyway, should you see any pink elephants in the blasted thing, you might not want to mention them to Aaloka."

I wrinkled my nose at the peculiar odor that still pervaded my nostrils. Noticing this, Malcolm set his glass down and sniffed loudly.

"The downside of educating our customers' palates, or a bouquet of things requiring no protoplasmic mechanism?"

CHAPTER III
DIGITARIA

*"This God took off his own head and the others kneaded
the earth with the blood that streamed from it and molded it
into men. By reason of which men were of reasoning mind and
partakers of the divine intelligence."*

\- Berossus (*Enuma Elish*)

"Is a God to live in a Dog?"

\- Aleister Crowley (*Liber AL vel Legis*)

I thought the Sirius mystery had been discredited many years
ago by new findings. However, despite evidence to the contrary
presented by cautious researchers (not to mention the prevail-
ing academic viewpoint), today more people give credence to
the possibility of extraterrestrial amphibians having imparted
detailed and accurate astronomical information to a primitive
African tribe than when the idea was first postulated in 1976.
None of my blog posts to date had generated more traffic from
both believers and skeptics than "THE ABCs OF THE SIRIUS
MYSTERY", which I was compelled to write after receiving a
glowing review from Zonnie of a recent cable television documentary about the sophisticated cosmology of the Dogon.

For those not familiar with what the Dogon have no business knowing, I included in my post the basic elements of the enduring mystery. This overview included:

Having done fieldwork with the sub-Saharan tribe for fifteen years, a French anthropologist named Marcel Griaule finally gained the trust of a blind Dogon elder named Ogotemmeli, who initiated him into their inmost teachings in 1946. This specific knowledge concerned peculiarities about the binary (and possible trinary) Sirius system. Rather than venerate Sirius - the brightest star in the night sky as viewed from Earth – the Dogon attach a greater significance to its dark companion, Sirius B, which is totally invisible to the naked eye. They also say that Sirius B is one of the heaviest stars in the universe and that its trajectory takes nearly 50 years to complete around Sirius A – the latter being commemorated by a mask dance ritual synchronized with the event. In addition, sand diagrams traced by tribal spiritual leaders appear to graphically depict this elliptical path with Sirius A positioned off-center. The existence of the white dwarf stellar remnant, its specific elliptical orbit, density and rotational characteristics are currently accepted by modern science, although the Dogon priests claim that it has been preserved in their secret oral traditions for many hundreds of years. As to how they acquired this information, according to Ogotemmeli, it was conveyed to their ancestors by androgynous, self-fertilizing fish-like creatures called the Nummo who arrived on Earth millennia ago in a massive glowing calabash.

Admittedly, the Dogon's knowledge of stellar mechanics as recorded by the French anthropologist(s) boggles the mind. But, the question is: is it good anthropology... or bad anthropology?

In my argument challenging the tribe's inexplicable knowledge of astrophysics having been transmitted by an aquatic alien species – what shall we call them, astrogators or croconauts? – I offered a series of more prosaic explanations.

Unless we are to assume the whole thing is just a string of coincidences, we should first consider outside interference other than intergalactic visitation to find a satisfactory explanation.

Even with the isolation of living among cliff faces just south of Timbuktu in the present Republic of Mali, West Africa, Europeans visited the tribe at the turn of the last century, including, possibly, astronomers studying a solar eclipse in 1893. Since these foreigners were certainly aware of the suspected existence of Sirius B (from irregularities detected in the orbit of the proper motion of Sirius A), contamination into the Dogon's ancient lineage could have occurred by the sharing of cosmological interests. Other means of cultural transfer might have been from Jesuit missionaries trying to convert the 'savage natives.' However, according to some researchers, the most likely source was from Griaule, himself, especially in learning that he was an amateur astronomer.

If the findings didn't reflect his own interests... and questions weren't asked in a leading manner, he might have inadvertently misinterpreted Ogotemmeli's answers. Others suggest that he might have supplied certain details pertaining to the mystery in an overeager desire to assert the complexity of indigenous African religions and cosmogonic myths to his xenophobic western audience.

Considering past scientific hoaxes, such as the Piltdown Man fossils, some investigators find it fishy (pun intended) that Griaule was the only outsider to gain Ogotemmeli's confidence. As they say, "we only have the word of one man." Since more recent attempts by anthropologists to corroborate his observations have failed to turn up anything substantial relating to the Dogon's anachronistic knowledge - with tribal informants being unaware of the invisible partner, or ascribing any special significance to Sirius A for that matter - claims have been made that he single-handedly fabricated the core elements of the mystery to gain notoriety among his scholarly peers. However, many doubt this to be the case, due to his academic integrity and that he displayed admirable restraint by not grandstanding the startling information, but, instead, merely adding it as a footnote in his published report.

As to other anthropologists coming up empty, this might be due to members of the Malian tribes being reluctant to divulge what they might know because of the political authority of the majority government testing their Muslim orthodoxy. (Griaule purposely avoided informants that converted to Islam and Christianity.)

Those offering other explanations for the Dogon not just being lucky guessers wondered if members of the tribe had special eyesight due to a higher concentration of melanin that enabled them to make a naked-eye observance. A more plausible suggestion was that the information originated in remote antiquity with the Egyptians, who conducted optical surveys of the night sky with a magnifying instrument that had a polished crystal convex lens like those found in statues of ancient provenance.

Besides elements of the Sirius mystery being riddled with ambiguities and downright errors, those most critical of the evidence (or lack thereof) of the Dogon's anomalous claims point out that Ogotemmeli said there was a third star in the system, and that this putative Sirius C hasn't been detected by modern astronomy. Although gravitational studies conduced in the 1990s suggested a possible third stellar component – a sub-stellar object called a brown dwarf – a more recent analysis in 2008 concluded that the system probably didn't have an additional star.

With regards to the all-important question of whether or not the Sirius system is capable of sustaining life, based on current scientific data, the prospect seems highly unlikely. Sirius A is relatively young and is a spectral type of star that emits lots of ultraviolet radiation. This would be detrimental to any forming planets in its goldilocks zone. Of course it's possible, as many of my readers noted, that the Nummo didn't originate in Sirius's circumstellar habitable zone, but migrated there out of necessity.

Jag was grinning from ear to ear as he walked into my cramped home office.

"Check it out, Sheldon... I just got chipped. Had a RFID tag injected into the subdermal fascia to wake the Vespa," he said while peeling back a bloodstained gauze pad to show me the outline of the tiny transponder that was barely visible under the swollen flesh on his left wrist.

"Great, let's just hope the signals don't get crossed and I have to come pick you up at the animal shelter."

Noticing a series of photos on my monitor showing the pic-turesque cliff-dwelling habitats of the Dogon tribe on the Ban-diagara plateau in Mali, Africa, he leaned towards the screen.

"That's not real!"

"What do you mean it isn't real?"

"Looks like a colony of ants on steroids built that. Gotta be only basic cable in those mud condos, right? Actually, it's pretty dope," he said while checking out the cluttered maze of twisting pathways and earthly brown facades protruding from the cliff faces. Scrolling down, more detailed photos of the village further emphasized its chaotic design. Blending in with the rocky scree above the sandy desert plains was a cluster of rectangular mudbrick huts and squatty towers thatched with pointed caps of millet straw.

"You should read all the nutter beliefs from users with ugly avatars that I have to respond to with dialectic tact," I said.

"What?"

"The Dogon tribe – well, not the hoi polloi – but the tribal priests have claimed that slithering creatures called the Nummo from the Dog Star in Canis Major visited them in the remote past."

"With those freakazoidal masks, I believe them," he said while looking at a photo taken during one of the tribe's colorful masquerades.

"They should monetize that shit with plant-based jerky and Yeti koozies for boozy seltzers."

"Yeah, I agree. How about a tee shirt that reads: NUMMO THAN YOU, TYSON, with SIRIUSLY printed beneath it."

"Bruh."

"How do you think they obtained the info?" I asked just to see what he might come up with.

"From reptiloid aliens who created us from ape-men to help them hoard gold before bouncing... just like it says in the history books... What do these dudes do for food on that pile of rocks?"

"Millet, onions, peanuts... and sometimes sorghum when they order from GrubHub... shallots, legumes, did I say onions? Did you notice the granary doors," I asked while pointing to photos of conical thatch-roofed granaries embellished with carved figurative imagery and abstract geometric patterns. "That's how they secure the stored grain. Mythical aquatic deities offer protection. Invocations of ancestral spirits - now, that's an impressive locking system. Light years ahead of your implanted microchip."

Other photos of the thatched granaries showed crude locking mechanisms that consisted of sliding crossbeams outfitted with wooden bolts and large metal prongs.

"If the spirits do such a good job, why do they need those ginormous keys?"

"As a backup in case the spirits need to be somewhere else... just like the key to the Vespa that you should keep in your pocket in the likely event of solar flares or something that causes your tag to shit the bed."

While noticing that the thread was getting image intensive (which affected download times), a message appeared across the screen with the same pronounced golden letterforms that were used before by what I assumed to be a cult of Enochites called Ramiel.

BLESSED ARE THOSE WHO WASH THEIR ROBES, THAT THEY MAY HAVE THE RIGHT TO THE HIDDEN TREE AND MAY GO THROUGH THE GATES INTO THE DUST BEYOND EDEN

THE RIGHTEOUS EAT THE FRUIT AND ITS FRAGRANCE SHALL ENTER THEIR BONES

"You've a lurker in the discussion forum... or... you need a better plugin as a spam filter," Jag mumbled with his unblinking eyes transfixed in awe of the vivid typography.

As suddenly as the message appeared, it vanished from the monitor.

"It's almost like it knew when you were done reading it. Cray, huh?" Jag said with a puzzled look while running his fingers through his dark hair.

Aaloka entered wearing black drawstring shorts and a rumpled white tee shirt that said:

CREATE SOMETHING BEAUTIFUL

"It came with the CRISPR kit," she said before I asked. "What's going on in here with my fellows?"

"Just chatting with the cyborg of Arcadia Terrace."

"You better keep that clean or you'll get a staph infection," she cautioned.

"The grinders at the transhumanist booth already told me that. The tag's encapsulated in bioglass, mom."

"So... how's it going with that crispred plate of E. Coli cells in the fridge?" I asked Jag. "You're trying to get it to grow antibiotic cells or something with white specks next to my leftovers."

"Streptomycin," Aaloka said.

"Yeah, I think I might have got some hummus in the pipette that ruined the first batch. I just need to add a pinch more of the transformation mix to a clean centrifuge tube and I'll be incubating again... and setting the plates next to Sheldon's 7-11 beef taquitos that took 660 gallons of water to make."

"I dip them into kale smoothies, okay... and they came from the best taqueria north of the border. So, if you're successful in modifying the bacteria this time around, I guess you and the ready-to-use kit will be all set to terraform the surface of Mars into boundless cow pastures."

"Why's he so snarky, mom?"

Aaloka's mouth curved into a smile.

"He doesn't remember why."

"I gotta bounce," Jag groaned in an exaggerated manner while trying to re-attach the bandage. After Aaloka fixed it for him, he hurried out of my office in his baggy bohos.

"I want to show you something," I motioned for Aaloka to take a look at the computer screen as I scrolled to some photos that one of my readers posted on the blog site. The Dogon sand pictures showed a confusing jumble of markings in the reddish earth inside a rectangular grid surrounded by stones.

"Those are just fox prints used for divining purposes," I pointed to what looked like complex hieroglyphics, "but I've been getting lots of comments on my Sirian thread saying that besides having knowledge of astrophysics, the Dogon also encoded in sand diagrams... as mnemonic devices... certain things associated with genetic concepts that were meant to survive until they are recognized by modern science... by someone like you. For instance, one of my readers thinks this relates to the spiraling coils of DNA. I can see how the tiny seeds of Digitaria exilis in the celestial granary are likened to Sirius B, but spirals, ovals and broken lines... or the symbolic meanings of spindles, weaving and fibrous skirts relating to genetics really seems to be stretching things. Anyway, before responding, the open-minded skeptic wanted to get your opinion."

"It could just be that they equate human procreation with elements of agriculture," she said while looking at photos showing spirals, zigzags and broken lines inside ellipses traced in the sand.

"Wow, this one's pretty strange."

She scrunched her face while pointing to a photo of one of the sand drawings that to my eyes looked similar to the others.

"Transdifferentiation."

"What's that?" I asked.

"It's a rare biological process that involves the transformation of cells into different types of cells. Where a sexually mature organism reverts back to its juvenile polyp state... like the Immortal Jellyfish – "

"Immortal?"

"Theoretically immortal. That doesn't mean it can't be eaten by something. When it gets old, *Turritopsis dohrnii* has the ability to reverse the biotic cycle... and it can repeat this process of re-generation over and over again."

"The Dogon teacher-gods – the Nummo – were said to be self-generating aquatic creatures. Yeah, okay, but this immortal jellyfish - they're just wispy blobs. Why was nature so generous to those floating globs?"

"You just don't like jellyfish because they remind you of um-brellas. Interpreting it is like a Rorschach inkblot, or finding pat-terns in linoleum swirls. You know – pareidolia. But, what the diagram shows – it's a pretty strange coincidence."

Though the *Turritopsis dohrnii* really can create numerous exact duplicates of themselves (I checked online), I wondered if Aaloka was pulling my leg about the Dogon sand diagram possibly relat-ing to the process of transdifferentiation. This kind of jesting was something that she did every now and then, just like the time she kidded the African-American women at the bar in the restaurant about some fortune-teller's involvement in our meeting. Think-ing about that (as my mind tended to wander), it always seemed a little odd that she never asked me about what might happen if I regained my memory and realized that I had a wife and kids. Maybe she blocked the thought from her mind - something many women would have a hard time doing. Was it possible that she knew things about my past, I wondered at times, before dismissing such an overly suspicious idea as being unlikely.

Overnight, the Sirian thread darkened considerably as armchair occultists offered their input. Sirian influence is well known in the esoteric tradition, many claimed, with the star being the

All-Seeing Eye of Freemasonry. As for quasi-masonic lodges, the initials A ∴ A ∴ (*Argenteum Astrum*), meaning "The Order of the Silver Star", stands for none other than Sirius. This was the initiatory organization dedicated to the advancement of humanity founded by Aleister Crowley, an infamous British occultist known for his tireless pursuit of admitting an extraterrestrial current into the human life-wave.

In the dark doctrines of one of Crowley's protégés, during magical operations involving erotico-magical techniques, priestesses in their oracular phase are able to perceive faint impressions of astral level manifestations of semi-tangible forms that are loathsome in appearance, similar to how the Dogon describe the repulsive amphibious Nummo. Through the diabolical caprice of sinister cults, such monstrous fancies have seeped through the cracks of a trans-spatial gateway – a "mirroir fantastique" codenamed The Nightside of Eden - and are, as we speak, intruding upon our terrestrial sphere. "Seriously," I uttered with a dumfounded smirk.

Taking a break from reading about the dreadful forms conjured from interstellar R'lyehs, I sought out a more desirable shape while stepping out onto the deck where Aaloka was sipping a can of hard seltzer while seated in a rattan chair.

On the crisp spring night, a full moon shone on the jacaranda tree whose indigo flowers overhung the wooden rails. The vanilla fragrance of numerous tea candles mingled with drifts of eucalyptus silver drop and the bouquet of spicy resins in the oriental perfume she was wearing.

"The thread turned into a lanterna magica shifting with the nameless bugaboos of H.P. Lovecraft's horror fiction literature," I told her. "Seriously, I just finished wiping the iridescent slime off the computer screen."

"I don't know exactly what that means unless you're saying that you're done demolishing peoples' weird beliefs for the night?"

With my arms outstretched before the glowing cups, I spoke in an ominously commanding tone:

"It means unspeakable things are awakening from their slumber and rattling around in the cranial vaults of necronauts residing leagues from the moldering tomes of Miskatonic U - go Black Goats! - in places like Ponca City, Oklahoma, as made evident by the scrawls of trembling hands before the shadowy flickers of tallow guttered out. Batrachian monstrosities with webbed appendages flabbily quivering as they emerged from the silver flooded billows of thalassic spume... shall I continue? Their glassy, bulbous eyes darting horribly under a gibbous moon that gave a spectral luster to horned casques protruding like ossified nacreous crowns set upon a hideous amphibian likeness."

On the verge of a smile, Aaloka stared at me as if I had lost my mind.

"That's my imitation of the curse of adjectives... without using squamous... and, yes, I'm done, so do you want to hang out?"

"What did you have in mind?"

"I'm up for whatever."

"Well, we could drink the last two cans of Jaggy's blueberry and acai hard seltzer while playing his nutritious facts cornhole... or you could watch me fix his latest Cas9 failure... or I could get out of these joggers into a dress and we could go to that bistro with the veggie fondue."

"I don't share Jag's taste with spiked beverages – how old is he anyway? – And as fun as editing the genome of bacteria sounds right now, lets go to the bistro and throw some road kill on a sizzling rock."

"You're not going to like his latest idea either. He wants to get a worm composting system to eat our garbage."

"So... he wants to become a transhuman cyborg, but wants worms to chow down on our table scraps instead of using the garbage disposal... just like he wants his next motor scooter to be self-driving, but wants me to grow my own peanuts to eat while I'm watching the game."

"That's how nineteen-year-old kids think these days."

"And that Twitter-born bafflegab – speaking of mumbo-jumbo - I saw some rather abstruse writings that your father-in-law had. Is he a member of some Fraternal Order, do you know? A Freemason? Even though I don't exactly associate him with brotherly love or charitable deeds.

If not a convivial society, maybe it's an occult organization he's involved with? Robed magicians engaged in nocturnal ceremonies. Arcane diagrams. Motley devils. Jeweled daggers. That kind of thing."

"That's funny because in India... when he was younger, he dabbled in some of that stuff. Like tantra... it's popular there... but I don't think he still has any interest in those things. Well, I should get ready if we're going out."

When I got back home and checked the message boards, I saw that the trail of mephitic ooze abruptly ended. Instead of posts about the Cthulhu mythos-type Sirians, the thread contained numerous observations regarding benign humanoids from the planet Xylanthia (located in the Sirius system). In reading the nauseating string of platitudes telepathically received from these slender, blue-skinned sapiens, which many believed to be our forgotten ancestors, I quickly concluded that I preferred the gut-

tural utterances of Lovecraft's cast of reptoid oddities clamber-
ing slipperily from some inter-dimensional abyss.

Mercifully, the cosmic revelations of our galactic brethren
fell silent when Zonnie sought to add a new wrinkle to the Sirius
mystery. This concerned Benjamin Banneker, a colonial-era Af-
ro-American farmer, naturalist, surveyor and astronomer who
supposedly theorized that Sirius was a binary star two hundred
years before it was discovered to be so.

According to one biographer, Banneker's grandfather was a
member of the Dogon tribe. It was from stories passed along by
the family that Benjamin came to know about Sirius being a
double star. As one of the surveyors of the federal capital district,
some allege he incorporated certain alignments of his favorite
star with specific architecture having occult significance.

In my reply to her, I pointed out that there was no evidence
that Banneker was in any way involved with points of interest in
D.C. that have recently become popular with those of a conspir-
atorial bent. Knowing that I would be called a racist by some of
Banneker's admirers, as a truth advocate, I added that some of
his supposed accomplishments had been embellished. True, he
helped survey the boundaries. Yes, he carved a wooden clock that
struck on the hour. He wrote almanacs that contained ephemeris
calculations and trigonometry puzzles (some with the wrong solution). Many credit him with predicting the period cycle of Brood
X cicadas. He might even have invented the reverse mortgage, but
he did not hide geometric symbols that are representative of either
a new Atlantis or of Satan's control over political figures into the
street layout of the nation's capital. Therefore, we can't hold him
responsible for the gridlock that plagues that city.

Before shutting down for the night, I read a member's post
about Voltaire's novella entitled *Micromegas*. In this seminal

work of science fiction from 1752, a giant from a planet orbiting Sirius and his dwarf companion travel to the earth. Taking pity on its tiny inhabitants, who believe the universe was created solely for them, before departing, the Sirian presents a member of the French Academy of Sciences with a book that tells "all that can be known of the ultimate essence of things." When opened by the secretary, he finds that it contains only blank pages.

I had to smile at this nice touch by a master satirist, even though I knew tomorrow someone like Zonnie would comment that the name *Micromegas* was a pretty good way of describing a super dense yet diminutive stellar remnant like Sirius B.

Turn on *Mindshift*!

Seeing the repeated messages in the thread from Zonnie, I grabbed my portable radio and tuned in her favorite late night radio show of all things weird. After listening to an advertisement about the miraculous properties of an elixir containing monatomic gold that some quack claimed to be an alchemical panacea, the theme music for *Mindshift* swelled as the calm, resonate voice of host Nell Trevers briefly summarized the breaking news that my friend was so anxious for me to hear.

According to Trevers, his special guest claimed to have the preserved remains of a mysterious aquatic creature that was likened to a Nummo. The man (who didn't want to give his real name) said that he was a former army soldier that served his country during the Vietnam War and was now residing in a veteran's home called Charlotte Hall in southern Maryland.

A work crew refurbishing an old tobacco warehouse that was currently used as a combination Amish farmers' grocery and flea market located on route 5 near the VA home initially discovered the creature. While installing a sprinkler system to meet county codes, they noticed a deformed fish-like thing that looked like a "freak show exhibit" in the oak rafters of the tin-roofed building. They guessed it was some kind of strange marine specimen that was either fished out of the Patuxent River or that washed up on the banks of another coastal estuary. After showing it to the owners, they decided to sell it as a curiosity piece along with the antiques in the bargain barn.

When the veteran first saw it while digging around for something of interest, he realized the "terribly shriveled thing" – which looked like it could "easily fit in with the aliens at the Star Wars cantina" – might be an important find. He would explain why after the break, but before doing so quickly added that part of reason he purchased it was because its creepy appearance frightened the Amish children.

Once again I had to endure another commercial for the spagyric decoction that was comprised of "orbitally rearranged monatomic elements." Using new-age jargon like "ascension DNA activation" that was designed to exploit the gullible, this time those peddling the nostrum claimed it was the biblical manna! Besides being the cure-all for nearly every malady known, it was touted as being a rejuvenation agent that even enabled cats to re-grow severed tails. Did I hear that correctly? Some of the other reported benefits were so outlandish that I laughed in thinking that the level of quackery involved was almost an insult to pseudoscience.

When Nell finished taking care of business, after encapsulating the breaking news yet again, he enquired about some mysterious journal his guest had previously alluded to. As he continued with his story, I began taking notes: Through a relative that lived in Baltimore, he heard about an antiquarian bookseller that had a fragment of what he believed to be one of Benjamin Banneker's journals that survived the fire that burned down his log cabin on the day of his funeral. Though badly scorched, some of the handwriting was still legible. This contained references to an unknown aquatic species that he was studying.

The guest then reminded the audience that besides being a city planner and building the first clock in America, Banneker was a naturalist that observed the period cycle of locusts.

According to the page from the journal, he acquired the curiously shaped amphibious life form that was somehow preserved or mummified from his grandfather, Benneka, who, as a member of the Dogon people, brought it to America from his native Africa. The creature – which the host repeatedly referred to as a Nummo – might have been the reason his cabin was set on fire.

In describing its physical characteristics, he said that it had a flattened, triangular or kite-shaped body covered with rough scales. It was a brownish-green color with faint rosette markings. It didn't appear to have any bones, but felt cartilaginous to the touch. There were appendages of a very unusual nature and it had a long tapering tail that was forked "like the devil's." From its head protruded helmet-like horns or a casque like certain lizards have. There were hollowed out sockets where eyes might have been and instead of ears it had auditory holes.

Before the interview ended, he said that he was currently negotiating a price with the producers of a documentary about ancient astronauts for what he believed might have originated "on an extrasolar planet in the Sirius star system." In conclusion, he said that he had been combing through that flea market for years looking for something of value... but never imagined any treasure he discovered might be otherworldly in nature.

When the segment was over, Nell announced that his next guest had evidence of a global plot by our shape-shifting reptilian overlords to withhold essential nutrients from baby formula in order to minimize human intellect. I wondered if that might explain Jag? Maybe it wasn't because he was raised on chicken nuggets and root beer after all.

Zonnie was surprised when I told her that the guest's story seemed pretty far-fetched. She was even more taken aback when I thanked her for the heads up about the show because otherwise I wouldn't have known about the golden secret of the multi-purpose elixir that I was planning to purchase as a natural aphrodisiac. As for the Army vet and his lucky find, it seemed like quite a coincidence that he both knew about the book dealer that had a piece of one of Banneker's scientific papers that was spared by the flames, and that this just so happened to be the section of the journal that contained the account of the creature in his possession. Add to that that he also chanced upon said creature at a flea market that was located practically right next door to where he lived. That was too many coincidences for me.

In her response, Zonnie said I should wait until I saw the photos the man promised to send to Nell before I made up my mind as to whether or not the story was true.

I didn't have to wait long before the photos were posted on the *Mindshift* website. In the series of detailed color images, the creature looked pretty much like how it had been described. I could understand why the Amish children found its appearance to be disturbing. Though I wasn't sure what it was that I was looking at, it didn't appear to be some latex fabrication used as a sci-fi film prop. The only feature that looked faked was the head crest. To my eyes, the lizard-like casque seemed somewhat rubbery as opposed to being a biological attribute. However, because the creature was so shriveled up, it was hard to tell. Which made me think — why had he originally described it as being diamond-shaped when that shown in the photos wasn't?

Now that the army vet's identity was no longer a secret — he revealed his name to be Lasco Thigpen — other researchers would be able to further investigate the 'Nummo' to not only determine if it was actually an organic life form of some sort, but also to either corroborate or discredit aspects of the story that I found to be suspect.

A few days later Jag handed me a postcard that he said was delivered to the condo by a courier that was wearing a funny looking yellow uniform, complete with a matching beanie and sneakers. Even his eyes were yellow, he said, describing how the man's contact lenses had a shimmering golden effect.

When I raised my brows at his description, he told me that he was thinking about getting contacts that were the same shade, but wanted ones that were switchable between normal and magnified vision.

"Yeah, probably better to wait until they actually exist," I nodded.

"Maybe you didn't know, but they're already testing prototypes with telescopic lenses you can toggle on with blinks."

"What was funny about the uniform?" I asked.

"Whose?"

"The courier's."

"Oh, yeah... I don't know... It was a weird shade of yellow... and it was boxy... Just seemed like it would be harder to handle the unicycle."

"You're saying he arrived here pedaling a unicycle?"

"No... It was an electric unicycle, Sheldon. The self-bal-anc-ing kind. If it were my company, I'd use hairy-ass drones with delivery release systems... so you get your stuff in seconds. I'd hand-deliver shit myself if I was strapped to a big enough Octocopter."

"Was this self-balancing electric unicycle yellow by any chance?"

"Bruh, how'd you know?"

The postcard was a vintage reproduction that said:

GREETINGS FROM TOMBSTONE, ARIZONA

"Has a cool photo of a big bat," Jag said.

When he tried to take the card away from me, I waved my hand at him as if shooing away a pesky fly.

What Jag called a "bat" was actually a sepia-toned illustration made to look like a doctored photo of the legendary Tombstone Thunderbird – a pterodactyl-looking bird that supposedly had been shot by a couple of nineteenth-century prospectors in Arizona Territory. After being transported into town by either a burro or wagon, the monster's immense wingspan had been unfurled and nailed to a barn by a group of old west rancheros who were posing next to the trophy.

Scrawled in ink on the back were the words:

WHAT MIGHT YOU FIND IN A MERMAID'S PURSE?

There was no return address, but, oddly enough, the postcard had a cancelled stamp from someplace called Mechanicsville in Maryland.

Having recently published an article on my blogsite about the disappearing photos of the Arizona pterosaur, I assumed the postcard was sent as a response to my attributing the phantom images as an example of false memory syndrome.

Over the years since the story first appeared in the *Tombstone Epitaph* – undoubtedly fabricated with hopes of spurring tourism once the silver boom ended – hundreds of people claimed to have seen an actual photograph of the winged monster that was later published nationally. But a photo was never published in the Tombstone periodical, nor can one be found in repeated searches through the files of other newspapers or paranormal magazines like *Fate* and *Saga* that revisited the mystery in the 1960s.

Some who were absolutely convinced that they saw a photostatic image of the Tombstone thunderbird have even suggested the possibility of time travelers stopping the original photo from being taken, which is why one hasn't been found since then. (In the twenty-first century, those who question consensus reality and believe we live in a simulated world explain these discrepancies as being the result of revisions created by the designers after certain glitches occurred in the program.)

As I mentioned on the blogsite, it would appear that descriptions of the scene – mustached cowboys with spurred boots and six-shooters hanging from their hips posing with an enormous prehistoric bird carcass nailed to the side of an unpainted barn – were so vivid that they created a semi-tangible metal imprint in the minds of the readers, as well as lasting memories of a photo that never existed.

Of course, I also had an interest in these shared false memories because of my opposite retrograde amnesia. Ever since I found the Sunnyvale address in a duffle bag, I had the feeling that someone was leading me to something of significance. Perhaps trying to help me regain my lost memories. Seeing how the postcard was sent anonymously by someone who went to the trouble and expense of having it delivered by a courier (albeit an oddball), I wondered if the rather cryptic message about what might be found in a mermaid's purse might offer a clue or act as a trigger in recalling my past?

Since I didn't know what a mermaid's purse was, I Googled it. In learning that it was the charming name for the egg cases of skates that are often found after being washed up on beaches, I was even more confused. When I found out on Wikipedia that a skate is a stingray-like fish with a flattened, triangular-shaped body and a slender tail, I quickly did a search for the town from which the postcard's stamp was cancelled. In seeing that Mechanicsville is only 5 miles from Charlotte Hall, Maryland, it suddenly occurred to me that, rather than having something to do with false memories of the photo of an Arizona cryptid, the sender of the postcard was drawing my attention to a more recent mystery involving a different reptilian creature.

Doing some more poking around online, using the key word "Mechanicsville", I found an article about a local crab shack that had recently been burglarized. Among the stolen items was a preserved skate (crudely taxidermied?) that hung on the wall as part of the restaurant's themed décor. As soon as I saw the photo of it, I knew that it was Lasco's Nummo. Other than the protruding casque that was most likely added to give the thing a more alien vibe, it was a perfect match. That might explain why he described its shape as being triangular – a slip of the tongue in knowing all along that it was a skate, whose body was triangular or kite-shaped before the large pectoral fins dried up.

Now, the question became - why would someone want to help me debunk Lasco's claims, and why do so in such a whimsical manner? A fellow skeptic perhaps, but why didn't he or she come forth with the damning evidence and take the credit?

I couldn't say for certain that Lasco was the perpetrator of this apparent deception, because he might actually have found what someone else stole and altered the appearance for whatever reason. However, I had serious doubts that he was an innocent dupe in all this. The fact that there was no information out there that additional pages from Banneker's journals had been found pointed a finger at his involvement.

Before posting my findings on the blog site, I decided to have a little fun. There was an upcoming ancient astronaut convention in nearby Santa Clara that I had planned on attending just for the amusement factor. With all the excitement that Lasco'c story and photos generated among the paleo-SETI types, what better place to expose the hoax?

Jag had invited himself to come with me to the Bay Area Ancient Alien Con. Wearing my "STRAIGHT OUTTA URANUS" tee shirt to the event, we walked past an auditorium where luminaries of the wacko circuit were wowing the audience with a panel discussion of *interpretatio technologica* (conveying mythological texts in a technical language). As the 'experts' marginalized accepted history and mainstream archaeology, vendors outside hawked Erich von Daniken bobbleheads and pre-Columbian Quimbaya "Golden Shuttle" replica pin lapels. (Of course Jag bought one of these silly trinkets.) Noticing a few of the scheduled speakers seated at a table by a food kiosk were discussing the images of Lasco's Nummo, I decided to share some of my own photos.

"Howdy, gents. Don't mean to be a party-pooper, but you should take a look at this."

Flipping open my laptop, I pulled up the image of the skate on the wall of the crab shack.

"I'll be damned," one of them said.

"Bears a striking resemblance to your Sirian lizard, doesn't it? Now, I know what you're thinking. A crab house on the Patuxent River had an alien being mounted on their wall for all these years. Well, yes, it once haunted the shallow, brackish waters of the Chesapeake Bay... inland where fresh and salt water mix... as a bottom feeder... as skates tend to be. Yep, that's right - it's a skate. Notice the spiracles behind the eyes in this dorsal view... sorry, I've been studying them... but what makes it look so freaky is the shriveled large pectoral fin."

"Well, that's some good work that you did," one of the ancient astronaut theorists said with a condescending grin, "and this should help us with our investigation – "

"Look, I'm not sure if you've been intentionally bamboozled or not, but besides the helmet thingy that was obviously fabricated, your preserved alien specimen is just a common skate that was stolen from a crab shack in Maryland. If you have to wash the bad news down with some nepenthes in your coffee, so be it. Twelve million people believe that shape-shifting reptoids with giant claws are running Wall Street. There have been hundreds of sightings in Bishopville, South Carolina... so keep looking. I'd honestly like to see one of these slime creatures."

"I believe they're here," Jag told those at the table.

"Make that twelve million and one including this goofball," I smiled.

"I appreciate you trying to humor us, and, like I said, your information might be of value as we check all the facts of this case, so thank you for sharing it with us," the guy said while offering a handshake.

"Have you guys ever heard that bananas shouldn't exist on earth and must have been brought from Mars or somewhere?" Jag asked no one in particular.

Leaving them to their sandwiches and coffee and a deflated balloon, we entered the auditorium as another speaker was lecturing to a full house. The bearded figure with a nerdy pocket protector – a former NASA engineer – asserted that the winged cherubim that guarded the gates of the biblical Garden of Eden so that humans couldn't approach the Tree of Life weren't the chubby, rosy-cheeked infants depicted in Western art. The angelic sentinels were actually terrifying alien machines. The flaming swords that flashed in every direction were laser beam-like weapons. He then compared the cherubim helicopters or alien shuttlecraft with the futuristic aerial devices carved along with ancient hieroglyphics on the walls at the Temple of Abydos in Egypt.

When he took questions from the audience, I could have asked if he knew what a palimpsest was? Told him that Egyptologists have explained the helicopter interpretation as simply being the result of what happened when the original hieroglyphics were effaced and re-used. Traces of what remained tend to look wonky. Besides the overlaying effects on the surface, erosion could also account for the anomalous glyphs.

But it wasn't worth locking horns. I'd done enough damage for one day. As for the audience, some in the eclectic mix were just looking for an escape from pedestrian reality – longing for the fantastic. The more vulnerable – those who embraced the activities of the high-tech gods as a new religion - were going to believe what they wanted to hear. More reasonable explanations for what was hailed as proof for ancient technology would fall on deaf ears. One thing was obvious, though. Judging by the number of attendees, and their favorable response to the presentations, acceptance of the notion that ancient space visitors intervened in human affairs was on the rise.

Before driving back to Sunnyvale, we stopped to get dinner at a trendy new cantina that Jag said had great Yelp reviews. The food might be good, but I wondered if any of the Yelp elites critiqued the dim lighting. I was having such a hard time reading the fine print on the menu that I almost pulled out my smartphone to use as a flashlight. So much for eating first with your eyes.

"Hello, a little Edison, please!"

"In a couple of weeks I'll have lights implanted on both of my wrists," Jag said. "Twin Northstars. And I really want to get a Vespa that's self-driving."

"Lights?"

"LEDs… like jellyfish have. I know this piercer that's also a grinder who buries LEDs into people's flesh to backlight tats."

"But you don't have any tattoos… do you? All right, whatever. Right now I'm experiencing a bit of fusion confusion. Look at this stuff. Blue flatbread with hominy and prairie dog – is that a misprint, or gourmet Navajo dish? Venezuelan pulled pork arepas stuffed with corn silk and purple chilies."

"There's not much I can eat as a pescatarian."

"I thought you didn't believe in God?"

"Means I only eat fish."

"How about ceviche?"

"Is it autonomous? My next scooter's gotta be autonomous."

"It's chopped fish and a long hair in citrus sauce. Order that and pickled bananas… seeing how they came all the way from Zeti Reticuli."

"What are you getting?"

"Thinking about taquitos with Korean beef bulgogi and telling them to hold the farmers' squash… like they're doing with the electricity… and a Carta Blanca without lime… if it's possible to keep from sticking their goddamn fruit in the bottle… but I'll bet the barbacoa ones from that gas station I wanted to go to are better. At least I can see the waiters in those white uniforms."

"Six hundred gallons of water consumed by a Moo to make those taquitos."

"Yeah, well just think how many gallons of water it took for all that fish you're eating."

A man not wearing a white uniform, but, rather, a chunky sweater and Italian chinos walked up to our table. With the 'landing strip' goatee on his diamond face shape and designer black round glasses, he seemed vaguely familiar, although I couldn't recall were I'd see him before.

"Excuse me," he said. "I thought I recognized you at the convention. We met a while back at a casino in Pahrump, Nevada."

"Yeah, that's right. You're a film maker doing a documentary about that missing prospector – what's his name?"

"James Kidd. It's still in the works for Paragon. I'm Julian."

"Sheldon and this wannabe transhuman pesco with the pendant of a highly-stylized bird or fish is my girlfriend's son Jag… short for Jaga… very short."

"Yeah, a delta-winged, vertical-takeoff fish," Jag rolled his eyes while tugging at his shirt to emphasize certain anomalous features in the tiny replica of the golden artifact that ancient astronaut proponents believe represent aerodynamic features that are mechanical in nature as opposed to biological appendages.

Fish fly underwater with upright fins," I reminded him. "The thing's probably also a skate. And there are lizard gliders."

So, why's the fish… or bird's head cut off?" Julian asked. "And what about the cockpit seat and mechanical ailerons or elevators?"

"I'm sure you've heard of artistic license," I replied.

"We're hoping to find a real one… the actual model the artist witnessed a thousand years ago that inspired the pre-Columbian artifact. It's just another angle in the documentary to try and explain Kidd's mysterious disappearance and where all the money came from that he left behind. Maybe he found one of those things while working one of his mining claims and was paid off not to reveal it. Or was murdered. Did you happen to catch the lecture about Shaver's star mech that were abandoned by the Elders in networks of caves?"

"No, we missed that, but saw a fellow from NASA talking about a cherubim helicopter that was stationed at the gates of the Garden of Eden to make sure no more humans stormed what was strictly alien territory and ate fruit from the tree like Eve did after being tempted by a talking snake who promised her that if she took a bite she'd become just like the gods."

"I take it you're dubious of all this."

"Well, of a talking snake for sure."

"Anyway, about the documentary – some interesting things about Kidd have come to light. He wasn't your stereotypical gold-crazed prospector. Not out of central casting. He was deep. Well read. While staring at the stars during the graveyard shift at the copper mine he worked as a pumpman, he'd ponder how life originated and what it all meant. But, he needed proof of things… including a soul leaving the body after death. He used to quote from the *Rubaiyat* of Omar Khayyam. His favorite verse was about the door.

"Strange, is it not? That of the myriads who
Before us passed the door of darkness through
Not one returns to tell us of the road,
Which to discover we must travel to – "

"Yeah, I'm familiar with the verse."

"Some of his acquaintances were quite literate, too. Grads from Harvard and Stanford."

A kid in a yellow nylon jacket (that I had no trouble seeing) timidly approached the table. After fiddling with his curly undercut, he placed a vintage pulp magazine with an eye-catching cover on the table. I laughed at noticing that under the coat he was wearing a tee shirt that read:

ALIENS DON'T BELIEVE IN YOU EITHER

"*Amazing Stories* from 1948. Careful, it's disintegrating. Hello, Mister Grane. I read on your nonbelieving blog about these Nummo things. This is a story about Oge-make," he said while carefully leaving through the crumbling and yellowing pages until he found a particular story.

"Don't you mean Ogotemmeli?" I asked.

"No, this is about Oge-make, Mister Grane… and it's not an ordinary story because it's true… like the guy says."

It was hard to tell if he was socially awkward or just had a chill demeanor.

"During a ceremony with Navajo, Pueblo and Hopi Indians that happened in New Mexico in the summer of 1947 Oge-make walked the fire-trail that was normally reserved for the medicine man. While in a trance he was lifted out of his body into outer space and was shown visions… remote viewed Planet One…

whose denizens... like it says... were fish-like. The planet was once heavenly... until things began to change. Once infected from the stuff, they became freaks of nature. Planet One exploded and turned into a sun with a dense core that revolved around the other sun. Planet One became Sirius B Oge-make told the elders. This story was told by a scientist with degrees from Stanford."

"What caused the destruction?" I asked.

"Radiation poisoning."

"Of course. Why'd I even ask?"

"I just thought you should know, Mister Grane... the secret of the past... so it's not forgotten... because terrible times are coming."

The man seated next to our table threw his menu down and stood up.

"Okay, first of all there's no such thing as aliens! Okay? So, put your comic books away and open the one book that holds the truth. Jesus said: I am the door... he's the only door... I am the door. If anyone enters Me, he will be saved, and will go in and find pasture."

"It's just science fiction," I said, hoping to calm the guy down. "Unlike your fish story."

Julian flashed me a victory smile.

"What's the name of your blog?" he asked.

"With a Grane - G-R-A-N-E of Salt."

"I'll check it out," he said while placing his business card on the table. "If you haven't decided on anything yet, I highly recommend the poisoned tacos... Tacos Envenenados. They're greasy suckers, but they've plenty of napkins. They're not really poisoned, natch, but I guess the secret ingredients are to die for. Order them with tamarind flavored pulque and you're in business."

"Meh," Jag said.

With Aaloka's car being in the shop for repairs, after dinner I stopped at Cellectech, where she had been working alone after regular business hours. When I phoned to tell her I was there, she told me to come inside and wait as she finished up.

Seated at a workstation full of lab equipment, I could barely see the surroundings with the lights having been turned off for some reason. The only source of illumination was the faint glow of multiple computer displays and the digital indicators of an array of biotech machinery. As I was checking out an automatic pipetting system I heard Aaloka's voice behind me.

"Honey, while I finish up here's a cup of chai for all that beer you nosedived into at the cantina."

"All? I had two and a half beers," I protested while turning around – not expecting to see a black-wigged robot wearing a golden sari moving towards me with a coffee cup in its outstretched mechanical hand. This little joke of hers explained why the lights had been turned off.

"Thank you... Aaloka... thingy."

After taking the hot cup of chai, the telenoid remained stationary. There were no eye movements or facial expressions. Trying to think of something to say, a thought finally came to me.

"Can you even dye my eyes to match my gown?"

When I still didn't get a response, I set the cup down and stood up.

"Well, then, can you tell me where the restroom is? I really need to go and could probably fill up these test tubes... with ALL that beer I drank."

Though I was hoping to hear its uncanny speech synthesis again, the fembot didn't reply.

Wandering through a maze of state-of-the-art equipment whose colorful numeric displays served as beacons, I opened a door near the back of the building that I thought might lead to the bathrooms. Instead, I found myself in a dimly lit storage area that was completely empty save for a couple of pallets with cardboard boxes. The only other thing in the entire place was a piece of art hanging on one of the walls. Examining it further, it looked to be a painted limestone replica (?) of an ancient Egyptian temple relief fragment that contained a hieroglyph of a bird with a long bill that resembled a stork. Beneath it was a typical looking Eye of Horus that didn't appear as weathered as the bird motif. Due it its glossy black sheen, it actually seemed like a modern fabrication that had been added to the earlier decoration.

As I walked back to the door, I heard a whooshing sound behind me. Startled, I quickly turned around and saw another humanoid robot gliding towards me – this one larger than Aaloka's telenoid, with dual front LED headlights that shone brightly in my eyes.

"Can I help you with something?" it asked with a voice that sounded more like the monotone of an electrolarynx.

At that same moment, Aaloka walked through the door.

"Professor, I didn't know you were still here."

The sound of her voice caused me to spin around. Her addressing the thing like that confused me at first, until, turning back around, I realized that what I first assumed to be another robot was actually a man wearing an immaculate white suit strapped onto a high-tech stand-up-power wheelchair. (From where I stood, I couldn't see the sets of wheels located at the back of the unit while tilted to its upright position.) With a shaky, venous finger, he pressed a button that dimmed the front lights.

The partly opened door cast just enough light to make out a man well in his nineties. Judging by the crisscrossing of deep furrows on his face, he might have been even older. One of his pale blue eyes was filmed over with a milky discharge that might have been from a corneal ulcer, while the other was clear enough that it might have been an acrylic fake. Why didn't I see him when I first walked in, I wondered?

With the Fantasy Island duds and high beams, the only thing I could think of was that he had been behind one of the pallets of containers while seated instead of being elevated on the wheels.

"I was just admiring the new thermal cycler," he said into the artificial larynx.

With the robot voice quality, there was only a trace of a German accent.

"Yes, Volker, I heard the PCR finally arrived. Hopefully, no more second-site errors. This is Sheldon." Sheldon, meet Professor Hellmann."

"Pleased to make your acquaintance," he said with a gentle demeanor. "Call me Volker. Sheldon, are you also interested in correcting typos in the human genome?"

"He eviscerates other things... you might not be familiar with... like speculation of ancient astronauts from Sirius," Aaloka laughed.

"Pelley," Volker said.

"What's that?" I asked.

"William Dudley Pelley. Back in the day, he wrote about migrating souls... star guests enwrapped in a physical ensemble. He spoke about eradicating the bestial ingredient – our brute ancestry – from man. Our waiting celestialanity is the true redemption of the Bible.

"Where did these souls migrate from?" I humored him.

"Spirit particles of organically-housed entities. You and I being their mundane residence," he said with an ambiguous smile that I wasn't sure how to take. Was it his way of mocking such eccentric ideas, or did he give credence to the notion, and was expressing pity for the human condition, especially in light of his own corporeal deterioration?

"Did he say where these spirit particles migrated from?" I asked again.

"The Sirius system."

CHAPTER IV
BREYFOGGLING

*"Consider the powerful cluster of glowing vectors on our intel-
lectual radar, the indicators we have created to tell ourselves where
to look and what to look for, the signs we keep leaving ahead of
ourselves all generated by the same inexorable genetic impulse at the
leading edge of our probing."*

*We do not know exactly how much of a 'budget' product "the
Adam" represented — and that uncertainty can be quite disconcert-
ing."*

- Neil Freer *(Breaking the God-Spell)*

"You shouldn't have been roaming around the lab without me,
even if you had to pee like a horse, Aaloka uttered, getting
visibly angry when I asked about the hieroglyph on the temple
relief fragment.

I had been curious as to why the piece was hanging in a
nearly empty stockroom. Having done some research, I learned
that the hieroglyph depicted a saddle-billed stork and found it
interesting that Aaloka's telenoid answering machine had, upon
my unintentional prompt, tried to connect me to something
called the Stork's Nest. I didn't tell her that the *ba*-bird glyph
represented a powerful aspect within a person that was given by
the gods — an animated spirit — similar to primitive notions the

high-mileage professor had talked about. I wanted to hear what she had to say before somewhat jokingly asking if there might be more going on at the lab than engineering perfect babies.

"The stork seems perfectly fitting for a biotech company that specializes in designer children," she said before taking another sip of chai.

We were sitting in my cramped office trying to figure out what to do for dinner before I had brought up the sore subject.

"They are traditionally associated with delivering children, are they not? They're even shown on jars of pickles because of the stupid notion that pregnant women crave pickles."

Although her explanation seemed reasonable, I was still a bit puzzled as to why it was placed where it was instead of being displayed in a more noticeable location.

"They're also voiceless creatures... being largely silent, are they not?" I added.

"They're symbols of parental devotion and good fortune, okay? Next time ask me where the bathroom is. Oh, regarding that story in the magazine about the Pueblo ceremony – "

"Yeah, the space opera where Oge-make is beamed up to Sirius."

"Well, I checked and there's no record of the author being a Stanford alumni. The writer – Lucille or something – adopted the persona of a man. I guess back then there was even a bias towards men being the writers of third-rate sci-fi. Anyway, his - her academic credentials were falsified."

"Really?" I blurted out with mock surprise.

"You're over-needling me, Sheldon. Any particular reason why?"

"You're telling me that the editor of a paranormal 'zine who claimed to remember not only his own birth but also his conception actually fudged the credentials of a contributing writer just to grab more sales? For nothing more than a grubby dollar! Well, I have to admit that I am astounded by these revelations of yours. You've single-handedly managed to shatter my deep-seated trust in the veracity of the P.T. Barnum of science fiction rags. The mental distress caused shall require psychic healing... or one of your Starflower cocktails."

This caused a faint smile.

"You're starting to sound like Malcolm."

At that moment Jag walked in and introduced his new lady friend.

"This is Zyla."

"Oh, what a pretty name," Aaloka said.

Though I tried my best to keep from staring, her overall appearance was so unique that I couldn't help myself. She looked to be in her early twenties, with a face that was stunningly beautiful, framed by a pearl bob whose bangs partly covered the subtle sparkle of tiny stars arched above her eyebrows. Wearing a spandex bodysuit with long sharp shoulders and chrome knee-high boots, she looked like she just stepped off a movie set playing the role of an ultra-feminine sci-fi queen. Even her unique perfume contained metallic notes. I also noticed that she had the same lapel pin as Jag – the pre-Columbian artifact dubbed by ancient astronaut buffs as the 'golden shuttle.'

"Where's the stash of cash for DoorDash?" Jag asked.

"My purse is on the table. What did you order?"

"Sriracha lime edamame," Zyla replied.

"Yum, that sounds good," Aaloka said.

"Delish, especially with charcoal water," I deadpanned. "I see you're also sporting the golden flyer, Zyla."

"Zyla geocaches them as swag with links to websites so the locators can learn the truth."

"So these anomalies aren't so easily dismissed by those who aren't woke," she added without the annoying glottal fry that many of Jag's other young female visitors used at the end of their sentences in some new speech fad. "So far, I've got the Quimbaya shuttle, the Abydos helicopter, Shamash's winged globe carving found on Sumerian cylinder seals, the space capsule of Pakal's sarcophagus lid and a grooved disc of the Dzopa… those left by the people from Sirius that crash landed in Tibet a long time ago. I'm also going to start using stickers with QR codes – like Munzee does – so they can be found using smart-phone apps… the trackables, that is."

"What about the astronaut of the cathedral of Salamanca in Spain?" I asked.

"I haven't seen that yet, she said with a confused look. "Was it on the History Channel?"

"He's only kidding – the freakin' skeptoid," Jag uttered.

Aaloka gave me a look letting me know that whatever I was planning to do probably wasn't a good idea.

"Hey, I try to keep an open mind."

After typing "Salamanca Astronaut" into Google, the screen quickly filled with images depicting what was clearly the depiction of a modern astronaut wearing a NASA-type flight suit floating amid some foliage carved into the masonry.

"Check it out. A hidden carving of an astronaut on the façade of a gothic cathedral."

As Zyla leaned closer to the monitor, I glanced up to see her reaction.

"Wow," she said as eyes with a touch of glimmer from silver contacts stared in wonder. "Look at the helmet he's wearing."

"Better than a shaman's headdress with deer antlers mistaken as antennae," I said.

"Even better than the suits worn by the Dogu figurines. Who could possibly say that's not an astronaut?"

"No one in their right mind," I replied. "And right next to him is a gargoyle... eating an ice cream cone... two scoops at that. Both of these hidden carvings were added to the façade of the 16th century cathedral during its restoration in 1992. The contemporary images served as the signatures, if you will, of the artisans involved in the project."

"You wanted to trick me," Zyla smiled.

"Nice going, hunty" Jag clapped.

"That's okay. I get it, Jag," she said while pulling out a small bottle from her hologram metallic tote. As she spritzed her face, I saw that the hydrating body elixir with an almond (?) fragrance was called 'FUCK BAD VIBES.' "That's why I didn't know about it," she nodded while putting the anti-negative energy face mist back into her bag. "It's not really that old. So... so... but what about those that we know are really old and out of place... that shouldn't be there like the Tassili spacemen painted in caves... Arabian rockets or Biblical-era vehicles piloted by gods in monasteries in Europe?"

Before I had a chance to reply, the doorbell rang. With Pavlov's Dog-like conditioning, Jag bolted out of the office, making a beeline towards Aaloka's purse. After waving goodbye to Aaloka and I, Zyla followed him, striding in her clunky footwear at a more civilized pace.

"You still up for some road kill tossed onto sizzling rocks?" I asked the woman with the annoyed look on her face.

When we got back from having dinner, I saw that Jag and Zyla were out on the back deck, leaning over the railing as if looking at something in the wooded area beyond the Jacaranda tree.

Sliding the squeaky glass door open, I stepped out onto planks that were still wet from the recent drizzle.

"What's going on?"

"We saw some weird lights out by the dog park," Jag said. "I thought it might be someone messing with a drone, but it wasn't. We were going to hide a night cache with a trail of reflectors... using FireTacks as markers, but it started raining so we decided to wait. When we got back – that's when we saw them. The freaky colors... they're gone now"

"Maybe it was someone else playing the same game," I suggested.

"The reflectors are a different color. FireTacks are kind of orangey –"

"They're blaze orange," Zyla said. "These lights were extra - the way they moved."

"Well, you better be careful with the scavenger hunt. Someone might think you're planting a bomb. Your mom brought you back some fish from the bistro – stewed mudskippers – just kidding. It's swordfish grilled on a volcanic stone," I said while heading to my office.

There was a message on my site from Julian of Paragon Makings asking me to call the number on his business card. When I finally reached him, he asked if I would be interested in participating in the Kidd documentary. The producers agreed with him that having the input of a "well-known" skeptic in the film would be good for balance when exploring some of the more far out explanations. Should I convincingly debunk these findings, so be it, they would be ruled out as a possible solution. After assuring me that they were only interested in solving the mystery, no matter what the truth might be, I said that I would think about it. He said that would be fine, but not to take too long in making a decision because they wanted to shoot the Superstition Mountain scenes before "it got to goddamn hot." He ended by saying that the exposure would definitely create more traffic on my blog, which meant additional revenue.

Even though I said that I'd have to confer with others, I had already decided that my involvement in the project could be potentially good for my site. Hopefully the production wouldn't be hackwork like most ghost hunting bunk in the paranormal reality television genre. I was already imagining fuzzy green screens of abandoned mine shafts with staticky digital audio files of 'disembodied' voices and ordinary Joes with spiky hair professing to be paranormal experts while brandishing their Home Depot techno-bullshit.

For reasons she wouldn't elaborate on, Aaloka said that I shouldn't involve myself in such rubbish, even after I mentioned the possibility that when it came to those making such films, maybe one size didn't fit all.

While discussing the matter further, something caught my eye through the kitchen window. These were colorful lights bobbing in an unusual manner off in the distance, possibly the same ones that had earlier freaked out Jag and Zyla. Walking over and peering through the glass to get a better look, whatever it was appeared to be spherical in shape with a small luminous diameter of alternating colors that seemed to be floating between the shaggy trunks of eucalyptus trees.

Curious as to what this was, I went out back in the light sprinkle and followed a dirt path to the nearby dog park. When I reached the first trees, I watched as the glowing sphere glided, twirled and dipped beneath the high branches. Suddenly, a yellowish fog enveloped the surroundings, the thick wisps drifting towards me with a nauseating buttery smell. When the cloud dissipated, and I advanced further on the path, I realized that the baffling object was nothing more than an umbrella whose luminous canopy served as the screen for the flashing lights. The person holding it looked like one of the tech-bros that hung out at Malcolm's Indian restaurant. In fact, with his vaping butter-flavored juice, I was fairly certain he was the same guy that I had mentioned the idea of umbrellas with video projections merely as a way of distracting him from unfurling his ordinary black one until I was a safe distance away.

When I asked about the design, he explained that it was a prototype that he was testing. Kinetic energy from raindrops was converted into electricity that powered an array of LEDs. Once perfected, he was going to try to get startup money through a crowd-funding campaign, and asked if I wanted to be a donor for special perks.

When I returned to the condo, Jag was seated at the kitchen table finishing the last of the swordfish.

"Where's your lady friend?" I asked. "Did she zip back to Venus?"

"Ass."

"So, I saw the lights you were talking about."

"Cray how they zigged and zagged, huh."

"Well, they turned out to be something not that odd."

"What?"

"A unicorn."

With no stagecoaches available, I arrived by cab at the Goldfield Ghost Town located at the foot of the Superstition Mountains in Apache Junction, Arizona. The historic old mining town had been refurbished as a tourist attraction with an authentic-looking dirt main street having a general store, museum, church, bordello, apothecary and saloon. It was at the Steakhouse and Saloon that a team meeting had been scheduled by Paragon. Over coffee, Julian introduced me to the small field crew and host of the documentary, Flynn McIntyre. Drinking a sarsaparilla instead of coffee brewed with "newfangled" Keurig pods, was our guide into the Supers – a crusty old prospector named Zeke, who everyone in Goldfield called Saltback.

With his battered cowboy hat and sun-creased face, the old sourdough fit right in with the saloon's décor of Wild West artifacts. From what I had been told, he had chanced upon a door fashioned from the slab of a boulder that concealed the entrance to a cave in a canyon wall. Dead grey mesquite branches and segments of jumping cholla disguised the stone door, itself.

Although he had entered the dark opening, he had not explored the cave because he was fearful that it harbored the spirits of deceased miners. Knocking sounds made by pick-hammers were warnings to leave them alone. He also spoke about the taurtums – the little people that surfaced at night from bottomless portals called hell-mouths. His mentioning of numerous headless bodies still clutching their bogus treasure maps that had been left to the vultures caused uncomfortable glances at the table.

Zeke would take us to the canyon on an old mule trail that wound through the "look-alike" rugged terrain, but he would not enter the cave for any reason, he stressed. "He's smacking his chops like a Dutch hunter," he rasped while scratching dense grey stubble with his callused hand before gesturing to Julian, who was wearing a tee-shirt with a skeleton sipping a margarita that read: YEAH, BUT IT'S A DRY HEAT, "but this ain't no place for armchair adventurers... and you can't git there in no Range Rover neither. Before we saddle up, pards, we ought to gather necessary supplies at the mercantile, including a slice of saffron cake to leave for the knockers to gain their favor."

I was told that my involvement as the "balance" in the project was to try and explain away these malevolent imps seen in the vicinity of the cave. Instead of wearing traditional mining outfits with leather boots, according to Zeke, the diminutive beings were attired in metallic greenish-silver coveralls with matching shiny boots. Other witnesses had described their distorted shapes as being almost reptilian in nature.

When I asked Julian what these gnome-like folk had to do with Kidd's mysterious disappearance, he said that he would tell me after I signed a non-disclosure agreement. When I said that I wasn't sure if I had ever ridden a horse, he said not to worry because I'd be going with the crew.

We wouldn't be heading into the Supers until the next morning. Julian planned on spending the rest of the day at an ancient astronaut convention in Phoenix. He wanted to get some footage of a presentation on "The Shaver Mystery" that could be used in the documentary as a possible explanation for what might have happened to Kidd. I was to accompany him, along with his female production assistant and the main camera operator.

The Phoenix con was even more crowded than the one in Santa Clara. I noticed that there were also more children in attendance, some young enough for the ancient astronaut coloring and picture books being sold.

From a table near a concession stand I could hear the former NASA engineer making his case that Ezekiel's visions of storm winds that bore living creatures (cherubim) were actually descriptions of his encounter with an alien spacecraft. His technical analysis included various components of the landing module, such as rotor blades, a propellant tank and mechanical arms. These essential systems all checked out – even the gleaming bronze of hydraulic legs and synthetic insulation - but the doubting Thomas in me raised a brow when he theorized that luminous plumes of gaseous emissions emitted by the shuttle craft were symbolized by... beards! Was he really suggesting that excessive facial hair in depictions of Sumerian deities and the terminal beards of Biblical prophets represented rocket exhaust? Wow...

After having a triangular hamburger for lunch, Julian and I made our way towards The Shaver Mystery presentation. Before we reached the auditorium, we paused in the hallway (along with many others) to check out an exotic-looking beauty who was seductively reclined on a rotating platform. Distinctive eye makeup and tipped black braids made for a pretty good Cleopatra. Beneath a beaded headband, the woman's face shimmered with a golden radiance that was supposedly the result of the skincare goop being advertised.

As the product's pitchman (wearing a white lab coat, no less) hyped the miraculous anti-aging properties of the "Chrysopoeia Serum", whose ingredients included monatomic gold developed by a "certified alchemist", the eyes of most of those who gathered around the slowly turning rostrum seemed to be on the 'natural vitality' of sensuous curves of bronzed flesh barely concealed by a sheer M-slit skirt and metallic underwire bra. Though I would have liked to hear more about collagen depletion, cellular regeneration and the "orbitally rearranged monatomic elements-infused cream" that was absorbed through the epidermis, the Shaver Mystery lecture had already started.

"The world is sure filled with crackpots!" the man at the podium began his lecture. With a half-crazed twinkle in his eyes, he doffed a scarlet bowler hat and placed it on his walking cane. Wearing a DERO DESTROYER tee shirt beneath a bright red blazer with matching corduroy pants and red faux-leather quilted sneakers, the speaker, Brodie Quinn, was billed as an "Inner Earth" expert. As he spoke, he stroked a neatly trimmed beard with patches of red.

"That's what the managing editor bellowed after reading a sloppily-typed letter addressed to the office of the science fiction magazine, *Amazing Stories*. Crushing the piece of paper into a ball, he tossed what he considered to be the ramblings of another crank into the nearest wastebasket. That might have been the end of it, but the man seated at his desk on the other side of the wall had acute hearing. As soon as he heard the word crackpot, his interest was piqued. The man was named Raymond Alfred Palmer - a diminutive hunchback who worked his way up as editor-in-chief of the company. RAP, as he was known, retrieved the letter from the circular file. After smoothing out the crumpled paper, he slogged through what the author claimed was an intergalactic alphabet known as Mantong - Earth's mother tongue - that should not be lost to humanity. Although RAP wasn't sure what to make of this, he had a brilliant hunch that might increase circulation. Having free reign of the magazine's contents, he decided to publish the salvaged letter. As soon as the issue hit the stands, letters began pouring in from readers... cave explorers and such... corroborating the high strangeness. Wanting to know more, he reached out to the author – a factory worker named Richard Sharpe Shaver... honestly, that was his name - who promptly responded by sending a manuscript about interstellar spacefarers and an antediluvian civilization entitled, 'A Warning To Future Man.' Though it was of poor literary quality, RAP was fascinated by the basic premise. Correcting the grammatical atrocities, he skillfully re-crafted the piece and published it. Sales skyrocketed. Thus began a publishing sensation known as The Shaver Mystery. The year was 1943 – decades before the ancient astronaut theories of Robert Charroux, Louis Pauwels, Jacques Bergier and Erich von Daniken."

After pausing for a drink of water, he continued by telling the audience that *Life* magazine called the Shaver craze "a celebrated rumpus that rocked the science fiction world." Indeed, Shaver's story sounded like bad science fiction, involving the Elder gods that migrated from their home world to the Earth many thousands of years ago. Here, they built a flourishing civilization filled with technological marvels that inspired the myths of Atlantis. However, over the centuries, the sun's rays became contaminated, bombarding the peaceful Atlans and Titans with harmful radiation.

When they began to mutate in terrible ways, they were forced to live underground in a network of caverns hollowed out by their wonder mech (mech being Shaver's catch-all term for the Elders' advanced technology).

"Shaver witnessed first hand the remnants of our glorious heritage. Ancient halls decorated with such magnificence that they would take Michelangelo's breath away, as well as polished corridors leading to domed gardens of unimaginable lushness. In subterranean chambers that pulsed with dim luminosity, he also saw god-machines - gleaming metallic enigmas that were still operable. After continuing to mutate from the poisonous radiation, many of the Elders fled in gigantic starships to search for a more suitable home. Those who were abandoned further degenerated over time, developing a bestial hunger while imprisoned in the luminous gloom of their chthonic playgrounds. Shaver called these mutated horrors the dero – short for detrimental robots. But, there are also some good guys. Those that somehow managed to develop a resistance to the deadly radiation. Although they are the minority, they constantly try their best to keep in check the savage malignancy of the misshapen dero. These are the tero.

At this point, Julian began typing notes on his iPad.

"As they've done down through the ages, the dero continue to bedevil surface people by accessing the ancient rays. These radiant instruments of untold age are capable of hypnotic suggestion, telesolidographic projections and implanted memories. There are dream-beams responsible for our nightmares and stim-mech whose beguiling whispers of pleasure rays lure people deep into the caverns."

So, that's why my mind kept drifting back to Cleopatra out there in her black lingerie. The little creeps must have zapped me right after I sat down.

"At times the Elders succumbed to their own technology, as with their habit of using the dream machines to escape into the bubble of a fantasy world."

Although this dream-drugged existence brought to mind the augmented reality devices that Jag often talked about retreating into, I didn't have long to ponder the similarities, as what he said next caused quite a bit of grumbling in the room.

"The treasure house of mechanisms included artifact-rays that were used to create the appearance of ancient remains scattered throughout the earth."

Artifact-mech? Perhaps I needed to reevaluate Shaver's nonsensical ravings. Was he actually an unappreciated genius that foresaw an ancient astronaut mythos that he helped to create?

Realizing the blasphemous nature of what this implied, after clearing his throat, the man whose embarrassed blush matched his suit jacket managed to get a few laughs when he told the *Chariot* buffs that science fiction purists of the time didn't care much for Shavermania either.

"As pages of *Amazing Stories* were filled with the rampaging dero, its editor incurred the wrath of fandom for promoting Shaver's hokum. By claiming that the stories were true, he was perverting the genre. Boycotts by pulpster critics threated to damage a lucrative brand. After the craze had run its course, when RAP was asked if he believed Shaver was telling the truth, rather than accuse his friend of consciously perpetrating a hoax, he replied by stating that Shaver truly believed the things he was saying, although there had always been a bone of contention between the two.

Rather than dwelling in the underworld, the mystically oriented Palmer theorized that both the tero and dero were spirits of the dead that lingered in the ethereal realm that encompassed the planet. The dero roam the lower astral plane, while the tero inhabit a higher vibrational level. Shaver countered this by steadfastly maintaining that the hideous depravity he witnessed right under our feet was the work of flesh and blood creatures. The blood of both spurts... red," Brodie said while pointing to his suit. "He couldn't imagine spirits – no matter how debased – roasting their human delicacies on a spit. And every time he pinched himself... it hurt."

With these words the lecture ended.

During the question and answer session, someone asked if the dero ever focused their rays on... Ray? After a few chuckles,

Brodie recounted a story often told by Palmer about an issue of *Amazing Stories* devoted entirely to the Shaver Mystery. The normally routine process was fraught with problems.

"I'll leave it to you to decide whether or not it had been sabotaged by the dero to keep the magazine from exposing the truth about their subterranean empire, or if this was just a shameful promotion by its colorful editor? All kidding aside, there was an incident that occurred in his past. Knowing better than to use the word cherub with this audience, let's just say that RAP was a beautiful baby... so much so that as a toddler his image was pasted on milk bottles as part of an advertising campaign that called him one of Milwaukee's Healthiest Babies. Fast forward to the age of seven when he's hit by a milk truck while crossing a street. The accident left him with broken vertebrae. A botched operation to keep him from being paralyzed crippled him for life."

On our way out of the auditorium, Julian told me he planned to include a segment in the film that explored the possibility that Kidd had unwittingly discovered an entrance to Shaver's cavern world and had an encounter with a subworlder while working one of his active gold claims on the eastern fringe of the Superstitions or along Pinto Creek. Such, an encounter, he said, might explain his odd behavior.

"Seriously?" I asked.

"The man who supplied Kidd with provisions at his mine said on his deathbed in 1982 that Kidd had begged him not to reveal its location, natch, but most important of all, after he died, not to tell anyone the site of his grave... which was probably at the mine. Maybe he insisted on this because he didn't want those looking for him to find out something or to put themselves in harms way?"

"You're saying he faked his death?"

"Maybe he joined the teros in the underworld... and that's why he wanted to die in obscurity?"

"Okay... Well, as excessively frugal as Kidd was, living among the tero was probably cheaper than his four dollar a month rent in Phoenix. Same with his meals... if he subsisted on the non-corroding canned nutrients left in the Elders' store-houses. He didn't pursue ladies, so that rules out him being lured by dero stim-rays. I think you're flipping over too many stones, Julian, but all things given, there's... oh... less than one-in-a-gazillion chance that Kidd joined the teros. Same odds that the dero and tero ever existed."

"And here I thought you were going to be skeptical," he smiled as we made our way into the crowded hallway.

"Keep in mind what Brodie said," I reminded him. "When asked for proof of his claims about the Altans and Titans, Shaver replied that all people needed to do was to look at the Devil's Tower national monument in Wyoming. He said that if it wasn't a gigantic petrified stump larger than any redwood ever hoped to be, he would eat his hat."

Paragon's lady production coordinator, Hayden, was at a complete loss to explain what happened. The hotel booking website she used showed that my reservation had been canceled and rebooked at a more economical chain. While the rest of the crew would be comfortably ensconced behind the Parfait Pink walls of Apache Junction's finest lodgings, I could only hope to be lulled to sleep by the complimentary screech of cicada in, of all places, the Sandman Inn. What was the color of that wall – Dreamsicle orange?

Before getting into my cab, she apologized profusely for the mix up, seemingly relieved that I didn't make a fuss.

"Maybe there'll be some Krispy Kremes left," I said, leaving her with a confused look on her face.

Judging by the surroundings, the Sandman was located in the junk-tion part of town. As the Hispanic cabbie dodged horses and Harleys, we passed a meth haven of cluttered trailer park porches and stucco houses with dirty faded paint. Sunburned tykes with mullets splashed in bargain store pools next to propped-up camper shells and duct-taped Camaros parked in dusty front yards. Wiggers crossed the street carrying Monster energy drinks and Chelada tallboys as the muffled strains of Lynyrd Skynyrd could be heard coming from windowless local bars draped with Confederate flags. Being that it was too early for drunken fisticuffs, desert rats in Circle-K bandanas gathered out front around their pickups to smoke Marlboros.

My room had a view of the Superstitions looming in the distance. As I gazed at serrated ridgelines outlined in dark copper shades against the bruised mauve twilight, I thought about the place's sinister reputation. In reading about the decapitated bodies of those drawn to the unforgiving wilderness by the irresistible lure of fabled riches, some had been killed by the Apache, who resented the foreigners desecrating their hallowed ground. Many had perished from thirst in the blistering heat, or had fallen to their death from steep vertical drops. Lone prospectors skittish of claim-jumpers were responsible for others, as became evident to the sheriff's department when bullet-shattered, bleached skulls were found after having been dragged through labyrinths of canyons by coyotes and javalinas.

Moving away from the window, I set the rooster alarm clock to crow at 5:00 am.

"But, how many had met their maker at the hands of deros?"
I joked while plopping my head down on a lumpy pillow.

When I found myself wandering among the aisles in a retail
nursery I knew that I was experiencing a reoccurring dream.
With rows of succulents, azaleas and eucalyptus, the setting
seemed like your normal home garden center, though at any
minute I expected things to change rather dramatically. Rounding a corner of more potted houseplants, I became increasingly
anxious of finding myself disorientated by a profusion of sculpted
greenery - botanical wonders of unknown varieties flourishing
inside spherical terrariums that had paralyzed my gaze while
having the same dream.

I tried to force myself to wake up, but was unable to do so. As
strange as I remember the constantly morphing, variegated luminous growth in the extensive hydroponic globes as being, even more
bizarre was the nurseryman wearing a futuristic protective suit and
slanted amber goggles that radiated with dark golden speckles.

Instead of the albino gardener that I was anticipating, standing before me in the dappled sunlight was a gaunt figure with a
deeply graven face and scant ashen hair. Wearing tan trousers
and an employee's vest over a collared shirt, his nametag read,
Maxx. When the elderly fellow spoke, a long black whisker protruding from the mole on his angular chin uncoiled in a disturbing manner.

"Can I help you find something, sir?" he asked with a raspy
Midwestern twang while smoothing back his brilliantined hair.
"Just what might you be looking for?"

"I'm not sure," I replied. "Some kind of gift, maybe."

"What's this gift for? A funeral plant, maybe?"

"Sympathy plant? I'm not really sure... but I need to find it."

Hearing strange hissing noises behind me, I turned to see

what might be causing them. In doing so, my eyes were dazed by the golden-white coruscation of a magnificent spiral staircase rising from the wetted concrete floor in the home garden center. As I slowly approached this architectural marvel, whose towering spiral twist was composed of some golden liquid-metal that shimmered with a delicate iridescence, the old codger shuffled behind me, shouting in his gravelly voice:

"Those are off limits to you, mister! For employees only. It's forbidden for you to climb!"

Ignoring him, I began to ascend the winding steps. As what sounded like a low, distant rumble became more distinct, I could hear monotonous chants of ominous voices repeating the words, "We have been expecting you." At the same time I could also hear the whirling propellers of drones buzzing around me. Glancing down, I saw that Moley was now wearing headset goggles of glistering amber while toggling a joystick that he used to control several quadcopters that were flashing vivid blue strobes as mechanical voices issued stern warnings:

"Walk backwards towards me with your hands on your head."

With the drones whipping around me, when I reached the final step, I walked out onto the polished metallic glass of a golden-white balcony that appeared to be a seamless extension of the glorious staircase. The terrace offered a panoramic view of Sonoran desert terrain, with the jagged peaks of mountains in the distance stabbing the bluish transparency.

Taking in the scenery, a tiny greyish bird with a bright yellow head alighted on my hand. Before I could react, the surroundings became engulfed in shadow. There was an ear-piercing shriek, followed by the glint of a massive silver pterodactyl that swooped down with its flapping wingspan blotting out the sun. The thunderous writhing and twisting of the enormous flying reptile jolted me awake. With my face beaded with perspiration, I sat bolt upright in the bed, confused for a second by the reflection of vivid blue lights bouncing off the peeling wallpaper.

Outside in the motel parking lot, I could hear static-laden radio transmissions and hard, distinct voices.

"Lie down on your stomach and keep your hands in the air. Comply, or you might not survive."

Getting up I walked over to the window and peered through the blinds. A couple of Apache Junction patrol units had their strobes flashing while several officers with their weapons drawn moved towards what looked like a shirtless skinny tweaker lying on the asphalt with his hands on the top of his tattooed shaved head and a lit cigarette in his mouth.

Standing behind one of the squad cars was a man that looked vaguely familiar. It took me a minute to place him, but suddenly it hit me. He was the same guy I had seen at the Greyhound stations and casino in Pahrump. Even in the middle of the night he was wearing the same gold-mirrored Cartier sunglasses. Wondering about the oxblood boots with the camo pattern, just like those on the floor in my room, I didn't get a chance to find out when he disappeared from my sight.

What kind of Hollywood movie cliché was I living in… and what the fuck was buried in my brain?

When I climbed back into the bed, the alarm rooster crowed.

A crewmember gave me a ride in an all-terrain vehicle up a winding trail to the bluff where Paragon's base camp was located. On the uneven bedrock, a configuration of transparent bubble tents resembling geodesic domes had been erected, making the place look more like a colony on Mars than a base of operations for a film shoot in an Arizona wilderness area.

"Who knew the mercantile had this many glamping supplies," I said to Zeke, who was scratching his sunburned nose while gawking at the spacious interiors of oversized camping pods furnished with hardwood floors, wicker furniture and inflatable couches.

"Glampin'. Heck, is that what you city slickers call this high-falutin' bivouac?"

"Leave it to a Hollywood production company to turn a godforsaken place like this into a 5-Star resort," I said while swatting at biting flies. "Go ask the camp butler for a pastry, Zeke."

As Hayden walked by, she licked her lips while tossing back strawberry blond braids hanging from a turquoise cowgirl hat. "Those lemon basil kronuts from Karls are to die for."

"Ingenious donuts... feather beds... and chilled Pellegrino. Roughing it, huh, Julian," I uttered as he emerged from the gable opening in a large tent with a portable flushing toilet and twenty-five dollars a roll bathroom tissue from Tiffany, according to what I had been told by a crewmember.

"With limes, natch," he smiled. "Just making up for last night's motel debacle, Sheldon. Have you tried the elephant coffee, yet? Black Ivory, or something. I understand it's been refined by passing though pampered elephants."

"Is that feller pullin' your tail?" Zeke asked, raising a questioning eyebrow while watching a crewmember unloading more glamping equipment from rolling storage duffles. "He's havin' a boiled-dog time of it now, but wait 'til the brick-oven heat comes and he gets clawed by a Spanish Dagger," the old-timer grinned with a brittle laugh.

"Yeah, but if he does, want to bet he's got some tweezers made in Switzerland."

Julian paced behind the fat-necked camera operator and the sound person holding a boom microphone. As he framed the next shot in his mind, waiting patiently for his cue was the 'face' of the documentary, a clean-shaven, well-toned adventurer dressed in desert khaki and wearing a crushable leather western hat. Standing beneath a towering monolith of lumpy crimson stone - one of the numerous hoodoos in the Superstitions, the "relatable" host, Flynn, pointed to a cactus wren perched on a needle-tipped cholla. After snapping photos of it, Hayden glanced about sheepishly.

"What can I say, people - I do lots of birding in Cali."

Noticing a tiny pale grey bird with a splash of yellow on its head that was chirping near a tangle of mesquite, I asked if she could identify it.

"That little birdie is a verdin. And guess what... they aren't related to any other birds here."

Once everyone was in place, Julian stepped to the side of the guy with the hand-held Sony.

"Okay, ready, Flynn... and action, people."

"It sounds like something straight out of a science-fiction drama, but ancient legends from many cultures tell of people that inhabit worlds deep inside a hollow earth. Farfetched? Perhaps, but supporters of the theory point to these inner-earth dwellers to explain out-of-time artifacts... known as ooparts... that have been discovered in various places. One of the cavern entrances and tunnel systems leading to these sub-cities is believed to be disguised somewhere in these foreboding mountains... one of the deadliest places in the west. With this in mind, an idea has been put forth that, while working one of his

mining claims in the area, Kidd may have encountered someone... or something that wasn't from the surface. Suppose...
just maybe, that the already extremely reclusive prospector
decided to live among these benevolent inner-earthers. Could
this explain his odd behavior – why he insisted to his partner
that he be left to die alone in his mine... and that no one should
ever know of its whereabouts?"

"Cut. Hayden, give Flynn the watch... and Burton... change
angles."

"What's with all the pictures?" Zeke asked.

With the prop in hand, Flynn held up a replica of the gold
pocket watch for the camera while continuing with his dialogue:

"The one object that Kidd didn't want to part with – even
after his death – was his Elgin gold octagonal pocket watch...
just like this one. Although the reason for this unusual request is
not known, if the timepiece - which is inscribed with his name
and date of birth - should be found among skeletal remains, part
of the mystery would be solved."

"Cut."

GoPro cameras were trained on Flynn and Zeke as they rode
horseback on a bumpy mule trail that wound through a boul-
der-choked canyon. Maintaining the same pace, the rest of us
were bouncing in all-terrain vehicles while traversing the inhospi-
table landscape. As the sun climbed higher in the cloudless azure,
Hayden vigorously rubbed some of Cleopatra's monatomic gold
lotion on her face, pausing only to point out a red-tailed hawk
soaring over a steep ridge bristling with prickly saguaro cacti.

"If Cleopatra had known about that midnight radio goop she wouldn't have had to take rejuvenating donkey milk baths," I joked while bracing myself against the dashboard as another jackrabbit darted in front of the Polaris.

"I'll turn into one of those chuckwallas in this ridiculous sun if I don't put it on," she said while fanning herself in the sweltering heat.

Crossing a washed-out gully shaded by gnarled juniper trees, the dusty track descended through a narrow pass flanked by foliated granite outcrops and bulging, mushroom-shaped rock goblins having deep ruddy hues. While raising his left hand to signal Julian, Zeke reined his mustang to a halt and squinted at a jumble of patina-browned boulders.

On a lichen-splotched stone beneath a barely visible ledge, someone had chiseled what Zeke believed to be a treasure marker. This was an M with a box underneath it that was positioned at eye level for a person riding a horse.

When the camera operator was ready, Zeke switched on his Lavalier.

"This M with a box under her ain't no Spanish clue. It's a Jesuit mark that lets you know there's a mine nearby. If you go followin' most of the markers in the Supers... chinked arrows or slash marks on a limbless cactus, you'll wear your boots out chasin' something that ain't nothing. Breyfogling it's called."

When he was done ad-libbing, Flynn began his scripted dialogue:

"There are conflicting viewpoints by lost treasure aficionados on Spanish directional markers, but most agree that a specific code was employed for trail markers... and that it was mandated by the king that trails leading to Spanish workings all be monumented – "

"The marks were always the same so it wasn't so difficulted," Zeke added.

"A heart means gold. Recall what Cortes said: We Spaniards know a sickness of the heart that only gold can cure. But a heart with a crack... or lightning bolt passing through it means you are close to a mine, but there's a deathtrap. The stone door... or however the mine is disguised, is booby trapped, so heed the warning. The Jesuit priest marker here is promising –"

"This one's bettermost," Zeke nodded. "Some might just well be carved with a BS," he chucked.

Flynn raised his palm as a shield while lifting his gaze to the sky.

"The temperature is climbing, but we're getting close and need to press on."

"Dinged hot!" the wiry prospector wiped his glistening bristles with his shirt cuff. "Best not piddle. We've clum this far, so grab the nubbin'."

As we advanced further into the stony inferno, orange-tinted spires of eroded volcanic tuff appeared like fossilized eruptions of fantastic-shaped sentinels. Snaking through a brooding canyon aglow on all sides by craggy peaks and stone chutes, we crossed a dry arroyo that rippled like a mirage as the wind whistled eerily through clusters of hoodoos that protruded like fingers of dull red fire reaching towards the turquoise sky. Pointing to a directional arrow incised on a white boulder enlivened by desert varnish, Zeke verbally commanded his horse to pause in a rocky clearing and signaled to the throttle-monkeys that we had arrived in the canyon where the hidden door was located.

The camera was focused on Zeke as he pulled away some scrub brush that further camouflaged the slab of an oval-shaped boulder that formed the stone door in the canyon wall.

When the last of the withered grey branches had been removed, we could make out the door's barely discernable outline, even though it had the same sanguined patina as the surrounding rock. With a slight push, the stone turned easily on its socket, revealing a narrow opening on both sides slightly above ground level.

After examining its "rotational axis", Flynn began speaking about how the engineering specifics were similar to stone doors he'd seen as entrances to caves in Armenia. When he was finished explaining how it operated, the camera guy squeezed through the gap so that he could capture the host's triumphant entry.

Flicking on a caving light, Flynn wedged himself through the scant opening. Seconds later, we could hear his muffled voice expressing excitement about the inside being covered with drawings.

Within minutes, several of us had joined him, walking on a gravel-strewn floor littered with debris. Shining my flashlight down, I could see grey and tan pottery sherds and piles of rotted leather sacks.

"Nothing to see here," Flynn joked as the powerful beam of his light swept across a cave wall, illuminating red and yellow pigments of ancient rock art.

In the wavering glow, the mixed ochers of pictographs stood out against the faded glyphs of pecked geometric shapes. As Julian moved closer with his hands-free spelunking headlamp, the prismatic halo of a bright white circle encompassed mystifying stick figures that seemed to be floating beneath a strange black object. In the same panel of these cryptic drawings, spindly beings with large bubbleheads had vacant eyes that radiated white dots towards stair-like patterns and a tree-like figure.

"What do they say?" Hayden asked.

"No biggie — just lizardmen emerging from a spaceship," Flynn laughed, knowing that alien-ologists claimed similar biotriangular silhouettes found elsewhere to be proof of ancient visitations by extraterrestrial beings.

When Julian asked what I thought about the fantastical imagery, I told him that it was evidence of ritual activity... not stylized depictions of teros or deros. To mainstream academia, the
strange anthropomorphic figures represented trance-induced visions of tutelary deities by Native Americans who used the caves
for ceremonial purposes.

Seeing Hayden pocketing a fragment of decorative buffware,
my eyes widened as if I was suddenly grasped by a feeling of
impending danger. When she placed the piece of ceramic back
where she found it, I let out a sigh of relief, laughing on the inside
that she thought I seriously believed by removing it as a keepsake
she would be cursed by some cranky Indian spirit.

"It might have been used by natives for a vision quest, but
it's also a hidden mine," Flynn said while wagging his light over
rusty tools and glass bottles webbed with dust.

"Looks like a tunnel," Julian said. "Let's check it out."

Having decided to further explore the cave (or mine), the
cameraman followed Flynn as he bent low and inched forward
down a narrow passageway that had been timbered with hand-
hewn ironwood.

After only advancing for several more yards, his voice echoed
in the dank gloom.

"I'm getting a funk... something not pleasant. Sulphorous
fumes, maybe?"

Moments later, the two emerged with concerned looks.

"No bony fingers with a death grip on a gold pocket watch I
take it," I joked to Flynn.

As we slowly exited the cave, Zeke was standing by the horses
with a wide grin on his sweat-stippled face.

"You seen the doodles... but there weren't no location notices
stuffed in mayo jars or nothin' for the diggin's. You got a whiff of

stink damp, too. Bad air risin' upwards, maybe… or mought be from a boodle of spirits. Hair in the butter, either way."

The plan was for Hayden to get a toxic gas detector (couriered from Phoenix if need be), and more "bricks for the GoPros and AX100" and return to the cave in the early morning.

"Best to get a wiggle on before sundown."

When we arrived back at the basecamp, Julian instructed the crew to "prep the fire."

As stars began to appear over the jagged ridges, several of us were huddled around a campfire on which a cast iron pot of beans was bubbling while hanging from a crude tripod stand.

While Burton and his camera assistant prepared for the next shot, Zeke was entertaining us with tall tales. Keeping a straight face, he spoke with a nasal bray about saguaros crushing people to death with their spiky arms as they followed ghost trails to Spanish gold, and how gifts of barrel cactus sometimes exploded, scattering thousands of baby tarantulas into one's home. Of course, there was the jumping cholla, whose flying needles stung those who came to close, but my favorite in his cock-and-bull repertoire was about how chaparral cocks (what he called roadrunners) were clever enough to fashion small corrals of cholla joints around a sleeping rattlesnake. When the trap was set, the birds coaxed the snake to strike, whereupon it became impaled with thorns and, hence, their dinner. Seeing Hayden's expression of awe by the birds' ingenuity, I didn't have the heart to tell her that the story was one of many published by a famous writer of southwest yarns whose tongue was often firmly planted in his cheek.

Before Zeke had a chance to regale us with another whopper, Julian walked up with the inner-earth expert from the Phoenix convention. Mister Quinn, he informed us, would be taking part in the "campfire scene", discussing a possible connection with

Shaver's cavern dwellers and a famous UFO sighting known as "The Phoenix Lights." After politely extending his walking stick while tipping a scarlet derby bowler, the man in a red denim jacket joined our circle.

When things were ready, Julian gave Brodie his cue.

"Picture's up. Rolling... and action."

"In 1997 there was a mass sighting of an immense, perfect V-shaped formation of intensely glowing lights by residents throughout Arizona. As the triangular mass glided soundlessly overhead, structural details could be made out though a rippling effect as if the object's anti-gravitic propulsion system was distorting the space around its massive black frame. Although know as the Phoenix Lights, the initial sighting was over the Superstition Mountains here, with the array of lights last spotted at the edge of Tucson, where it shined down a beam of red light."

Flynn picked up the story.

"I've heard the legends of such gigantic craft that were supposedly abandoned deep in caverns by a warring race of beings that traveled to earth from the stars in ancient times. According to one witness named Richard Sharpe Shaver, this star-mech, as he called the alien machinery, is still in good repair. As you're aware, Brodie, such advanced technology is believed to exist beneath these forbidding mountains... a place where many people have either disappeared or met with sad endings."

As coyotes yelped and howled in the distance, Zeke poked a stick at the settled logs, causing the coals to pulse as sparks skittered into the star-filled night. With his prodding, the juniper logs crackled and popped, sending resin-scented wisps of smoke over prickly ocotillo.

"Arrow-shaped, you say," he turned towards Brodie with twitching shadows on his face. "Whelp, it might be stretching the blanket a bit, but the thing sounds like a big directional marker of sorts... just like them carved on boulders to signal the whereabouts of hidden mines... only this arrow was glowin' in the night sky and pointin' to rich pickin's near Tucson. That's quite a stumper, all right."

It was my turn.

"Although I like Saltback here's idea of a giant treasure marker floating in the sky, you don't have to look too far to find a more mundane explanation for the lights. Even if you discount the weather pattern and don't think the flares were wind-driven, how about drone flares?"

"Why then did Luke Air Force Base scramble F-15 fighter jets?" Brodie asked.

"They were part of the exercise," I suggested. "Flares not attached to parachutes, but to drones."

"The decoys came later that same night," Brodie insisted, "To trick all the people that witnessed something otherworldly. The kaleidoscopic orbs were the engines."

"What seems more likely," I asked, "alien troglodytes taking a football field-sized spaceship out for a quick joyride... or a military exercise using experimental countermeasures... maneuvers involving drone-launched or plane-ejected infrared suppression flares?"

"Obviously, flares sound more logical," Brodie agreed, "But that doesn't mean what really happened wasn't something far more fantastic."

"Cut."

"Who's for some frijoles and hot coffee?" Zeke asked while leaning over the licking flames to stir the steaming pot of beans with a large spoon.

"Zeke, you don't need to eat the props," Julian laughed. "I've got a surprise for you. We flew cowboy chef Lane Westin in from

Beverly Hills - and there's plenty of gold in them thar hills, I can tell you – to prepare a bowl of his famous slumgullion. Lane's catered the Rolling Stones tours, but I figured he could hitch his wagon to your star as well."

"Long as the stew's got skunk eggs, I'm good. These beans ain't got no sow bosom in 'em anyway."

"Well, if skunk eggs are onions, it does," Julian smiled. "C'mon, let's fix you up with some proper eating irons."

"White beans?"

Zeke scratched his stubble as the celebrity cowboy chef with a droopy mustache and a long silver ponytail hanging from the back of his Stetson ladled white beans that were simmering in one of the pots on the professional outdoor grilling system.

"Cassoulet beans," Lane said.

"That's some fancy conchos you got there, pard," Zeke whistled while gesturing to the buttons on the chef's back leather vest that were glinting in the Halogen cooktop lighting.

"Cowboy bling," Lane smiled. "Hope you enjoy the chuck," he said while adjusting an infrared burner. "And there are chilled Shiners in the Yeti."

"No imbibin' for me, thanks," Zeke said while giving his titanium spork a funny look.

As Lane was about to serve my side dish to go with the slumgullion, I heard Julian's excited voice coming from one of the production tents. Seconds later, Hayden emerged from the clear tunnel entrance of the domed "Stargazer" and shouted for me to come take a look at something.

When Zeke and I entered the spacious bubble, I found Julian seated on an inflatable couch, viewing some of the day's footage projected onto a silver-coated fabric that served as a screen.

The unedited footage was captured by one of the GoPros when we stopped near a boulder-strewn gully shaded by a lush tinge of paloverde trees to check out a stone carved with a directional signal in the form of a heftless arrow having an upward slant. In the background, Julian had noticed someone quickly ducking behind a formation of pinal schist. Though the footage wasn't clear enough to make out details, the shape did appear to be more human than animal.

"It's clearly not an animal," he said. "Someone was watching us. This will be great for the film… and we don't even need to add CGI shadows."

"Snooper, alright," Zeke nodded. "I figured we was being tailed. Not just a gadabout way out there. Probably another Dutch hunter."

"Hayden's got the gas sniffer so we're choppering into the canyon in the morning. Someone tell McIntyre that I want to re-shoot him holding Kidd's prop watch standing under a different goblin. Someone found a hoodoo with a more enigmatic capstone."

Later on that night I noticed Zeke sitting alone at the campfire. Apprehensive of the chef's lily-white kidney beans, he used a biscuit to sop up some of the "prop" frijoles that he spooned from the pot. "Old time vittles", he called them.

"So much for watery leftovers," I smiled.

"Good chuck for city folk, I reckon."

"Yeah, where's a cowpoke gonna find jeweled tomatoes and wagyu ribeyes out on the range?"

"What did he call that flat macaroni?"

"Tagliatella."

"And what was on those sinkers?"

Just then Hayden approached with a bag of marshmallows and roasting sticks.

"That brown butter truffle froth on Lane's biscuits is to die for," she said while trying to find a spot where the billows of smoke wouldn't sting her eyes.

"Still crankin'," Zeke said while holding a pine splinter over a glowing chunk of bark. When it flared, he lit the cheroot dangling from his lips.

"Did you roll that yourself?" Hayden asked.

"Nope. Ordered 'em from Amazon."

After Hayden gave up on toasting marshmallows and Zeke returned from using "the necessary," we dowsed the fire and headed to the yurt-like sleeper tents.

"That feller in red Levis... some of that stuff was crazier than a six-handed fiddle. I think he's got the wrong pig by the tail... but this person, Kidd, and his spirit people... who you ought to talk with is my pard, Nicodemis. Every one calls him Yance. He's a lawman in Tortilla Flat... at the old west town. I reckon he knows some stuff about Kidd."

"Have you told Julian about this?"

"Not yet. Seeing how I'm becomin' a big star and all, I might need a feller to haggle for me... to divvy up the pot."

"You mean an agent," I smiled.

"Sleep fast on that velvet couch."

Shortly after the sun came up, I was awakened by animated voices coming from the production tent. Since it felt like it was already in the high 80s I climbed out of my cot and quickly got dressed.

When I went to see what all the commotion was about, I found out that the gold pocket watch had gone missing from where it was kept in a box of props set on a folding table. In its place was a tattered scrap of brittle paper that contained part of a treasure map. Zeke was standing next to Julian as he blew away the dust while examining the faded trail markers and key landforms on the crudely drawn map.

"Looks like a trade rat came into camp last night," Zeke said. "Took your dummy watch and left a bogus map. Fair trade, I reckon."

"Trade rat?" Julian's brows narrowed. "You mean a pack rat?"

"Yep."

"And the map's fake?"

"One of hundreds. Chinese Whispers."

As Hayden busied herself charging electronics and filling canteens with Pellegrino water, I noticed a stone that had a heft-less arrow carved into it that had been placed inside a plastic storage bag. Taking a closer look, I realized that it was one of the directional markers that we had found on the trail yesterday.

"What's that for?" I asked Julian.

"My patio in Malibu," he replied dryly.

Flynn and the camera guy ducked their heads under sagging timber while slowly advancing in the stuffy confines of the narrow tunnel. Julian and I were right behind them, walking on slippery rubble as we pivoted the sharp beams our flashlights looking for anything hidden in shadow.

"Air's good according to the sensor," I heard Flynn say as he braced himself against the crumbly damp rock walls after almost losing his footing on loose stones.

"Wonder what caused the gaseous odor yesterday?" Julian asked.

"Probably Saltback," Flynn replied.

"Zeke stayed outside," I reminded him.

"I'm aware of that," Flynn joked. "Anyone else hear voices?"

We paused to listen to what sounded like the crunch of foot-falls and a strange whispered chatting coming from an adjacent passageway. Other odd noises like the hum of far off machinery could also be heard.

"Probably just wind," Flynn said while rounding a corner.

"Whoa!" he shouted as a bright flash of light reflected off the jagged rocks. Both he and Burton stopped dead in their tracks. A series of grunts followed by a loud roar caused them to scramble backwards. As they bumped into me, through the glare of bobbing lights, I made out the silhouette of something moving towards us with an awkward gait. There was a blur of green.

Rows of sharp teeth and fiercely glowing red eyes under a grotesque ridged face popped up, causing me to freeze for a second. A loud growl echoed off the cave walls, but this time it sounded artificial, with a distorted high-pitched hiss.

"Zup, Mofos?" a voice rang out.

What at first appeared to be a bipedal reptilian humanoid turned out to be some skinny dude with frizzy hair and blood-shot eyes wearing a child's novelty dinosaur-faced headlamp that was attached to his head by a Velcro strap. The plastic mask continued to make "authentic" loud roars that crackled from a built-in speaker until the guy figured out how to shut it off.

"Julian – we've got to stop meeting like this," the guy said with a wheezy laugh. "And we've the same hair guy, too. Sorry about all the noise. It's my kid's toy, but it works better than the special ops lights. I don't know what's more dangerous - a mis-step in these Brazilian sneakers or the breakfast burritos the crafties are serving?"

A college-looking kid appeared behind him with a video camera on his shoulder.

"This is Bosker – the help. Bosker's my main videographer. We're working on a docu-style pilot that's getting lots of interest from Netflix. Flynn McIntyre! You were my first choice to be the host, but your agent said you were booked," the guy said while extending a twitching hand that Flynn obligingly shook.

"It's about underground alien bases," he sniffled. "Or, should I say, jointly operated military-alien facilities... with genetic labs and caged soccer moms like that tabloid shit you hear about. We're scouting for ventilation shafts. What are you looking for, Julian?"

"A gold pocket watch," Julian replied, unable to hide his annoyance about having his shoot interrupted by the coked-up rambling of some wannabe filmmaker.

"Oh, I can tell you the time," corkscrew hair said while glancing at his wristwatch. "It's 10:08. No. Make that 11:08. I keep forgetting there's no time change in Arizona."

"You wouldn't be following us, would you?" Julian asked.

"Following you? Hell no," he shook his sweaty head, spattering us like a poodle coming in from the rain. "We just arrived on location. There must be two entrances. From all the sotal plants we've seen, this place was most likely only used to make Apache moonshine."

"We saw someone watching us yesterday," Flynn said with a dubious grimace.

"In this hellish terroir – probably just your average dry gulcher," he said with a nasal laugh.

"Well, it was bound to happen at some point," I laughed. "This place is really going to get crowded when the film crew of some paranormal reality show about haunted mine shafts arrives."

"He's only kidding," Julian said after seeing the guy's puzzled look.

130

"You think alien stuff is saturating the market?" he asked Julian with a paranoid glance.

"Okay, we'll sashay out of your way. Just doing a recce for intake vents and exhaust pipes, but would settle for finding a government-issued ballpoint pen if you happen to see one lying on the ground."

As cowboys wearing spurred boots clomped across wooden boardwalks, Julian and I pushed the swinging doors and entered the Old West town's lusty saloon. A detuned upright player piano hammered out parlor songs as waitresses in floor length corset dresses and feathered headdresses delivered bowls of chili and mugs of beer to tourists. With lavishly upholstered furniture, brass fixtures and gaming tables with baize surfaces, like other frontier boomtown recreations, there was no shortage of rough-and-tumble western kitsch at Tortilla Flat.

Seeing a 'lawman' in a black frock jacket with a holstered six-gun at his side seated at the bar, Julian walked up and introduced himself.

"Howdy, Yance. I'm Julian, the director from Paragon making a documentary about James Kidd. This is my associate, Sheldon Grane. Your friend Saltback from Goldfield told us that your father was an acquaintance of Kidd and that you might be able to provide us with some helpful information for the film. Mind if we belly up for a spell?" he said while gesturing to an empty barstool saddle.

"Call me Nicodemis," the aged fellow with a walrus mustache said while eating prickly-pear gelato. "Yance is my deputy marshal persona," he said with a well-modulated, soft voice while tugging at a tin badge on his vest. "And right now it's too damn hot to shoot it out with any outlaws on that dusty street. Sure, I'll give you a hand if you want. Jimmy found himself in an imbroglio of sorts after chancing upon a strange garden inside a floating spherical made of unknown glass."

Noticing the reflection of my incredulous reaction in the large mirror behind the bar, Julian lowered his head in anticipation of my questioning this rather bizarre statement.

"After this happened, he put that whole business of the soul – the survival of one's identity after death – into his Will. As for his disappearance, I don't know who got to him first... the government honchos or the Black Nobility with Phoenix Orientem... and I'm not talking about one's skin color, but those who are part of the Phoenix Empire... and I'm not talking about a sprawling city... but those with a deep interest in the native Terrans that some refer to as star-progeny. Or maybe it was the keepers of the garden, themselves?"

"Are you by chance talking about a human-reptoid alliance?" Julian asked.

"You mean tube shuttles in a tunnel system coated with blue phosphor and security forces with extra selenium in their bones that vaporize intruders with flash pistols? That Yellow Fruit nonsense? I assure you there was iced tea in my glass and not red eye. I'm not offering fool's gold here, but nuggets of high-grade ore."

I nodded to indicate my appreciation of his honesty, although inside I was thinking that if they made sensors that measured the kook factor, right now it would be buzzing louder than the tinkling keys of the old-fashioned tack piano.

"I can tell you three things about Kidd: One – Six months after he went missing bank records indicated that someone using his name opened his safe deposit box. Two: Some of Kidd's mining claims weren't really his. They belonged to an elderly Spaniard... a Basque from the Pyrenees... who wasn't an American citizen and couldn't file the claims, so Jimmy filed them for him. Three: One of these claims was a decoy, with the mine that should be of interest located closer to Tucson."

"What do you think might have been removed from his safe deposit box?" Julian asked.

"Safe deposit box... or Pandora's Box? That's the half million-dollar question, isn't it? Have you ever heard of E.D.O.M. – Electronic Dissolution Of Memory? Did you know that both the government honchos and members of the Phoenix Empire are able to implant thoughts into peoples' minds? Imagery taken from their dream library. Once you figure out what was taken... you can fade to black."

With my flight out of Phoenix leaving later that night, I decided to spend some more time in the old west town. After enjoying a great burger for lunch, I moseyed over to the general store to look for a tacky souvenir for Aaloka. While browsing at the local meeting place, with its pot-bellied stove, spittoon and pickle barrel, I got to talking with the proprietor. When the subject of Yance came up, I learned that both he and Saltback were card-carrying members of a Liar's Club. In fact, Yance had been awarded the first place prize by judges for three years in a row during the annual contest.

As the mercury continued to rise in the old glass thermometer hanging on the porch, I was seated on a cube of hay, drinking sparkling apple cider while trying to piece some things together.

Even if what Nicodemis had told Julian and I about Kidd were just inventive tall tales (strange parlor stories at that!), I still had to wonder how some of the stuff he conjured up seemed to be connected with odd happenings in my life. Things such as the strange garden I had anticipated in my recent lucid dream, along with the reptilian-looking keeper of the garden I had glimpsed in the other dream I had at the Sandman motel.

And then there was the old man with the long mole whisker that worked in the home garden center. I distinctly remember him telling me that my activities were forbidden. Forbidden? Which reminded me, after we finished shooting the campfire scene, Brodie had warned us about the reptilian agenda. They weren't just the latest alien squatters on the planet - they had been interacting in human affairs ever since deceiving Eve in the Garden of Eden. They are master shape-shifters and super genetic engineers who have been manipulating God's original creation. He even suggested that our current infatuation with synthetic biology, including options right out of a Cellectect brochure, was part of their plan to farm a better specimen for their own interests. (Maybe I should check to see if Aaloka ever consumes the special formula mixed with peach puree that Brodie said the reptoids subsisted on along with their appetite for human flesh.)

This *creation a novo* (creation afresh) sounded like the "renewed fertility" in Ramiel's messages on my blogsite — those that also involved the fruit of a hidden tree. Even though I found such ideas to be absurd, again, I couldn't help wonder why the motif of the forbidden fruit of a particular tree kept cropping up (pun unintentional) in my life?

Weirdest of all — even if it came from the mind of a champion leg-puller — was the idea of dissolution of memory and implanted visions by Black Nobility, as Nicodemis called the elite cabal. This almost sounded like a warning. Where had I heard these things before? Mind stalkers and a dream-incubator that generated lucidity in a treasure locator? Was it Malcolm?

With all the high strangeness I dealt with – spaceships and lizardmen – was I starting to imagine things? Finding patterns in linoleum swirls and Rorschach inkblots like Aaloka said? Were the seemingly synchronistic events just meaningless coincidences, or did any of this mean anything, even if on an unconscious level?

For the first time in quite a while, I wanted to know about my past.

The person I once was.

After hearing Brodie Quinn's lecture in Phoenix, I invited him to be the special guest in the latest installment of my podcast.

"When asked about his involvement with the tero and dero, Richard Shaver answered: There is no way to tell you but incoherently, so I will do it that way. While that might have been okay for Ray Palmer's pulp magazine audience, for the listeners of this episode, I would prefer a more coherent account of the sequence of events that led to the phenomenon known as The Shaver Mystery in the mid-nineteen forties. So, strap in for a wild ride and away we go:

In 1932, while employed as a spot welder on the assembly line of the original Ford Motor Plant in Michigan, during his shift, Shaver heard what he described as far off voices of endless complexity. Because this occurred while he was holding a certain welding gun, he rationalized that by some freak of its coils' field attunement, the tool had become a teleradio. If you think that's quite a leap on his part, well folks, you haven't heard anything yet.

Once the incoherent babble became clearer, he was sickened to realize that he was hearing the torture sessions of females that had been abducted from the Earth's surface. Even after stuffing cotton into his ears, he couldn't escape the monstrous snuffles, anguished screams and maniacal laughter. As the tormenting voices continued, he quit his job and when on the bum.

While tramping around in depression era America, at some point he was locked away. While in confinement, a woman appeared in his cell… a form as light in its step as the seafoam that drifted up and touched the beach… those were his words. Her name was Nydia, and though beautiful and enticing, at times her luminous form became hazy and colorless. Even if she was only some kind of beamed projection, the image was solid enough to trick the guards into releasing him. After making a daring escape, Nydia took him to a cleverly disguised cavern in the wooded countryside.

While standing on an ancient polished floor, the radiant vision of Nydia abruptly vanished, only to be replaced by the flesh-and-blood real thing. The woman claimed to be a descendant of an ancient alien race, and as one of the secret people, she said she would restore his sanity… because he heard voices, I guess she meant by this… by divulging to him a mysterious realm of unfathomable technology that has for millennia existed in tandem with unsuspecting humanity."

After describing Shaver's version of how Earth's surface dwellers have been victimized by the terrifying effects of dero ray activity over the ages, it was time to reveal the sad truth that inspired the cavern world, as well Shaver's mission to expose those responsible for these evil doings.

"Years after the Shaver Mystery faded into obscurity; it was revealed by Ray Palmer that during the entire time that Shaver claimed to be in the caverns, he was actually in mental institutions. One of these was Ionia State Hospital for the

Criminally Insane that he was committed to after being diagnosed with paranoid schizophrenia. In light of these revelations, it seems likely that his dream woman, Nydia, was in reality a compassionate psychiatric nurse in the overcrowded asylum that befriended him and supplied him with writing materials. In describing Shaver's nonsensical ramblings, or, what others consider to be highly imaginative science fiction stories, someone said, I quote, "He wrote delirium with footnotes and absurdities with diagrams." Many of these writings were on the back of hospital charts and report forms.

Patient number 3234 escaped the asylum... escaped in his mind deep into the cavern systems... creating the world of the vanished pre-diluvian civilization. In doing so he replaced the depressing confines of the state hospital with vast underground chambers.... again, I quote... "That were pillared by mighty simulations of trees, hung with crystalline glittering fruits." In every one of these great rooms stood several of the enigmatic ancient mechanisms, themselves beautiful of form and shimmering with prismatic color.

When he wrote that the deros' creative instinct to find new and different ways to inflict torture, was he actually referring to the doctors' experiments with metrazol convulsion and transcranial electroshock procedures? The onslaught of influencing beams responsible for scrambling his neural circuitry could have been due to the current from electroshock apparatus while under restraint, with the same shock treatments causing his retrograde amnesia and periods of time distortion... the time between ticks of a clock, as he described it. Your thoughts, Brodie?"

"Well, the other side of the coin is if the dero truly were tampering with Shaver's mind via the rays, wouldn't that prompt him to seek psychiatric care? Indeed, that asylums are filled with patients in similar catatonic states might prove the validity of the Shaver Mystery."

"Spoken like a true Shaverphile. Look, it should be obvious by now. We are the dero... and we are the tero, as well. The warring races. And if you think about it, the terror of the caverns that Shaver was trying to warn us about is closer to the surface than we'd like to believe. I'm not talking about some ancient ray-science. I'm talking about current advances in human technology... and the possibility of living in a machine-gone-mad world.

Shaver might have been the first ancient astronaut theorist, but in the next episode I will be discussing the early Russian influence on the paleo-contact movement in the west, and the possible reason behind it... something that we should NOT take with a grain of salt."

The day after the podcast could be uploaded, several of my subscribers sent messages that they could make out a barely audible voice speaking something that was unintelligible under my own words during part of the show. When I had a listen, I could also hear this other voice, but couldn't understand what was being said.

My first thought was that my remote guest, Brodie, was playing some kind of prank on me by making it appear that the dero were tampering with the webcast. When he assured me that this was not the case, I looked for other reasons that might explain them. Because I was new at this medium and hadn't worked out the rough edges yet − including adding the proposed theme music − I thought there must have been a glitch with the digital audio file. When I checked with the company hosting the podcast, they were equally baffled by the voices.

It wasn't until a follower informed me that the words being spoken were in the Enochian language that I realized that I had been hacked by the same person that attacked my blog posts. Ramiel had struck again. Even though the podcast used a different RSS feed, he had somehow breached the automatic safe-guards. The same listener was also able to translate the words into English by using an Enochian dictionary.

I was aware that some occultists experimented with the calls and keys of the Enochia, and that it was considered by many to be a deep end of the pool system of ritual magic, but for the language to have its own grammar and syntax and such, that was news to me. When I checked to see if such a dictionary existed, I was surprised to learn there were several versions that were all fairly consistent.

The Enochian language, also called celestial speech and the language of the angels was said to be that used by Adam before the expulsion from paradise and was last spoken by the biblical patriarch Enoch until it was rediscovered in the 16th century.

The language in modern concordances came from fragments contained in the meticulous diary entries of the Elizabethan Magus, Doctor John Dee. These were derived from skrying ses-sions (séances involving crystal gazing) assisted by the spiritual medium Edward Kelly. Dee was believed to have provided the pronunciation of the individual words alongside the text delivered by the angels as dictated by Kelly. Modern linguists aren't sure if the language is natural or invented, but many suspect the angelic conversations recorded by Dee are either the result of glossolalia (speaking in tongues) or an early form of cryptography.

Whatever the case, when the words spoken during the pod-cast were translated into English, the message revealed was: "Open the mystery of your creation and make us partakers of undefiled knowledge."

CHAPTER V
LVCIFTIANITY

"I have started something. There are 56 million copies of my books worldwide. But now it is not just Erich Von Daniken. It is others, many others, as well. You cannot kill the idea anymore, never."

- Erich von Daniken
(ufoevidence.org: interview with Billy Cox)

"We are generally afraid to become that which we can glimpse in our most perfect moments... We enjoy and even thrill to godlike possibilities we see in ourselves... And yet we simultaneously shiver with weakness, awe, and fear before these very same possibilities."

- Abraham Maslow

Aaloka needed some help behind the bar for a private party in the themed bhoot room, so I offered my services. While preparing the syrup for the restaurant's signature cocktail, I chatted with Malcolm, who was sipping a more traditional gin & tonic on the other side of the lustrous teakwood while waiting for the group to arrive from their tour of spooky spots in the area.

While fetching a bucket of special ice cubes that contained borage flowers, I happened to glance up at one of the paintings of the various Bengali specters hanging on the wall behind the bar. This was the depiction of Pishachini – a beautiful young maiden, whose facial features bore a resemblance to Aaloka's, though the seductive glance she exhibited was that of a celestial nymph that beckoned viewers with her sexual powers. Although I had seen the painting before, this time it looked different. From where I was standing, the woman's face was split in two, with the skin on one side being a darker tone of green and scalier as opposed to the flesh on the other side. Adding to the reptilian half was a deep golden eye, whose pupil had a black vertical slit. Also, the one side of the purple sari was abnormal in that it looked more like a cloak. Examining it further, what I first thought was a pruning knife now appeared as a stout claw barely concealed by her sleeve.

"Pishachini, here, appears to be slipping, Malcolm... half of her face shifting into some kind of reptoid creature."

"It's all about optics and perspective, dear boy. Anamorphosis. The image changes depending upon the viewer's vantage point. Features that were disguised become recognizable from a different angle. I take it you're seeing the side of Pishachini that drains one's blood and virility with her insatiable sexual hunger. What's the artist saying by employing this unique technique?"

"I don't know... but I've a sneaking suspicion you're going to tell me."

"If you'd rather not know, let's just say it's to evoke a sense of strangeness. Not unlike those nocturnal fancies of yours."

"That reminds me, I had another freaky dream while in Arizona. All this craziness I have to debunk on the blog is piling up as neural trash that my brain needs to dispose of... as brains were designed to do."

"Did this dream involve more virescent perplexity? Another nursery tended by some freakish form with a green thumb?"

"No, this time it was just a garden variety… garden center with a dour employee. But, oddly enough, his reaction to my looking for a houseplant as a gift was as if I was storming the very gates of Eden. You probably don't know this, but Wal-mart isn't exactly an Edenic paradise. Well, to most people, at least. The only strange thing growing this time was an out of control mole whisker."

"Mole whisker? Malcolm raised his brows. "What else did he say? Do tell."

"Are you really that hard up for content for that ripping yarn of yours?"

"No, but it's interesting isn't it? Shifting perception like the artist here used in the painting. The deformity of the lengthy mole whisker is a mild affliction. Seems the old chap's appearance was distorted to attract your attention."

"A lengthy mole whisker… no matter how long… is not a deformity. It's just something that needs to be plucked."

"It still seems to be a signal… a symbolic marker. But what else happened in this dream?"

"Not much. A little bird landed on my hand, followed by a swooping pterodactyl that caused me to wake up before the rooster alarm clock went off. Oh, and the cops detained a meth head right outside my door… not in the dream – in real life – where meth heads are more prevalent."

"This happened at the deluxe accommodation the cine-film people put you up in?"

"No, there was a mix up with the on-line booking site, so I stayed at the Sandman again."

"The Sandman is a chain, I gather."

I turned to have another look at the painting of the shape-shifting woman, seeing it from the perspective I was more accustomed to.

"These reptilian humanoids that are body snatching every Tom, Dick and Harry these days – I've heard this was Blavatsky's doing. You know about this flaky stuff. She was a Russian mystic, right?"

"Helena Petrovna Blavatsky. With a name like that one would certainly hope so. True, she wrote about the Wise Serpents and Dragons of Light in her opus, but it was an occultist named Doreal from Oklahoma, of all places, who spoke at length of the serpent race. All the basic elements one hears today were contained in Doreal's teachings in the 1940s... with the exception of the reptilians' hosts having low blood pressure and being convinced to design square buildings. The serpent people inhabited what today is Antarctica. At the time it was a lush, green paradise located at the equator. The reptilians and humans in those ancient days were incompatible. The two bloodlines did not mix and the reptilians wanted the earth for themselves. Using their superb mental abilities and hypnotic powers that explains their perceived shape-shifting, they secretly killed and assumed the place of many human rulers.

To keep the scaly infiltrators at bay, the humans devised a trick. Before anyone was allowed to enter the gates of their cities, they first had to say the word, *kininigin*. Although Doreal never revealed its meaning, he said that the word could only be pronounced by human vocal cords. Which gives rise to a thought... the last syllable does. Would you mind terribly constructing me another drink? With Fever-Tree quinine and this time being just a tad more conservative with the ice."

"I'm glad to hear you're able to pronounce the word, Malcolm. It's keeps me from having to imagine a lizard barrister wearing one of those frizzled white wigs in court," I said while opening a can of premium Indian tonic water and pouring it over a few cubes of ice in a glass of gin. "One disguise ought to be enough to foil the bad guys. But if the reptoids hijacked human bodies, wouldn't they have human vocal cords?"

"One would think that's the case, but if you're a guru why let such a trivial detail muck up a perfectly good conspiracy theory? At any rate, as it came to pass, the humans developed a powerful weapon and unleashed it on the serpent race. The result was cataclysmic for both sides. In what must have been one hell of a spectacle, the destructive force caused the poles to shift. The reptilians froze to death in their now not-so-Edenic state."

"So, why are they still hanging around today?"

"You have Russian scientists to blame for that. During an expedition to Antarctica, they discovered bodies they thought were ancient humans entombed in ice... and managed to revive them from their preserved condition."

"And this crank, Doreal, learned about this from some rogue lizardman I take it, before he was netted by men in white jackets?"

Just then Aaloka entered the Bhoot room.

"There's my hazel-eyed beauty," I smiled. "Aaloka, can you say *kininigin* for me?"

"Say what? Why?"

"I just want to make sure you don't add me to Hamburger Helper, that's why, honey."

"Malcolm, what kind of nonsense have you been telling Sheldon?"

"Just some serpent lore to be taken with a grain of salt."

While preparing for the next episode of my podcast, I got a call from Julian about Kidd's pocket watch having been found. Zeke had found out from a prospector friend that it had been discovered by someone looking for Apache arrowheads in a limestone cave in the Superstition Wilderness Area. He didn't tell

Julian the exact location – only that it was above the drainage in the Haunted Canyon area of Pinto Creek, adding that the entrance was concealed by manzanita shrubs. Because the walls of the cave's "Grand Chamber" contain dazzling calcite crystals, it's called The Cave of a Thousand Eyes. He assured Julian there were no human remains inside, and no placer gold.

The reason for the secrecy was to protect the cave's natural beauty from vandals, who in the past tried to exploit it as a diamond mine. With so many people searching the area for the Lost Dutchman gold, this was one place he hoped would remain undisturbed.

The watch was sold to a pawnshop in Globe, Arizona, and was still in the glass display case when Zeke went to ask about it. Using the money Paragon had paid him, he purchased it and now wanted to know if Julian had any interest in buying it from him. If not, he planned to donate it to Goldfield's historic museum.

After checking out the photos Zeke sent, Julian bought it for the $2,000.00 asking price (the prop cost him $1,500.00) and promised to give it to the museum once the film wrapped. As for why he called me, the plan was to take the watch to a woman in San Francisco named Blaze, who was a medium highly regarded for her ability with psychometry. After handling it, Julian hoped she might receive some impressions of Kidd. Once again, I was to be the balance.

When I voiced my skepticism of spiritualism, even readings by psychic detectives, he explained that the process involved was similar to playing back information stored in a digital medium. Psychometrists like Blaze believe that the past still exists as vibrations at a sub-atomic level that are accessible to human perception.

Instead of reiterating my case against this pseudoscience, I told him about Zeke and Yance both belonging to a Liar's Club. They're a couple of characters; I tried to explain, masquerading as storytellers like those that entertained folks with this fine art in the old West. Tales about how it once snowed tortillas and scorpions being hatched from cholla houseplants. How did he know, I asked, that the watch wasn't the same prop that Zeke said had been carried off by a "trade rat" (no doubt slapping his knee while telling his friends), but that had actually been taken from the tent by Zeke himself with hopes of selling it back to the hotshots from Hollywood?

Julian's reply was that the watch in the photos looked slightly different. Both timepieces were manufactured by Elgin in 1888, each having a 14 karat gold case with a piecrust Guilloche design. Both had a white dial, black roman numerals and cobalt blue hands. However, the case recently discovered had more scuffs than the prop. Plus, the inside of the cover was fitted with a rounded old photo of Kidd like those placed within lockets. Since this was the much-published photo of Kidd wearing an uncreased grey fedora while standing in front of some climbing vines, I told Julian that it didn't prove anything.

Even though I thought the whole thing was ridiculous (including the idea that Kidd would keep a photo of himself inside his pocket watch), I nevertheless agreed to go with him. Watching a charlatan in action might supply material for a future blog post, as well as providing a few laughs.

"It's no surprise that people in America today are worried about Russian bots pumping out propaganda designed to disrupt our elections. And while we should be concerned about how interference from software applications causes political chaos and threatens our very democracy, long before we were targeted by an army of web robots, the Russians were meddling in our affairs with a different form of propaganda... something I'll bet few Americans have ever thought about. I'm talking about the hidden agenda behind promoting views involving ancient astronauts. Hello, I'm Sheldon Grane and you're listening to Episode 3 of With a Grane of Salt."

After making a few technical adjustments, I continued with the program.

"That's because it's irrelevant, you say. You're not going to lose any sleep over stories about aliens and make-believe conspiracies. Well, its more than just camouflage for the Russian's own secret military tests, or a plan conceived by the Kremlin to clog up valuable assets from our alphabet-soup agencies by sending spies on a wild goose chase. It's a form of psychological warfare, meant to destabilize and undermine our way of life... to smear both religion and science... to discredit scientific achievements, such as landing on the moon... with the lunacy... sorry, of alien structures and bases built by a super civilization long before the Americans took a giant step for mankind. And why does NASA hide these photos? Their answer: Because, when it comes to the cosmonauts of antiquity, it's our government that suppresses the truth... not the Russians. Nearly all of the heavyweights of the ancient astronaut theory were influenced by Russian authors... Soviet megaphones behind the Iron Curtain, like the scientist, Matest M. Agrest, who in the early 1960s claimed the megalithic platform at Baalbek was used by intergalactic travelers to launch their spacecraft. There's the destruction of Sodom and Gomorrah as being caused by a nuclear event. Think about that for a minute. A warning directly from the pages of the Bible about the catastrophic fate of this Hiroshima and Nagasaki of the past.

And it was an article from a literary gazette by the Soviet scientist that first sounded the alarm about these alien nukes. This kind of propaganda against U.S. interests has continued in more recent times, such as the claims that the real reason American troops invaded Iraq was to steal Anunnaki star-gate technology.

Someone sent me a message about the Dzopa stones having been examined by Russian scientists before they went missing. For those not familiar with the story, called by some the Chinese Roswell, it began with a scientific expedition by Chinese archaeologists in 1938 to Bayan Kara Ula in the mountains near the border of Tibet. There, in a burial cave, the team supposedly discovered the skeletal remains of slender beings with elongated heads. They also uncovered from the dust hundreds of stone discs, whose surface contained tiny hieroglyphic-like markings incised inside grooves that spiraled outward. When the markings were decoded, they contained a message about the makers of the stones being stranded aliens that crashed on earth 12,000 years ago.

When they heard the news of this amazing find, Russian scientists asked if they could examine the stones, so they were shipped to Moscow. Since the grooved discs each had a hole in the middle, one of the scientists, Dr. Vyatcheslav Saitzen, performed an experiment in which he placed one of the discs on a turntable-like device and played it like a record. Remember those? After doing so he realized that traces of cobalt made it an electrical conductor that hummed and possibly contained another message. After the experiment, the Dzopa stones mysteriously disappeared. The story of these alien artifacts was published in a Soviet magazine called Sputnik. This was a tabloid-type rag full of paranormal happenings... said to be non-political, but was clearly another voice of propaganda meant for western consumption.

Well, of course, none of this can be confirmed. There's no academic proof…nothing but the disinformation promoted by the Kremlin. Actually, the most popular version of the story – including the idea that the Dzopa came from a planet that orbited Sirius - comes from an admitted work of fiction.

I received a message asking me what I thought happened to the discs? My reply is… nothing. It's not a real archaeological find. They don't exist! It's a hoax that was subsequently turned into a novel."

After detecting some hissing sounds, I paused and tried to fix the problem by adjusting the noise gate slider in Garageband.

In doing so, I realized it wasn't just unwanted background noise picked up by my microphone, but, rather, a faint sibilant chant of sorts. When I played the 'mumbo-jumbo' to the subscriber who clued me in about the intruding voice during my last episode, he informed me that once again someone was speaking in the Enochian language, and, just like as before, using the somewhat cumbersome Golden Dawn method of pronunciation. Although there really wasn't a universal pronunciation guide, he tried to explain the grammatical structure, breaking down the various words into segments. One of the words uttered was "luciftian", which translated into English as "brightness." Because this was so similar to "Lucifer", some linguists concluded that the Enochian language is Anglophonic in structure. Although this didn't make sense for what was supposedly the speech of angels, the occultist admitted that in a few cases the words had a familiar ring, such as "babalond", which meant "wicked." His personal theory was that, rather than being "Adamical" or the primordial language, Enochian was the tongue spoken in Atlantis. When I asked him what this was based on, he was at a loss, saying it was just a hunch. Having carefully written down what was spoken, after consulting his dictionary (called "Gmicalzoma"), the message this time was: "Behold the face of God, the beginning of comfort, whose eyes are the brightness of heavens."

The security measures already in place obviously weren't working, so I needed to take further action before Ramiel or whoever was harassing me took over the show. Not only was I frustrated by having to purchase extra safeguards and then fiddle with the shit, I was getting sick and tired of answering the same questions from the security industry kiddies that I contacted for assistance. Those who kept asking me if I was using an omnidirectional microphone, or if I had recently blacklisted a subscriber, or if someone had attempted to get me to pay a ransom with bitcoins. What I needed was a former kingpin of cyberbadness to figure out who was breaking into my house with brute force and then lock them out for good. It was suggested that the person for the job was a notorious former hacker from Florida known in the computer underworld as "CYCLOPZ." A hacker with good intentions - that's who I planned to hire.

While running some errands for Aaloka, I passed a man riding one of those self-balancing transporters in the bike lane. Glancing in the rearview mirror, his funny-looking yellow uniform matched Jag's description of the courier that delivered the postcard with the Tombstone pterodactyl. When I took another look, the face under the beanie looked like one of those yellow-headed birds – not just bearing a casual likeness, but the actual features of a bird, complete with beady eyes and a black beak. The face was that of a virden, just like the one I saw in the bizarre dream and those that flashed in the arroyos in Arizona. Before I had a chance to do a double take – thinking the guy must be wearing a mask - another one of these oddball couriers on the same model yellow electric unicycle rolled past me on the other side of the road. As he glided by, his face underwent a rapid transformation into that of the same bird. Seeing this happen, I nearly rear-ended the car in front of me.

Finding a spot to pull over on the busy street, I parked and tried to collect my thoughts. Unless there was something in the water (and it wasn't 1967), I couldn't figure out what might have caused me to hallucinate. It was like I was wearing Jag's augmented reality headset. Did being exposed to the optical layering cause delayed reactions or other neurological effects?

After sitting there for a while, when everything seemed normal, I eased back into the traffic. While doing so, a large shadow swept across the hood of the car, followed by a deafening screech.

Glancing out the window, I was shocked to see an enormous pterodactyl-like creature with greyish leathern wings flapping overhead. The freakish vision lasted for only a second, after which I realized it was a commercial plane coming in for a landing at the nearby San Jose airport.

Had I been dreaming while awake? I was grasping at straws, of course, but it was the only explanation I could think of. Either that, or something very unusual was happening in my head. Something, perhaps, related to my memory disorder. After seeing the prehistoric reptile with its landing flaps down, I figured it might be time to finally seek help from a specialist. For the time being, I would keep this a secret so as not to worry Aaloka.

Having slowed down to a crawl, I thought about pulling over again, but turned around instead, wanting to get home as soon as possible. After driving for a few miles without any further episodes, it happened again – another full-blown hallucination. This time I saw what appeared to be the top portion of a rocket or futuristic spacecraft on a launching pad that rose above the jacaranda trees in the middle of a residential district. As its metallic surface glinted with a fiery orange tinge in the setting sun, I rubbed my eyes, hoping the phantom image would go away. Instead, it persisted, looming larger and more detailed as I drew closer.

Rounding a corner, I slammed on the brakes, staring in disbelief at the absurd sight unwavering before my eyes. This time I wasn't seeing things. The rocket-like structure was very real, having been erected in place of the towering steeple on a church that was in the process of being renovated. Scattered about were skids of building materials, including piles of lumber and dry wall under plastic sheeting, evidently to be used for a domed addition to the roof. Seeing the familiar Methodist church being converted by someone into a planetarium topped by the mock-up of a rocket was even stranger than if I had merely hallucinated the damn thing.

When I pulled into the parking lot and found a space between all the construction supplies, I noticed that the traditional notice board that welcomed new members or displayed the day's sermon had been replaced by a digital signage system that read:

PARADIAL LVCIFTIAN

What the hell was going on here?

With the doors being partly open, I decided to take a peek inside. In the dimly lit interior that was also under construction, I could hear a woman's voice intoning a prayer of some kind in a low monotone. Though the words were unintelligible, I began to recognize some of the strange pronunciations she seemed to be struggling with as lettered segments of the transmitted Calls in the Enochian language that were nearly identical to those the hacker uttered during my podcast.

When I got close enough to make out the woman seated with her back to me, her stylish bob hairstyle and silvery-grey color looked just like Zyla's. She was also wearing a shiny bodysuit with sharp shoulders like that Zyla had on once while hanging out at the condo. In my nostrils were weirdly familiar metal-themed tones. However, because of the way she was enunciating the words – almost like she was singing - it was hard to tell if it was Zyla's voice.

Where some of the church's pews used to be, there was now a large gold-framed table whose round black surface was painted with a complex geometric diagram. Twelve crystal skulls set on red silk cloth were arranged in a circle, with a single dark obsidian skull placed at the center. The woman was leaning forward while staring into the eye sockets of one of the glowing transparent skulls.

As she recited the Enochian chant, both of her hands were placed in a prayer-like position on an upright, thin metallic console that had been designed with indentations on each side for five fingers. The hand impressions in the slanted panel might have made the unit function as a tactile computer interface similar to a data-glove, but that was just a guess on my part.

Above the table were several flat screen monitors angled at various points. Each one displayed a different region of the night sky with a coordinate grid, reference points and column of numbers. Glowing blips moving against the celestial backdrop led me to believe that someone was keeping tabs on certain satellites or other man-made aerial objects, but, with the anatomical 'keyboard' and occult elements, who knew what kind of game was at play?

If all the colorful graphics and orbiting figures on the screens weren't complicated enough, superimposed over them was what appeared to be wave discharges of electrical activity occurring in someone's brain. Although, again, this was just a guess, the wavy lines on the monitors fluctuated and spiked in relation to the incantations the woman was uttering.

Honestly, I had no idea what she was trying to achieve, but judging by the expense involved with the system (crystal skulls aren't cheap), someone must have thought they were doing some pretty important work. Unless, of course, the whole thing was just an elaborate con job to fleece the gullible of their savings by having them believe they were investing in a "unicorn" startup. (Perhaps a space-based technology powered by Enochian forces!) Either way, I was interested to see what developed, especially if I had chanced upon the Temple of Ramiel.

As the woman remained engaged in her specific task, I pulled out my phone and began to record her. A bit of synchronicity followed when, moments later, I received a call from the former hacker that I wanted to hire to thwart my cyber attacker.

The infamous hacker's real name was Oliver Spitzer. On the phone he described himself as once being a black hat cracker who had turned over a new leaf and applied his skills to help both small businesses and large corporations protect themselves from becoming the victims of a sophisticated intrusion. Soon, he told me, everything would be connected… and even kitchen appliances would be infected with malicious code. "Try to imagine a coffee pot being held for ransom after brewing up a cup of Donut Shop Joe." He suspected that I might have a "hacktivist" on my hands. Someone wanting to spread a religious message, who gained unauthorized access to my computer by using malware purchased on the dark web. The first thing he wanted me to do was send him screen shots of my blog files.

When I asked what led him to become a hacker, he told me that while growing up in the 1960s he "gypped" vending machines with slugs and Canadian quarters. And speaking of counterfeit coins, he told me that he had a friend in his Midwestern home town that had a "super slug" that was made of a metal that was so light weight that they called it "frozen smoke." Even though you could hardly feel it, it always tricked vending machines; even returning the strange coin-like object after a product had been dispensed. In the 70s he was phreaking the telephone company with Captain Crunch whistles and makeshift blue boxes. Later on in life he was dubbed "Uncle Spam" until indicted for high-profile data breaches like the Milwaukee 414s.

After learning that I was a skeptic of paranormal phenomena, he asked me if I had ever heard of the "Looney Tunes" house. When I told him that I hadn't, he said it was called that because weird shit happened there similar to the repeating backgrounds of landscape features in the old cartoons. Just like the Road Runner and Wile E Coyote passing the same mesa, cactus or rock, the house seemed to have its own eternal-looping generator.

In the front yard, identical - not just similar, but identical, he stressed - birds would fly from branch to branch with the exact same flight patterns, and this was repeated over and over again just like those cost-cutting animated wraparound backdrops used by Hanna-Barbera. One day in the middle of a summer heat wave, a huge icicle fell from the gutter onto the porch, just like it was seen to do during a frigid winter. Again, he emphasized that it was the same long icicle hanging from the same location on the gutter. And this happened not once, he said, but several times, as if on a repeat mode. Crazy shit like that freaked the town folk out, and when a stranger came to investigate the place, he wound up disappearing without a trace. Because the old house was located near one of the seven decommissioned railroad overpasses in the area known in a local legend as "The Seven Gates to Hell", some people believed it was built over the pit where the Biblical Fallen Angels were cast. However, because the metal slug was found in the same house, maybe, instead, the aliens from the Roswell crash lived there, he joked.

When I scoffed at this, he said that someday he would tell me about having used the special tools of his black hat cousins to crack the "crappy passwords" of secret NASA computer files. Besides seeing "cleaned up photos," he had evidence of something they discovered which he hinted was not man-made.

If he had copied classified NASA data, and was willing to share it with me, then so much for donning a white hat. Still, I needed his "special tools" to prevent another breach.

Instead of making an appointment with a medical specialist, the next day I was on my way to purchase a used copy of *GMI-CALZOMA: An Enochian Dictionary* from an antiquarian book dealer in San Francisco. While sitting in heavy traffic not far from Sunnyvale, I kept thinking about the hallucinations I experienced the last time I was driving. After enduring a few more miles of gridlock (with my mind continuing to wander into negative places), I decided to return home and order the same copy online.

Once I got back to the condo, I saw that Malcolm had stopped by to visit with Aaloka. While pouring myself a gin & tonic in the kitchen, I watched the two talking while sipping chai out on the deck. Judging by their animated conversation, followed by contemplative silence, whatever they were discussing must have been serious.

When I pushed open the sliding glass door and went out to join them, both seemed surprised that I had returned early and abruptly stopped their verbal exchange.

"Sheldon, is everything alright?" Aaloka asked with a concerned look.

"Yeah, traffic was nasty so I'm going to have the book delivered."

"Bay Area motorways? What are things coming to," Malcolm joked. "I see you're keeping London hours these days," he grinned while gesturing to my drink. "Jolly good show. Next you'll be bringing tinnys to the park."

"It is a little early," Aaloka frowned.

"What's going on?" I asked.

On the rattan table an iPad was open to a hotel-booking site. Seeing photos of the Sandman Inn (with marked down prices), I gave the two a funny look. Next to the tablet was a coffee table book whose subject was the paintings hanging in the Louvre in Paris. It was opened to a page that showed a famous work by the 17th-century artist Nicolas Poussin entitled *Autumn, or The Grapes of the Promised Land*. Done in the classical French Baroque style, the canvas depicted the Old Testament story of the Israelite spies returning from Canaan. In the foreground, two rustic-looking figures were using a branch or wooden pole to carry an enormous cluster of grapes.

"*The Grapes of the Promised Land*. Mythical landscapes? Why this sudden keen interest in biblical stories instead of the usual macabre curiosities, Malcolm?"

"What might appear to some as a biblical theme others see as a toast to Bacchus. A gift from God that inspires divine madness."

"Malcolm was talking about treating us to a vacation. He thinks we could all do with a little break from our work."

"You're planning to splurge on the accommodations, I see," I smiled while pointing to the images of the Sandman Inn. "I'm not sure if the free breakfast in the lobby would be up to your jaded palate."

"We won't have to worry about that noxious sludge. I rather doubt the bog-standard of the Sandman chain even exists where we're going."

"Where's that – biblical Canaan?" I smirked before taking a gulp of my drink. "To pluck giant grapes like these."

In the painting, a ladder that seemed to rise out of the cluster of over-sized grapes was placed against a tree that a lady had climbed to pick its fruit. Oddly enough, this tree was the only one that bore fruit, with the branches of the others in the landscape being noticeably barren.

"Pardon my suspicious nature, but is it really just a coincidence that the painting here contains details that are very similar to things I told you about seeing in those dreams I had while staying at the motel? If you know something, please tell me – "

"Know something about what?" Aaloka asked while she and Malcolm exchanged puzzled looks.

"About... things I can't recall, that's what!"

While glancing down at the photos on the iPad, I noticed the address of the nearest Sandman Inn.

"North First Street... by the San Jose airport. That's where I was yesterday. I must have passed right by the place without noticing it," I said while thinking out loud about a possible connection. Did the motel in some way act as a trigger that caused me to perceive while awake the same bizarre imagery that appeared in my recent dream? As I considered the possibility, I wondered if Malcolm had already reached the same conclusion?

"You really need to take a break," Aaloka said. "What's been going on with your website – it's making you paranoid... Questioning those who love and care about you. This isn't like you, Sheldon. Not for someone who's normally so reasonable."

She was right. I was becoming increasingly paranoid. What was the likelihood that some flea- bag (that I didn't even notice) affected my brain? There had to be a more rational explanation. One that involved a neurological condition.

"How does an all expense paid holiday to the south of France sound, lad?"

"It's the small village on the hilltop in the painting that he wants to visit," Aaloka said.

"I take it you've heard of Rennes-le-Chateau... and the impossible wealth of its former priest."

"Okay... alright, I get it now. Instead of taking the whole family to Disneyland, you've a different theme park in mind. One for heretics," I chuckled, shaking my head with amused tolerance while at the same time feeling a bit relieved. "Tell me, does this latest caper of yours involve a quest for the Holy Graal? And let me guess - you think this painting contains clues... More hidden meanings... secret exchanges. I can see cogs in the machinery turning, Malcolm," I said while rattling the ice cubes in my nearly empty glass. "Ideas hatched in that mind of yours. Well, it will probably be full of kooky tourists, but I hear the view is spectacular. One problem, though – how am I going to travel without a passport?"

"Let me worry about that," Malcolm winked.

That night we had another visitor. Although I didn't see a bell-shaped craft land out back, Zyla had arrived to visit Jag.

I could hear them out on the deck through the screen door. It sounded like she was trying to teach him a sentence in the Enochian language. From the way she pronounced the melodious syllables – flowing almost poetically - I was now certain that it was her that I had seen earlier in the church with a rocket on its roof. After switching on my phone's recorder to find out if what she was reciting was in any way similar to the messages uttered by my blog hacker, I carried my Bombay tonic outside as a warm breeze mingled her distinctive metallic perfume with the night-scented plants in bloom around the trellis.

"Densification must be a bitch," I joked while admiring her sparkly sleeveless bodysuit. "And look at that new tat," I gestured to the luminous tattoo of an abstruse geometric symbol that was backlit by blue LEDs that had been implanted in the skin on her arm.

"It's a beneficial talisman - the Enochian sigil," she said flatly.

"Lit with super-night blue," Jag added. "I'm getting mine next week."

I also noticed a new crystal skull ring on one of her slender fingers.

"This holy ice is my mini-Maxx," she said as if anticipating my next question. "I also call the real one Maxx, though that's not its real name."

"What's real Maxx used for? Something like crystal gazing, I would guess?"

"For conversations with an angelic presence, hopefully. I say hopefully because the pronunciation... it's a difficult process... with the unique inflections and stuff... conjugations and declensions. Even with a few samples - Dee's phonetic notes – it's educated guesswork."

"Dead languages can be a tad tricky," I nodded. "Especially the tongue of angels, with all the intricacies involved and such little information left to assist us."

"Oh-Rah-Seh-Beh-Ah," she said while winking at Jag with her shimmery eye makeup. I assumed the word or phrase was Enochian, but whatever it meant, the boy seemed to be equally clueless as he swallowed a mouthful of root beer.

"With the energy present in Maxx, we're trying to make contact with the Watcher that didn't fall onto Kecksburg back in the 1960s, which was then retrieved by NASA."

"Kecksburg? Pennsylvania? Wasn't that a downed satellite? A Soviet space probe that was launched to explore Venus. Kosmos something or other."

"Downed is the right word… but as to whose probe… that's the real question."

Once again, Punyaaloka's bhoot room had been booked for a private party by the owners of a local ghost tour. Having arrived early, I was chatting with Malcolm at the bar as he watched with interest at my mixology skills. Instead of prepping for the popular Starflower drink, I was making vanilla simple syrup that I planned on using in my ghostini. Once done, this would be added to vodka, Godiva white chocolate liqueur and cream. The final touch would be cocktail glitter to give it a pearlescent sparkle.

"So, is Jag still snipping away at squiggly things and sticking them in the fridge?" he asked.

"No, he's got a shiny new ball these days. Why bother fooling around with lowly bacteria when you can hob-nob with the cosmic elite. According to his new friend, Zyla, after mastering human knowledge, John Dee wanted to expand his education into the angelic realm."

"Jumping right to the top of the food chain is he? Perhaps someone should inform the lad that the Enochian angels bite."

"I don't know about that, but as soon as the copy of Gmical-zoma was delivered, I used the lexicon to find out what she said to Jag with her winky face. The Enochian gobbledygook trans-lated to drunk. The little shit thought the boomer was drunk because I poked fun at her pedantic carrying-on. Through my voice recorder jiggery-pokery I also wangled what she was re-peating in that space cadet church: Open the mysteries of your creation and make us partakers of undefiled knowledge. There was also some stuff about her crystal skull, Maxx, the Windexed conduit. Be thou a window... kind of crap. Anyway, I think I might have found the cult of Ramiel. One of its duties as an angel – even a fallen angel – is to offer true visions. And other-worldly visions are what they're attempting to tune into at that church of odd. Instead of learning about declensions and conju-gations, I hope Jag's just trying to get laid by her shimmery ass... though I don't know how he's turned on by perfume that smells like a cold knife."

"I've seen her. Curious fragrance or not, that's one tidy ma-chine. And she certainly doesn't lead a drab existence. Like you said, the lad drifts from fad to fad. But as to your pillorying her," he said while adding some imported quinine to his glass of gin, "I trust you recall what I once told you about the theory of the bicameral mind in remote antiquity... when all of humanity was beholden to the gods and obedient to their auditory commands. Might I suggest that this lost language... this primordial god-speech was Enochian, or something closely akin to it?"

"You're free to suggest anything, but where's any proof of this earlier mentality?"

"You, dear boy, are a splendid example of the change that occurred. But not everyone has adapted so well. Fragments of tablets from ancient Mesopotamia have been unearthed which depict rulers kneeling before an empty throne. The throne is empty because there were no longer any gods, neurologically speaking, on the Earth. These same tablets contain verses lamenting how miserable life had become with the absence of the gods. After the breakdown there were no more crystal clear voices in peoples' heads, which, one suspects, at times, were accompanied by vivid hallucinations... the rich pageantry of god-theater. With our new-found subjectivity, chaos ensued. Our innocence was lost and we gathered fig leaves to cover our nakedness. Authority from the divine realm was replaced by kings and rulers... most of whom weren't up to the task. Thus began the world's great religions... with themes about promises from figures of divinity returning at some future date. Troubled humans resorted to prayers... begging the gods for help dealing with various situations. Intermediaries were invented as stand-ins... The messengers of the gods. Angels, prophets and oracles. Dream-interpreters, diviners and so on, all being watered down versions resulting from the further weakening of the bicameral brain... when divine guidance was included for no charge. Built-in instructions that we simply followed."

"These verses about why bad things happen to good people just sound like an earlier version of Job. A model to placate the righteous when things didn't seem to make sense. A salve for their suffering, that's all it was."

"Okay, save your derisive smirk for another time. Maxx, you say... Wasn't that the name of the old chap with the thriving mole whisker in one of your dreams?"

163

"If you say so," I said while sniffing the Half and Half. "So, which ghost tour do we get tonight? People pulled under water by a giant hand. Country joyriders chased by albinos, or the poor fellow killed in the roast-beef freezer at the amusement park?"

"One of the stops was the ghost that stalked the aisles of the Sunnyvale toy shop and pelted customers with Beanie Babies or Cabbage Patch Kiddies before the bloody things became valuable assets."

"Oh yeah, the loser that axed himself to death. Honestly, Malcolm, you don't believe any of this silliness? I mean – a woman's red ball gown doesn't have consciousness... and what about phantom Chevys? With inanimate objects, there's no soul-stuff sticking around."

"True, but as to residual hauntings... encounters with wispy apparitions that flicker into view and sightings of shadowy figures, again, this might be a throw-back to the bicameral mind."

After combining all the ingredients and adding a sprinkling of cocktail glitter, I tasted my version of a ghostini.

"Not bad, but next time I think I'll use whipped vodka. The idea just popped into my head... without so much as a peep from any gods."

For several nights Zyla had been coaching Jag in the poetic resonances and linguistic quirks of the Enochian Calls (based on marginal notations in Dee's journals), with the latest being angelical dipthongs that she repeated while gliding certain vowels to create a more powerful effect.

Here he had been systematically ditching vowels as part of his millennial speak, and now Zyla had him piling them on to make the Angelical Calls more efficacious. As soon as she left – probably frustrated at his inability to grasp the chimeric makeup of celestial speech – I called him into my office to have a little fun with some phony NASA images recently posted on the Net.

In what was obviously a parody of all the whacky claims by people of artificial objects or fossilized life forms captured on the surface of Mars by the Curiosity rover, I showed Jag an enhanced close up of a weird rock formation (circled in yellow with a pointing red arrow) that had a caption which read "AMELIA EARHART'S MISSING PLANE." The craggy features had been cleverly (and humorously) photo-shopped to vaguely resemble the outline of the female aviator's Lockheed 10-E Electra that went missing over the Pacific Ocean in 1937. In the design, portions of the registration number 6020 could be made out on the 'plane's' glinting tail section.

"What the hell is Amelia Earhart's plane doing on Mars?" I asked while trying to sound like I was totally dumbfounded.

"Who's that?"

"The female aviator that vanished while flying this plane over the Pacific in the 1930s. The plane's number was NRI 6020… and the image even shows what looks like the added fuel tanks to the wings."

"That's fire," he said, swallowing the bait. "I've seen the crab guarding a cave, blurpleberries, jelly doughnuts, Viking ship and, of course, the face."

"So, you think this is real?"

"Why wouldn't it be?" he shrugged.

"Jag, the other images you mentioned are examples of pareidola. Like the tendency to see faces in clouds and Marilyn Monroe in the full moon."

"Who's that?"

"The famous actress."

"Is that the blonde bae the government killed because the President of Merica told her about the Roswell crash? I saw that on Netflix. Zyla and I are going to the con. It should be turnt up."

"So, you're not the least bit suspicious of this doctored photo? It's not even pareidola. It's a parody of pareidola. Someone lampooning the other images."

"If it is, someone slayed it... but I'm more sus of the Sims."

"What does that mean?"

"Those screwing with us with their simulation... that we now know about because of all the pop-ups. Glitches besides déjà vu, like particles in labs that only do certain things when we're looking and Nelson Mandela's first death before they changed it. What about hammers found in coal seams and what you saw yourself in my crappy augmented reality glasses? The simulation within the simulation as we're now adding our own layers... though low-level ones so far.

We're finding the chunks of code designed by the more advanced race on earth that live behind the normal scenery. Some guy on Reditt said that he once got a peek at this othering and it was cray. Some of the simulators who want to come clean... to stop cheating us... might have put the lady's plane on Mars as another giveaway, like those programmers making agriglyphs. You know... crop circles... to give us a heads up. Red flags, Sheldon."

"Crop circles? Aren't those hoaxed by jokey Brits using wooden planks? Besides, they're not new. It used to be thought the shenanigans in the fields were made by mowing devils."

"Cancel, skeptoid. That's what the simulators want us pixel-people to believe as a way of counteracting the rogue guys. Maybe the plane was snatched out of the sky by aliens and then dumped on Mars. Who knows, but it still happened in the sim. It's real, but not really real."

"You're brain hurting again," I said while rubbing my temples. "Okay, these sims... the high-fidelity ones... why bother with things like micro-organisms? I mean the tiny little fuckers like *Nanoarchaeum equitans*? And why go to the trouble to make every snowflake unique and dark energy so abundant in the universe without being observed? What's the purpose of widespread extinctions and continental drift?"

"Why would God do that as well?"

"For once I agree with you. When you said we'll know soon, what did you mean?" I asked while scrolling through the Net to see if there really were NASA images that showed what some nut case thought might be the remains of a Viking longship on the Red Planet.

"What do you think mom's really doing at Cellectech? Not just designing babies that have blue eyes. Zyla thinks that's a sham. When I told her about the telenoid denying you access to something called the Stork's Nest, she said that mom's working on a secret project that probably has to do with colonizing another planet by using seed freezers. Fro-zen em-bry-os, Sheldon, that are thawed out and raised by android caregivers that human minds have been uploaded into.

"So, as we speak, your mom is developing artificial wombs... growing uteruses or something in the lab to be placed on one of these spacecraft?"

"It's way better than sending people in hibernation on the generation ships. Adults on the sleepers... Slow boats."

"Actually, I had a sneaking suspicion she was trying to find a way of switching on the genetics of the immortal jellyfish so that you could Jaggravate me forever," I joked.

"She probably is... but for those in the Sub Zeros on the ship. Anyway, I gotta bounce. Zyla and I will be making rainbow tacos while you're sitting here on your glitch tailbone looking for glitches on Mars. Wait until you see the Sand Whales."

Though Jag's strange notions used to leave me exasperated, they were becoming a source of perplexed amusement. However, something in his last volley of bizarro ideas caused a curious reaction in my mind that was similar to experiencing... déjà vu (damn!). When he was talking about this more advanced race on the earth (if I understood him correctly?), whose simulators are pulling the strings, he mentioned that someone got a peek behind the curtain into the world they referred to as the "othering."

Besides being an odd term, as soon as he said it, it was like a switch flipped on in my head. For a second I thought I was having a memory flash, but, sadly, that was the extent of it. Just a twinge feeling and nothing else.

"What's that smell?" Jag asked while wrinkling his nose.

"Piles of bullshit," I replied while glancing about at the kaleidoscope of alien-themed imagery on the dusty main street. "Your olfactories might also be detecting a whiff of manure in the breeze from the surrounding pastureland, but at least there's a breeze," I said while looking up at a vibrant blue sky unbroken by clouds. Apprehensive of the sudden unfurling of any black umbrellas, I stepped onto the cracked sidewalk where throngs of tourists were clinging to the shade offered by awnings attached to faded brick buildings.

The carnival atmosphere ensuing on the Fourth of July in Roswell, New Mexico not only marked America's independence, but, more importantly, it seemed, celebrated the anniversary of what many believed to be the crash of an alien spacecraft on a nearby sheep ranch back in 1947.

Locals who jumped on the bandwagon hawked souvenirs at rickety card tables near storefronts emblazoned with UFO and spacecraft iconography. Frisbees, coffee mugs, doormats – no matter how tacky, as long as they were the signature glowing green color, were gobbled up by tourists. Even though the rancher who first discovered the debris field said that the dead aliens weren't green, and after the rest of the world had come to realize that most intergalactic pilots were gray-skinned, for some reason, Roswell's mascots were still the little green men of early pulp sci-fi magazines.

Though I couldn't begrudge a town that was once dull as dishwater for capitalizing on their ufological notoriety with businesses tailored to attract tourist revenue, it was amusing to see how some incorporated the cosmic motifs, such as the Mexican cantina whose mural depicted alien matadors fighting bulls, or doughnuts made with silver food coloring (an idea borrowed for the Sunday pancake breakfast) and the auto body shop with a sign stating that until the recovered memory metal could be duplicated, they were ready to fix any fender benders. Some tie-ins to the alleged incident, however, were confusing, like the cow chip throwing contest that was included in the festivities, unless, of course, the whooping ranchers had to toss them in a zero gravity environment?

But where else could you find a barrel cactus wearing a sombrero seated in a jalopy parked beneath a doe-eyed manikin attached to a camouflage parachute dangling from a power line? Or a McDonald's shaped like a flying saucer? Hell, even Wal-Mart had embraced the heavenly invasion. And at night, lampposts whose bulbous globes had slanted black eyes glowed with an unearthly greenish tinge. Whoever missed the idea of stringing multicolored lights around the massive mothership of a gleaming water tower that loomed in the middle of the town should have been fired from the tourism council, though.

As we moved through the curious onlookers, Zyla seemed to be wilting in the stifling heat (even though, as I reminded her, the average surface temperature on Venus was 864 degrees Fahrenheit). With the afternoon sun glinting on the metallic embroidery of her futuristic ensemble, she deflected her head back and made a funny face when an elderly woman beneath a floppy hat asked if she wanted to buy a moon quilt.

"So, how does the Cattle Baron sound for lunch?" I asked.

"Like the worst idea I've ever heard," Jag replied.

"Sorry. Okay, then it's Cattleman's Steak House, I guess. You tell people around here that you're pescatarian, they'll ask you what part of the galaxy is Pescat located."

"I'm not pescatarian. Zyla and I – we're both vegan."

"Good luck with that. This is a Jinglebob cow town. Though there's probably a Golden Corral somewhere amongst this unbridled kitsch. You've a better chance there than the Arby's or Rib Crib. Are you sure you can't share a shrimp basket? Shrimp that look like Zeta Reticulan neonates." Before either had a chance to respond, someone speaking into a bullhorn was attempting to spoil the party.

"God's chariot doesn't explode… and it's not made of tinfoil, rubber and sticks," a burly man in a white suit coat uttered with the fiery passion of a fundamentalist Christian sermon.

"Just take one bite from the fruit the serpent begged, but you people are gnawing on the entire orchard. You've even cast God out of the Garden of Eden. Refrain from mystery mongering!" he shouted while raising a Bible, "over a pile of Tinker toys. It would be better – Roswellians – to go back to being a sleepy town with potluck dinners than to serve these darned alien burgers. Look around and see what you've latched onto. People who used to work at the cheese factory are walking around with propellers on their head. This alien hubba-hubba – it's as cracked as the asphalt here. Put down your evil refreshments," he said with a Texas drawl to a couple of little girls licking virescent alien lollypops. "Why you ought to be ashamed...cavorting about... with this pagan shindig right on main street in the shadow of the House of Prayer. You've abandoned your true God and are now worshipping flying pie pans. False signs in the sky! This alien gospel, it's a satanic plot. Bug-eyed demons hanging from power lines and the devil's trinkets for sale at this unholy street fair," he barked while moving through the crowd, seemingly mocked by a wiggling blow-up lime green alien with black teardrop eyes. "Freaks as green as grama grass - space brothers, my patootie! The Bible doesn't mention anything about aliens or even about other planets... so, therefore, they cannot... and do not exist."

"It doesn't mention anything about Australia either, but I'm pretty sure it exists," someone in the crowd shouted.

"There's nothing holier than the American dollar," uttered another.

Zyla pulled out her bottle of (anti) negative energy hydrating elixir and misted her face.

"Fuck bad vibes," she said as almond tones mingled with the onslaught of manure.

171

Even though the Roswell United Methodist Church was still white-steepled (having not yet been converted into a mock rocket launching pad), the pasty-faced preacher with the megaphone was facing a full frontal assault by the adherents of a new religion. His home turf had become ground zero to this new movement – a pilgrimage site for the super-believers who came to touch the sacred hardscrabble (or to bottle soil samples from parts of its grazing land). Scraps of anomalous metals found at the purported crash sites displayed in the local UFO museums were the equivalent of ancient relics venerated in the Gothic cathedrals of Europe, such as pieces of the true cross or fragments of the wooden manger.

What was happening here (and elsewhere) could be described as re-mythologization. Suggestive narratives in the scriptures being re-interpreted - the Bible being a goldmine for exotheology.

As well-established religions continued to lose their luster, increasing numbers swapped their orthodox beliefs for the more millenarian religious impulse (something that those of no particular religious persuasion, or even atheists found far more appealing). In the ongoing cosmic drama, biblical celebrities of the Old Testament were re-cast in a more technological guise... those without limitations. Though short of stature and coldly clinical (nay, cosmic predators!), the high-tech angels were welcomed as celestial saviors, whose mission was to genetically alter or hybridize humans as part of our next 'evolutionary' phase.

Although the belief in both traditional religion and the arrival of interstellar space fleets both require a leap of faith (both being wishful thinking), many UFO believers consider the choice of their 'gods' as advanced extraterrestrial entities to be more provable and thus better able to fulfill our need to be rescued.

Just as biblical literalism was being replaced by *interpretatio technologica* from the paleocontact types – those who believe otherworlders supercharged human civilization (and continue to do so), scientific illiteracy was also facilitating the acceptance of the ancient astronaut hypothesis, especially where there are gaps in current scientific knowledge. As I've said before, just because questions remain with certain archaeological artifacts, that's not an excuse for drawing conclusions based on faulty reasoning, not to mention wild speculation.

"That steak was good," I said while rubbing my belly. "I'm sure glad Bessie wasn't snared by some alien tractor beam. How were your salads? Cucumber wedges shaped like crescent moons... Radish bulbs with toothpick legs and root antennae... Carrots with – "

"Jeez, we get it, mi-GRANE," Jag uttered while casting a nasty glance at me as I held the heavy glass door open. Obviously, he was still perturbed by the "Ancient Alien Theory Academy" parody tee shirt that I donned for the UFO festival events held at the Roswell Convention and Civic Center.

As we made our way through attendees in alien costumes and vendors peddling space-themed baubles, after reminding the kid that both UFO enthusiasts and skeptics were invited, I scanned the scheduled list of speakers.

"What do you want to anguish through first? Let's see now, there's ancient technological marvels... Talos, a machine of the gods that guarded the alien zone on Crete from unwelcome humans with fiery glances... laser weapons... until it was rendered useless by Medea, who removed its bronze plug and drained its divine blood, ichor, which was actually a certain fluid...like todays synthetic oil... that was necessary to keep the giant automaton's machinery lubed... Sacred bulls of Egypt that were really alien tank-like vehicles... Okay, if that's not stupid enough there's the biblical tale of Jonah in the belly of a whale... a whale of a mistake that the Big-J called a mammal a fish, but, who cares, these days it's Jonah having been abducted by an alien submersible – "

"Satan puts barriers around the Bible," another Christian fundamentalist preacher said after hearing my mentioning of the scientific error in the scriptures about Jonah's 'big fish' (probably the fault of the translators, but shouldn't that also be a concern?). "Plants with thorns to keep people away."

"There's a presenter's theory about the Sykesville monster," I continued to read from the schedule. "Could the mud-caked Wildman captured by the military in a heavily wooded park in Maryland in the early 1970s have been a Neanderthal that was returned to earth after having been taken to a distant star system to be studied many thousands of years in the past? Of course it was. Not sure why I didn't think of that... clueless me. So, what will it be?"

"The Black Knight," came the reply in unison.

Inside the hushed auditorium, a broad-faced man wearing a blue blazer stepped up to the podium.

"I know what all of you are thinking. Why couldn't the damn thing have crashed in April?

Well, I'm not here to talk about that crash retrieval, though plenty of other speakers will be. What I'm here to talk about is what occurred on December 9 in 1965 in Kecksburg Pennsylvania. According to numerous witnesses, an acorn or bell-shaped object made a landing in a wooded ravine... made a semi-controlled landing," he said while fiddling with the microphone after a series of loud screeches. "Those who saw the object under the tarpaulin on an Army flatbed truck said it had strange

174

markings, just like many observers in the woods claimed, but it wasn't Cyrillic script, meaning it wasn't Soviet spy hardware. It was, I firmly believe, an alien space probe. An artificial satellite that has been dubbed the Black Knight. The Black Knight... or whatever you want to call it... had been circling the earth in a retrograde orbit for thirteen thousand years until it was knocked out of space by an American G E Mark 2 reentry vehicle as part of Project JOUST and spirited away by MoonDust personnel. So, that photo you've all seen taken during the STS-88 mission in 1998 probably was just a thermal cover that got away during extravehicular activities."

During the course of his lecture, the speaker offered no real evidence, but, instead, merely repeated earlier speculations in a labored monotone. There were the radio signals coming from an intelligent source detected by Nikola Tesla in 1899 and coded messages in long delaying echoes later picked up by HAM operators. In the fifties, military units at White Sands using long range radar tracked a couple of objects in a near-polar orbit, whose reports were quashed by the top brass claiming they were moonlets or other natural bodies. Then there was the greenish light emitted by a UFO seen by Mercury astronaut Gordon Cooper that NASA said was a hallucination caused by an excess of carbon dioxide inside the space capsule. This was followed by sightings from people all over the planet who said they could make out the mysterious orbiting object with their naked eyes. More recently, the legendary Black Knight was filmed passing by one of the blue moons, which meant that at one time there must have been two of the mysterious probes observing the Earth.

Before I could exit the auditorium, a reporter asked me what I thought of the presentation.

"He got one thing right. Well, make that two. It is too bad the Roswell incident didn't occur in April. The other is that a GE M2 reentry vehicle that may have collided with Cosmos 96 was involved with the Kecksburg affair. That's almost certainly what landed in the forest. The cone shape matches exactly, and its copper heat shield would explain the greenish glow. The so-called hieroglyphs seen were unintelligible welder markings at its base. The MoonDust unit was quickly on the scene because it contained a nuclear generator that might have started leaking.

As for the rest... the signals in Tesla's radio experiments were most likely from a pulsar. The intruders detected near the equator," I emphasized "could have been phantom blips called radar angels. Wouldn't a civilization that's light years ahead of us have also developed stealth technology? Cooper denied ever reporting a green light and odds are the NASA images show a thermal blanket rather than a fastwalker or alien machine watching us from above."

"What do you think crashed at Roswell?" another reporter asked.

"I'm rooting for it being nothing made on the earth... whether intergalactic Magellans or just a space tumbleweed, because I'd like to come back for more silver flapjacks. Kidding aside, instead of all the digging at the skip site, where there's nothing left except rusted tin cans, why not send a couple of these instant field archaeologists with their metal detectors and trowels to conduct a search at the former base intelligence officer's house on West 7th Street? His son claimed that after his dad loaded the pieces of wreckage into the back of his Buick, on the way back to the base he stopped at home first to show the family the strange material. After trying to make sense of the fragments dumped on the kitchen floor, most of it had been gathered back up and taken to the base. Mom must have been one hell of a clean freak, though, as junior remembered her sweeping some of the smaller bits of the mystifying stuff out the back door. Around that time, concrete was being poured for a patio or washing machine or something. Well, even if this was before the odds and ends got swept into the backyard, to dig up the truth, why not excavate this postage stamp-sized area which no one disagrees the debris, whatever its nature, had once been placed, rather than focus all the forensic tools on the nearly quarter square mile grid on the Foster Ranch? I'll tell you, though – there sure are a lot of mishaps with these flying saucers. Why is it that after hopscotching through the vast gulfs of space, they suddenly go on the fritz above the Earth?"

"Do you give any credence to the ancient astronaut theory?" a journalist asked.

"You've blue ribbon panels at these symposiums who seem to think our ancestors were a bunch of dimwits. Who weren't capable of doing anything on their own. Well, guess what – they weren't incompetent savages that lacked engineering skills. They had the same brain as we do, okay. I realize the ancients had a different technological frame of reference, but why jump to the conclusion that cherubim helicopters with laser beam weaponry guarded the Garden of Eden when flaming swords could be a rather poetic way of describing how the intense rays of the sun caused drought and turned into desert what used to be a lush, fertile region. I don't have a problem with the UFO phenomenon. The problem I have is with the way it's presented. Show me empirical evidence instead of mind-numbing speculation. Let's not wash a century of accepted science down the drain a and replace it with unreliable data and outright fabrications."

"What about the red Sirius anomaly?" a woman with a gravelly voice asked. Turning around, I was surprised to see Zonnie smiling at me. Her raven bob still had blue streaks and other than having more tattoos on her arms she looked the same as when I first met her.

"Obviously, all the ancient Greek and Roman astronomers were color blind," I joked. "Maybe they were observing Sirius only when it was low on the horizon."

"You just got done saying that the ancients weren't a bunch of idiots," she laughed.

"If not hydrogen fusing with helium, maybe it wasn't Sirius alone they were looking at. The ruddy appearance could have been the planet Nibiru passing through the solar system in its retrograde orbit," I kidded her. "Or, maybe it was the aquatic inhabitants from the Sirius system using laser light to transmit fragments of their DNA. How the heck are you Zonnie? I should have known that my favorite big rig driver that believes in Martians wouldn't miss the Roswell gala."

"I'll bet you're as about as welcome as a dog turd on a Persian rug, she cackled."

"Never heard that before. Just getting a crash course on how the sacred bulls of Egypt were really alien armored vehicles. Could use a cool respite now… hopefully with imported gin."

As we walked out into the crowed hallway, I saw Jag and Zyla leaning over a merch kiosk.

"The kids and I are camping out tonight at one of the alleged impact sites. You should join us."

"That's some kid," she said while gesturing to Zyla. "I lycra that Spandex. Can you imagine that on this chunky frame," she laughed. "And what's with her boot assembly?"

"It's ultra-velcro called Metaklett, but you can't find it on Earth."

"I see you're still wearing the same pair. Second time I've seen those snazzy steppers today."

"Really? Here?"

"Yeah. Some fellow that looked like a darksider checking out things was wearing the same ones. How'd you get so lucky?" she asked Jag.

"The simulators work in strange ways," I said, somewhat distracted. "This is Zonnie. Zonnie, I'd like you to meet Zyla and Jagy."

"We're going to hunt for Pecos diamonds before heading to the crash site," Jag said while shoving back his dark hair.

"Do I hear wedding bells?" she asked.

"They're not really diamonds – they're healing crystals that you can only find here," Zyla said flatly while checking out some crystal infused skin products.

"So, it wasn't atomic testing," I deadpanned. "Pecos diamonds... that's what they were after. The craft was loaded down with too many rocks."

Jag shock his head annoyedly while trying to suppress a smile.

"Hey, it's better than my other theory. Cosmic buckaroos rounding up moos to try and duplicate the formula for Cheez Whiz invented by Edwin Traisman... E.T. himself."

"There's no moo in that stuff," Zonnie made a serious face.

"What can I say – I'm prone to fantasy."

"We gotta bounce," Jag said.

"Sparkling conversationalists, the two of you," I said as they walked away. "Take a sniff. What do you think of her fragrance?"

"There might be a metallic smell on the outside, but I'll bet she keeps a cherry Lifesaver tucked in her you know what," she blurted out with a croaky voice.

"Go get that drink and I'm gonna grab me some barbecue from the Zero Percent Vegan," she wagged her brows while pointing to an old-fashion wagon-shaped food cart with spoke wheels and a canvas top. "But, if you've room, I might join you tonight. Did you hear about the recent sightings? People were calling in to Nell about them on the radio last night."

"More hot rodding grays. Hope they're not coming back to rescue the ones that have already been pickled."

"I hope they are!" she snorted while making a beeline to the chuck wagon.

Occasional flashes of heat lightning bounced over the dusty stretches of a barren landscape. In the gradually decreasing light, the last of the rattletrap buses filled with tourists had left and we were the only ones that remained on the unchanging vista of scrubby ranchland that extended as far as the eye could see. As Zonnie and I chatted at our little campsite, a short distance away, Jag and Zyla were burying a cache of Pecos diamonds near the embankment of a shallow arroyo where many believed the Roswell craft had come to rest. Looking out at their silhouettes against the twilight-streaked sky, the table-top flat, purple-hued wastes appeared to be undulating with slithering insects.

"They're Jerusalem Crickets and they have little faces that look just like the standard description of a gray alien," I said while sloshing my drink in a plastic cup before taking another gulp."

"Why would E.T. look like Praying Mantises and these Jerusalem Crickets?" Zonnie asked.

"I really don't know what the damned things are. Some kind of grassland pests. One thing you don't want to encounter out here is a giant desert centipede getting up into your underwear."

"When I was talking to Zyla earlier, she told me that your significant other works at a secret biogenetic lab that's creating something called Tomorrow's Child. She thinks this might have to do with signals coming from the alien satellite... the Black Knight... whose laser pulses contain instructions on how to build a better human – "

"Tomorrow's Children. And she heard this from Jag I take it. So it's no longer frozen embryos that will colonize Mars."

"She didn't mention anything about that. But, the optical transmission – she called it – contains DNA sequences of alien genetics. She thinks the code-name for the project is the Stork's Nest."

"Zyla is the type of person who is anxious to be misled," I said while sneaking a glance at Zonnie to see if she was offended. "And her planetary citizen partner in crime, Jag, takes things he reads on the Net to a mind-melting degree. Zyla has a crystal noggin named Maxx that she thinks is a device for talking with angels. It's a polished hunk of rock, not a gateway to anything except maybe fantasyland. Cellectect, where Aaloka works, is not attempting to rebuild creation... well, not exactly... In the Stork's Nest, they're making better babies. Using their editing tools... a snippet here, a snippet there to prevent hereditary disease. Correcting God's mistakes... and, yes, making improvements. There's nothing unethical or covert happening. They're delivering a product... tailored goods. It's a money-driven business where the standard of beauty applies. Now, if you want to let your imagination run wild... they're more likely to be trying to figure out the immortal jellyfish's code than to be tinkering with some cosmic blueprint or biochemical recipe beamed from a circling alien satellite nudging us to create one of their own."

As heat lightning continued to flare on the horizon, stars began to appear in scattered patches. Having finished with their geocaching, Zyla purified the area with a sage smudge wand as

Jag checked out the trail of reflective markers emitting a bright orange glow in the beam of his new tactical flashlight.

"Do you really hope what crashed here was made by aliens?" Zonnie asked.

"Why wouldn't I?" I replied while grabbing a handful of popcorn from the cheesy lime green alien bucket she was holding in her lap. "But if there was a crash, it might have been staged by the aliens, themselves, to give us dodgy earthlings a gentle push in the right direction. The goodies that spilled out were a gift... a level of technology that we could handle. This included the mechanical puzzle of the craft, which in no way represented the pinnacle of their scientific achievement. Otherwise it would be like Humpty Dumpty's fall... where all the king's men couldn't put him back together again. Even the little beings with the chalky yellow skin might have been designed specifically as part of their well-intentioned plan. They were included in the package. And if one of these grown bio-gadgets survived – the batteries didn't fall out – the military probably gleaned as much useful information from them as a little girl gets after pulling the magic cord on her favorite doll. After all the studying what breakthroughs did we make? Goggles to fight wars at night. Velcro straps for beach sandals. PlayStation version whatever."

"Umm, how about integrated-circuit chips, fiber optics and laser-based products."

"Point well taken," I said with a sardonic grin while watching Jag playfully aiming a green laser pointer that projected a tiny alien face on Zyla's shiny outfit before shining it up at the starry night sky to try and signal aliens. "Like the one he's putting to good use. Isn't there evidence of precursors to all these things that some believe came from the R&D stash? But, speaking of human advancement, there's another possibility that might explain what happened here…. and if it were true and people got wind of it, the ironic thing would be another cover up, not by the government this time, but by the local boosters and merchants."

"What are you talking about?"

"A couple of years after the Roswell incident, a spy-thriller titled *The Flying Saucer* was published, whose British author was almost certainly one of your darksiders… a secret agent with MI5. Ostensibly, it was a satire of international politics, but it might have been even more than that. The book is about a league of scientists… a handful of the brightest minds on the planet that mastermind a plan to prevent another world war. The scheme involves creating an alien threat… a common foe that would cause all of the earth to unite. For the plan to work, the first step is to make humans receptive to the idea of alien intelligence in the cosmos. To translate science fiction into science fact. After seeding the newspaper with rumors and juicy stories using as a template the Aurora, Texas crashed airship winder and Orson Welle's radio drama, *War of the Worlds*, a mysterious craft crashes in the wastes of New Mexico… just like this," I gestured to the barren surroundings where Jag and Zyla were now shining their flashlights down at the ground. "You're wasting your time," I shouted. "The local auto body shops have vacuumed up every last piece. Anyway, the recovered material is described as being a paper-thin, lightweight but extraordinarily hard metallic substance marked with unrecognizable hieroglyphics.

The world is baffled by the object and the plan appears to be working, except, for one big obstacle… religious fanatics who don't believe aliens could exist. So, as part of the charade, they fabricate an alien… the victim of the crash… using the chemically-treated skin of a dead Asian to give it an off-green yellowish cast, with its fillings made by cobbling together parts of exotic animals.

It had six-fingers with octopus-like suction cups. Sound familiar? Kind of like the out-of-focus latex-based corpse shown in the hoaxed alien autopsy footage."

"Are you saying that's what this is all about? The celebration here of everything alien... is to get people receptive to the idea. Okay, there's a similarity, but –"

"So, the question is: did an alien crash really happen, dumb-downed or not, and was the author privy to the details? Or... was he aware of a staged event. Not by aliens, but by our own government as a well-crafted psychological warfare operation. Disinformatsiya... designed to send Russian spies in the highly sensitive area on a wild goose chase. This would account for the seeming blunders by the military, such as the press release, which is the foundation stone of the event... before the weather balloon cover story. If it was an intelligence caper, all the key players involved would have been in on it from the get go, with all of them, including the rancher, doing their patriotic duty. The covert tomfoolery on the author's part... writing a book about an elite group pulling the strings behind the scenes could have been to settle a score with the Yanks for pulling a fast one with the Brits during Operation Paperclip."

"But... what about all the deathbed confessions so many years later? And that poor G.I. who literally washed his hands down to the bare bones to try and remove the alien stink after handling one of the bodies?"

"That takes us back to the other scenario. The Roswell incident involved crashed aliens – godlike entities not just giving us technological devices for the advancement of humanity, but, more importantly, putting an idea into our head... giving us something to think about after the war we just fought... that of a common threat from outer space. Maybe they're saying we need to become one planet, one people, which is why the aliens in the ship all looked alike… But don't go telling anyone I said that," I laughed. "I'm being charitable in the spirit of the occasion."

Jag and Zyla were now tossing a Frisbee whose rim was flashing bright colors from attached LEDS. Twice I heard him ask her "What's keeping them?" to which she replied, "Don't worry, they'll be here."

"Who are they expecting?" Zonnie asked barely above a whisper.

"Who do you think?" I whispered back.

"Aliens? That reminds me – *Mindshift* comes on soon."

"It's nice to see wannabe trans-humans playing silly games, isn't it?"

"It almost looks like a flying saucer," Zonnie said through a mouthful of popcorn.

"I just hope the rancher doesn't see it and come out here with a shotgun."

While getting up to make another drink, I realized that I needed to relieve myself.

"I'm going to brave getting spiky burrs on my socks and go find a shrub. Jag, come tell Zonnie about the Nazi car found on Mars!" I shouted over the chirping of crickets.

As I walked between clumps of desert scrub behind the make-shift campsite, I noticed plumes of dust in the distance. A faint rumble could be heard over the insect shrill and gust of wind rustling a creosote brush. Looking in the direction of the sound, I spotted a rotating beacon with curious violet-whitish flashes. Clicking on my flashlight, I could make out through the lingering dust the outline of a large silver object that remained stationary against a rock-strewn ridge near the sandy track we had used to enter the rancher's property. Switching off the flashlight, I watched as a luminous globe inside the thing was changing colors and patterns.

Soon I heard something crunching the dried grass and thought I saw dark shapes moving in a strange manner behind a blue irradiation that shone on the ground. When I turned my flashlight back on, I was startled to see three smallish figures gliding towards me. All three were wearing the same tight fitting bodysuits of a shimmery transparent material that revealed layers of android-like metal joints, gears and panels. All had identical feminine features with clean shaved heads. In my halogen beam, they looked like dolls with glistening porcelain white skin that emphasized fluidy black eyes. As they rolled closer, I noticed that the sleek figure in the middle was carrying a box of some greyish fabric. Before I had a chance to react, all three spoke in unison with velvety female voices.

"We're looking for Zyla."

Looking down, I realized they were standing on the rugged wheels of some kind of aluminum hoverboards that were illuminated by banks of radiant deep blue headlights.

"Is this about the geocache? The Pecos diamonds?" For the moment it was all I could think to ask.

"We've brought Cauliflower tacos," the one holding the container said while looking up with freakish dark eyes at a sky that was now filled with stars. "For tonight's space picnic."

"Where'd you come from?" I asked with a mischievous grin.

"California," came the reply, again in unison. "Sunnyvale." I'm Syd," the one in the middle said. This is Kyd and that's Xyd."

"Triplets," I laughed.

"Were you crapping your pants?" Zonnie snorted.

"For a second when they rolled up on those gyro things, I was thinking – put away the spades and sifting screens. With those Spandex bio-leggings... you saw how detailed the print was. Eyes tattooed jet black... and that moonstone powder or whatever on their kissers – "

"And the motorhome, too," Zonnie said with an animated face. "What are they driving – a silver Winnebago?"

"Some early model Airstream with a weird light on top of a flagpole. Who inks their eye whites?" I shook my head while gazing at the beams of flashlights bobbing in the darkness.

"I'm still not sure they're not walk-ins," Zonnie chuckled.

Jag, Zyla and the triplets had gathered out by the triangle-shaped "blaze orange" FireTacks stuck in the scrub brush that marked the geocache. As they munched on vegan tacos and sipped seltzers that had been packed in the neoprene picnic cooler, Zonnie and I were sitting in our lawn chairs listening to her staticky portable radio.

The host of the late night program, *Mindshift*, said there was breaking news coming out of Egypt and that he wanted to get right to it without first taking care of some business (possibly added for dramatic effect, I thought). After introducing his first guest – a journalist who spoke with a German accent – the man started by telling Nell that his announcement hasn't been broadcast anywhere else yet and that *Mindshift* would be reporting it first.

The news concerned a recently discovered pyramid complex north of Saqqara that was first discovered by an amateur archaeology researcher by analyzing satellite imagery from Digital Globe. Acting on her finding, a team of field researchers located the ruins of three unusual mounds arranged diagonally. They appeared to have once been pyramidal structures, although it was evident that in the past someone had attempted to disguise them by damaging the outer surfaces and even re-shaping the structures with mud brick into something else. Corridors were sealed-up by repurposing the original building materials, but not before many of the ancient inscriptions were obliterated.

While exploring an elaborate system of galleries beneath one of the foundations, radar surveys revealed a secret passageway adjacent to the maze of tunnels that led to a hidden chamber. When excavated, what they found was unlike anything they had previously seen. All of the treasures of Tutankhamen paled by comparison, not for the splendor of the objects that were meant to accompany the boy Pharaoh in the afterlife, but because of the sheer strangeness of that eerily preserved inside the underground enclosure. After further investigation, members of the field laboratory realized they had found the glittering prize of Egyptology – the final resting place of the Old Kingdom architect-turned God, Imhotep.

In case this became subject matter for one of my blogs, I decided to record the rest of the show.

"What had once been a great mystery – the whereabouts of Imhotep's tomb – was now an even greater mystery. The burial ritual that occurred, if it was, indeed, a burial vault, and not something else, is puzzling to say the least. Nell, when I call it a mortuary chamber, I do so without knowing what the room actually is... because of that found within the gilded mummiform... the metal sarcophagus... again, if that's what it is? Same with the seal imprints and wall paintings... the curious symbology on colorful faience tiles... Are they merely decorations or something hyper-technical? That's the biggest mystery. Forget about all the mummies you've seen. Forget about organs in canopic jars, oils and ointments and other preparations for the life beyond. Forget about everything. Wait until you see what they found in Imhotep's tomb... or whatever it is."

Before ending his brief report, he teased that video footage taken inside the chamber and smuggled out by an early team member would soon be made available on the Internet. Along with this, more details would be provided.

Before commenting on the newsflash, Nell went straight to a commercial. A company was offering further testimonials about a product with monatomic gold from those who were skeptical at first, but were now singing the praises of their alchemical elixir.

Not only was it a cure-all that reprogrammed the body at a cellular level, its full spectrum of orbitally rearranged monatomic elements even enhanced psychic abilities.

"By the way," I said to Zonnie, "in that book I was telling you about with the staged alien invasion... the aliens demand the earth's stockpile of gold, which they needed for the cure of some disease. What is it about gold?"

"It's why humans were created. The gods – as we called the aliens – created us to mine the gold they needed."

Having just returned from the circus in Roswell I found myself in San Francisco, where I was about to take part in the filming of a psychometric examination for the Paragon documentary. Stepping out of the passenger side of the rental car, I stood before a Grand Queen Ann Victorian that was sandwiched in a picturesque row of similar well-maintained tri-level houses on a tree-lined block near Golden Gate Park. Evidently, human gullibility had done the famous medium well. As the camera guy, Burton, poked fun at Julian's eggplant Italian chinos, I joked that the color blocks on the director's wool sweater had me wishing that I were the one wearing the designer shades.

Waiting for the lady psychic to answer the door, I imagined her to have an Egyptian ankh pendant hanging from her neck and several spotted cats at her heels. Instead, Blaze was devoid of jewelry, wearing a paisley blouse and casual pants with an elastic waist. Her hair was silver-lavender and she wore minimal makeup.

The interior of the house was equally impressive as the outside, having polished oak flooring, soaring ceilings and Victorian-era detailing. After exchanging pleasantries, we were given a quick tour of a succulent garden in an open-air atrium before she led us down an oriental runner into a parlor with blackout drapes of appliqued damask. Dancing flames in a marble fireplace and muted floral bouquet patterns on a carpet made for a great backdrop, but for Julian the centerpiece was a gleaming hand-painted, two-manual harpsichord.

After framing a shot with Blaze seated on a richly upholstered couch with the lacquered antique clavier in the background, Julian handed her the Elgin pocket-watch and told Burton to start filming.

With the camera rolling, she asked for patience while letting her psychic faculties receive impressions of residue entombed in the object. With the timepiece being of a psychically conductive metal, hopefully she would pick up vibrations of a past owner.

"I'm seeing a man who's wearing a hat," she said with her cheeks drawn tight while fondling the watch's piecrust Guilloche tooling.

As soon as she mentioned a hat, I thought to myself: Okay, here goes the cold reading technique. She would skillfully extract pertinent information with a series of guesses until Julian led her right to Kidd's grey fedora.

"It looks like a battered cowboy hat," she continued while squeezing the gold case with her liver-spotted fingers.

"This man... he's seated at a screen... like a computer... pecking at a keyboard... he can't type very well... Was this item recently purchased... on eBay? I'm not getting anything else... just a man in a beat up desert hat shopping on-line."

When she stood up and handed me the watch, I inadvertently brushed her hand. At the same instant, she stepped back with her glassy wide-open eyes fixed on mine. Visibly shaken, her trembling fingers dropped the timepiece onto the carpet. As the blood drained from her cheeks, making them resemble lumps of milky dough, she backed up further while continuing to stare straight at me.

"I'm terribly sorry, but I'm really not feeling well," her blanched lips quivered. "It just came on – all of a sudden like that. Stop the camera, please... Can you find your way out," she said with a wavering voice while trying to swallow back her fear.

Taking a break from my work, I joined Jag and Zyla out on the deck. Seated together on a bench, their faces reflected the mottled glow of shards of copper glass sparkling in the propane fire pit. As he sipped one of his Blueberry & Acai hard seltzers, she was bringing him up to speed on the latest theory about the alien probe known as the Black Knight. Since it was such a lovely night, with the moon rising over the jacaranda tree and the scent of eucalyptus drifting in the warm breeze, I plopped into a rattan chair and listened to her ufological yackety-yack without any derisive grins or snarky retorts (Aaloka's words).

Having monitored human progress for centuries, in modern times, the satellite (constructed of sentient meta-materials that were part of the Watchers' technical arsenal) switched on an advanced invisibility cloak that projected no telltale distortion that could be detected by intel sleuths. "It's a spectral camouflage that functions in three-dimensions," she said, "Cloaking its biomorphic metal tissue. It's continually speaking to those receptive to angelic transmissions. These repeated signals that translate into beautiful singing contain the holy code of the lofty ones, not to be confused with the Reptilians," she stressed. "It's the super-helix of the luminaries... imprinted with their genetic profile."

"They're luminoids," I said matter-of-factly.

Rather than whipping out her bad juju spray or slandering my name behind a veil of Enochian lingo, Zyla favored me with an expression of approval that I took to mean that she liked my off-the-cuff moniker for these particular entities.

Though I was anxious to hear more about this beamed star code, after finishing their drinks, the two bolted off to shop for purple fruits and vegetables that supposedly contained traces of monatomic gold. In their absence I continued to ponder the strange reaction the lady psychic had when I accidently touched her hand.

A moment later I received a text from Zonnie letting me know that *Mindshift* had an update on the story about the unearthing of Imhotep's tomb. Knowing that she would be asking for my thoughts on the matter, I grabbed the transistor radio on the deck railing and turned it on, expecting to hear a New-Age jargon-laden endorsement for Cleopatra's nourishing skin goop.

Instead, the investigator with the German accent was talking about ancient rituals involving the flayed skin of sacrificial victims. Many ancient astronaut proponents believed the trophy skins were worn by the cult's priest as an imitation of their remote ancestors having been witness to the partially dematerialized bodies of cosmic beings reclined inside ascension chambers.

Besides the sloughing of human skin, other parallels with the technology involved for near instantaneous travel between distant points was the later substitution of funerary equipment as provisions for the afterworld – thus mimicking the luggage taken by those who came and went through the transporters. Accounts in the scriptures of fiery abysses, pits to hell and great furnaces were a technical misunderstanding of flickering discharges, fluttering energy waves and other optical effects associated with the portals. Other diminishing echoes included the idea of liminal deities, superstitions of passing through thresholds and the magic of transitional spaces.

Just when I thought the reporter was going to talk straight through the break, Nell had him stand by for a commercial about a facial serum that boasted Dead Sea salt. I wondered if the Flayed Lords knew about these anti-wrinkle minerals?

The sliding door squeaked open and Aaloka emerged in ivory joggers and a black plaid pajama top.

"I'm calling it quits for the night. What's going on? Oh, look at the moon."

"I was just thinking about the odd reaction of that woman I told you about," I said while switching off the radio.

"I don't believe this. Some palm-reader's given our skeptoid the heebie jeebies. What did Giovanni make of her antics?"

"His name is Julian... and he didn't say much. He was probably horrified to think that old Zeke from Goldfield pulled a fast one on him. I've just been feeling sorry for myself again. The man without a past living in the plot of a potboiler... wanting a social security number... and to know what happened after I was banged on the head or whatever's responsible for my silly umbrella phobia? Things like what's behind the freakin' curtain that maybe the shadow-hunter saw. But, from the look of terror on her face, hell, maybe I don't want to know."

"Maybe the idea of a skeptic being present – someone keen to her tricks caused her to feign dizziness... or to mess with your head before you caught onto her little game. Doesn't that seem logical?"

"You mean to get me to leave? I suppose... although you didn't see her reaction."

"Where did Jaggy and Zyla go? I heard the stampede."

"Yeah, once I showed up they got the eff outta here. Went shopping for purple fruit."

"Did he badger you into trying that purple carrot yuk from the juicer?"

"So... what's got you so frustrated?" I asked as she sat on my lap. "Something with your work at Cellectech? I could hear it in your voice when you were speaking with a colleague, I'm guessing it was."

"The same old thing – the junkyard battle. I don't know why everything's got to be either black or white. Those raising alarms and calling us reckless - they're not really concerned about vandalism during our repairs, or about our genetic boosts for that matter. They're terrified we might discover a biological graal."

"What? Is that immortal blob of jelly finally revealing its secrets?"

"They want us to leave things as HE made them - including the congenital diseases we're trying to stamp out... even the cruelest ones wonderfully made by our God in HIS low budget creation. It's about the ENCODE hullabaloo. The creationists are desperate to show ANY biochemical activity to what many evolutionists insist is just background noise. Useless vestiges of natural selection with no apparent purpose."

"Like male nipples," I joked.

"Well, that evolutionary baggage is obviously not a priority to do away with. I'm talking about those creationists who want to do away with the whole idea of the very high-percentage of our non-coding stuff in the Darwinian dumping ground being worthless and thus doesn't fit in with intelligent design so, therefore, it must contain functional significance. Yes, I agree it's not all evolutionary litter... unreadable gibberish like that forgotten language Jag's always talking about."

"Enochian."

"Yeah, I never called it dead or worthless. The quote un-quote dark matter probably has purpose. It might very well serve as integral controllers of cell machinery... functioning as on-off switches for genes... and I'm very interested in any activity theses enhancers kick-start."

"Seeing how this has you so lathered up, next time let your telenoid take the call," I laughed as I began to gently massage her shoulders, breathing in her fragrance of exotic resins. "And while we're on the subject of robots, Jag's latest tattle is that Cellectech's searching for traces of ghost DNA in genome sequences for which there's little fossil evidence... no bones dug up. He thinks these ancient ghosts found in modern gene-pools are dwarf aliens called the Dzopa that crashed landed on the Tibetan plateau in pre-history."

"The little snoop. I miss the old days when he thought CRISPR was a new toaster I wanted to buy. So, he's also quoting me out of context. My own son."

"Zyla probably put him up to watching you," I said while rubbing her upper back. "You haven't found any silver bras or metallic G-strings lying around, have you?"

"I was probably talking about the Denisovans – an extinct species that once roamed Asia. That's something else the creationists are always bitching and moaning about. It complicates matters... footprints like this. In wanting to trace everything back to Adam and Eve, many doubt such archaic groups ever existed... or claim they were just from a different tribe because we all know DNA degrades over time. Instead of rejecting the data, how about joining us on a genetic ghost hunt, using deep learning techniques to detect signals from unknown ancestors like Denny that split off. Why not see if these super-archaic lineages – like the ghosts found in sub-Saharan populations – contain anything of interest?"

"That's Dogon country," I mumbled.

"And why isn't Jag spying on you when you get up in the middle of the night to work on your blogs? Never mind, I know why –"

"What are you talking about? I don't get up in the middle of the night."

"Well, then you can add another disorder to the list. Sleepwalking also involves a dissociative reaction... and, at least, partial amnesia. So, how would you know? I'm not saying you're peeing in the closet with your eyes glazed over, or that it happens a lot... it hasn't happened for a while, but there are times when you climbed out of bed and were gone for hours. Would you mind terribly getting my wine from the living room? I keep leaving it there. It's in my little chai cup... and then you can finish what you started."

When I checked my blog the next morning, I quickly realized that the heightened security features on the site had once again been breached by the cult of Enochites. As before, the color of the typeface design was intensely vivid, with the pulsating golden letterforms seemingly drawing me in to their curious rippling effect. The message was similar to the others – a hodge-podge of End-Times scripture and New-Age tripe:

GIVE EAR TO THE VOICE AND EYE TO THE FIERY SCROLL FOR THE TIME IS NOW TO THE ONE WHO IS VICTORIOUS, I SHALL GRANT AUTHORITY TO EAT FROM THE GALACTIC TREE IN THE PARADISE OF THE GODS

When I contacted Oliver to report the latest intrusion, he told me that he didn't think it was the work of a hacktivist, nor could it be attributed to any exploits purchased from the dark corners of the web. The problem was that my computer was possessed. I needed an exorcist – not a malware expert. The reason for the hauntings was most likely due to the content of my blogs, he explained. It was all the paranormal stuff, including aliens and discussions involving occult themes that had attracted this Ramiel, who had contacted me through the medium of an electronic device. That would explain the glowing orbs and buzzing voices (glowing orbs?). As for the animated glowing text, he had never seen anything like it and doubted it came from some futuristic font generator (like Jag suspected). While examining pixel grids, he felt a strange sensation that made his hair stand on end. I should go to Reddit, he suggested, to read about similar cases where floating cursors clicked on URLs and opened pages on dot onion sites with graphic displays that should never be viewed. Others pulled up creepy wallpaper imagery of shadowy figures, but no one knew of any digital ghost traps for these unwelcome specters.

Before hanging up, he asked once again if anyone on my site had ever brought up the Looney Tunes house in Southern Illinois? When I told him that no one had, and reiterated that I didn't believe in haunted houses, he told me that it wasn't haunted in the usual sense. Back when he was a black hat cracker, he had found on an encrypted military site things referred to as "beyonders." From what he could gather, these were invisible spheres and networks of structures of unknown origin that intersected with our familiar reality and could be made accessible by some means.

Although many believed the Looney Tunes house had been built over the pit where the fallen angels had been cast, it might have been constructed on the spot of some of this hidden architecture interpenetrating with our own world. The doohickey (as he now called the metallic slug that he joked was the scourge of all vending machines) had been found in the rundown Victorian. Having held it on several occasions he was pretty sure it wasn't made by human hands. Or, if it was, the past, present and future somehow got jumbled together at that rural address. He told me to check out the story and see if I could explain it.

When I put my phone down, all I could do was shake my head. That's when Jag entered.

"I left you some healthy stuff in the juice fountain. What's going on – roasting users?"

"Not much – my computer's haunted – that's all."

"I could have told you that."

"What do you mean?"

"I wasn't going to tell you, but one time I was on it... looking for those lit fonts when the mouse clicked on some stupid game on its own. It was basic free point-and-click shit. Like a cartoon about Adam and Eve trying to find a new paradise or something. After I left the site to look at the menu of this vegan-friendly pizza place... when I checked out their purple salad, the two cartoon people were walking on top of it... like it was their new Garden of Eden. Cray, huh."

"I'm gonna have to take care of this by myself," I said out loud while rubbing my temples. "I'm just gonna show up there and have a talk with someone other than Maxx."

"Go where?" Jag asked.

The entire façade of the former Methodist church had been painted with a metallic silver finish. Like the streamlined contours of its rocket ship-shaped steeple, its surface rippled like an iridescent mirage from a distance. Walking haltingly up a lustrous ramp, I must have triggered a sensor that caused the outline of a door of matching silver to automatically slide open and allow me to pass through its narrow opening.

Silver panels and chrome accents in the dimly lit interior were designed to give the impression of being inside a spacecraft. While checking out some of the other details, I was startled by a crackling voice. This emanated from a custom vertical display (in portrait orientation) on which a life-size image of a pasty-faced figure in a cheap suit spoke into a megaphone fashioned from a waxed cardboard "King Coney" root beer container. The flickering projections looked like transfers of old home movie footage shot with Super 8 black and white film stock that had been spliced together. In other scratchy clips, the ranting preacher stood at a pulpit inside tents of holy-roller revivals.

"In a *Time* magazine article, scientists – the same aca-de-monic pissants that would have you believe limb-hopping monkeys are your uncles – were talking about billions of planets out there that are just like Earth. Now ask yourself, how many times did God have to sacrifice his son? Billions of times? Billions of Jesuses!

Some think the Loch Ness Monster is a surviving dinosaur. Well, if Nessie is, they, too, were created on the sixth day – the same day God created man… and it's only because Noah welcomed them on the Ark. The Brontosauruses took up so much room, Noah had to leave unicorns behind, which is why you only see them in fairytales. Says who? The Book of Genesis and this Pocketronic calculator, that's who! Come to my church and I'll give you a direct line to God without having to give Ma Bell a single dime. Now, they're talking about flocks of space gargoyles swooping to earth in junk jewelry cloudships because the kindly persuaders are anxious to teach us stuff. Have you seen the pictures of their popping dark eyes? Looks to me to be part of the same angelic pack that taught the black mentalists their evil doings. Part of Satan's masterpiece, that's what it is, folks. Heavenly Father, I declare that you are my strength and my shield. Now, can I get an Amen?"

The footage changed to washed-out color tones that showed the same preacher at a later date. He was looking straight into the camcorder while speaking in a low subdued manner that was quite a contrast from the hoarse diatribe of the bible thumper in the earlier sequence.

"It happened during a practical joke known as a snipe hunt. On a summer night I had taken a group of children to a nearby corn-

field in a tractor-pulled hay wagon. I was steering the John Deere...
yet I wasn't moving. The dog running along side us also didn't move
forward. Children who were chewing on their PBJs did not chew...
and those who were drinking pop did not drink. Their faces were
turned upward in amazement, electrified by the shadows of splendor... and... then, suddenly, everything returned to normal. Later,
I recalled the guide who took me into the haze of this silver dream.
Paralyzed by visions, I saw the empathetic gaze of a mysterious
countenance. While in its midst, along with others having a similar
visible radiance, I felt great shame at my polluted emanation, and
desperately wanted to exchange the vapidity of my mortal garment
for the same glorious envelope of these aerial beings."

At that moment a figure with shoulder-length blonde hair
approached. He was wearing a shimmery bodysuit that was
reminiscent of the depictions of the Venusian space brothers encountered by the famous contactees in the 1950s. He also had
glimmering blue eyes, although I suspected that any magnetic
quality was due to the finish of special contact lenses.

"Greetings. I am Magiar," he said with slightly effeminate voice.

"I'm looking for Ramiel."

"Aren't we all," he smiled in a disarming manner.

"Not the angel of Enochic lore – the computer hacker. Do
you know who I am?"

"I only know of Ramiel as the Watcher who presides over
divine visions... those that preserve the true history of the world.
That's my father, Roopert, before and after his change," he said
while gesturing with his strange blue eyes to the vertical screen.
"As he says in the digital resurrection, it happened during one of
those snipe hunts of his... back when, in his version of the game,
the imaginary prey was described as a winged snake with red
eyes glittering evilly and a forked tongue."

He motioned me to follow him further into the building. On each side of the main aisle modern theater seats had been installed. Some were reclined to the domed ceiling where a starfield (like that in planetariums) was barely visible.

"You heard my father describe the uncanny stillness and deafening silence right before it happened. I also remember how the cornstalks stood perfectly still, as if frozen in place until allowed to once again rustle. Being the one chosen to capture the snipe, I was left all alone near the edge of the woods. While holding a pillowcase above my head, the other kids were supposed to make noises and bang sticks while attempting to drive it towards me. As I waited, I repeated the prayer my father told me to do. 'Touch me O' Lord, and fill me with your light, and your hope...' And then I saw what looked like a huge black ball rolling towards me. Whoosh! The next thing I remembered was sitting in the wagon licking a Popsicle. Nobody talked about what happened or remembered being inside the waiting place."

"Some practical joke," I said, feigning sympathy.

"A Fool's Errand in which the table was turned," he said with his serene demeanor.

"Where did this occur?"

"In the boonies in southern Illinois. The region known as Little Egypt. King Coney root beer country. Did you notice dad's megaphone? The next day in church those who went on the snipe hunt began speaking in tongues. This, in itself, wasn't unusual for members of a Pentecostal Church. What was unusual is that – this time – it wasn't glossolalia... what those in less charismatic faiths refer to as meaningless gibber-jabber. A new member of the church who got too deep into the occult... what my father used to call a black mentalist... and who now wanted to be saved... claimed that what we were speaking was an actual forgotten language. It was the tongue of angels – "

"Enochian," I said.

"Exactly, how'd you know? We had been chanting: Open the mysteries of your creation and make us partakers of undefiled knowledge, which is similar to our current Call at Paradial Lvciftian, meaning Living Dwelling with Ornaments of Brightness. The Call is: Move, descend and apply yourselves unto us, as unto the partakers of the secret wisdom of your creation. As embryo godforms, we are preparing to crack out of these biochemical shells."

The ornate table with occult glyphs and a series of crystal skulls arranged in a circle looked the same as before, as did the slanted metal panels of tactile neural interfaces. The screens above were turned off. Directly in front of me, where the church altar used to be, brilliant panels of a circular stained glass window portrayed the scribe Enoch surrounded by celestial beings watching over human affairs. This bathed a section of the room with vibrant blue, red, green, violet and yellow patterns. Beneath the faceted colors an inscription read:

SO THAT YOU CAN DISCOVER IT OUT OF YOUR
OWN POWER

I leaned over the translucent skull whose eye-sockets I once saw Zyla peering into.

"I've been told that a rascal named Edward Kelley served as the medium for John Dee's early experiments with summoning angels," I said. "The angels only showed their presence and conversed with him during the séances. According to Kelley, the spirit that appeared in the scrying crystal ordered that the two

Englishmen swap wives. And, guess what? Dee's wife, Jane, was far younger and prettier than Kelley's."

"As humans, who are we to judge the motives of angels, such as the counsel of Madimi."

While my gaze remained fixed on the skull, silver, grey and white swirls appeared to blend together in its pellucid depths. As I continued to observe the curious effect of these intermingling pale wisps, fleeting shapes that wavered like smoke coalesced into an ivory-hued lump that gradually formed what looked like an alabastrine face with delicate lineaments framed by tangles of scintillating white hair. As the ghostly visage became more distinct, its most dominating feature was oddly slanted eyes with fluidy golden-hazel irises. For an instant, I seemed to connect with their penetrating gaze until the exotic physiognomy blurred into myriad faint tendrils that quickly melted away.

Jag leaned his head into my office and told me to come check out something on his computer. Seconds later, I received a frantic text from Zonnie telling me to go to the *Mindshift* website.

When I walked into Jag's room, he and Zyla were gathered around his large screen, watching what was said to be the first video footage taken inside Imhotep's recently discovered tomb. Although no mainstream Egyptologists acknowledged the find, a team of archaeologists (some admittedly lacking proper credentials) claimed to have kept the exact location secret to ensure the footage would be made public. They justified this by pointing to corruption involving authorities within the Egyptian Ministry of Antiquities, who recently facilitated access to artifacts that wound up missing and were probably sold to private collections. Others were taken by maverick archaeologists to foreign countries and used as evidence to support controversial conspiracy theories. The footage filmed in Imhotep's mortuary chamber, they insisted, belonged to the world.

The video showed a figure dressed in khaki moving about in the hushed gloom of a tomb. Through a haze of suspended dust in the glare of a flashlight, the camera panned a limestone wall on which brilliant pigments of abstract glyphs unlike any known hieroglyphics stood out in relief. While focusing on illustrations blackened by torch that showed the lateral undulation of snakes, a voice with a heavy German accent opined that the fluttering movement represented streams of energy inside the secret furnace or true ascension chamber.

According to his interpretation, the inscription beneath the serpentine patterns read:

> I stand open now:
> Enter and quickly go!

The next shot was a plinth that supported a perfectly square block that was sheathed in gleaming copper and contained uniform rows of "gems cut into fancy shapes, including squares, ovals and chevrons." The "tiny brilliants were a crude imitation of a blinking control panel," the man stated, "in a pathetic aping of the star gods' technology. The polychrome depiction of the exoskeleton of the scarab beetle in the center, with its elytra ablaze in emerald fire, mimicked the fully winged power setting required for zero-time transport. An inscription on the funerary stela translated as:

None comes from there,
To tell of their need,
To calm our hearts,
Until we go where they have gone!

"This skepticism... or outright denial of the conventional tradition associated with burials and the afterlife during the Old Kingdom is affirmation that rational, scientific minds like Imhotep's were more intrigued by the process of dematerialization when undergoing a stargate transfiguration than constructing pyramids as resurrection machines."

Peering into the camera, the man warned that what we were about to see would be very disturbing to some, especially to young children, and that viewer discretion was strongly advised.

"Instead of the usual embalming method of the body cavity being filled with resinous pastes and wrapped in gummed linen, we see this."

The camera widened to show a half-spherical enclosure plunged in shadows. Lying inside an ornate metallic mummiform was a perfectly preserved body whose layers of skin, as well as his muscular structure, had been meticulously peeled away by some unknown surgical procedure.

What remained looked like a model of physiology found in the transparency overlays of anatomical illustrations. The camera moved closer for a graphically shocking view of the full-color organs and circulatory system. The only outer layer of skin that remained on the entire body was on the figure's forehead, the exact center of which was 'embossed' with a wadjet eye fashioned from a gold foil-like material. Its highly reflective gaze was focused on the star-spangled vaulted ceiling within the circular room.

"Undisturbed for millennia is our first known example of - what shall me call it - anti-mummification? Together with techno-signatures preserved in Imhotep's mortuary chamber, one can only conclude the witnessing of an operational teleportation system that was referred to in the Pyramid Texts as a heavenly ladder and sacred staircase."

CHAPTER VI
PAIRIDAEZA

"Seeking God knows what, but surely not God!"

- Jean Markale

"At Limoux one should not fail to sample the sparkling local wine, as further on it will be too late; the Razes is richer in water than wine."

- Gerard de Sede
(*Le Tresor Maudit de Rennes-le-Chateau*)

It was already stiflingly hot. Instead of black coffee and puff pastries, I took another gulp from a chilled bottle of sparkling water that had real mineral virtues. As birds squawked in shade trees and several calico cats drowsed on the mowed lawn, a gentle breeze lifted the scent of wild mint. Seated under a spreading mulberry tree at a table in front of a large brick farmhouse that had been converted into a hotel, I thumped my pen on a notepad and glanced around to soak up the atmosphere. Under deep blue skies, rolling countryside swathed by picturesque vineyards surrounded the provincial tourist retreat in the Languedoc region of Southern France.

True to his word, Malcolm had arranged a passport, no doubt thinking I would be amused by the last name, "Sand", as in "With a Grane of Sand" instead of "Salt", which I often had to correct when he mistakenly told others my blog was called "With a Dosage of Salt." Although the setting was the perfect opportunity for quiet reflection, I found myself jotting down notes on how to debunk what I suspected to be a hoax playing out on the *MindShift* website.

My skeptical nature told me that the macabre spectacle in the tomb was pure theater. If not old school tricks of the trade, the preserved remains of Imhotep were created using Hollywood's latest magic. However, rather than dissect what resembled a layer of sequential human anatomy on a transparent poster, my wandering thoughts kept returning to one of the ancient Egyptian inscriptions:

"None comes from there,
To tell of their need,
To calm our hearts,
Until we go where they have gone!"

This was very similar to James Kidd's favorite verse from the *Rubaiyat* of Omar Khayyam:

"Strange, is it not?
That of all the myriads who
Before us passed the door of darkness through
Not one returns to tell us of the road
Which to discover we must travel to!"

Which caused me to think about something that happened before the prospector's mysterious disappearance. While working the graveyard shift in the pump house at a copper mine in Arizona,

Kidd was involved in an accident. Shortly after the explosion, he felt sharp chest pains and lost consciousness. An ambulance was called and he was rushed to the hospital where the diagnosis was a heart attack. It was during his recovery that he first began to wonder about what happens to a person after death, and if the soul could be photographed leaving the human body.

Could his sudden interest have been the result of a near death experience? One in which the neurochemistry involved produced a sense of being separated from his body that seemed all too real? I jotted a note to run this by Julian, who, as coincidence would have it, was in the area filming an interview with the son of the Spaniard from the Pyrenees that once had a couple of mines near the Superstitions that were registered in Kidd's name.

"Bonjour, Monsieur Sand!"

As Malcolm rounded the corner with Aaloka and Jag in tow, his bellowing voice caused the cats to scamper beneath the heavy tangle of vines that covered the façade of the centuries-old building.

"I must say I am delighted to see everyone sticking with the plan to stave off jetlag. With a shot of espresso in these old veins instead of a nice cup of chai on the terrace… along with a chest-nut confiture spread on a French stick in the tum, I'm feeling ready for quite the adventure. If we're to beat the tour coaches, we should be on the motorway in the hire in no longer than say a half an hour. I should warn you, with all the twists and turns, the macadamized incline to the village will provide superior thrills than one of those old e-tickets at your Magic Kingdom."

"Jesus, how many shots of espresso, Malcolm?" I asked while looking at my sleepy-eyed partner.

On the way to the village we passed a dramatic landscape of thickly wooded hillsides, craggy gorges and jagged crests of mountains enshrouded by a scudding, glistening haze. Gaunt edifices of medieval fortresses rose strategically above secluded valleys where tawny stone outcroppings took on fantastic shapes in the tricks of light and shade. Beneath slopes blooming with gorse, a patchwork of green pastures was dotted with farms, cottages and more ancient ruins. Wafts of fragrant lavender filled the rental car, mingling with the smell of horse manure.

As we sped along in the Peugeot, Malcolm explained the rich and turbulent past of the region, including the evocative legends of a lost treasure. Besides being the setting of fabled riches, there were persistent rumors of an explosive secret whispered through the ages and encoded for posterity by its shadowy guardians. Although the secret is believed to be one of staggering proportions, exactly what it is continues to be the subject of intense speculation.

Winding through the rugged beauty of the hilly terrain, he continued to speak about the geological oddities discovered in the brooding valleys. Along with carvings of a cryptic nature found on natural features in the surrounding countryside, there were a disproportionate number of mysterious deaths in the area. There were also the historical antecedents in the Languedoc, which included the blood-soaked stage of the Albigensian heresy, one of the blackest marks in history, as the Church of Rome launched a campaign of fanatical persecution to stamp out the unorthodox doctrines of the mystically oriented Cathars.

When Jag asked him what he thought this treasure or powerful secret might be? Malcolm's answer was that "The wooded slopes echo with tales associated with the unlimited wealth of the Holy Graal, and, supposedly, this legendary object is responsible for both the enduring enigma and secretive atmosphere of the place."

When we reached the little town of Couiza, Malcolm turned left to begin the winding, steeply upward drive. Negotiating sharp bends as the narrow road followed the contours of the hillside, Aaloka's droopy eyelids were now wide open under her floppy sunbonnet. As we zigzagged higher and higher, sunlight filtered through the tangled gloom, offering glimpses of the huddled roofs of the tiny village perched on the summit. Finally, a signpost appeared that read:

RENNES-LE-CHATEAU

Near the entrance, we pulled into an empty space in one of the sandy car parks.

Happy to take a break from the hairpin turns, I climbed out of the cramped rental. As Malcolm and Jag went to purchase tickets for the priest's creepy little church, I took Aaloka's hand and headed towards a popular landmark of souvenir postcards. Jutting from the edge of the village so that it appeared to be hanging over the sheer drop to the idyllic valley below was a circular turret that resembled an enormous chess piece. The mock-Gothic tower was just one of the peculiarities of the abbe's estate, but rather than merely being a rich man's folly, there might have been a strategic purpose for the wide horizon provided to one standing among its castellated heights.

Climbing some well-worn steps, we strolled at a leisurely pace on the belvedere, taking in the magnificent panoramic views of sun-bleached vestiges of the past and more recent additions jumbled in a fairytale landscape that stretched to the purple foothills of the French Pyrenees.

A few minutes later we rejoined the two at the entrance to the notorious parish church. Before entering, Malcolm paused in the muffled sunlight to gaze up at the Latin inscription incised prominently over the tympanum of the doorway.

TERRIBILIS EST LOCUS ISTE

"This place is terrible," he translated the phrase with a mischievous smile.

"Well, there you have it," I said. "How about we skip the church for a bistro lunch with an iced panache?"

"Sounds like someone knew about us living in a simulated reality" Jag nodded knowingly.

"Chock it up to the pitfalls of Latin and modern English, Malcolm said. "It's actually a reference to Jacob's famous dream or vision of a ladder on which angels are coming and going… It was his reaction to the frightful or awe-inspiring vision of beholding the gate to heaven."

When we stepped inside the tiny vestibule, a grotesque polychrome demon that supported the holy water stoup greeted us. The glassy stare of the hunched figure's bulging eyes was focused on a black and white checkered floor. On the opposite wall, a plaster statue of Jesus being baptized by water poured from a silver cockleshell had been sculpted in a mirror-image crouching pose and painted with equally showy hues as the grimacing, horned devil. Like his adversary, Jesus's enamel gaze, too, was fixed on the mosaic tiles.

After a bemused pause, we left the players to contemplate their next move in this curious game of chess. Before we reached the final square on the 'board', a lanky figure emerged from the nave wearing a khaki cargo vest, field pants and hiking boots. He was thin as a rake, with a weathered face that was pockmarked with old acne scars. Longish grey hair was combed back on his high forehead. Without any discernible accent (like some people from the mid-west seem to be proud of), his eyes twinkled with mirth as he introduced himself as an aficionado of the Rennes affair.

"I'm a Sauniereologist," he half-joked before asking if we had any questions about Berenger Sauniere, the village priest that was responsible for the eccentric decorations.

Malcolm told the fellow that he was already familiar with the story of the ambitious priest, who may have discovered a significant treasure in the vicinity, which transformed his life dramatically, going from abject poverty to a life of luxury, that included spending vast sums to refurbish the church with what many have called near-blasphemous indulgences.

"Do you know the source of his wealth?" the fellow asked.

"Gold, one would assume," Malcolm replied. "Or precious heirlooms of the dead."

"Following a confusing trail, those will only lead to dead-ends. Look around. What do you see? The common theme here appears to be baptisms of holy water. Perhaps you've heard rumors of underground streams in the environs, whose water is said to have miraculous properties? Are you aware that in 1895 a fire broke out in the village while the priest was away on business and that in his absence his faithful housekeeper, Marie, tried to deny the fire brigade access to a water cistern that was under a small building in front of the church that the priest kept under lock and key? When he found out that they had broken into the enclosure and used the water to fight the flames, he was visibly upset, even filing a complaint with the mayor. What could have been so special about this water?"

Before we had a chance to escape from the lunacy of this self-imposed guide, he pointed to the curious statuary group in which the weighed-down demon held on its back the holy water font as four brightly painted angels genuflected the Sign of the Cross directly above him.

"Examining the baptismal font, many equate the four angels above the demon with Enoch and the scrolls of his prophecies that he hid inside a pillar... just like the parchments in a sealed wooden tube found by Sauniere, which has led to all this talk of a holy bloodline descended from Jesus and Mary Magdalene. I believe the phial that the bell ringer discovered inside the hidden compartment in the pulpit and gave to the priest contained the water from a sacred well. One with curative minerals. Did the secret of his wealth concern royal blood... or royal water?"

"The dots are becoming connected," I deadpanned.

"My friend here is equipped with a protective bubble of cynicism," Malcolm said. "He has a battery of explanations for anything mysterious. But the boyo here believes anything," he joked while mussing Jag's hair. "I appreciate the guesswork, and shall give it due consideration, but how might thermal springs account for the priest's confession?"

I wasn't sure what Malcolm was talking about until he gestured to a large fresco above the confessional. The striking, semi-circular tableau depicted in relief the "Sermon on the Mount." However, in Sauniere's altered version, Jesus was preaching to the faithful on a flower-strewn hill. Near the bottom was an old-fashioned drawstring moneybag in which a nugget of gold was visible through a hole torn in its budging cloth.

"Of course, many believe the purse to be the X marks the spot on a treasure map," the Sauniereologist shrugged with a dismissive grin. "If only things were that simple."

Another tourist walked up and pointed to the figures in the mural that were gathered in circle around Jesus.

"The twelve figures represent the signs of the zodiac, which is to be superimposed over a map of the local countryside. The moneybag lies in the thirteenth position of *Ophiuchus*, the serpent-bearer. Did you notice the little details the priest added on both sides? Like this bent figure holding an umbrella - perhaps

Sauniere, himself, that is staring at a bush in the scenery. But, this bush is pretty crappy looking compared to the one on the other side, which makes me think that someone came along later and daubed globs of paint around it to camouflage what he was originally staring at —"

"Yeah, check it out, the guy has a black umbrella," Jag said while leaning closer to the fresco. "I hope he doesn't open that sucker," he chuckled.

"What do you mean?" the fellow asked with a confused look.

"The laddie is just kidding," Malcolm said. "One of us has issues with umbrellas. Pellabaphobia, it's called."

"You never know, skeptoid," Jag rubbed his hands together fiendishly. "Anything can happen in a church that has a devil waiting at the door."

"That's Asmodeus," the man smiled. "Legendary guardian of treasures and custodian of secrets. Okay, so, if you place both sides of the Fleury tableau together, the two pieces fit nicely to form part of a landscape that might be another clue."

"We'll keep that in mind," Malcolm patted him on the shoulder.

As we moved along, the heavily decorated interior was stranger than I had imagined. The bedizening mass of color was too gilded, too florid, with everything crammed too tightly together for such limited confines. As gaudy as theological aesthetics were in most Catholic churches of the period, the priest's phantasmagoric riddle had taken things to the next level by his addition of hand-painted background details on standard religious adornments ordered from a catalog. Even The Stations of the Cross had been embellished with Sauniere's idiosyncratic flair. Running anti-clockwise along the walls in the nave, added touches, many seemingly irrelevant, made the scenes look more like garish advertisements for a theatrical production than the traditional portrayal of Christ's path to Calvary. Standing on ornate pedestals between the colorful plaques were polychrome statues of saints with glossy enamel eyes. Although the unlikely assemblage had been placed with apparent purpose, as to what exactly the priest was trying to convey with their specific virtues was anyone's guess.

"Eye-biting, isn't it," Aaloka cringed at the tasteless colors.

"As advertised," I replied.

"He may have over-egged the pudding," Malcolm said, "but I assure you there is a method to his madness."

"Any one else feeling a bit uneasy?" someone asked with a faint air of amusement. I recognized the voice to be Julian's and turned to see him coming down the aisle in a baggy sweatshirt. "What we Italians call *jettatura*, the curse of the evil-eye."

"Blank eyes to alert a discerning few," Malcolm said. "To remind us of a passage in the gospels: To open the eyes of the blind and ears to the deaf."

After brief introductions and exchanging a few pleasantries, Malcolm took on the role of our tour guide.

"As I understand it, the puzzle here is cartographic in nature. The fourteen stations contain the co-ordinates on a treasure map. One has to correctly interpret certain inconsistencies... the priest's added flourishes as being certain features or land-marks in the surrounding countryside. This explains the differ-ences in the biblical terrain shown in the various scenes. After one becomes orientated with the starting point, they must follow the directions, whose signposts are indicated in the background scenery and such... in some cases with precise measurements. For instance, the length of the shadow cast by a certain figure might specify the number of paces one needs to take to find the next marker."

"Oh, like Jag's geocaching for trackables, only without GPS," Aaloka said.

"Or glowing FireTacks," I added.

"It's a rather ingenious system really," Malcolm said. "As for the saints, besides being chosen for their associated legends, one needs to observe what they're looking at with those glossy stares. Of course, to make things even more difficult, some of the tantalizing imagery has been devised to mislead those who are not worthy. The priest is speaking in an unspoken language. Using puns and play on words like the green tongue or phonetic cabala employed by those operating behind a cloak of secrecy who only wish to be understood by fellow players. Those with shared interests."

For whatever reason, he fixed his gaze on Julian during this last remark.

"With that being said, here's another possibility," Malcolm said after checking his watch.

Gesturing for us to follow him, we paused before Station XIV (which, paradoxically, was also Station I due to their anti-clockwise nature). Painted in lurid colors, the ornate bas-relief of the Way to the Cross appeared to show Jesus's body being carried from a cave rather than into it. Like the other stations, although there was nothing glaringly obvious, it contained several background peculiarities, including a night sky with a prominent full moon.

"There's a full moon shining in the night sky," he pointed out. "The inference being that no Jew would handle a dead body during the Passover... but, at some hour after night had fallen, Jesus was moved. With all the clues given here, are we to conclude that Christ's ordeal, including the Crucifixion, itself, was a staged event?

An illusion worthy of Houdini and other master magicians, with those involved in a carefully orchestrated plot – that included a few trusted supporters, even some undercover ones - being essentially actors reading from a script and playing their parts in a living mystery play. Details in the final plan might have required, among other things, an anesthetic of some type in a sponge that was supposedly soaked in vinegar. If this is true, Jesus was no run of the mill wonder worker of the time. Not only did he live out his role, he went to great lengths to preserve a secret of forbidden knowledge. Knowledge as hinted in riddles, ciphers and scandals of the heresies that concerned a bodily resurrection. Recall his words: My Kingdom is not of this world."

"Malcolm, with all the unfounded theories from your mystery-mongering, one of these days you're going to be right," I told him. "A mock-Crucifixion?"

"Conveniently, in a private garden… with a private tomb no less —"

"From which Jesus cheated death only to pose as the gardener. Like I said, one of these days."

"Allow me to show you another of the priest's tricks," he smiled.

While consulting his watch, he had us position ourselves in front of the north wall. When he told us to keep our eyes on a certain spot, I figured we were in for more oblique clues (or blind alleys). A few minutes later a beam of sunlight passed through a pane of stained glass and projected small blue orbs onto the opposite wall. After several seconds, the fruit (as he called it) appeared to ripen on the 'tree', with all of the glowing spots turning red except for a few that remained blue. Glancing over my shoulder, I noticed that the window responsible for the optical effect depicted Lazarus being raised from the dead by Christ. After a few more seconds passed, the three blue orbs moved along the altar decoration before gradually fading away.

After bearing witness to the light phenomenon – the famous "blue apples" of Rennes – we followed Malcolm across the chancel to the altar bas-relief, in which Mary Magdalene was inside a grotto, kneelling before a crucifix formed by branches with three flowering roots.

"Another eyeball looking at... something." Julian recoiled his head in mock horror. "This one's in a skull on the ground. Check it out, my fellow treasure hunters."

Though I saw the skull under the crucifix with the sprouting sapling, I hadn't noticed that an eye, complete with the iris, had been painted into its left socket. It would take a lifetime to find all the background details colored in by Sauniere; I shook my head, amused by his antics.

After the tour coaches began to arrive, in the span of a single hour, I heard at least a half dozen theories to explain the priest's good fortune and strange behavior. Some claimed to have solved the mystery from the plethora of clues embedded in the church's decorations, while others based their conclusions on the numerous legends spawned.

To account for his long walks in the local countryside, one solution involved a kind of reverse alchemy. With a basket on his shoulder, Sauniere wandered about the sparsely covered hills under the pretext of collecting rocks that were appropriate for the grotto he was in the process of building near the church. However, what he was really searching for were gold nuggets that had been coated with clay and hardened in ovens. Disguised as ordinary stones, the massive hoard of gold was deposited in local streambeds by someone who occasionally made 'withdraws' so not to arouse suspicion of their find.

After finding the right ones with his keen eye, he cracked them open in the privacy of a secret room that was attached to the sacristy. He then added a few ordinary rocks to the grotto to cover his tracks.

Another claimed that he had chanced upon a salt mine beneath the village that had been used in the remote past to safeguard the lost treasure of Jerusalem. Either that or he was a money launderer for its true discoverer, and received payment by commissions.

Some of the crazier explanations for the odd goings-on at night in the church cemetery and the darkly ostentatious religious adornments were that the priest practiced black magic, including the diabolical Convocation of Venus, which was facilitated by his young maidservant within a pentagonal temple in the landscape that was formed by natural features.

Even more disturbing to Catholics was the suggestion that Sauniere was in collusion with fellow priests that trafficked in masses for wealthy clients who wanted certain guarantees for their deceased relatives. These mortuary rituals were akin to Babylonian death cults, secret ceremonies of the Persian Magi and Egyptian funerary magic, but were probably more similar in design to the heretical deathbed sacraments of the Cathars. Perhaps he had stumbled upon evidence of macabre practices by his predecessors in a crypt while renovating the church. After seeing the trepanned skulls of the Lords of Rennes, along with other grisly remains of the prescribed rites, he borrowed techniques of angel magic from the apocryphal Book of Tobit and began performing his own masses by first experimenting with the bodies interred in the church cemetery. Not only would this explain his nocturnal activities of grave digging and profaning tombstones, it also might account for the consecrated water in the jealously guarded cistern that was required for future baptisms for the dead.

If this wasn't blasphemous enough, someone pointed out what they thought to be a telling clue left in one of Sauniere's papers. The cryptic meaning of "An angel had turned fish bones into a golden comb" indicated that he had discovered the skeletal remains of Jesus and used them to blackmail the Church.

A woman in a dramatic dress and laden with symbolic jewelry disagreed. The money didn't come from simony or any of the other crazy ideas being bandied about (I wondered if she overheard some of Malcolm's nonstop speculations?) The priest had gained custody of the third frontal eye of a disposed angel when it tumbled to the ground as punishment for a transgression. The mystical artifact gave him a privileged position in the universe and enabled him to locate treasure by channeling cosmic entities. Others knew about this, which is why several years ago someone gouged out the plasterwork demon's eyes. It was also said that at the time of his death Sauniere had a glass eye. Even if he had to sacrifice one of his own eyes, it was safest place to hide the celestial relic, though it probably has since been removed from the socket of the priest's corpse and is currently in the possession of someone else. To support her claim, she urged people to look closely at the altar relief.

I'd had enough stucco basilisks, skulls and gilded monsters for one day in a church. It was time for another one of those sudsy amber treasures. Before exiting the debased funhouse, someone uttered to another tourist that a race of troglodytes that sometimes appeared in the densely thicketed gorges had revealed the entrance to a strange underworld with vaulted chambers filled with prized treasures. This caused Julian to raise his brows.

As we waited for the others to join us for lunch, Julian and I were seated at a table under noisy bird-filled trees in the garden. While chewing a hunk of crunchy baguette with strawberry jam and sipping a pint of Kronenbourg Blanc, I was waiting to hear the latest developments on the Paragon documentary, but first its director shared his thoughts on Sauniere's domain.

"However he obtained his wealth one thing's for sure – he set out to create a little slice of paradise," he said as marble white butterflies fluttered over the stubby grass. "What, with the botanical and zoological gardens, glasshouses, fountains and esplanades… the orangery and exotic fruit trees. Also, how he entertained notables with lavish banquets… ordering cases of Malvoisie and barrels of Martinique rum. The paths and ponds… I read that the layout of the garden was a mirror image of the floor plan of the church. I don't understand the other projects he embarked on… like his notorious church – "

"It's a grand distraction. A dazzling smoke screen. Forget about my friend's relentless piffle. Whatever the priest's lucrative endeavors might have been, the cryptic fashion of the overdone decorations was intended to protect his financial self-interests. To keep people forever guessing."

"Treasure and death… at every turn," Julian mumbled. "Death and treasure."

"What did you find out from the son of Kidd's partner?" I asked.

"Funny, isn't it," he said. "Both Kidd and Sauniere are known today because of their unexplained wealth. And yet there were major differences with their personality traits. Almost complete opposites. You would think that a priest would have more interest in the soul than gold… where as a prospector would be more inclined to gold than the soul. Sauniere pissed his money away, spending lavishly while Kidd was a tightwad, ordering the cheapest item on the menu and never tipping. One was flamboyant… animated, while the other was the antithesis… simple and restrained. And both died under mysterious circumstances."

"Cirrhosis of the liver isn't that mysterious to someone with a serious drinking problem. You mentioned all the wine consumed during the priest's bacchanalian gatherings."

"True, he was known to tipple the grape, but he was said to be in enviable health at the time he ordered his casket. Bacchanalia and non-indulgence. Not exactly carbon copies, the two men... but, again, mirror images so to speak."

"You're not suggesting there's a connection between the two?"

"There probably isn't – except, maybe, Castelar, the Spaniard from these parts. He was a mining engineer from nearby Girona, seeking to find Jesuit gold stashed in an old mine disguised as a ruined mission in Arizona. The location was believed to be near a region called The Place of Many Springs. You'll like this. Sergio kept referring to his father's map as a *derrotero*."

"Derro-tero, you're kidding?"

"Turns out in Spanish the word means path or chart... as in the directions of a treasure map. Anyway, here's where things get interesting. I recently got a message from Zeke –"

"Oh, brother," I sighed before taking a deep gulp.

"He had a proposition for me – "

"I'm sure he did."

"He could show me photos taken from an old Kodak that showed the ruins of a mission on a forgotten trail in Arizona – get this - near The Place of Many Springs that marked the location where Kidd was searching for a lost treasure. The photos show a crumpling adobe brick structure with four empty belfry portals. Even though there is no record of any mission founded in the area, the shrewd Jesuits had constructed the façade to conceal the entrance to a mine or treasure cavern. Even the adobe had been whitewashed to blend in with the canyon walls. A story about this was published in a magazine, which at the time, seemed like a credible lost treasure yarn, but was later thought to be a hoax. However, according to Zeke... or his handler... the story is true, with the names of the principal characters involved having been changed. Natch, Zeke won't tell me the name of the magazine. He wants to do so while being filmed again as part of the documentary. And now he has an agent."

From the corner of my eye I saw the "Sauniereologist" approaching the café tables on a gravel path. Although there were other victims (many willing, I'm sure) for him to latch onto, I turned away with uneasy eyes, hoping to avoid more of his inane ramblings. Despite being swallowed in shade and surrounded by those enjoying sandwiches, cheese and drinks, he made a bee-line towards me, almost knocking over a child's iced chocolate in the process.

"Seeing how a couple of paintings by Nicolas Poussin are inextricably linked to the mystery, I thought you'd be interested in this letter about him written in 1656 by the Abbe Louis Fouquet to his brother."

He opened a book about the Rennes affair and began to read:

"He and I discussed certain things which I shall with ease be able to explain to you in detail. Things which will give you, through Monsieur Poussin, advantages which even kings would have great pains to draw from him and which, according to him, it is possible that nobody else will ever rediscover in the centuries to come, and what is more, these are things so difficult to discover that nothing now on this earth can prove of better fortune nor be their equal. This letter has never been understood, but in the opinion of art experts, it had to do with a garden design. A garden design... that kings would have great pains to draw from him... and are so difficult to discover that nobody else will rediscover in the centuries to come."

"A garden design," Julian smirked. "That's funny."

"Yes," the aficionado said… "But, you know what, incredibly enough, they were right. He was referring to the design for a garden. This is a profound secret. Well, enjoy your lunch… in what was Sauniere's private garden."

As he walked away, Aaloka, Jag and Malcolm arrived.

"The priest's villa must have cost a fortune to furnish," Aaloka said while taking a seat. "It's as overblown as the church. Patterned wallpaper with bounteous colors. Marbles, fabrics and terracotta —"

"I sure hope they have Barq's," Jag uttered impatiently while scanning the iced drinks on other tables.

"I'm craving something tart," Aaloka said. "A citron presse to go with lavender honey on a fresh baguette and salad."

"That guy who was here told me that the best root beer was King Coney, but I've never heard of the stuff. He said he used to work there."

In this place where the slightest thing out of the ordinary was greatly magnified, I, too, might have been imagining things, but I thought I saw Aaloka give Malcolm a concerned look when Jag made this rather mundane comment. King Coney? Didn't someone else recently mention that? I tried to remember where I heard it, but after drawing a blank, figured it didn't really matter. It was just a meaningless coincidence, and what I initially mistook for concern was just Aaloka feeling bad that her overindulged son wasn't going to get his favorite soft drink.

"I really enjoyed that sarsaparilla that old Zeke turned me onto in Goldfield," Julian said. "*Avez-vous de la biere de racine,*" he asked a waiter at the table next to us.

"No root beer," was the curt reply.

"I doubt they have it at the hyper-market either," Aaloka scrunched her lips in a teasing frown.

"Root beer is unheard of in France," Malcolm said, "but after-lunch cognac isn't."

While seated for dinner on the veranda of the rustic hotel, we were treated to a gorgeous twilight of orange and deep amethyst. As the sparsely covered hills and vineyards of the Corbieres faded in the dwindling light, moths wheeled around the candles that illuminated our table. On its scarred wood surface were plates of sea bream, marinated eggplant and braised artichokes. There was also a nice selection of goat cheese and anchovy and olive tapenade, along with the ubiquitous French loaves. Drinks included chilled rose, beer, sparkling water and "grappy" sodas.

"Merci," Julian looked pleased when the waitress brought a white bean cassoulet.

"White beans!" I uttered with feigned shock. "Remember how horrified old Zeke was. White beans!"

"More frites for the boyo," Malcolm told the pretty young woman after noticing Jag gloomily picking at his cabbage and beets wrapped in gelatin.

"Have some of this French's mustard – it's more than a condiment," I joked.

"These artichokes are dreamy," Aloke moaned pleasurably, "and I'll bet the thyme didn't come from the *supermarche*."

"So, Julian," I said. "Did you ever consider that Kidd might have had a near-death experience when the explosion occurred in the pump house? I emphasize 'near', because memories are indicative of brain activity. You know, endorphins gone wild.

A blissful floating sensation… bright tunnels and mystical visions. A heavenly trip."

"Actually, I hadn't, but I suppose it's possible. Maybe we should include a little segment to explore the possibility."

"Aaloka once told me about a new scientific theory to try and explain human consciousness. What was it called – that neuroscience of the soul?" I asked her.

"Oh, you're talking about microtubules. Yeah, rather than humans being animated by some immaterial essence, the hypothesis suggests consciousness… or the idea of a soul, if you want… are quantum vibrations in microtubules in brain neurons. If released, the stored quantum information could possibly exist outside the body and survive death as energy hanging out in the universe… indefinitely. What did your blog hacking friend, Ramiel, say?" she asked me.

"The treasury of the souls of the righteous confined in a special chamber under God's throne until the final judgment bla bla bla."

"And in the case of a near-death experience, once the person is resuscitated, the quantum information returns… maybe with some bonus footage," she laughed.

"The director's cut," Julian clapped.

"And that's exactly what Kidd wanted a photo of and was willing to give his life savings for," I reminded him.

"Just like it does when someone goes through a star portal," Jag chimed in. "Like that Egyptian guy, Imhotep, with his fillings showing before he bounced to a new turf."

"Are you talking about the internet trailer for a new sci-fi release?" Julian asked.

"It's just a movie?"

He looked more bummed out than when his vegetables arrived encased in a gelatin loaf.

"I forget the title," Julian said. "Despite confidentiality agreements, word gets out fast in Hollywood. What you saw is their slick promo with loads of CGI. Clever of the producers to hype it that way to try to create a buzz, but it's probably gonna tank at the box office and have to be recouped with pay-per-view."

"Poor Jag," I teased. "Wobbly veggies, no root beer or real-life alien stargates."

Right when I said that, the owner approached with an unopened bottle of root beer-flavored vodka and set it down in front of Jag.

"Fuck yeah," he uttered. "Now this party's lit, fam."

"Hey, what did your mom say about using the F-word at the dinner table. It's fam-i-ly, not fam!"

"What about the sign posted on the church talking about that Bible guy who was sleeping with a rock for a pillow and woke up to see angels coming down a ladder? That was a stargate," Jag said with his spirits brightened. "Though, a pretty shitty one. Anyway, I'm more into what Zyla told me that the professor with all the wheels on his chair that works at Cellectech said."

"Volker?" Aaloka asked. "Zyla was talking with Professor Hellmann? How does she know him?"

This time I was positive that she and Malcolm exchanged furtive glances.

"I remember Volker," I said. "The Phantom of the Stork's Nest. Jesus, they let him out in public on that souped up roller bed?"

"Don't be such a little sneak," Aaloka blurted with more than a trace of anger in her voice.

"I told her about you and him talking on the phone, that's all," Jag raised his hands as if it was no big deal. "Remember, the thing that causes a change like when a caterpillar morphs into a butterfly. A higher birth, you were calling it."

"Trying to have a private conversation without him listening and blabbing everything to Zyla is like trying to sneak a sunbeam past a rooster," I shook my head.

"Okay, seriously, what does that even mean?" Jag asked.

"You didn't hear that damn thing crowing at the crack of dawn right outside our rooms? Probably with a well-pleased grin in knowing that we had jetlag."

"That was someone's ringtone," he said.

"No it wasn't," I insisted.

Julian tapped the screen on his phone and a ringtone of a rooster began to crow.

"See, ass."

"He wasn't even here!"

"Super biology," he called it, Jag said. "The Egyptians knew about it and that's why they had mummies. And later a woman came to where Zyla works with her crystal skull, Maxx, and was asking her what she knew about super biology."

"Woman? Did this woman say what her name was?" Aaloka asked, still visibly unsettled for some reason.

"I don't know, just some woke lady into the same stuff as Zyla... like the tribe that knew about the invisible star. She was wearing a rainbow slouch hat. She was black... and had a fake eye."

"Sounds like the same woman I once had a conversation with at Punyaaloka. Only, she was a bioethics advocate... having issues with labs like Cellectech. I can't imagine her sharing the same interests with Zyla. Especially this super biology," I laughed.

"Volker is a brilliant geneticist," Aaloka said with a calmer voice. "But, admittedly, he has some non-conventional ideas when he's not at Cellectech.

"You're saying he's a bit of a kook on his own time?" I asked.

"The conversation Jag was eavesdropping on was about ecdysterone supplements. Yes, the substance that activates the two pulses of a radical metamorphosis in some life forms.

But, we were initially talking about biomarkers for toxicity when using it as an anabolic agent. The professor then began talking about a metamorphic apotheosis in humans. A body-morph that's possibly triggered by neurosecretory signals – which, themselves, are controlled by polypeptide hormones in the brain. Needless to say, such a notion is speculative in the extreme. As Volker sees it, a bodily resurrection might be made possible when our normal DNA is shut off and other coded in-structions are switched on. These latent powers might enable us to become something in an alternative or higher dimensionality as different as a butterfly is to a caterpillar. For the sake of ar-gument, I asked if he thought in this chimera relationship the caterpillar that's now a butterfly remembered having digested itself into juices inside the chrysalis before being recycled into undifferentiated cells?"

"Caterpillar soup. M'm! M'm! Good!" I said over the drone of summer insects. "I'll bet they have the recipe here for that to be served as an appetizer, or for Jag's lunch tomorrow."

"Why am I always in his cross-hairs, mom?"

"Right now, you're in mine, too," she said with a stern look.

"When I argued that there's no trace of as yet un-activated genes that allow us to grow wings and take to flight like angels, if you will, he resorted to the Egyptian stuff, casting aside ac-ademic standards. Actually, with their preoccupation with the afterlife, he believes they were merely mimicking hyper-biolog-ical sciences that an even earlier civilization was aware of. Like those golden buds in that painting on the altar we saw today, the Egyptian root of the word to embalm also means to sprout or germinate –"

"Nothing new there," I said. "Like my own disorder, lots of visitors to my blog assert that we earthlings as a whole suffer from a case of amnesia when it comes to an advanced pre-deluge civilization that was wiped out by the impact of a comet. As proof they always bring up the placement of the great pyramids by the ancient Egyptians, forgetting that's where they fucking lived."

"Indeed, we have a perplexing history," Malcolm said. "And if you look around, you just might find things that would tax modern technology."

As a woman cleared our plates, the waitress served dessert of baked apples and ice cream, sliced baby melon, pralines and meringue cookies.

After savoring pieces of the muskmelon, Malcolm stood up and put his napkin down.

"Now, you'll excuse me. While you continue to discuss ye gods in potentia lurking in the goo, I'm going to retire so to get up early for tomorrow's graal quest."

"Why do we have to look for it on our vacation?" Jag asked while debating whether or not to eat one of the foreign-looking cookies on a platter.

"Because its not going to turn up in your backyard, that's why."

As clouds parted to reveal limestone outcrops jutting from slopes of bristling thickets, in a light sprinkle, we continued to drive past unspoilt views of a striking landscape. In the grey murkiness, plunging, pine-choked valleys were making Aaloka nervous and once again she commented on Jag's driving.

"That castle has been there for over a thousand years and I don't think it's going anywhere in the next ten minutes."

"I can't take that chance," Jag replied while nudging the accelerator. "The original vegans."

"Jag!"

Looking out the windows, blue-pied cows grazed in sprawling pastures beneath thick woodlands. Slopes of stunted oak and gorse soon gave way to small villages, inns and more gloomy umber ruins set amid olive groves. Rounding a bend with terraced chateaux amid purple wisteria, in the distance we could see the towering walls of the Cathar stronghold of Montsegur set atop a precipitous rocky spur.

"There it is," Malcolm said. "The site of the Albigensian Crusade. It's said that hundreds of Cathars were singing as they walked willingly into the flames – preferring to be burned alive in the holy bonfire rather than renounce their beliefs... or give up their secret. Men, women and children. Kill them all, God will recognize his own, said a representative of the Pope."

"That's like medieval," Jag said without a trace of humor.

"Many believe Montsegur to be the Graal Castle of Wolfram von Eschenbach's *Parzival*. The location of the Cup of Destiny... source of all legends and the treasure of ages. Later, the Nazis would come here looking for the graal, unaware that it's not simply the cup, but what it holds that has value."

As Jag pulled into a crowded car park, we got out to view the razed bastion in the shade of a copse of trees. Before starting the climb on the narrow rocky path that wound up the mountainside to the inner courtyard of its ruins, we went into the museum. As the others went to get something cold to drink, I checked out some postcards of Poussin's famous works. One was *The Grapes of the Promised Land*, which depicted a couple of rustic figures shouldering a pole to carry a cluster of huge bluish-purple grapes. Though I had seen it before, this time I noticed that the ladder on which a woman was standing as she picked an apple from a tree (the only fruiting tree in a barren landscape) seemed to be rising from the over-sized grapes.

In another canvas – the other version of his *The Shepherds of Arcadia* – I spotted a weird background detail of a large detached eye above a skull placed on a tomb. There was also a similar disembodied eye in the artist's self-portrait. Weird.

While looking at the more famous version of *The Shepherds of Arcadia*, a painting that is widely associated with the jigsaw of Rennes, a gaunt, elderly man in an over-sized black suit walked up to me. His piercing blue eyes reflected a gentle demeanor, and there was an ascetic manner about him, which was explained when he told me that he was a neo-Cathar. He pointed to the Latin phrase incised on the tomb the shepherds were examining in the painting. ET IN ARCADIA EGO, he said could be translated as, "And in Paradise I…" However, since it was chiseled on a tomb, it could also mean the less unambiguous, "I, Death, am even in Paradise."

He told me that a stone tomb similar to the one in the painting used to exist near Rennes-le-Chateau before a farmer demolished it with a sledgehammer after growing tired of treasure hunters trespassing on his property. Not only was the tomb similar, the topography, including a holly-oak tree, was nearly an exact match to the landscape in Poussin's canvas. The original tomb might have concealed a well of a sacred spring, he said without further comment.

൭ഌ

On the way back to the hotel, instead of visiting the antique baths in granite blocks, we stopped to have a picnic in a shady nook near a purling stream by the roadside. From a wicker basket Aaloka pulled out baguettes with cured sausage and samples from a local cheese-monger. Jag told the person at the shop to hold the tuna and pile his French stick with black olives, tomatoes, cucumbers and salad leaves.

"Do you really think that was the graal castle?" Jag asked Malcolm as he rolled up his baggy multicolored bohos and began wading in the shallow water.

"I believe the castle of wonders is under continual construction and the graal adventure still developing. The word, graal, is derived from the Medieval Latin, gradualis, meaning gradually. The human eye cannot see it...in the scenery. Not without pure vision, as one must learn to Pierce-the-veil... Parzival. Must of us – Jag excluded, and I thank him for the extra pear tart – still wear the motley garment of the fool. As for the graal... its root surpasses all earthly perfection – was planted in the stars... and gradually its shoots will bear fruit."

Recalling all the detached eyes in the postcards of Poussin's works gave me an idea. As the gentle murmur of crystal clear water eddied around dark stones with bubbly swirls, I pulled out my phone and began taking photos of everyone, making sure to get close-ups of their faces.

"Say cheese!"

"I found it!" Jag shouted. "The Holy Graal."

Exiting a small gas station that we stopped at so Malcolm

could "spend a penny", he triumphantly held up a bag of Doritos 3-D chips.

"Eureka!" Malcolm said. "No trifle, that."

"Great, but you can't eat them," I reminded him.

"Yeah, but I can put 'em on eBay."

"Well, yeah, sure, if you can get them through customs. The French are vigilant of tourists trying to sneak antiquities out of the country."

CHAPTER VII
JETTATURA

"Light does not enter your meeting-place where the gods dwell."

- Enheduanna

"I wouldn't want to belong to a club that would have me as a member."

- Groucho Marx

Though I hadn't unpacked from our vacation, a scheduled podcast had me gulping a third cup of coffee in a futile attempt to reset my body clock to the local time. Realizing how so many people had been tricked into believing the tease for a soon to be released sci-fi feature was an actual recent archaeological discovery of a notable Egyptian figure, the subject matter for the first part of the show was a rational look at the concept of distance-nullifying portals known as stargates.

I began the episode by sharing with my listeners some of the zaniness I heard while visiting the hilltop parish of Rennes-le-Chateau. Nearly every tourist had an explanation to account for the local mystery; some being feasible enough while others strained credibility to the extreme. According to one theory, the answer to both the priest's rags to riches and the esoteric details added to the church decorations involved a magical portal located in the vicinity. Supposedly, when illuminated by the sun at a precise time, the profile of a particular rock outcrop known as "the demon guardian" gazed down the tawny flank into a densely wooded valley where a natural temple complex concealed the opening to a parallel world. As to how the priest monetized this gateway, the possibilities were unlimited. But, the most likely scenario was that the doorway into the invisible was a refuge for the coming apocalypse to which the priest solicited hefty entrance fees. While some in the area claimed to have peered into this shimmering inter-dimensional window, others had ventured into it and returned to tell of the many wonders on the other side.

Some were convinced that the artist Nicolas Poussin was aware of this portal and encoded its whereabouts in his famous works. Along with canvas x-rays showing the controlling features of hidden geometry underlining the pastoral landscapes, as well as an enigmatic letter that mentioned something that "it is possible nobody else will ever rediscover in the centuries to come", one of these 'stargate' paintings was his *Grapes of the Promised Land*. In the bucolic setting, the central figures, which ostensibly depict the Israelite spies returning from Canaan with a specimen of the gigantic fruit harvested there, bore witness to inhabitants like those described in the biblical passage, whose stature was such that they felt like grasshoppers among them.

While further discussing the possibility of synthetic transgalactic tunnels or exploited primordial wormholes, when I opened up to callers, a listener (who sounded level-headed, at least he talked the talk) claimed to have witnessed something he referred to as a "beyonder." This wasn't a pulsating stargate like in the movies, but an artificial structure of unknown origin that was invisible to the human eye and only detectable by using a high-tech device.

Although some kind of exotic warping mechanism was involved, the beyonder didn't seem to have been built as a transporting device. It was more like a stationary bubble that co-existed as an extension of the physical terrain. Blending in seamlessly, its presence caused no distortion to the scenery it overlapped. There were no carved glyphs or janky Hollywood controls associated with it, though he was told that a key-code symbol of some type was required to gain access.

"Open Sesame," I joked.

"Actually," the caller said, "the rumors of an ancient stargate discovered in the ruins of Ur near Nasiriyah south of Baghdad in 2003 were planted by a faction of our government, who wanted to put a lid on the reality of the beyonder. Only nuts believed in cosmic portals, so they weren't concerned about that. Adding to their growing sense of unease, and need for a diversion, was that the thing was surrounded by numerous alabaster statues similar to those called spectacle or eye-idols because of the unnaturally large eye-sockets on their otherwise featureless faces. If you've seen photos of the Urfa snowman, you kind of get the idea, though unlike him, the statues at Nasiriyah weren't covering their hairy balls. And, unlike the Tell Asmar hoard, instead of their eyes being painted black or inlaid with obsidian, they had bulging orbits of encrusted gems that reflected the desert sunlight and in the moonlight gave them a spectral quality. These figures were mounted upright in the brick stratum, with their baked beige clay gleaming as it did, and enormous globular eyes of golden crystals hypnotically staring... at we now know what. These Watchers, as they were called, really spooked the guards - a small garrison of troops brought in from the Green Zone... especially when peering at them through NVDs. Add to that the freakish sounds of wind and shifting sand that seemed to emanate from them. My DEROS was coming – "

"Deros?" I uttered.

"The date expected to return from overseas. I was one of the special-op personnel involved in the highly classified program. So, I wanted to find out as much as I could about it. Again, there were no indicatory effects or consequences to the man-made structure that the beyonder was partly superimposed over... the latter intrusion, being the ruins of a Sumerian temple unearthed by coalition airstrikes, appeared as any other perceived norm in the area. Well, there was this odd sensation one felt while in close proximity to it... pressure building in the ears and, at times, a giddy joy, which doesn't make sense if you're standing on haunted ground... like some believed."

When pressed further about specific details that might corroborate the story, the caller clammed up, saying he wasn't ready to provide this info yet, but should he decide to go the full nine yards as a whistleblower, he would return. He also declined to answer any questions from my subscribers about what the purpose of a beyonder might be. However, before hanging up, he responded to a member who asked him if he was aware of any allusions on ancient cuneiform tablets about the existence such structures?

"The world's first known poet, Enheduanna, daughter of Sargon, wrote a verse that read: Awesome, its ways no one can fathom... your pedestal is closely knit as a fine-mesh net." He then added, "Did you know that the Arabic word for paradise literally means concealed place."

"The restricted zone of the gods," the subscriber replied, "which humans were not permitted to enter."

Straightforward as it was, the caller's story not only made for great audio texture, but presented a fresh topic for another episode. Naturally, I was a bit dubious of this invisible structure, though my BS radar told me that he might not be making it up.

This was based in part on his admission that the Iraq star-gate was a disinformation tactic to muzzle something they wanted to keep under wraps. Maybe what he and the others had experienced was part of some psychological warfare project that was tested during the Gulf War. A weapon system using pulsed energy to affect the enemy's mind. Rather than ponder this mysterious beyonder thing any further that night, the jolts of caffeine had worn off and jetlag from the trip was wreaking havoc with my biorhythms. I needed to get some sleep, although to get even with me for some pranks I played on him, the minute I dozed off I knew Jag was going to hold his phone next to my eardrum and let one loud-ass rooster alarm ringtone cock-a-doodle-doo.

Having conked out for twelve hours, while processing the audio file to get some shorter grabs from callers in the audience, I was relieved to find no evidence of the hacker's presence. Either the new safeguards were doing their job or Ramiel had lost interest in his little game. Perhaps the Enochian angels had bit him in the ass for misrepresenting them as goody two shoes, when they stated to others that their goal was to destroy humanity.

That's when Jag told me the news about Zyla's space cadet church. Evidently it had been shut down by the city for violating numerous codes. Hold everything. Was the reason there was no cyber intrusion this time due to Ramiel's concern with having to find a new home for the cult to attempt contact with an alien probe?

As I figured, Julian agreed to hear Zeke out and wanted me to toss in my two cents during the filming. Though I dreaded going to Arizona in the summer heat (Flynn said the meeting should be Skyped), the pay was too good to turn down and, besides, I was kind of interested to hear what someone who yarns the hours away was going to try and pass on as the truth to the city slicker. Whatever it was, with the added bonus, he was wasting Julian's time, not mine.

Once again Aaloka didn't think I should get involved, but when I kidded that I was already one of the stars, she rolled her eyes and told me to pack some good sunblock for my ageing skin.

Having arrived in Apache Junction before Julian and the small Paragon film crew, I decided to visit the historic museum at the Goldfield ghost town. While checking out various displays that included everything from blasting caps, sluice boxes and carbide lamps to coffee grinders, tobacco tins and rusted cans of beans (cowboy caviar the sign said), I noticed some crude treasure maps nailed to the wall. One of them contained vague directions to an old mission in a mountain range located just south of Tucson.

"What's the deal with this map?" I asked the mustached curator.

"The thrill of the hunt will only cost you five hundred dollars," he said with a straight face. "Let's see, that scribbling was supposed to lead you to a lost Jesuit mission that contains mule loads of silver. Cerro Ruido, it's a known fake, but the Apache lightning in that jug is real," he said while pointing to a pottery flagon. "The treasure of the noisy mountain called Cerro Ruido was featured in a copy of *Arizona Highways* magazine from 1945. We've an original copy here if you'd like to give it a read."

After reading the article with its blurry photos of the outlines of a ruined Spanish mission, I was pretty sure this was the same story that Zeke had told Julian, having left out some key elements that would no doubt be recounted once the camera rolled. If, indeed, he had hijacked the tale for the documentary, I made a mental note that the events occurred in the 1920s and that names were given in the article with no mention whatsoever of James Kidd.

The story concerned a European miner who believed Jesuit priests centuries ago had stashed a treasure near the peak of Cerro Ruido after having been expelled from Sonora for dodging the tribute mandated by the Spanish Crown. An American friend of his living in Tucson tried to talk him out of searching in such a dangerous area, but the foreigner persisted.

After helping him set up camp, the rancher agreed to bring him fresh supplies every few days. On one of these runs, the miner told him that while following an old forgotten trail he discovered in a narrow canyon, he was astonished to see a ruined adobe mission that he first thought might have been a mirage. To match the smooth wall of a cliff that it had been built against its stone façade had been rendered pinkish-white. Intrigued, the rancher lent him his camera and told him to take photographs of anything of interest.

While checking out the crumpling interior of an adobe outbuilding the next day, he noticed a jagged crack in a sealed mortar entrance to a tunnel at the base of the cliff. At this point, the story got a bit hokey when the miner claimed that he felt a strange tingling sensation running through his body and was soon paralyzed with fear by the unearthly sounds of some unseen creature echoing off the surrounding walls. After describing the terrifying event to his friend the next morning, he gathered the supplies and returned the camera.

Before the next supply trip, one of the worst storms in memory hit the area. When the rancher returned days later, he saw that torrential floods had washed away the camp and drastically altered the landscape. No trace of his friend was ever found. However, a month later when he had the film developed, it showed the ruined mission and shadowy cavity the miner claimed to have found.

When I returned the magazine (after taking photos of the article), I asked the curator what his thoughts were. The story was definitely a hoax, he said, and as proof he told me that one of the photos taken of the cliff as a landmark had been intentional reversed so that it wouldn't be recognized as being in a different (more populalated) location.

Armed with this information I prepared for the showdown at high noon. As fluky as glancing up at the phony map had been, it would now be a simple matter to call the old-timer out on any of his liar club chicanery.

The saloon near Tortilla Flat served a mean bowl of chili, and even off-season, when partnered with an ice-cold draft or two, sounded like a pretty danged good prop. Seated at the table, I crumbled some crackers into the killer recipe and spooned a spicy mouthful as Zeke amused Hayden with salty jokes. When Burton finally got the camera angle set and Julian called for a take, the old prospector nudged his soiled cowboy hat so that it nearly touched his stooped shoulders and rubbed the grey stubble covering deep sunburnt furrows. He then held up for the camera a faded photo that showed the ruins of a mission identical that in the *Arizona Highways* magazine.

"This here picture shows the mission the padres in Sonora whitewashed to blend in with the walls of the canyon. That's where they hid the treasure rather than pony up the royal fifth.

You can see the melted adobe front with the four empty belfry portals... no bells... where the bat-like creature, or whatever it was that scared people away with its blood-curdling screeches. Maybe you've heard of the Tombstone Thunderbird? The Indians and Mexicans in Nogales won't go near the place. Even with the chance for a big strike, neither will hardened prospectors," he said with a mischievous glint in his deep-set, grey eyes. "That's because the lost treasure is only meant to be found by one who is favorably destined... degreed by fate."

While listening attentively to his tale, the rest of what he had to say was almost a verbatim account of the magazine article.

"Unless you believe in time-slips with angry pterodactyls," I said, "there's no chance that Kidd was swept away in the flashflood while looking for the gold of these robed friars because the photos were published in 1945."

"I can set with that," Zeke replied. "I know that Kidd was still above snakes when these pictures were taken," he said with his voice having become defensively louder.

"There's no need to raise one's bristles," someone in the saloon uttered. Looking up I saw that it was Yance, the Old West town's black-frocked lawman, who was walking towards the table while eating a prickly pear gelato. "Zeke didn't say it was Kidd that was caught in the flashflood. Kidd had heard the same tale... probably read the same article... in a library, because we know he didn't buy it. And years later he went looking for the mission ruins. That's all we're saying. There were witnesses in Nogales that saw a prospector that fit Kidd's description. He was a gringo wearing a funny hat... and he was said to drive a hard bargain while negotiating for a tin of beans. Some think the photos are fakes, but that can easily be explained. You see, the originals had been borrowed to construct a film set, and when they were returned, some photos showing the finished set got mixed in with the originals. Like I already told mister flannel mouth here with his wobblin' jaws," he shot me an angry glare, "what you ought to be asking yourselves is why someone opened his safe deposit box after he went missing."

When the shoot was over, Julian and I were having a nightcap at hotel bar.

"Well, not exactly according to the script," he said, "if we had a script, but pretty decent footage, especially when Yance gave you the evil eye while trying to unravel fact from fiction. Unless I hear something more from Sergio in Girona about the *derrotero*, I might close by questioning if Kidd did find the Dutchman hoard and faked his death so no one would come looking for him... or the gold. I think that's what Yance was trying to suggest with that stuff about bank records that showed his safe deposit box had been opened after he went missing. To keep people thinking he was dead, he placed the will inside... probably no longer concerned about a piddly half mill. Maybe, like you once told me, it really was him that was seen gambling in Vegas in the fifties. Natch, it would be nice to find a photo of him, or hell, even someone that resembled him at a card table."

"Cashew milk doesn't work," I said to Malcolm. "Makes my liquefied ghost a little too beige."

With the restaurant's private room booked for another ghost tour party, I was standing behind the bar trying to tweak my ghostini before any of the guests arrived.

"What I'd really like to come up with is a ghostini that evaporates into thin air seconds after it's served."

"And you think people would be willing to pay in excess of ten dollars for a cocktail that disappears into nothing?" Malcolm set down his drink and began fidgeting with his cufflink.

"Anyone gullible enough to pay a hundred to go on one of these stupid tours would fork over the ten and then probably order a few more. What's tonight's tour – the guy who jogs at midnight?"

"The angry albino colony."

"Yeah, they'd gladly pay. Shit, they'd pay to see the curry stain that can't be removed. How do I make whipped vodka, cream and Godiva liqueur vanish from the glass before it's raised?"

"Well, you keep trying to figure it out. When you see her, tell Aaloka I went home early."

While pouring ice cubes for the Starflower drink into a special bucket, I noticed that the small paintings hanging behind the bar could use a good dusting (maybe the phantasmal visitants in Bengali tradition spooked the cleaning crew). As I started to whisk the ghostly images with an ostrich feather duster, I paused to look closer at the one with a green-skinned 'Jesus' holding a grafting knife. There was something about the random shapes on the left border of the canvas that always bothered me. Suddenly, I recalled what the guy in France said about the large mural in the church. When placed next to each other, the oddities in the background on each side blended together to form certain landscape features.

With this mind, I removed the two paintings and set them side-by-side on the top of the bar. Amazingly, the wonky details on the borders lined up perfectly. The matching halves as a whole showed a withered sapling that was shaped like a crucifix. From a branch sprouted three golden buds. In what was becoming a familiar motif, there was also a skull on the ground with an iris visible in what would normally be a hollow eye-socket. The image was nearly identical to the one on the altar bas-relief at Rennes-le-Chateau, with the only difference being that there was a depiction of a winged angel tied to an anchor above the skull in the combined specter paintings.

Why hadn't Malcolm showed me this little trick, I wondered. He made a big to-do about the perceptive technique used by the artist – anamorphic art I think he called it. Surely he was also aware of the matching borders. And it couldn't have been a coincidence that the same image was found at Rennes. What was Malcolm involved with and did it have anything to do with my situation? Things were beginning to add up, but as to where it was all leading, I was still in the dark. Since I was on a roll, seeing the left eye in the skull gave me another idea. Something I had planned on checking out, and with Malcolm having left for the night I now had the perfect opportunity.

After hanging the paintings back up, I walked over to the glazed curio cabinet set against the far wall with its miniature lithographs of graveyards lit by Bavaesque moons. Among these lurid canvases propped on small easels was an acrylic portrait of Malcolm that was humorously contrived with ghastly features, including eyes that brought to mind the peephole trope of a Disney haunted mansion.

I took out my phone and swiped the touchscreen to pull up one of the close ups of Malcolm's face that I took in France. I zoomed in even closer on one of his eyes and held it in front of the glaring stare in the painting. When nothing happened, I thought that my hunch involving some kind of flush mounted hidden door that was activated with a facial recognition mechanism was wrong. I hadn't forgotten how he once crept up on me, joking afterwards about this being the ghost room. Just to make sure, I tried again with the image on the phone but didn't hear any buzz or clicks.

When I pushed gently against the cabinet, to my great surprise, it swung inward with ease on a steel roller system to reveal a dark opening.

I stuck my hand inside and fumbled to find a light switch. After groping for a few seconds, when I flipped it on, I tried to figure out what I was looking at. It was the lodge room of a Fraternal Order, of that I was certain, but as to the exact nature of the craft affiliation, that I wasn't sure. It wasn't garden-variety Freemasonry, though coded allusions to esoteric gardening figured prominently among the Masonic trappings.

Sconces holding electric candles flickered on gold-flecked green wallpaper patterned with mysterious horticultural symbology. Between pastiches of vines hung masks of foliate heads and carvings of vegetation deities. Peeking from the riotous tapestry were masculine visages with sprouting mouths and leafy beards. Facial elements of females as personifications of nature and symbols of rebirth were also formed of stylized foliage.

While stepping onto a Persian carpet of emerald wool that was laid over part of the checkered floor, I glanced about at the arcane furnishings. Front and center was a large mural of an espaliered tree whose branches were barren save for three golden shoots. Above the tree was the familiar All-Seeing Eye of Freemasonry, only the usual square and compass had been replaced with two antique pruning knives crossed against a crude water basin. Beneath the tree was what appeared to be an actual human skull whose left socket contained a glass (?) eye.

Draped over the back of chairs at a richly carved wooden table were the Order's ceremonial regalia – sashes, collars and aprons of fantastically embroidered dark blue serge. A cursory examination of some framed documents led me to believe that the lodge room was the property of "The Secret Order of the Gardeners."

As I was about to leave, I noticed a sheet of paper lying on the table. Typed at the top was:

ANNOYING SAUNIEREOLOGIST
PLAYED BY NESTOR, THE NESTORIAN

Beneath this was typed:

"Seeing how a couple of paintings by Nicolas Poussin are inextricably linked to the mystery, I though you'd be interested in this letter about him written in 1656 by the Abbe Louis Fouquet to his brother."

This was followed by:

"He and I discussed certain things which I shall with ease be able to explain to you in detail. Things which will give you, through Monsieur Poussin, advantages which even kings would have great pains to draw from him and which, according to him, it is possible that nobody else will ever rediscover in the centuries to come, and what is more, these are things so difficult to discover that nothing now on this earth can prove of better fortune nor be their equal."

These were the same words spoken by the guy who called himself a "Sauniereologist" at Rennes-le-Chateau. The lanky bastard was reading from a script! What kind of crazy game was Malcolm playing?

When I saw Aaloka later that night, I was about to tell her that while I was dusting the cabinet – lo and behold – without so much as a super secret knock the damn thing rolled into the wall, allowing me to walk right into Malcolm and his cronies' hidden playroom. Instead, I kept quiet – even though she was always complaining about needing more storage space.

That way, prying eyes could explore it for further clues, such as the reason for making a trip all the way to France just to try and convince me that illustrious figures in history were preoccupied with the oversized grapes of an obvious fertility myth for reasons, I presumed, other than making prestigious wine.

When I walked out onto the back deck during a light sprinkle, Aaloka was leaning over the railing, peering into a night vision monocular while facing the wooded dog park.

"What are you – a ghost hunter?" I laughed.

Startled, she lowered the unit and turned around.

"It's Jaggy's new toy," she said with her face blotched from the luster of copper glass reflected from the propane fire pit. "He bought it from the money he got selling those 3-D Doritos. Said it would have to do until they sold contact lenses with cat vision."

"What were you looking at?"

"He and Zyla forgot it when they hurried down to the dog park. They were talking excitedly about some silliness of a portal opening between the trees that a green alien crawled out of."

"Isn't everything green with that thing? Yeah, I saw Maxx on the dining room table. At the head of the table," I chuckled. "It's drizzling. That guy's probably testing a new version of his... I mean my umbrella design... my idea that he stole and ran with... of projecting YouTube videos inside the canopy screen."

Aaloka positioned herself so the jacaranda tree wouldn't be in the way and trained the device back on the dog park.

"Hey, you're right… and so were they. I can see a green alien. Want to have a look?"

"Are you crazy? What if he closes the umbrella and then opens it again? Seriously, are you crazy?"

"Sorry, I don't know what I was thinking. Here, I promise the canopy's wide open," she said while handing me the unit.

Peering into the viewer, the circle displayed a fuzzy greenish image of the man holding the bobbling umbrella. Inside the bubble-shaped 'screen' was a projection from a YouTube clip of a Flintstones cartoon from the 1960s that featured a tiny floating alien whose smiling face was similar to the Rice Krispies cereal mascots, only with antennas on its green helmet.

"Yabba dabba doo, it's the Great Gazoo… And I see the two dumb dumbs are walking back… but I don't see any grainy greenish tails tucked firmly between their legs."

"What does Gazoo yabba dabba do? Good deeds for Fred and Barney, who found him after he crashed his saucer into the pre-historic town of Bedrock," I answered Jag's question. "Of course, things usually got screwed up. You have to wonder, though, about the Barney and Betty Rubble connection."

"What's that?" Jag asked while biting into a piece of watermelon sushi topped with green seaweed jelly.

"Betty and Barney Hill were the first public alien abductees. But mister Grane is just messing with you," Zyla smiled slyly.

"I'm trying to keep an open mind," I said while once again averting my eyes from her latest futuristic summer ensemble. The recent drizzle enhanced the sheen of a silver metallic liquid turtleneck crop top that looked like it had been poured over her jutting breasts. The matching shorts were also form fitting tight with a thin, multi-pocketed utility belt. Even her sandals were metallic with silver-toned hardware. Like the rest of us, her face was stippled from the fire glass, but when she tilted it at certain angles, her celestial eye makeup sparkled like miniature galaxies.

"You're mind is anything but open," she sneered while smoothing her blunt pearl bangs. "It's funny how you remember these animations so clearly, but don't have any idea of where you were or who you were with at the time. The mind lock is really snapped tight on you. What ever happened in the past must have been so shocking that your brain won't even allow a teeny glimpse –"

"So, what happened to your friend's church?" Aaloka quickly changed the subject.

"It's evident that someone was opposed to Magiar's intent," Zyla frowned. "The idea that the Black Knight is a biomorphic soul accumulator – a floating machine that vacuums up the ascending souls of the recently dead as part of a cosmic recycling program."

"It sounds like he's familiar with the theory of microtubules as containers of quantum information released from brain neurons," Aaloka nodded.

"I knew his church didn't hand out posters of God's ten plagues to potential members," I said, "but an orbiting Electrolux sucking up the spirits of the dearly departed –"

"His main concern was for the one that got shot down. What was going to happen to all those souls? He wants to know if his father's spirit had been collected by that one."

"And what does Professor Hellmann have to say about this?" Aaloka asked. "Jag said that you spoke to him about his interests outside of Cellectech."

"Volker — now he's lit!" Zyla's eyes widened. "He's into the Soulcraft teachings. We are star guests from a planet that once orbited Sirius B. Some of its inhabitants migrated to earth to escape an enemy. Real life Star Wars. They created humans from apes... our brute ancestry. So, we're half-beast, half-angel. Their spirit is still within us — encased in a physical ensemble... waiting to be regenerated back into them at some pre-determined time."

"Makes perfect sense," I said. "The half-beast part of humanity continues to slaughter one another so the half-celestial part can wing itself off into the transcendent sunset, unaware that there's an intergalactic Hoover waiting for them."

Ignoring my sarcasm, Zyla continued without pulling out her trusty elixir spray.

"But Volker has other thoughts, too. About our larval state."

"Oh, he does? Such as?" Aaloka probed.

"The highly capable civilizations before the re-set were aware of our distorted godhood — the indwelling spirit-particle of the Sirians awaiting the return to celestiality. Actually, the embalming of mummies in ancient Egypt was a corruption of the divine embryo of the golden womb."

"Maybe we have something in common with that immortal jellyfish after all," I said with a straight face.

Aaloka responded with an annoyed glance before gesturing for Zyla to continue.

"Volker has been experimenting with specialized frequencies to activate a neurosecretory valve. He's looking for a master control switch that triggers a hormone cascade... a signal like caterpillars have that starts the radical transformation. He's hoping to discover this metamorphosing substance before more souls of the dead are collected by something like the Black Knight, which might be a technology of the Sirians' enemy. He thinks it's buried in junk genes, or maybe even deeper. But, he wants to achieve this without any detrimental effects. Like what happened in prior experiments before the last extinction level event. All the chimeras in ancient myths... which aren't really myths but are historical records."

"What about this woman asking about Volker's work?" Aaloka asked.

"Josephina," she nodded while pulling from her metallic tote a sleek glass cylinder with a stainless steel cap. This turned out to be a fancy water bottle that contained a colorful gem-pod at the bottom.

"Are those amethysts?" Aaloka leaned over and touched the glass.

"Yeah, and ocean chalcedony and other elements. I used to drink alkaline ionized water for its negative antioxidant potential, but, besides boosting the PH spectrum, this water is reconstructed by the gem stones."

After sliding an amethyst crystal straw into the lid, she took a sip. She then ate another one of the small balls of lemon sorbet in a mochi wrapper before Jag knocked the bowl over with his elbow while taking a gulp of root beer. Using the night vision scope, he bent over and picked up some of those still rolling across the wooden planks.

"Yeah, that was weird," Zyla continued. "She wasn't really into Magiar's ideas, but when I told her about Volker's cosmic account, she was all ears. What was really weird, though, was that she already knew about his work... By the fruit you will know the tree, she repeated this several times. By the fruit you will know the tree. When I told her I wasn't sure what she meant by this, she told me that Volker's mentor supported the Nazis and was locked away in prison for his fascist ideas. She asked if he mentioned anything about dark souls. When I said he didn't, she said goodbye and then left. Weird."

All I could do was smile. Nazis and genetics! Talk about clichés. If the good professor had any xenophobic tendencies, it would be with the human race in general. With all his pseudo-scientific blather about a mysterious process of stimulating our nascent divinity in one's holy laboratory, he was post-human all the way.

Judging by her expression, Aaloka seemed pleased by Zyla's answers, which, for some reason, seemed like a subtle inquiry. I could tell that something had been bothering her ever since Jag mentioned Zyla having a conversation with Volker about this fringe science. When I asked why she was worried about this, she denied being upset and said everything was fine. When I pressed the subject, telling her that her assurances weren't that convincing, and asked if it involved a security breach, she told me to "stick with critical thinking and quick-fire wit."

As to critical thinking, or a lack thereof, Zyla's exchange with Aaloka only added to my growing suspicions. From her description, this woman who called herself Josephina sounded a lot like the black lady that 'randomly' started a conversation about bioethics at the restaurant bar last spring. She had what looked like a prosthetic eye, as did the professor. Also, her repeating the phrase, "By the fruit you shall know the tree" sounded like one of the hacker's cryptic messages, causing me to wonder if she was in any way connected with Ramiel's Enochian cult. Add to that Malcolm's secret lodge room with its plant-themed décor and the coincidences were beginning to stack up, at least with my obsessive reflections of the people in my small circle.

While having a slice of pizza for a midnight snack, I jokingly gazed into the hollow eye-sockets of the crystal skull that Zyla had left on the kitchen table.

"Maxx, you handsome devil of a well-shaved chunk of quartz, what can you tell me about all these things in my life? Surely, you, of all crystal noggins, must know what it is I'm missing here."

While chewing the tough pizza crust, I noticed a peculiar shading effect on the surface of the skull's clear quartz. Thinking Aaloka or Jag had entered the room, I quickly glanced about, not seeing either of them. When my gaze returned to the carving, I realized that the splotch of faint darkness was swirling within the translucent depths, and not on the surface. Not only was the vapory mass expanding, its pearly, milky twirls were congealing to mold the distinct shape of a male face with a curious pinkish ivory cast. Once fully formed, intricately layered white braids framed the delicate pale features. Most unsettling of all were the golden-hazel eyes that stared back at me. As I lifted my hand to rub my eyes, at the exact same moment, a hand with pallid, tapered fingers raised itself towards the lustrous, speckled irises of the ghostly visage.

As my gaze remained transfixed on this vaguely familiar being, my phone dinged, causing the hazy, mysterious presence to rapidly splinter into myriads of pinkish-white filaments. For a minute I sat there stunned, growing increasingly agitated by having witnessed those glistening eyes observing my reaction to the movement of the hand. Seeing it make a gesture that mirrored by own was difficult to process. Confronted by yet another full-blown hallucination (I didn't know what else to call it), I decided right then and there to seek the opinion of the medical specialist that I had long been putting off.

When I finally regained my composure, I saw that the text was from Julian. Sergio had sent him a copy of his father's *derrotero*. The location of the lost Spanish mule trail was southwest of Tucson,

Arizona in the Pajarito Range near the Mexican border. The area was called *Oro Blanco,* meaning "white gold." From other research he had conducted, Julian believed he had discovered Kidd's isolated shack in the vicinity of the peak called Cerro Ruido. He said he was hoping to "lasso" me to add balance for the final scenes. The message ended by saying that the usual suspects would be there for the wrap, including "no white beans!" Zeke.

When I told Aaloka about this, rather than try to dissuade me as she had done before when Julian asked for my involvement, she encouraged me to participate. What caused her to change her mind I wasn't sure, but in another odd twist, she didn't seem at all concerned about "what I thought I saw", telling me that I could always get an evaluation from a neurologist when I got back.

What I wanted to know, I told her, was if these hallucinations might be related to my disorder, either as collateral damage to a traumatic event, or as flashes of the condition attempting to resolve itself. When I suggested a third possible explanation – that I might be the victim of a powerful hypnotic suggestion – I couldn't help but notice her strange reaction. There was a nervous shuffling, as she seemed to be debating whether or not to tell me something. When she finally did speak, she told me to file my "power words shit " under P for paranoia. Hypnotic reflexes weren't the cause of any unusual sensory experiences or my focal retrograde amnesia, she asserted. The only reason for even considering such a wild idea – that of responding to a cue – I explained, was because some of the visions were similar to the bizarre dreams I experienced while staying at the same motel chain. Again, was this just a coincidence?

Despite the intense heat in Arizona, Jag wanted to come with me. When I asked why, he said that he hoped to spot a PFO in his new night vision monocular. When I asked what a PFO was, he replied "Prehistoric Flying Object." He wanted to see the Tombstone monster. To increase his chances, he was going to buy an inexpensive pterodactyl-drone to use as bait. Even with the expected jaggravation his company was sure to cause, picturing old Zeke pulling out his Winchester when the winged demon passed overhead made the decision a no brainer. I told him to be ready to saddle up in three days, and to pack a canteen – one without a vial of pretty gems at the bottom.

"What happened to the damn pavement?" I uttered as Jag and I bounced around while strapped into our rental Jeep. We had hit another rough patch of the narrow road that wound between Tucson and Nogales, but as the grassy savanna gave way to the shallow canyons and ocotillo-covered foothills of the Pajarito range, the thought of no guardrails became more worrisome. As the road conditions continued to get worse, with large potholes in the brittle asphalt, Julian braked ahead of us and pulled his SUV over in front of a hand-painted billboard that read:

YOU ARE TRAVELING ON THE MOST POORLY MAINTAINED ROAD IN PIMA COUNTY

As cameraman Burton got out to get a shot of the warning to drivers on Ruby Road, production coordinator Hayden followed him with an equipment case. Wanting a photo of the sign myself, I climbed out of the black Wrangler and walked up to it, careful to stay out of frame.

"If I don't melt first, I should get some nice photos," she said while pointing to a turkey buzzard that alighted on the unpaved stretch ahead. "Pajarito means little bird, so I'll bet it's a great sighting spot."

"I hope you didn't forget your skin goop," I said as she took a gulp of water from a sleek bottle that had a pod of gems at the bottom.

The Paragon team had set up cameras and sound in the spacious kitchen of an elderly Nogales couple. Arched openings, majolica planters and talavera tiles made for a nice backdrop, as did the crimson, yellow and turquoise cabinetry that bordered a large stove with rustic iron cookware and apothecary-style spice jars. Covering the walls were religious folk charms, including painted tin hearts with *milagros*, colorful crosses and velvet oil paintings of Catholic saints.

Seated at a multicolored wooden table, host Flynn McIntyre sipped iced hibiscus tea while interviewing Miguel and Juana Sanchez. Framed by decorated panels and copper *retablos*, the two spoke of a wandering stranger who used to be known in these parts as *el Ermitano Cananea* – "The Hermit of Cananea."

According to the Mexican couple, both of who spoke good English, the reclusive stranger popped up out of nowhere, appearing in Nogales in the early 1950s. Miguel had seen him as a young boy when his father befriended him. He claimed to have lived previously in Cananea, a Sonoran town near the U.S. border that had large copper mines. Since James Kidd had worked for a copper mining company in Arizona for much of his life, 'natch' Julian wondered if the hermit and he were one in the same. There was also the matter of the funny hat the "logo gringo" used to wear. From the description, it sounded like a fedora. And then there were the rumors that he subsisted solely on unspiced corn gruel.

Although no one was sure of his nationality, guesses included him being a French Basque, a Pyrenean Catlan, a Sardinian and even an American. Because of the eloquent manner in which he spoke, often reciting lengthy poetic verses, he was thought to have come from a noble family. Besides being puzzled over his nationality, the locals were also conflicted as to his religious beliefs. While he seemed to have no tolerance for organized religion, there was a mystical shimmer about him that caused some to think of him as a Compostela-type pilgrim, who, for whatever reason, had traveled to the wilds of Arizona. Though well versed with Christian scripture, he interpreted it in an unorthodox manner, which also was hard to reconcile. When asked to give an example, at first Miguel was hesitant, saying he couldn't recall the odd beliefs, but as he struggled to remember certain details, bits and pieces of a vow the hermit said he must keep sounded similar to the gnostic ideas that I had heard in the south of France.

Because of his austere lifestyle and scant belongings, others thought he was an anchorite-monk. However, with his stated desire for solitude, rumors persisted that he was a prospector looking for lost Spanish treasure, who merely assumed the guise of a religious ascetic to avoid being followed.

In his later years he dressed in a monastic robe and carried a wooden staff. Because of his peculiar garb and long flowing beard, he was compared to an Old Testament prophet. Perhaps because of his dark vestments, he was thought to be able to cure ailments and restore peoples' health with the pail of water from a sacred spring that it was his habit to carry, even when he ventured off alone.

Miguel doubted the hermit's ability to heal because he was admittedly at odds with the Catholic Church and didn't believe in their teachings. On a couple of occasions he had seen the mountain spring near the isolated mud-plastered shack, whose crystalline water supposedly had miraculous properties. The strange thing about it was that when it bubbled forth, it never spread out. There was no stream; the water just seeped back into the ground. The other funny thing was the hermit's pot of *atole* - the tasteless corn mush that he lived on always seemed to be full, no matter how much he scooped onto the plate of a curious visitor.

This latter folktale brought to mind the cornucopia or Horn of Plenty of the Graal legends. The cauldron that symbolized abundance and nourishment. What had any of this to do with Kidd? I kept thinking. The eccentric hermit sounded more like a modern-day Jesus impersonator than someone seeking deep seams of gold while pondering the human soul.

When the interview was over, Juana served churro shells with a pecan-encrusted Nutella filling. As we enjoyed these with our chilled *aguas frescas*, Miguel assured Julian that he would take the crew to the hermit's shack near Cerro Ruido. Although most locals refused to set foot on the mountain, and even Spanish forays by the early mission padres quickly ceased, he wasn't afraid of the strange noises, he said with a faint smile while clutching his silver crucifix.

Since the ghost town of Ruby was on private property and not open at night, the crew decided to eat dinner at a picnic area near a small lake that was surrounded by a grassy valley. Hayden was happy because Pena Blanca Lake was known as a good bird watching spot, and Burton thought he might try his luck at catching some of the stocked fish. Not that we were lacking for food. Juana had brought a homemade tamale pie and *frijole charras*, and even made a tangy vegan *chorizo* with pickled jalapenos especially for Jag.

If this wasn't enough, Zeke was sizzling sirloins and venison sausages on a pedestal grill under a stand of oaks. In the gathering twilight (the fussed darkness the old timer called it), he squinted while brushing generous dollops of his spicy scorpion sauce onto the steaks.

"These grill doings are bettermost than gettin' fuddled at some bit house," he said while scratching his dense stubble. The remark concerned Flynn, who had opted to take his pretty lady friend to a nearby cantina to escape the evening heat. "E'em a'most ready!"

Before the chow bell clanged, however, I got inveigled to be the judge for the two cooks' famous fixins. Zeke's scorpion sauce pitted against Juana's cactus salsa. After sampling both with a modicum of dread, I said it was a coin toss, invoking the expected diplomacy such a regional contest required.

Having finished everything except Juana's rapidly melting *paletas* for dessert, we gathered around the fire circle to listen to more of the tall tales Zeke told with skill honed as a member of his liar's club.

As bright sparks jumped from the glowing juniper logs, while puffing on a cheroot that popped like a firecracker, he spoke of the Superstition killings. This included the degraded corpses, phantom orbs of ghost warriors that guarded hidden gold and turned treasure buffs into the melted faces seen on hoodoos and exploding cactus houseplants that were filled with baby tarantulas. Though I had heard most of these before, seemingly new to his repertoire were stories of cud-chewing goats whose stomachs were bursting with Jesuit silver *reales*, blue meanie entities that harassed ranchers' wives for tortillas and peach salsa and Martians spilling out of black circles that appeared in the starry skies.

When speaking about a Spanish mission, whose front façade contained a carving of a snake chasing a mouse, he said that according to legend - when the snake catches the mouse - the end of the world is at hand.

"The mission of San Xavier has carvings of a cat chasing a mouse, not a snake" Juana corrected him.

"We're straining at gnats here," Zeke replied, "but the cussinness of the thing is to keep watch."

In the middle of Saltback's tale spinning, Jag had wandered off to play with his night vision monocular. When he returned, having removed his shirt, both Miguel and Juana were fascinated by his grinder stuff. The luminous tattoo and north-sense biomagnet implanted in his chest.

"We're being watched," Jag said. "By some dude flexed up with super expensive stealth goggles. I'll bet there's no fuzzy green shit. Probably a white phosphorus display with those military wearables. I saw a coyote, too."

"I'd like to take a look at this man," I said.

"When he saw me looking at him, he left. Got any more of those almond milk cornsicles?" he asked Juana.

When I asked Miguel in private what he thought about the lost mission near Cerro Ruido, he said that it was most likely just another romanticized tale similar to the lost silver bells of Tumacacori. Legends of Jesuit priest-miners and *uno metales* in the Oro Blanco region were spread by Anglos, based on rumors, poor translations of Spanish and Mexican documents and other non-reliable sources. First of all, the Jesuits were forbidden to engage in such activities. Secondly, there was the threat of hostile native tribes. Who knows, though, he smiled, despite such tales being greatly embellished, the Jesuits might have concealed a cache-mine on an old *carreta* road after their expulsion.

An old cart track or mule trail is what we were looking for in the narrow canyon – not one that led to a mineshaft, but to a flat-roofed adobe shack built near a gushing spring. We had done most of the off-road driving in the rugged terrain in Polaris ATVs that had been modified with lift-kits. Ginormous tires with crazy tread patterns made tackling sandy washouts and rocky stretches a breeze until the rutted dirt track ended at an overgrown hiking trail that skirted a winding arroyo. The rest of the search would have to be conducted on foot.

"Why does everything want to poke you here?" Hayden winced while stepping around clusters of spiky leaves.

"I'm sure the next person who rents this thing will appreciate the natural pin-striping," I joked while climbing out of the ATV, whose knobby tires were resting on a patch of thorny mesquite.

"I've seen more rabbits than birds for a place named Pajarito," she frowned.

"Well, at least it looks like we might get some cloud cover," I said while pointing to the formation of woolpacks gathering to our north.

Hayden shielded her eyes from the sun's penetrating rays while looking up at the sky. "I could use a good downpour right now. I'll bet McIntyre is having second thoughts," she said with more than a trace of sarcasm.

Though the film's host was a no-show, Julian didn't seem bothered by his absence, knowing he could dub in narration over the footage. What did concern him was the puzzled look on Miguel's face as he scanned the harsh surroundings. Though he was certain we were in the right vicinity of the cabin, he was surprised to see that once familiar landscape features were no longer there.

As the crew explored the area beneath the high cliffs, Jag and I followed a path that ran beside a steep-sided gully that meandered between slopes of stunted oaks. Jag was carrying the case with the pterano-drone, looking for a level spot to launch the thing. As clumps of dried yucca crunched under our footsteps, we continued to climb a short ways until we reached a dramatic overlook that offered a better view of the nearby peak of Cerro Ruido. The ledge was also the ideal spot to send aloft his monster bait.

Watching as the approaching clouds darkened around the edges, Jag was busy adjusting some switches, preparing the radio-controlled drone for take off. When the quadcopter blades began whirring, the flying reptile with its menacing beak and large wingspan slowly lifted off the ground, quickly gaining height. As it circled in patches of blue sky between the rolling, billowy masses, the glint of reddish-orange wings flapping against picturesque towering buttes made for a strange sight.

"You don't really think Zeke will shoot it down, do you?" Jag asked.

With the pterodactyl silhouetted against the sheer drop offs, I suddenly experienced a sense of déjà vu. I had seen this before – the scenery on the horizon – in my last 'Sandman dream.' There was a distant rumble. I wasn't sure if it was one of the peculiar sounds believed to be associated with Cerro Ruido, or if it came from the clouds that were swelling ominously overhead.

"Mister Grane," a gruff voice uttered.

When I turned around, there was a man wearing camo fatigues standing in the bustling dust plumes. I recognized the gold-tinted lenses of his grey-metal Cartier sunglasses. It was the guy that I had glimpsed on several occasions, starting at a Greyhound bus terminal. He was even still wearing the same boots, the oxblood leather ones with hand-painted camo patterns just like the pair I owned.

"I don't have time to explain, but I need to get you and the young man out of here... now."

"You've been following me, haven't you," I said while taking a step towards him. "Why?"

"You're an important asset to someone."

"The skeptoid?" Jag laughed.

"Important? To who am I important?"

"Never mind about that now. There's no time," he said as a deafening clap of thunder shook the ground. "In my assessment of the situation... in this gullied area... the threat is urgent. We're about to get pummeled with one hell of a summer squall... and this place is a flood prone."

"Tell me why you've been following me. I don't remember anything about my past."

"The plan is to get away from this gulch as quickly as possible."

"Cray – we're being extracted," Jag laughed as the pterodactyl swooped before disappearing into the thunderheads that blanketed the horizon.

The hot, moist air suddenly smelled of fetid caliche.

After a jagged streak of lightning was followed another sharp bang, the skies opened up and all hell broke loose.

With heavy raindrops pelting us in violet gusts of wind, I tucked my glasses into the pocket of my shorts before grabbing

Jag's shoulder and shouting at him to leave the controls behind. During the cloudburst, shallow depressions filled with water in a matter of seconds. Following the hand motions of the stranger, we hurried down the slippery path, dodging the blur of cotton-tail rabbits that darted from the soaked desert scrub.

It was amazing how quickly things turned dangerous.

While making a run for the canvas-roofed Polaris, Jag stumbled as pounding rain saturated the ground and slickened the gravel. As he splashed into the murky water that overflowed the wash, I reached for his hand, managing to clutch his arm before he was dragged under by the surge. In an instant we were both swept away by rising, turbid water that coursed like a river in the narrow channel. As we tumbled about in the swiftly moving current, we tried to keep from being pulled under. Trying to draw air without swallowing the muddy water, while gasping for breath, over the lashing rain, I heard what sounded like hundreds of trees snapping like matchsticks. Even without my glasses, what I glimpsed was jaw dropping, as the towering dark brown wall of lather ripped away earth and rocks, gouging everything in its meandering path.

Struggling to keep my head above the dirty torrents that frothed around protruding boulders, my legs scraped against the thorny prickles of a submerged mesquite bosque. Though my thighs stung a little, adrenaline numbed the pain of what I imagined to be ripped flesh.

As the rain persisted, the churning run-off continued to funnel down stream, carrying with it branches, leaves and piles of debris. Keeping an eye on Jag the best I could, I saw him barely avoid being struck by a splintered limb that rushed past him like a leafy torpedo as he snagged a bottle of water bobbing in front of a gliding rumpled cowboy hat.

After what seemed like an eternity staying above the surface in the rampaging streambed, we both managed to latch onto a tree that was bent over the sloping ground. While clinging to it, we were able to pull ourselves out of the rushing floodwater. Grabbing onto spiny ocotillo stalks, we used jagged rocks as a ladder to reach higher ground.

As we clambered up the muddy bank, the rain finally let up. A warm breeze rustled the desert grasses shaded by the bruised purple sky. While seated on a ledge wiping the lenses of my slightly bent frames, foul-smelling water dripped from my clothes. When I checked my legs for abrasions, there were some bleeding cuts and scrapes but it wasn't nearly as bad as I had anticipated. Jag was also in good shape, having only a small bump on his forehead from his initial fall. He was more concerned about losing his smartphone than anything else.

"If you weren't wearing those clown pants," I teased him while picking out stickers from my palms.

"Like that waterlogged thing in those grabbers is going to work, luddie."

"What's wrong with slim-fits? You shop at Macy's. Well, at least one of us is a human compass."

Watching a yellow-headed verdin alight on the bright crimson flowers of ocotillo stems, we both started laughing uncontrollably. It had finally dawned on us that we survived the ordeal none the worse for wear. When Jag handed me the water bottle that he had grabbed a hold of in the torrent, we both noticed the cluster of gems encased at the bottom. Seeing this, we became silent, wondering how the others had fared. With only so much water left, we knew that if we didn't find one of those mountain springs, we'd have to ration it carefully.

Looking around at the high foothills, I was surprised to see that the steep rock flanks of Cerro Ruido loomed larger. Having rested for a bit and calmed our frazzled nerves, we headed off in the direction that I thought would get us back to where we started (using chest vibrations from Jag's compass to get our bearings).

A heavily grown over trail led us into a rocky canyon, whose slopes were dotted with the ubiquitous ocotillo. Passing under rocky bluffs, we stepped over purplish limbs of dead juniper, swatting at deer flies as the sun climbed higher. Avoiding the small gulch in a loam bank, we continued on, pausing at times to listen to what sounded like a low chant accompanied by the shaking of a gourd rattle. When Jag asked me if the Apache were friendly now, I told him that the sounds were probably due to the wind passing through fissures in the rock formations. Strange sounds like these are why they call it the Mountain of Noise.

After following the trail for nearly an hour, we sought shade in a sun-dappled glen. While taking a carefully measured drink of water, through the yellowish blooms of paloverde trees, I made out the vague outline of what appeared to be a structure wavering in the heat. Pushing branches away to get a better view, I was stunned to see a grandiose edifice rising from the desert wilderness. To make sure it wasn't a mirage, I told Jag to take a look. For someone who believed at times that we lived in a simulated reality, he was at a loss to explain the impressive remains in such an incongruous setting.

Excited by the discovery, we clambered up a path to check it out.

With the foundation overgrown by greyish clumps of brittle mesquite, the façade of the old Spanish mission blended in with the base of the cliff against which it had been erected. Vertical walls of pinkish-white shimmered like the flecks of quartz strewn on the sandy stretches from which they stood. This had to be the lost mission of the Jesuit treasure legend, as the four ruined arches of the bell tower were visible. Along with the empty belfry portals, other structural elements glinted in the blinding sunlight, including the façade pediment with its decorative scheme, window openings and arched entry with a large wooden door. Rising from a horizontal cornice under a triangular gable was a plaster ball holding the cross. Like the heavily eroded bricks of the crumbling walls, its base was striated with deep cracks, with flakes from its lime mortar littering the melted adobe of the portico. Rather than the imposing structure of legend, the mission appeared to be a scaled-down model, though complete in every minor detail, such as the main quatrefoil window and elaborate carvings on the curved false front.

Before entering the church, we exchanged bemused glances while noticing the hand carved designs on the door depicted a snake chasing a mouse. Taking a tentative step into the shadowy interior, we were greeted by a low rumble that mimicked a bass note of a pipe organ echoing off the earthen walls. Rather than look for some robed phantom playing a sonorous behemoth, I told Jag this was most likely just another trick of Cerro Ruido.

Wafts of bat guano accosted our nostrils while standing in muddy rivulets below their roost. With twigs snapping under our footsteps, we proceeded forward, pushing back tangles of dirty cobwebs and ducking beneath collapsed pine beams hanging from the rafters of the roofless nave. Along with sotol brush growing from cracks in the burnished tiles, fragments of gypsum plaster covered rustic benches. Moving towards the baptismal font, we were surprised that there was clear water in its ornate stone basin.

A dusty sunbeam struck what remained of the oak pulpit, revealing writing that had been scribbled with a black marker on its stained surface:

MAY GOD HAVE MERCY ON ALL WHO ENTER THIS PLACE
12/28/56

Under this another message was scrawled in red:

THIS IS NO JOKE

There was an uneasy look on Jag's face as we moved forward.

In the sacristy behind the altar, an exposed secret door had been forced open to reveal a timber-framed passageway. Using Jag's luminous tattoo as a light source, we followed the narrow corridor to a small outbuilding of orangish-red mudbrick that had been built against the adjoining canyon wall. The moment we entered its stuffy confines, a tingling sensation coursed through my body. Jag said he also felt his skin prickling, describing it as his flesh being poked with thousands of electrified needles.

As faint sunlight filtered through gaps in the ceiling, a lizard scurried across the faded vermillion, disappearing under the spiky branches of flowering coachwhip that protruded from the broken flooring. While trying to avoid stepping on it, I had brushed against something seated in an old armchair. At first the bony fingers resting on the wooden rails didn't register, but when I stepped back, I was shocked to realize they were part of a headless skeleton dressed in the black gown of a Jesuit priest.

Telling Jag to walk the other way, when I turned around, I saw his gaze was frozen on an equally macabre sight - that of a human skull wearing a biretta perched on a shelf supported by ironwork corbels.

"Jesus... it feels like I'm in one of those paintings by that Italian guy," I uttered in a shaky tone. "With the skulls always eyeing something... like a clue."

"There's supposed to be gold here, right?"

"Maybe... or silver. From the size of it, the mission seems to be little more than a disguise. Normally, it would be much larger. I guess it could have been built to conceal a shaft or tunnel in the canyon wall... though I don't see anything."

"What's spooky looking at?" Jag asked while noticing the skull had been positioned so its hollow eye-sockets were peering down at something.

"The rest of spooky's bones," I said while gesturing to the fully dressed skeleton slumped in the armchair.

"Cray," Jag grimaced before flinching as another lizard scuttered across the stucco.

"Maybe he's got a key to unlock another secret door," I said.

On a hunch, I leaned over the moldering fabric of the chair and reached into the pocket of the priest's cassock. Feeling something metallic, I pulled out a pocket watch with a broken chain attached to the winding stem. The shape was octagonal with a golden luster that had similar filigree as the prop used for Kidd's cherished timepiece. Looking for any evidence that it might have belonged to him, I opened the hinged protective cover. The maker was Elgin and it was dated 1888, but there were no engravings on the inner back case. There was, however, a separate thin disc that had been tucked inside it. Its reddish-copper surface was dominated by the image of an oddly slanted eye with a golden-hazel iris. There was something about the curious liquidity of the enchanted gaze that I found a bit unnerving.

While carefully lifting the disc out of the case, I could bare-ly feel the thing – whatever alloy it was fabricated from being extremely light. When viewed at different angles, subtle fluc-tuations within its surface emitted a strange luminosity in the room's faint light.

When I touched the perplexing eye, it quickly became de-tached from its circular face like a soaked decal that easily slides off its backing paper. Holding the flimsy thing, it seemed to glide into the palm of my hand before instantly being ab-sorbed by my skin.

"Whoa, that's cray!" Jag's eyes widened.

"What the fuck just happened?" I asked while staring at my palm.

"How'd it get sucked into your hand?" Jag flashed me a puz-zled look while forking his fingers through his hair.

"What, that's crazy."

"I saw what happened in your hand - it implanted itself like an intradermal tattoo."

"No, I must have dropped it. Where'd it go? It was just a Cracker Jack prize," I said while checking the ground.

"Then why are you so shook? If it's not a prank, that's one highkey biomarker. You're a super-grinder, Sheldon," he said with what sounded like tinge of jealousy.

As I continued to look for it – thinking about the fluidity of the iris's golden speckles lying amid the rubble – Jag began sneezing, with the fits becoming so prolonged that he said he was going back outside. Before joining him I put the disc back into the watchcase and stuck it into my pocket. Knowing that we didn't have time to look for any stashed goods – even gold plac-ers – I took a quick peek at the back wall. In doing so, I glimpsed a barely-visible marking that looked like a crudely drawn heart-shaped design that was cracked in half by a jagged bolt of lightning. If I remembered correctly, this was a Spanish symbol that served as a warning that the entrance to a hidden treasure was booby-trapped.

When I ran my hand across the eroded adobe to see if I could feel any telltale signs of a false wall, a tiny black dot appeared in my field of vision. What was actually an ellipse rapidly expanded until I was standing within a shimmering black void.

There was a strange weightlessness to my body like I wasn't physically in the surroundings I perceived. The only thing I could see was the strange variegated glow surrounding an espaliered tree some distance away. The moment I focused on it, I was able to see details with perfect clarity. It was as if my eyes had become super-lenses. A second later I was standing right in front of it, having been transported point to point by some unknown means.

Three pieces of glossy bluish-purple fruit were dangling from one of the branches. Their size was smaller than an average apple, but considerably larger than a grape. When I reached to touch one, minute unintelligible symbols of a sparkling heliotrope color appeared suspended in thin air beneath it. At the same instant they flashed on, I also discerned an oddly familiar subvocal impression with a soothing tonality that emanated from some self-activating source. Knowing what I was supposed to do, I plucked all three of the meager yield and cradled them in my hands. No sooner had I done so than I found myself standing behind the crumbling earthen wall that I had been examining for a concealed entrance.

When I stepped out into the blinding sunlight, Jag was running towards the dilapidated church.

"Wait until you see what I found!" he shouted excitedly.

He stopped dead in his tracks with a dumbfounded expression on his sweaty face.

"What happened to your clothes?"

Looking down, I saw that both my shorts and shirt were spotless. Not only were the muddy stains gone; the fabric appeared to be freshly laundered. Even my shoes looked like they were right out of the box.

"Did we die?" he mumbled somberly.

"There's an explanation... for everything," I said with a tone I'm sure he didn't find convincing.

"What are you holding?" he asked.

"Fruit. What did you find?"

"An old truck. It's cray... and it started."

Following him around the corner of the ruined mission, I could see the distorted image of a truck fluttering in waves of heat rising from a patch of thick yellow grass on which it was parked a short ways off. It was an early model Chevy – from the 1950s - with rusted, wide blue-gray fenders. On its wooden flatbed was an array of parallel steel alloy tubes that were aimed like antennae towards the sky. Connected to the pipes were numerous frayed rubber hoses and cast iron valve wheels. It took a minute, but I recognized the apparatus from an old photo.

"It's a cloud-buster. Maybe even one that's been converted into a space gun. It was an energy device that an old crackpot scientist named Wilhelm Reich tried to use to turn the desert green. We're not far from Little Orgonon – the base of his experiments to try and unblock some universal force he claimed to discover. Something like dark energy. Reich had some nutty ideas, but if this clunker gets us out of here, I'll consider him to be a genius. Why wasn't the battery dead?" I uttered over the rumbling engine.

"It's running good. I can't figure out how to get the windows down, though."

On the rough dirt tracks that wound all the way back to Ruby Road, I persuaded Jag not to mention the lost mission to Julian, or to anyone else for that matter, in case there was gold to be found when we returned. Ditto with the pocket watch and strange piece of metal that had been placed inside its hinged case. I also warned him not to eat any of the fruit because its species was unknown to me and therefore might be poisonous. When he asked me why I wanted it, I made up something about it being a curiosity for Malcolm's gardening club (which, of course he didn't know anything about). This was the best story I could think of until I figured out what had happened in that 'room', and why I felt compelled to take the fruit.

When we got to the Sanchez's home in Nogales, where I had left the rental Jeep, their maid cheerfully welcomed us into the *casa*, saying the couple hadn't returned yet from the "movie." When I was able to contact Julian using their landline, he was relieved to know that we were safe, and was going to call off the search for us. They hadn't found the shack or natural spring that was marked on the *derrotero* yet, but were going to resume looking for it now that everyone had been accounted for. After filling me in on where they were going to continue the search, he told me that just prior to the storm, Hayden had taken a photo of something weird in the sky, which he didn't elaborate on, but said he was anxious to get my opinion. While listening to him go on about how the crew (along with the Sanchez's) had taken shelter on higher ground, there was a sudden commotion coming from the kitchen. Something had alarmed the maid to the point that she was shouting frantically.

"Dios perdoname!"

When Jag and I hurried to see what she was reacting to, I realized that I had left the three pieces of fruit on the table, and that she had helped herself to one of them. Within less than a minute, she had consumed the entire thing, including the stem, core and seeds (?), which she currently was in the process of re-gurgitating after jamming her fingers into her throat.

A chunky stream of vomit spattered onto the talavera plates.

Using a cloth dinner napkin, she frantically began wiping up the lumps of light bluish pulp on the vibrant tableware and stringy bile that dangled from her lips onto her floral dress. When I tried to assure her that everything would be all right, she flailed her arms, deeply agitated by her actions.

"Mister, Sheldon... *la fruta del Diablo es deliciosa. Manzana azul! No pude evitarlo...* I could not help myself," she uttered as tears welled in her eyes. "*La fruta del Diablo es deliciosa. Comerlo esta pro-hibido! Manzana azul,* mister Sheldon..." she shouted while grasping her crucifix and wiping away the ropy mucous from it.

I saw Jag cringe as she picked up a dripping lump that she had just thrown up.

Unable to calm her down and thinking she might stick the smelly glob back into her mouth, I grabbed the remaining two pieces and motioned for Jag to head for the front door.

As we waited behind a line of cars at the Arizona-California border agricultural checkpoint, Jag reached inside the cooler where the fruit was and pulled out a can of Barq's root beer.

"Did my mom ever tell you about when she was in college at Los Cruces.... in New Mexico... how she and some other students in the genetics program swapped some of the junk genes … the inactive guys… in an apple tree with some of our human stuff?"

Really? No she didn't," I said. "Why'd they do that? Just to see if it could be done?"

"She said in case anything ever happened to us… to humans… with the hybrid… human DNA would be preserved in all parts of the apple tree."

The inspector motioned for Jag to roll down the window.

"Where are you coming from?"

"Arizona," Jag said.

"Bringing any fruit back?"

"Just two blurples."

"Two what?"

"Blurples. You've never been to Sprouts? It's not citrus. Blurples."

Not amused by Jag's 'joke' – he waved us through.

CHAPTER VIII
MOOFKOOZTEE

"Now comes the mystery!"

- Henry Ward Beecher

*"If this were played upon a stage now, I could con-
demn it as an improbable fiction."*

- Shakespeare

"The people around here walk on gold without knowing it," I
said while approaching a figure seated on a rattan mat with his
back turned to me. I had followed a shady path through white
wisteria to an urban community garden off a dead end lane near
the Nestorian Church in San Francisco.

"Guess who said that?" I asked as the man slowly turned,
wide-eyed surprised to see me standing there. Wearing a long,
wide-sleeved tunic, the lanky figure closed a prayer book covered in saffron-colored silk and set it down next to a Styrofoam
box that contained his lunch. Besides his priestly garb, the only
thing different from the last time I saw him was that he had
grown a beard, either to give him a more acetic look, or to cover
deep-pitted acne scars.

"The priest of Rennes-le-Chateau," he replied.

I made a loud, discordant buzzing sound like those when a
game show contestant gives the wrong answer.

"Nope, it was his maid servant, Marie. That's quite a mistake for a Sauniereologist, Nestor. The bishop told me you liked to eat your lunch here. Persian fast food."

"Charbroiled chicken with a rose sharbat, today. Do you know me now?" he asked.

"I only know your first name."

"Mister Cutshaw didn't tell you about the plan of using me to try and jog your memory?"

"That was the plan?"

"I knew you way back when. You used to come to the Ne-store... not for the good prices on snacks, but to ask about certain out-of-place artifacts as you called them."

"Nestore?"

"That was my little store in the basement of my grandmother's house on the mini bike trail to the strip mine. I sold the riders stuff. Soda and chips. Back then I didn't think big... like I do now."

"And this root beer... Sup Dogs or Soda Pup —"

"So, you remember the Stray Dogs. Yeah, it wasn't Dog 'N Suds, but, that's good, too."

"Where might one find this good root beer?"

"Back then... King Coney, in Moofkooztee. It's in Southern Illinois. Little Egypt they call it, which is why you showed up looking for stuff. I always knew you weren't with an epigraphic society like you said. You were looking for artifacts all right, but not from tribes of blue-eyed natives. You were looking for doodads of civilization X... those who knew of a time when the gods walked amongst us. It was evidence of supreme beings, plural, that you wanted."

"You mean like rubble of ancient spaceports, Baghdad battery type stuff?" I asked while almost laughing in thinking about the irony if what he said were true. But was it? For all I knew, he was just reading from another one of Malcolm's scripts, "Okay, if you knew me, what was my name?"

"Zerrill... Sand."

That was the name on the passport that Malcolm had obtained for me. Had he finagled it through his connections, or was it my actual passport? Although there were a hundred things that I wanted to ask the conniving beanpole, for some reason I was intrigued by the connection with his name and the Nestorian diocese of California.

"What's with the Nestorian church? You're not a member just because of your name, are you?"

"My full name is Nestorius – just like the church's founder. Maybe I'm his reincarnation... come back to set things right after his teachings were railroaded by the false church. I'm a deacon now, but I've got bigger things in mind," he said while showing me his eastern Syriac cross. "This is the version of Christianity that's the closest to the original source. The Nestorians spoke Syriac – Jesus's own language. They were elite... the schnitz. With the money I'm saving, I plan to stay at a monastery in Iraq. While I'm there, I'll be looking for a scroll with unfiltered stuff... a smoking gun document. The same secret wisdom the Knights Templar discovered, which I'll sell to the highest bidder... so long as it's made public first. The truth. If I can't find it there, I'll go to Socotra Island in the Arabian Sea. At one time, all the inhabitants were Nestorians. Have you seen the weird vegetation? Looks like an alien world. It was once the home to the Phoenix... Cosmic dragons, too. Maybe why it's home to Earth's strangest plants."

Using my little trick, I once again gained access to Malcolm's secret room. As before, the profusion of whimsical greenman plaques was daunting. Trying to ignore the vegetation gods grinning at me from all sides, I further examined the large mural of the espaliered tree. Were the three golden buds on its otherwise barren limbs meant to represent the fruit I recently picked? The depiction of the ancient practice, along with the watching eye of a skull, could hardly be a coincidence – especially having seen the same arcane symbolism elsewhere on Malcolm's turf.

While looking for other clues as to what the Order of Free Gardeners might have their dirty fingers into, Malcolm walked in, seemingly not the least bit surprised to catch me rummaging through an antique wooden filing cabinet carved with stylized foliage that matched the rest of the Lodge room's folkloric décor.

"Would you look at what I found while doing a little busy work," I said. "After getting rid of this gaggle of leering greenery, Aaloka can finally have that extra storage space she's been wanting."

"You needn't bother with anymore of your clever bullshit. That photo you took of me wouldn't fool any retinal scan. We actually engaged in a good amount of trouble to get the system to allow you to enter without recognizing blood vessel patterns. Your face alone did it."

Placing his hands on the embroidered blue sash draped over one of the chairs at the table, the bergamot in his cologne caused me to edge away.

"This was your seat, Zerrill… when you were our star pupil. Despite allowing yourself to get sidetracked by other esoteric interests, you soared through the advanced grades. Which is why you were sent on an adventure."

"Pretending to be an ancient artifact hunter?" I asked, recalling what Nestor had told me.

"True, we gave you a good cover story - one sufficient enough to fool the locals."

"What was this errand I was selected for?"

"Errand?" Malcolm smiled while fidgeting with a lapis cufflink. "This wasn't the kind of thing where one draws straws."

"I'm going to listen to what you have to say, but don't take that to mean I believe what you're saying is the truth, Malcolm. I honestly don't know what to believe anymore... but something might have happened recently to cause me to rethink certain things."

"I can image. This adventure was quite a serious undertaking. The man you were sent to make the acquaintance of went by the name of Maxx Schaufler. Maxx was without equal for the knowledge he possessed. You could say he was a step above a human - though not by leaps and bounds - his brain was just wired a little different than the rest of us. Something in the genes. He was the last of an ancient dynasty known only in legends. Those the Enochian texts refer to as the Watchers. That's what made him unique... gave him his special abilities. The divine portion hadn't faded away as much in this family... wasn't as diluted with the mortal admixture alluded to in Plato's account. Another hint that has genetic implications can be found in Genesis: My spirit will not dwell with humanity forever. Despite these inherent faculties - or maybe because of them - Schaufler didn't reveal anything about his lineage. To the contrary, he masqueraded as a bog-standard type... with an affliction that made people not want to associate with him. This was part of his disguise."

"Maxx," I said softly. "Like Zyla's skull."

"We found that to be of interest as well. Schaufler's time left on earth wasn't long – even with his good genes. So that he didn't take this specific knowledge with him, our hope was that he would entrust it with us, even if locked away in the form of a terma to be divulged when the time was right. Sometimes a terma – which means treasure – might be written on a scroll that is concealed. After being discovered by the terton, or treasure finder, with the teachings now liberated, the script written on the scroll disappears... though this is not to be taken literally. However, in Schaufler's case, it would appear that the treasure was locked away by a different means... buried in the appointed terton's own head. Buried in your head, I'm afraid."

"I take it I didn't deliver the goods."

"The mind lock has proven to be nearly impossible to crack... protected as it is by the bewitching paralysis of hypnotic fluids. Yes, that which I negligently left on the bar didn't pertain to some ripping yarn. It was from – well, I'll get to that in a minute. There has only been a trickle of revelations so far, from your own account... triggered by a dream-incubator – "

"The Sandman Inn?"

"It would appear so. So, I'll ask - this time without the pretense of nicking material for some work of fiction - have you experienced a terma epiphany?"

"When you spoke of humans in the distant past being instructed by voices heard in their head, I think you might have been right about some people having left over traces of these embedded commands. In these dreams or visions, I had the impression of being in some futuristic setting, but after hearing something Nestor said, and having seen photos, could the island of Socotra hold the answer? There is flora... like the dragon blood tree... that looks like an umbrella... not found anywhere else."

"As much as I admire the varnish on a Stradivarius, the dragon blood tree or any other trees endemic to Socotra aren't worthy of a heroic voyage. Whether once the true Garden of Eden, or some latter ark of refuge, the tree in question was removed long ago. It was taken across the globe like the wandering of the Holy Graal to keep it from dying... by those who continue to tend to it."

"Then what is it that you don't know?"

"What the dreams haven't told - the ladder of divine ascent. How the fruit relates to the physicality of the gods... and their return."

"As crazy as that sounds, Malcolm, if I knew the answer, I'd be happy to tell you. But, the truth is – this treasure finder hasn't a clue. Like the text on your scroll, the messages on my computer from Ramiel pertaining to forbidden knowledge have magically disappeared."

"Seems Jag has been wagging his tongue again – telling a certain someone about an object you found. You know whom I'm talking about – his face is usually stuck to her rump. Evidently, the pair decided to sample the delicacy... like the Mexican Mabel did... believing the fruit was planted courtesy of ancient astronauts. They were unable to stop until no trace of it remained, though hopefully they didn't resume their pleasure with any chunder. When I told you about the bicameral mind and its lingering traces, at the same time I also mentioned the Qareen of Persian lore. Our ghostly double that lurks deep inside us, often casting wicked advice. Pardon me for painting such a grisly image, but there are those who would stop at nothing to possess such a marvelous thing as that implanted in your hand, and I would really hate to see it become someone else's charm."

"That sounds like a threat, even though I don't know what object you're talking about. It's a shame really that there's no paperback. I'm sure it would have all the makings of an imaginative narrative."

"I'm referring to the divine All-Seeing-Eye. Ancient biometrics, though hardly outmoded. That which can be used to cross unseen borders into neighboring realms. We know you didn't procure this... blurple from a dusty fruit stand —"

"We?"

Despite what you might think, I'm not overseeing this endeavor. You and I and the others in the Order worked at the behest of an organization. Just think of them as those who seek salvation from above. This organization is not to be trifled with. Like the hidden Qareem, they exert control from the shadows, Zerrill, and their shadows are all around. Knowing that you won't carry a lucky rabbit's foot, what I would suggest is that you give the specimen — now that there is only one left — to Aaloka and let her use her expertise at Cellectech to determine if it contains any unusual properties."

"Unusual? Meaning this ladder of ascent?"

"The organization has shown great patience... as well as incurred much expense to keep things — shall we say — in the bubble. Limited outside interference to your constant probing, but now their tolerance is waning."

I wasn't sure what he meant by this, but the thought occurred that he was referring to someone sabotaging my search for records (including DNA testing) that might confirm by identity.

"Your adventure is almost over," he said while patting the ceremonial regalia hanging on a chair.

"The thing you're missing here is that none of the occult machinations ever amounted to anything. Anything I might have found was purely the result of random occurrences while participating as a skeptic in the Paragon documentary. Clues from the filler and junk that clutters these popcorn tricks... so, how's that for a terma."

&

"We didn't eat it, periodt!" Jag shouted at me as I continued to question him about the missing piece of fruit. "I don't know what happened to it, but you've got another one so what's the problem? And your hiding them in a fake bowl of fruit with ceramic bananas and oranges was lame."

"Under a bunch of grapes just for a few days until I could find a better place. And how'd you know that? Also, how'd you get that skin rash?" I asked as Aaloka daubed his arm with calamine lotion.

"It must have been from the bushes out there when Zyla and I were geocaching."

"Please tell me you didn't geocache the blurple... even the remains."

Aaloka put her hand over her month to try and refrain from laughing.

"I'm sorry but that sounds funny."

"I wanted to call them grapples," I said with a dignified air.

This caused a snort of laughter.

"If you're gonna keep grilling me, mi-Grane, I'm gonna need a sparkling probiotic or root beer. The trackables were a link to Zyla's website... with ultrasonic mantras that Professor Hellmann told her might be a switch for our superbiology... like a caterpillar has. What's it called, mom?"

"Ecdysteroid."

"Link?" I asked.

On little papyri scrolls she bought at Walmart... if you want to know everything. I told her about the freaky piece of metal, but not about the gold... or the Cracker Jack prize," he added with a cryptic glance, "that we found because of my hacks."

"Gold?" Aaloka's eyes widened.

"There's no gold," I grimaced.

"I mentioned the blurples, but she didn't care because we found them in Arizona. The only plant she's interested in is called tchefit. It contains the star medicine the Atlanteans used to transform themselves into non-molecular bodies. It doesn't matter, anyway. I don't think Zyla wants to hang anymore... bet. She's all into Volker's sacred pregnancy stuff. I'll probably move to Iceland and become an elder in the Zuist church."

"Zuism? I shook my head. "Isn't that a mock religion... like the Flying Spaghetti Monster or Invisible Pink Unicorn?"

"No, it's based on modern ideas of the Sumerian religion. Like the Anunnaki."

"I thought that was Zitchenism?"

"As a member, I can donate my taxes to charity."

"What taxes?" Aaloka and I asked in unison.

"Look," Aaloka said while making herself a cup of chai, "I don't know what this blurple thing is, but in the bio-game, hybrid fruits are being created. Improved crossbreed variants like the Nectaplum that are supposed to have intense flavor. There's the orangequat –"

"It didn't come from a dusty fruit stand!" I snapped.

"I'd try a Nectaplum," Jag said while opening the fridge.

"When you do, let me know if it tastes as a good as a grapple?" my temper flared again.

"What's got you so wound up?" Aaloka asked. "Well, you and Malcolm can deal with this. Honestly, I might expect to hear about this stuff from a nineteen-year-old, but honey... honey you're... What caused you flip, Sheldon?"

"You mean, Zerrill, don't you?"

"Good, you're back to your blog," Aaloka said while bringing me a cup of coffee as I sat at my computer. "What's the latest thread from your loons?"

"The Blue Star Kachina," I sucked my teeth.

"Blue star creeper?" she laughed.

"Kachina. Zonnie is planning to go to one of the Hopi mesas in Arizona to watch the masked kachina dancers perform in the village plaza. She's been going on about one of their prophecies of the end of the current world and beginning of a new one... which wasn't an actual message from the elders, but came from a leaflet typed by a Christian pastor as part of a doomsday sermon. Granted, he was inspired after picking up a Hopi hitchhiker and listening to his ideas of a global crisis brought on by the white man's techo-worship. New agers supplied the rest of the story. It's not an inbound comet that they're waiting for, but the arrival of star beings from Sirius... of course. Zonnie is claiming that even NASA has admitted to having spotted the approach of the blue star, so the clock is ticking to the crunch moment."

"She's a weirdie, all right. Okay, so do your thing."

"Yeah... naw... Why?"

I had been neglecting the site ever since I got back from Arizona, and didn't feel like bothering with replying to the latest thread, especially since other researchers had already debunked the prophecy concerning the Blue Star Kachina.

As I was about to shut the computer down, I heard the door-bell ring. Figuring it was too early for one of Jag's DoorDash deliveries, I went to see who was there. When I opened the door, I was greeted by one of those couriers that rode electric yellow unicycles and dressed in funny yellow uniforms with mustard yellow beanies and matching sneakers.

"You're not the unicycle wheelie champion, are you?" I joked.

"Came in last place but I'm practicing hard," was the quick reply.

After handing me a small folder and getting my signature, he quickly departed.

When I opened the folder, I found another vintage postcard. This time it was an advertisement for the Sandman Inn in Mur-physboro, Illinois. Beneath a faded color photo of the budget lodging was the slogan:

FOR BETTER SLEEP AND BETTER DREAMS STAY AT
THE SANDMAN MOTEL

On the back was scrawled:

Beauty is in the beholder of the eye.
Check in early this Sunday to check out with answers.

I recognized the handwriting to be the same as on the last post-card. Once again there was no signature or return address, but this time the cancelled stamp was from Carbondale, Illinois.

The next morning I rented a safe deposit box to temporarily store the piece of fruit, which I sealed in a zip lock bag with a damp paper towel.

With the prospect of getting more answers, after chewing things over (factoring in that the anonymous sender had provided helpful information with his previous postcard), I decided to take the carrot and make the trip to the motel in southern Illinois. Since the location wasn't that far from where I had boarded a Greyhound bus bound for California back in December, I figured this increased the chances of someone putting together more pieces the puzzle.

Once the decision to go was made, I told Aaloka that I stashed the blurple in a safe deposit box at the bank and arranged for her to be the only other person who could open it. Should something happen to me (I planned to call her at a certain time each day), I told her to take the fruit to Cellectech to see if there was anything special about it. For the time being, though, she was to leave it locked in the box, and tell no one about its whereabouts, including Malcolm. I also told her that if anyone (again, including Malcolm) asked where I was, to say that I was attending an alien convention with a strange piece of fruit that might be from Zeta Reticuli.

Although she though I was being overly melodramatic (this without my mentioning the no-nonsense organization that Malcolm warned me about), she ultimately agreed that if I could learn more about my identity, it was worth making the trip. While in Little Egypt, she added, I should try that good root beer.

The Sandman Inn in Murphysboro was the oldest in the roadside chain, though it had recently undergone a renovation to include more modern touches. When I went to check in, I was told that someone had paid in advance for a three night stay that also included any incidentals.

When I entered my room, the first thing I noticed was that the traditional colored wallpaper of salmon, turquoise and marigold had been replaced with a fresh coat of pale blue paint. The second thing was a set of clothes neatly laid out on the bed. There were beige seersuckers, a pair of white Rockport Prowalkers and a tee shirt with the depiction of a generic flying saucer beneath which was written:

I DON'T WANT TO BELIEVE, I WANT TO KNOW

On the pillow was a note in now familiar handwriting that read:

Once checked in, put on the clothes on the bed. At noon, walk over to have lunch at the adjoining "Feed Bag" restaurant. Order whatever you want – the pepperoni stromboli is crud, but the smokehouse turkey burger is good – after taking one bite, return the plate to the KITCHEN with a look of disgust. DO THIS YOURSELF, DON'T LET THE SERVER TAKE THE PLATE.

Wearing the clothes that had been picked out for me (they fit perfectly), at the appointed time, I walked into the restaurant with its old-fashioned country kitchen kitsch décor. After being seated, the waitress brought me a mayo jar of ice water and a menu. Telling her that I already knew what I wanted, I pointed to one of the daily specials on a chalkboard easel and ordered the lousy stromboli.

After the dish arrived, I forked a piece of pepperoni and began chewing. No sooner was it in my mouth when I stood up from the checkered tablecloth with the farmhouse china in hand and headed towards the kitchen's swinging wooden doors. As I passed through them, the fellow with the Cartier sunglasses was waiting for me. He grabbed the plate and sprinkled a dash of canned Parmesan cheese onto the entrée before handing it to the person standing next to him. Seeing this man was like looking into a mirror. He could easily pass for my double, especially while wearing an identical outfit. With plate in hand, he exited the kitchen.

"The stromboli was a good choice," the man said with a gravelly voice and disarming smile. "No reason to waste a decent meal, right. Hello once again, Mister Sand. I hope you don't mind the clothes I chose, but its better if my partner deals with these unfuckwithable types. He's ex-Task Force Black and can handle most any situation."

"You knew that chip was under your boot, didn't you?" I asked.

"I got reimbursed."

"Why those boots?"

"They're great, aren't they?" he rasped. "Let's go through the back door here... and find some better mess for ourselves."

On the drive to a local farmers market, my hired "guardian" filled me in on certain things. His name was Kelby Timmons, and from what I gathered he was once a hotshot while in the Special Forces. Although he had retired years ago, he took on contract work in the private sector from time to time. It was he who sent the first postcard, saying he did so for no reason other than to see that his favorite crab shack got back their stolen curiosity piece. He used to eat there while training as an elite forces candidate in a fictional country on an estuary of the Patuxent River.

The second postcard was intended as a warning. He wanted to get me to a safer environment until certain things got sorted out. When I asked if Malcolm knew of my whereabouts, he responded with the word, "negative", before commenting that my friend was "quite the oxygen sucker." Kelby was also the caller during a recent podcast, who spoke about something called a beyonder that was discovered among the ancient ruins of Ur near the city of Nasiriyah in Iraq. Having experiencing a similar 'open sesame' at the lost mission of Cerro Ruido, I was very interested to hear what more he might have to say about this mysterious structure.

Kelby's beautifully crafted log and timber cabin was perched in a secluded cove on Cedar Lake in southern Illinois. Surrounded by sandstone bluffs and forested hills, it was fairly isolated for a popular recreational spot. While seated on a deck facing the wooded backyard, we sipped some good red wine under a starry sky.

"You do much hunting here?" I asked as he tossed handfuls of hickory nuts over the railing for the squirrels and opossums.

"Only for mushrooms like those I tossed in the salad," he said with his scratchy voice. "You were asking me about the thing we found in Iraq. That was one hell of a shock – gave the DoD boys quite a stiffie. Adaptive cloaking is one thing – but you can't get any more hyperstealth than a totally invisible structure.

There were Christians in the ranks that were mortified. To them it was a work of the devil, who they contend has many worshippers in the region…. like the Yezidis. As to what purpose the beyonder served other than a glorified connex, the only clues we have are from cuneiform sources. Temple hymns and the likes… about how the gods became disgruntled with their creation of humans. Humans were too damn loud… like a bunch of rowdy teenagers. The clamor kept them from sleeping. The only place to escape the hubbub was in these paradises... as humans called them. Paradises were restricted zones... that even the moonlight couldn't enter. Until, that is, some of the gods became so annoyed they decided to diminish the population. And when that didn't work, they left the planet."

"You're not suggesting these cranky gods were aliens from the stars, are you?"

"I don't know what these supreme figures actually were – transition kings after the withdrawal or, yes, our makers, but from the descriptions in the ancient tablets, the humanlike forms, even if conscious machines, embodied something called *melammu*. Now, *melammu*, or *melam*, is an interesting word. It was a divine radiance like the halos of Byzantine angels. A fearsome nimbus that caused a human's flesh to tingle when in its presence. In an interesting connection, the Yezidis worshipped the peacock angel... also known as Shaitan or Satan, so you have to wonder if this peacock angel alluded to the supra-luminal aura of the gods? The sect traces their culture back to the dawn of civilization and claims the story of their chief angel bearing forbidden fruit became distorted over time... besides the hatchet job done by the Church. Images of bird-gods found at the ruins at Gobekli Tepe dated at 12,000 years or older might add credence to their story... concerning the gods of Eden that bequeathed agriculture to their ancestors."

"Any idea how such things could have been made?"

"I've heard several theories to try and explain novel physical properties... besides the density profile of atomically thin layers of metals... stuff I've no understanding of. Whatever the thing is, it exists in an artificial dimension. Which brings us to ORMEs... Orbitally rearranged monatomic elements... that actually might be diatomic. Non-metallic forms of metallic chemical elements, meaning metals in a different atomic state."

"The same energizing properties of rare earth elements in that Cleopatra's Milk hokum they advertise?" I laughed.

"With the discovery of m-state elements, there are bound to be quacks with fake online diplomas from any university of their choice palming off the stuff as cure-alls. I'm sure the DoD encourages these hucksters with their snake oil. Hell, they probably initiated the idea."

"Poppycock to divert attention from the true anomaly?"

"As the story goes, a dirt farmer near Phoenix, while either conducting an analysis of sodium levels in his soil, or trying to leach gold from the black alkali, stumbled upon an unknown substance during the process. While I don't understand the scientific principles involved, by some mysterious process, while treating his sample, part of it disappeared, though the missing percent had to be somewhere. It couldn't have been translated into nothing. So the question is: Had he inadvertently discovered... or re-discovered a new form of matter? Something quite exotic. Perhaps, during the transition, a portion of this high-spin metallurgy, dubbed ghost gold, had been projected into a hyper-dimensional environment... which might explain the super camouflage of the beyonder... if the structure was fashioned in a similar manner.

And speaking of this farmer living near Phoenix, the process that produced the exotic material brings to mind the mythical bird that burns itself alive only to arise back to life from the ashes. It's said there are three phoenixes in paradise. The first is immortal, the second attains a thousand years and the third is consumed. The description of the phoenix is also interesting – its body was enhaloed with a striking peacock coloration."

When he went into the kitchen to pour some more wine, while watching moths batting softly against the hanging lanterns, my mind swirled with all kinds of scenarios. With the mention of "ghost gold", I thought about James Kidd. Might he have witnessed or heard about a similar phenomenon while using old mining techniques such as trying to extract gold from salt-encrusted dirt with cyanide or other solutions? If portions of gold or other precious metals had disappeared from the working material, he certainly would have wondered where it had gone. This non-identifiable, non-assayable gold that reappears with different qualities might have an analogue with a human soul that departs at death and ascends to some ethereal location called heaven. If someone were able to get a photo of the soul leaving, might it also be possible to capture the ghost gold in its higher form. Was a soul-endowed mineral behind his obsession with photographing the human soul? Or vice versa?

If the pocket watch I found was Kidd's, had he died of natural causes or exposure to the elements while at the lost Spanish mission marked on the *derrotero*? If so, his partner that brought him food and supplies might have left him there according to his wishes of not wanting his whereabouts to be revealed, even after he died. But why was his head cut off and why was he dressed in priestly duds? Was this done later by someone, like those who wrote the warnings on the pulpit, out of fear of some evil presence there? If the remains weren't Kidd's, maybe they belonged to the hermit of Cananea. Or maybe after Kidd's disappearance, he became the hermit people saw roaming about the area.

Another possibility to consider was that Kidd found the metallic disc with the mysterious eye near the church, but didn't know what to make of the thing. As a curiosity piece, he put it in his safe deposit box. Later it was removed either by him or someone pretending to be him. If this was the Spaniard, Castelar, who actually owned the mining claims, maybe the strange metal with its warped gleams and something about the striking golden eye on its surface spooked him – so much so – that he placed it in the pocket of the corpse hoping it would never be found.

While turning this over in my mind, Kelby returned with the glasses of wine.

"As you mentioned," he said, "now you have all kinds of dodgy characters hyping the mysterious substance. It was the secret of the medieval alchemists, and pot of metal in ancient Egyptian texts that represented one's soul weighed against a feather. It was manna and star food. Of its many virtues, some claim it interacts and corrects DNA. M-state materials can be retrieved from spring water, and they work wonders on plants. Makes them healthier and last longer."

"Don't forget it allows cats to grow back severed tails," I joked.

"Back to the beyonder – here's something else. You've probably heard of the Order of the Assassins and the Old Man of the Mountain, Hassan."

"I'm not that familiar with him. Only that the cult sprung up in the Middle East... and that Omar Khayyam was a contemporary."

"They were members of the same sect."

He set down his glass and quoted part of a verse from the *Rubaiyat*, which sounded funny with his grating voice.

"Oh, Thou who Man of baser Earth did make, and even with Paradise didst devise the Snake.

The cult formed in the Persian Mountains in the eleventh-century. Hassan was looking for candidates to do his bidding. He demanded blind allegiance from them. To find recruits, he came up with an idea. An artificial paradise that he created in a secluded valley that was accessible only by a secret passage. There was a luxurious garden with fragrant fruit and all kinds of delights. Maidens, wine, food - the whole nine yards. His candidates were young men in the area who were drugged and while unconscious transported there. When they awoke they found themselves in paradise, indulging in all its pleasures. Anything they desired. After a while, they were drugged again and returned to their dismal surroundings. If they became devotees of the Old Man, upon their death in his service, they would return to the paradise they witnessed first hand. The legend is considered to be just a fanciful tale like the Arabian Nights, but I started to wonder if the basis of the story might involve the restricted zone and privileged humans who were granted access to it for their loyalty. Maybe they were even given a certain object that was similar to today's biometric iris recognition devices. I trust you know what I'm referring to."

"Possibly." I nodded.

"The mother of all ooparts." He took another sip, before looking me straight in the eye. "Degrees of initiation... Revelations of a great secret... Things I guess you know all about."

"Well, that's what Malcolm told me, though I don't have any memory of being involved with this Order of Free Gardeners as it's called."

"I wonder how many more of these artifacts are out there?" he said while swirling the wine in his glass. "In someone's coin collection, perhaps. Maybe in a pawnshop or thrift store. A trinket in some Middle Eastern bazaar. Unlabeled curio in a bin at some museum. Or... in the ruins of a Spanish mission awaiting some lucky finder. Or, would that be an unlucky finder?"

Before I had a chance to react to this obvious inference, he excused himself and went back into the cabin, only to return a few minutes later with a tactical knife encased in a black scabbard. When he placed it on the table, its presence made me a little nervous. I doubted he set it there for my protection, as I was fairly sure with him being an all ex-special forces ranger that he had at least one gun stashed nearby.

"Some Yezeti kid found one," he said after taking a sip of wine. "He called it his Ized. Said it crawled inside his head to hide. Afterwards, he gained access to the beyonder, which, from what I heard was an empty dark void. Spic and span. Whatever it once might have contained was gone. He used it to escape the clamor of war. When the boys from Camp Liberty learned about this, some suggested he be given x-rays to locate it and have it surgically removed. To them, the kid was just another Haggi in the fucking sandbox."

"This was the high-tech device you alluded to during the podcast?"

He nodded gravely.

"They put two and two together after dozens of eye-idol figures were excavated. All of them with huge globular eyes of polished golden-topaz staring at the invisible beyonder."

Once again he quoted from the *Rubaiyat*:

"There was the Door to which I found no Key: there was the veil through which I might not see... Besides covert agencies within the government that want to secure all these things with crazy winking eyes, you've also the secret brotherhood of the Phoenix Empire... Phoenix Orientem. I'm concerned the gent on the council wearing the black crown might go kinetic to possess one... and not for smart camo applications, but because of the prestige that the beyonder was reserved exclusively for the gods and their representatives... the best specimens... humanity-plus, those with boosted genetics called semi-divine or demi-gods... By the way, what do you know about this Professor Hellmann that works with your wife at the biogenetic lab?"

"She's my partner," I corrected him. "Volker… he's supposed to be brilliant when it comes to genetic engineering, but he's got some peculiar ideas when he's off the clock. And he's getting up there in age… way up there."

"I'm not sure what game the venerable professor's playing, but I've heard some backchannel chatter that leads me to believe he's part of another shadowy association… or should I say, disassociation… that works for an organization known disparagingly as the distinguished Order of Mackerel Snappers, otherwise known as the Roman Catholic Church. The change-resistant Catholic Church," he emphasized.

"Volker? You're kidding. Really? That I would never have guessed. He's anything but change-resistant. He talks about ancient Egyptian concepts of regeneration while in cocoon-wombs. Of our larval state and potential refulgent imago. That's how he talks… but with what you just said… yes, that would make perfect sense if he were an infiltrator… having ideas so far out there."

"I'd imagine the Church has a mole embedded in every biotech lab. Human enhancement is one thing, but there's a dividing line. They don't want the gap to widen to the extent that it interferes with God's plan for humanity… or, especially, with their lucrative business. Both being eternal verities in their eyes," he joked. "Volker talks a lot to his Cardinal friend about a biolistic system that fires gold nanoparticles. Evidently, they don't use flintlock pistols at targets anymore. It sounds like they've got tools of high specificity at your partner's lab… tools for epigenetic modifications that reduce damage to cells. But, what I'm most intrigued by… is something he refers to as the Maker's Mark."

Without excusing himself this time, Kelby hurried back into the cabin. I wondered if he was privately communicating with someone, and if so, did it have to do with my situation. As I kept glancing at the knife, I recalled Malcolm's cryptic warning. For a second, I thought about jumping over the railing and making a run for it into the woods, though the prospect of being attacked by a bear or other wild animal while looking for another cabin caused me to think twice. With all that was going on in my head, I dismissed any ideas of him "going kinetic" on me as just being paranoid. After all, he slighted both Malcolm and the secret organization. Was he, himself, a kind of double agent in the brotherhood?

After a minute or so, he returned carrying a pie that had been heated in an aluminum container. He was also balancing a couple of Styrofoam plates and plastic forks.

"I hope you like apple streusel."

When he pulled the knife from its scabbard, I finally breathed a sigh of relief as he used it to carefully cut a couple of slices.

"I'm not a geardo... I just don't do the dishes often enough," he chuckled. "After dessert, you might want to rack out. In the morning, we're going to visit an old friend."

On a grey overcast morning, Kelby parked his SUV in front of a small rural cemetery that was surrounded by cornfields. Before visiting this old friend, he wanted to show me something. As I climbed out, he pointed to a gap in the rickety picket fence that we could easily pass through.

While stepping over pieces of mossy broken statuary on one of the overgrown paths that wound through the unkempt grounds, I noticed that most of the inscriptions on the worn headstones were unreadable, the names and dates filled in by lichen. Besides the scaly growth and slimy stains, many were also covered with graffiti.

Bending down, Kelby picked up a discarded can of red spray paint beneath a pitted marble stone that had also been defaced by vandals. Continuing on for a bit, he paused near a burial marker that appeared to have been recently erected. Unlike the others, its flawless surface sparkled as the sun peeked through the clouds. Etched into the marble were only two strange words:

YWLLWY * ELXXLE

"Why would anyone want to be buried here?" I asked. "With all the vandalism… knowing kids are going to be drinking and marking up the stone."

"This has been here for a long time. Decades actually. Over the years I'm sure many have tried to tag it, but, as you can see, none have been able to do so."

"What do you mean?"

He shook the can of spray paint and handed it to me.

"Here, go try yourself. Go on, see if you can."

At his insistence, somewhat reluctantly, I approached the tomb. There was a slight tingling that spread through my skin, and faint ringing in my ear. Next, my eyes began to vibrate, enough so that it distorted my vision. Before I was able to take another step, something in my head told me that I shouldn't or *couldn't* come any closer. Confused by this inexplicable feeling of dread, or whatever it was that, in essence, paralyzed me, I turned around and walked back over to Kelby, handing him the can.

"You're right, I can't. Why is that?"

"Probably a fear frequency... something akin to infrasound. Whatever it is, it's resonating at the right – stay away – frequency."

"Stay away from what? And where's it coming from? Who's buried here?"

"Are you missing rationality?" he smirked. "Where I'm taking you next – it's where they used to live. They're the reason you came here way back when. His name was Maxx Schaufler, also known as Molewhisker, otherwise know as Ywllwy, and the woman was his... partner."

Having crossed a decrepit railroad overpass that was also scarred by painted graffiti, Kelby made a left onto a lonely semi-rural road called "ShadowCrest." The first houses we passed on both sides of the oiled gravel stretch appeared to be vacated, with overgrown lawns, empty driveways and a few broken windows. Glancing back, an old tire swing hanging from a tree branch was filled with dried leaves.

Seconds later we parked in front of a large Victorian house, whose steeply pitched roof rose above the sycamore trees that dominated a well-maintained yard. With grey scalloped shingles, the roofline was multi-faceted, having a garbled dormer and protruding oriel windows complete with fanciful gingerbread trim.

"This is the so-called Looney Tunes house that you asked about. It once belonged to Schaufler, but your old friend lives here now."

Walking up to the wraparound porch, its white columns and ornate spindles appeared to be freshly painted. I could see nothing unusual about the façade – everything seemed perfectly normal. Weren't birds supposed to do something weird? I tried to recall what the cyber security guy said as I watched a cardinal flit from a tree limb in a typical manner. Then I remembered. Something about their flight patterns wasn't natural. They flickered and darted about in repeated loops, like the exact same background scenery rolling past on a low budget cartoon does. There was nothing bonkers going for the time being, at least that I could discern while climbing the flower pot-lined steps.

As we walked across the creaking wooden planks on the veranda, I observed a bluejay alight from a branch, again, just like you'd expect it to. Before Kelby could tap on the screen door, a woman was there to greet us.

"Hello, Patrice," he said while handing her a Tupperware container. "Some freshly picked morels. Look who I brought with me."

"Hello, Zerrill," she smiled widely with shrunken rosy cheeks."

Wearing a maroon *Salukis* sweatshirt and faded jeans, she had a pleasant face with little makeup and rimless glasses. Her long, straggly grey hair probably should have been cut much shorter at her age (she looked to be only slightly younger than me), but maybe it just needed to be washed.

"Addison, look who's with Kelby," she called to someone inside at the same time a man appeared alongside her. He was about the same age as her, clean-shaven with thinning grey hair and a narrow face. Unlike her gaunt form, his stomach bulged a bit where the pullover shirt reached dark brown chinos.

"Zerrill, how are you?" he smiled warmly.

As he gestured for us to come inside, I noticed that he had a slight facial tic that caused one eyelid to blink rapidly.

Glancing around, nothing on the inside of the house appeared to be out of the ordinary either. I was told the couple was proficient in the magical arts, which they engaged in regularly, but there was no indication of this with their choice of furnishings.

I definitely didn't expect to see Hummel figurines in a display cabinet, a Scrabble board on the coffee table next to a glass bowl of pinecones, nor framed black and white photos on the beige and sage green walls.

"I was expecting to see birds acting goofy or an icicle to come crashing down on the porch," I joked.

"Well, you should know," Addison said, "having spent years documenting these things. My favorite was your photos taken a year apart that showed smoke curling from the chimney making identical patterns. That and the beetle."

"I made grape salad," Patrice said while carrying a tray of brandy old fashions onto the porch where we were seated in rocking chairs. "Better for you, Kelby, than Butterburgers and Culver's sundaes. We'll have a hotdish for supper... with those morels you picked."

"Followed by gooey butter cake," Kelby laughed hoarsely.

We don't get bothered much these days," Patrice said after noticing me constantly glancing about. "Certainly no visits on early Saturdays by Jehovah Witnesses, though the Perkins Pancake people still gather in prayer across the street on some Sunday mornings."

"What can you tell Zerrill about when you knew him?" Kelby asked.

"You were interested in this house," Addison said as his one eye continued to twitch. "The protective barrier that surrounds it and makes it blend in with the neighborhood. Enables it to co-exist with our perceived norms, you used to tell me."

"From Addison's descriptions, the house might be a type of functioning beyonder," Kelby added, "that Schaufler lived in for decades... centuries, who knows... using some advanced technological means or powerful mind tricks like hypnosis taken to

the max," he smiled at his pun, "to disguise it from the world...
just as he disguised his own appearance."

He took a large gulp from the iced brandy.

"Let's just say that it was far more than the ramshackle Victorian that it appeared to others. The beyonder might extend
further into the town. This is a strange place – Mfkzt* – what
with the hidden inky black spaces."

It occurred to me that these strange black spaces recalled
the dim-green gloom of Shaver's cavern world, though, in his
stories, some of the caverns still contained abandoned metallic
enigmas and were 'pillered by mighty simulations of trees hung
with crystalline glittering fruit', as he described the bizarre visions he often experienced.

"You thought there was more to Schaufler than he let on,"
Addison said. "There was something very special about his
unique heritage, and the specific knowledge he might have
had of some prior advanced civilization that's now lost. He had
something you wanted – a diary of sorts - that you believed was
hidden under our little public library."

"Library? Why there?" I asked, almost with a laugh.

"Because of the color of the brick mortar. You thought traces
of the Atlantean metal, orichalcum, had been mixed in with it
as a signal... to draw someone's attention. It was during a caper
there one night after it was closed that you vanished without a
trace. Patrice thought you might have been conked on the head
by something that fell from a bookcase – "

"But Addison thought you might have walked into one of
those black whooshes that sometimes appear out of nowhere,"
Patrice said while looking at me with widening eyes. "Anyway,

---

* Pronounced Moof-kooz-tee

we didn't know what happened to you. There were reports... Well, the workers here claimed to see you wandering about in a confused state... based on your missing persons photo —"

"They didn't last long, did they... with all the bizarre goings-on," Kelby chuckled.

"But, then you showed up back at the library where my mother worked," Addison said. "Since you didn't have any memory of your past, she got you some treatment and gave you a job there. In your spare time, you read nearly every book. After a while, you left. There were rumors that you worked at the main branch in St Louis, but we didn't check. This was so many years ago. Anyway, we lost touch until Kelby responded to someone looking for you in California. He did the rest, and now you're back."

As we continued to talk, an unmarked black cargo van pulled in front of the house by the adjacent garage. There was a slight look of concern on Kelby's face until a middle-aged man and woman climbed out and walked up to the porch.

"Hello there, we're pickers from Freeport", the man said. "Any chance we could have a look at what's under the tarp? The wheels look interesting. I could see those cloisonné hubcap medallions from the road. Who's the owner?"

"I am," Addison said while standing up. "Sure thing, you can take a look."

The three of us got up and followed him to the gravel driveway where a weathered tarp covered a vehicle. When he removed it, the couple was amazed by their find.

"Whoa! Look at that honey. A hearse hot rod. 1951 Packard Henny. Nu-3-Way!"

"Is that the original Thunderbolt eight cylinder and selective silent slush-box?" The woman asked, barely able to contain her excitement. "Awesome lettering."

The chopped matte black frame of the old funeral coach that had been converted into a street rod was pinstriped with a flamboyant cursive green script that read:

WILL O' THE WISP

Its chrome grille and showy green hubcap emblems gleamed in the sun. Other custom details added to the gravedigger theme, such as square black lanterns for exterior lights and a strand of rusty barbed wire that engirded the roof. There was even a wooden coffin in the back.

"The guy who built it – Maxx – was the town's undertaker and a 50s greaser. He headed a local hot rod club back in the day. They called him the grim-beeper."

"I can't believe the condition," the man said while running his finger along the body. "Not a speck of dust. Ever think about selling it? Mind if we get inside?"

"Go right ahead," Addison said.

Thrilled to have the opportunity, the two climbed inside.

As they geeked out over the unique gauge bezels on the dash panel and added chrome skull stick shift, I noticed a glass eye had been inserted into the left eye-socket. The eye was bulging and bloodshot so that it resembled "Rat Fink" art. When I braced my hand on the window to get a better look, I heard a guttural shriek.

"What's it doing?" This was followed by a high-pitched scream. "Oh my God!"

Both quickly pushed their doors open and jumped out.

With all the color drained from his face, the man backed away in a state of sheer terror.

"How'd it do that?" the woman repeated while hyperventilating as she walked around in circles. It looked like she peed her pants. "You've no right to play tricks like that!" she shouted to us as both hurried back towards the van and jumped inside before it sped away.

"What caused her to piss herself?" Kelby rasped before draining his old fashioned.

Patrice and Addison were staring at me without saying a word.

As Addison started to put the tarp back over the vehicle, I looked back inside at the one-off dash components, but didn't see anything that would cause such a terrified reaction.

While Kelby helped Patrice prepare dinner, Addison and I were in the back yard, walking on grass that had been freshly mowed. The view beyond the lawn was a bleak dirt field of soybeans and copse of denuded trees.

"I have to mow the lawn myself," Addison said. "I tried to hire some kids but after the first time they never return. Even to get paid. The lawn does funny things, too."

"Funny things," I repeated softly. "Kelby told me that when you were a young boy Schaufler played tricks with your head. Even had you believing you were some kind of mind form that he created and controlled for some purpose."

"You also thought I was a terton... Do you remember what that means? I was part of Ywllwy and Elxxle's plan to preserve the knowledge that was purposely held back from the condensed Eden story. I am the lacuna, if what I was led to believe is true. But, is it? Or, is this burden your fate?"

While enjoying Patrice's salmon potato cakes, wild rice pilaf and Kelby's sautéed mushrooms, we were startled by a loud clatter. It sounded like handfuls of small rocks were being thrown against the house's wood siding. This was followed by something clinking the glass of the front windows. Rather than jumping up to see what the noise was, the others remained calm while continuing to eat, albeit with annoyed expressions.

"We've been corned," Addison told me. "A little early, though. The leaves haven't even changed color yet."

"It's a local fall tradition," Patrice explained after seeing my puzzled look. "Youngers around here pelt the sides of houses in the neighborhoods with kernels of field corn dried to a pebble-like hardness. But, it doesn't usually happen until around Halloween."

"I thought maybe icicles had broken off and fallen onto the porch," I joked.

"Kelby and I used to do it," Addison grinned. "We had bags of the really loud stuff from Hubb Ohlendorf's field. Tossed it at everything. Windows, siding and gutters, you name it... after knocking back a few cans of gusto. Liquid courage. Remember that time Spitzer wanted to corn his own parents' house?" he said to Kelby.

"Ollie was a real piece of work," Kelby shook his head while chewing his fish. "Didn't he used to tell us that his mother asked him to remove ticks from the hard to reach places on her naked body while she was in the shower."

"Are you talking about Oliver Spitzer... the computer hacker?" I asked while taken by surprise.

"We always knew he'd amount to something," Kelby chuckled.

"I contacted him about some issues I was having with my blogsite. I didn't know you were friends. But, now... yeah... it was he who first mentioned the looney... this house... your house. The site was being breached by someone called Ramiel - the leader of a cult of Enochites – leaving weird messages about scrolls encoded with fire letters... keys to higher communications and a hidden tree that's beyond the dust of Eden. You should have seen the intensity of the typography. The text almost looked like it actually was ablaze."

Once again Addison and Patrice stared at me without saying anything. Finally, Addison broke the silence.

"Zerrill, you are Ramiel."

I was seated in a rocking chair on the veranda, drinking another brandy old fashion and swatting at fluttering moths, as Addison swept the scattered corn into a pile. The only minor damage caused by the "corning" was a broken pot of geraniums that got knocked over.

"Your condition could be compared to the collective condition of cultural amnesia," Addison said. "Schaufler ... Ywllwy, whatever you want to call him, was nostalgic. During one of his numerous experiments on his own neural workings, something extraordinary happened. There was an intrusion during the procedure – like with your hacker – from what he thought to be a divine presence. The being didn't impart immediate illumination. Instead, it possessed Schaufler in a curious manner. For the rest of his time with us, he had serious regrets for enabling this emigrant to enter the human life-wave. Patrice called it a buttinsky, but it was actually a foreshadow projected by the pre-dominance of a latent, yet advanced genetic sequence."

He set the broom against one of the Doric columns and peered out at the heat lightning that flared in the distance.

"Just like the primal state that exists in the unstable hybrid we humans are, there also exists its antithesis, and that's what Schaufler was initially hoping to bring about. It might seem odd, for someone with the hubris of the so called fallen angels, that he would become conflicted, and later adopt the position that any further mutations of major consequence should be a natural gradual process in accordance with the makers' plan, but that's what he did. Perhaps he realized the implications of any tampering. However, the emigrant – again, a manifestation of the rapid ascendancy of the more advanced non-human genes – had a different agenda. Whether or not our full potential is time-released, even with the upward drive of their genes, or permanently limited by the masters as an inherent incompatibility, Schaufler suspected a rogue engineer, or faction of them that looked upon their creation without cold indifference, or even came to regret genetic tailoring to such a degree simply for practical purposes, anticipated an upgrade brought about by occult means."

"You're saying these limitations can be bypassed?"

"This is where your Ramiel fits in. If you experienced a terma perception, Schaufler didn't initiate it. He didn't think you were a suitable candidate, because your trans-human aspirations were at odds with his own conviction against any neurological interference.

As a precaution, to counter any activity by his infected other half, he introduced opposite views … providing mental filters that shaped your reality-tunnel, especially when it came to astronaut gods. With these messages concerning the hidden tree, it appears that the emigrant may have been busy in your subconscious mind, having slipped through the cracks once again."

"This thing in my subconscious must also have been one hell of a computer whiz," I said.

"Granted, the emigrant manifests itself rather bizarrely."

It was a lot to absorb, even if these explanations were just abstruse meanderings in his own head. Arcane chunks he stirred into an esoteric stew. After all, didn't he once think his own existence was merely a thought-form. And yet, some of the pieces did fit together - his conclusions providing answers to my own concerns.

For some reason I thought about the dero trapped in a series of caverns where they tormented humans. Did the story of their rebellion have an analogue with the limitations the engineers placed when fashioning their slave workers? Were the impressions that swirled in Shaver's bewitched grey jelly derived from the perspective of the advanced code? That buried deeper within? Hidden in the genetic scrap pile, though capable of being activated by some means, just like the abandonderos' ancient star mech.

I must have nodded off for a bit while watching television from a recliner in the living room. When I awoke, I could hear the muffled voices of the others talking out on the porch. The picture on the screen wavered as an old black-and white movie was playing. The volume was so low that I couldn't hear what was being said, but from the grainy scenes of scuba divers examining a barnacled hulk on the murky seabed, I knew that it was a sunken treasure film.

Sharks were gathering around the stumps of mastheads of the ancient galley, on whose rotting prow was painted an eye. Sloppy jump cuts to an anchored yacht bobbing in the foam-capped waves above the shipwreck were awash with amber tints and sickly lavender tones.

After a sequence of two divers engaged in a dramatic knife fight near a reef in the shark-infested waters, I quickly realized that I had seen this terrible movie before – enough times that I knew some of the cheesy dialogue by heart.

With my attention focused on the action on the screen, I hadn't noticed the television set itself. It was a bulky floor model from the early 1960s, with a rabbit ears antenna on its scarred wood console. Before dozing off, I had been watching the news on a modern flat screen, not this obsolete thing.

Brushing my hand against tattered fabric, I released that I was also no longer seated in the leather La-Z-Boy. Looking around at the mildewed wallpaper in the flickering of the old Zenith, I saw that the corners of the ceiling were swathed in dirty cobwebs. The windows were blacked out by cheerless drapery, and there was a funny smell – like putrid tobacco spit or someone's bad breath. Maybe it was coming from the small aquarium that needed to be cleaned. In the cloudy water, a small fish glided in loops around a resin model of a shipwreck amid painted coral skeletons.

Realizing that I wasn't dreaming, when I got up out of the dingy recliner, Addison appeared in the entranceway. As he walked across the water-stained oak floor that was littered with small pieces of plaster that had fallen from the ceiling, he didn't appear to be surprised by neither the neglect nor the room's out of date furnishings.

"When I saw the look on the faces of those pickers this afternoon, I had a feeling you had an othering token. And now I'm sure of it," he said.

"I don't remember where or when," I said with a blank stare, "but I've seen this movie before. Many times. Everyone dies except the buxom blonde daughter of the main treasure hunter, who is saved by Captain Nemo in the Nautilus. In the end, she finds a purse of priceless ancient coins tucked into a hole in the hull in the small painted model of the shipwreck inside an aquarium at her father's dockside bar."

"The hole is a hideaway designed for fish in a tank... as the opening scene hints at," Addison smiled. "It's not a real movie... not like you'd see at the mall or even the old Bijou Theater reruns on television we used to watch as kids. It was whipped up by Schaufler... somehow... just like this room was, including the chronic halitosis. I think he did it to test me, because the stupid plot and the scantily clad woman in the bikini led me to find an othering token inside the model shipwreck... an ancient galley, as you can see, just like in the film. At first I thought it was just some worthless doohickey of his, but I found out it could be used to cheat vending machines for free pop and so on. Just like a slug does, only it was always returned. Later, I learned about the other things it could do. I think it belonged to Elxxle before she passed. I imagine you got yours from Schaufler... that it was presented to you by the zealous half of his split character."

"I found mine in the Arizona desert... in the same place I found the fruit."

There were repeated spasms in his eye as he put his hand on my shoulder.

"Come, let's talk about this, but not in this nasty othering"

"But with that, you also get this," Addison said while opening the back door.

When I stepped out back, I was shocked to see that the drab lawn, extending well into the monotonous patches of soybeans, had been transformed in the blink of an eye into a massive vivarium of spacious manicured grounds, whose ingenious gardener had conjured botanical wonders that glimmered dreamlike within its invisible framework.

"What do they say about a little slice of paradise," he said while spreading his arms wide to embrace the palpable enchantment of some futuristic agronomy.

Soon, we were strolling on luminous paving stones with swirling green patterns that wound through a labyrinth of exquisite miniature forests and small moon-dappled ponds over which floated softly-lit transparent globes teeming with leafy enigmas. All about, night-flowering delights morphed with a variegated

rhapsody, exuding curious perfumes while unfolding amid virescent chimeras. Between abstract topiary pulsing with a subtle
radiance, a couple of silver lounges were suspended in the scent-
ed breeze under flickers of stars. While inhaling these vegetative
wonders, surges of euphoria throbbed in my brain.

"To give you an idea of the complexity involved, a grape has
more genes in its DNA than the human genome does, but that
doesn't mean someone in a white coat can't find what they're
looking for. What then? I'd start by looking for signs of incom-
plete melding between the strains that resulted in the intermit-
tent sequences that creationist geneticists are loath to call junk
genes. Retrieve. Delete. Insert. I can't tell you what to do with
this thing you... chanced upon, but I've told you about Schaufler's dilemma. We're not talking about semi-synthetic biology.
Not the funny stuff... or even highly customized results. We're
talking about a new genetic system. Think about the traits of all
of humankind's past geniuses rolled into one.

Einstein, da Vinci, Aristotle, Ramanujan, Tesla and Py-
thagoras. All their combined abilities - even magnified by you
name the percent - would fall pitifully short of the capability of
a being with each function zone of its brain turned on. Suppose
the being can self-impregnate. We would no longer be the paragon of life - the masterpiece of creation. How might the being
react to these lowly creatures that it could easily dominate? If the
evidence in the ancient narratives is accurate, we already know.
After the reunion, would it enslave us again? Would we gradually become specimens in its zoos? Maybe it would quickly fashion
a spaceship to search for its own kind. Who knows, but do you
want to roll the dice?"

When I asked him if he had any information as to where
humankind's lofty progenitors came from before their arrival

on the Earth, he said that the only clue he had might be from something he had once seen. This occurred many years ago, after Patrice had managed to activate what he came to believe was Elxxle's personal satellite – this being the mysterious device that he earlier referred to as an "othering token" that Schaufler had arranged for him to have. (He even suggested the possibility that the object might have once floated inches above or orbited around Elxxle's head, where it glowed like the halos depicted in ancient art with holy people.)

Though the autumn night sky was somewhat overcast at the time, the small metallic disc had projected the image of what at first appeared to be an exceptionally bright star (even brighter than Sirius). While it remained in view, they quickly realized that it resembled a planet more than a star, as it didn't twinkle. After it winked out, they consulted an ephemeris and determined that it wasn't one of the known visible planets in our solar system. Later, they wondered if it might have been a marker of some kind – perhaps someone's way of indicating where their home planet was located. Whatever the object was, it was only visible for a short time and neither of them ever saw it again.

When he finished telling me this, Addison looked me in the eye and said, "Who knows, maybe they originated on the Earth...left, and then returned."

After we thanked our hosts for dinner and said our goodbyes, as Kelby and I were walking to his SUV, the porch light came back on before the front door squeaked open.

"Hey, you forgot your Tupperware and gooey butter cake," Patrice shouted while standing behind the partly opened screen door.

When I walked back to get this, I saw that Addison had joined her. While reaching for the container, once again I got a glimpse of the othering that existed behind the old house's afflicted layers. This only lasted for an instant, but what I perceived was just as startling as the transformed back yard.

Both were standing on an invisible floor that made it appear as if they were floating above the elaborate furnishings in a spacious lower level whose curved silver-toned walls were identical to those of the sizable ground level. Each had striking, unblemished faces that were framed by intricately-sculpted white braids. The garments they wore looked like streams of eddying gold, whose glistening swirls matched the color of their marvelous (albeit, unsettling) irises.

Beneath a sloped ceiling of metallic glass, the ultramodern décor was suffused with a soothing bluish 'innershine.' As some of the decorative fittings morphed while continuing to blend seamlessly with the other household effects, I caught sight of some of the perplexing appliances behind these features before their flickering textures wavered and the generic living room that I had first walked into reappeared.

If what I saw was real, the two radiated an ageless beauty while living in the unimaginable comfort of a hidden futuristic abode that they had somehow become heir to.

The first thing I did when I returned to California was to check the safe deposit box. Seeing that the blurple was missing, I called

Aaloka. When she didn't answer after several tries, I called Jag. He said he didn't know where she was, but informed me that Volker had died.

While stuck in traffic on the way home, all kinds of scenarios raced through my head. Had Malcolm or the Phoenix group forced her to take the fruit, and, if so, were she and her colleagues at Cellectech analyzing it for its alien DNA? Recalling what Kelby said about the Professor's possible allegiance with the Church, I wondered if foul play had been involved with his death? At his age, it was mostly likely due to natural causes, but how easy would it be to make it appear that way if they needed him out of the picture so that he couldn't interfere with their plans.

In a state of panic, I called Kelby and told him about my concerns. He told me to sit tight while he looked into the matter. Before hanging up, I tried to convince him that we needed to get a hold of Volker's biometric glass eye, either from the morgue or funeral home, in case we had to break into the secret area of the bio lab called the Stork's Nest. I wanted to get the blurple back, I told him, not just because of Addison's impassioned plea, but also to use as a bargaining chip against any further harassment from the Order. Again, he told me to sit tight and that he'd be in touch.

When I got home, Aaloka was sitting at the kitchen table.

"Why'd you take it?" were the first words out of my mouth.

"Because it's safer here," she replied. "When Malcolm insisted I give him the contents of the safe deposit box, I gave him the piece of metal that's supposed to be from a crashed flying saucer that one of your readers sent for you to have analyzed."

"What the hell are you talking about?"

"You know, the thing that Jag saw," she said with a sly smile, "and blabbed about to Zyla. I know this guy from my Stanford days who works for a government contractor developing metal foam, and, as a favor, he gave me a sample of one of the pieces that didn't meet the criteria. So, you don't have to worry about Malcolm or the others any more."

"Why'd you do that?"

"When I was younger I fell in love with this guy named Zerrill. He was into all kinds of weird things. He went away for a while to learn a secret, but he didn't return for a long long time. Even though, during all that time I still had strong feelings for him, I eventually got married. Had Jag. Then one day I heard he had been found, but without any memory of his past, or even why he had left. Believing this secret was locked away in his mind, to obtain it, an arrangement was suggested… and I agreed, mainly because I still loved him."

"So, where's the piece of fruit?"

"It's hiding in plain sight."

She walked over and opened the refrigerator, sliding out a crisper drawer from which she picked up one of those Blueapple containers that she used to make produce last longer. Unscrewing the plastic lid, she removed the blurple. Instead of handing it to me, she held it up to her mouth. Before I had a chance to react, she closed her eyes tightly and bit into it. There was a look of extreme pleasure on her face as she chewed. When she licked her lips, a faint bluish liquid trickled down her cheek.

"Can I tempt you to take a bite?"

When she handed it to me, after hesitating for a second, I sunk my teeth into its funny texture. I was expecting it to be flavorsome, but didn't anticipate the intensity of the exotic, floral sweetness balanced by slightly bitter, rich earthly tones. When I handed it back to her, a tapestry of strangely delicious flavors lingered on my tongue. Only then did I understand the word, ambrosia.

We continued to pass it back and forth until the flesh was gone and only the stem and sliver that contained some seeds remained.

Without saying a word, Aaloka gathered this up and tossed it into Jag's indoor worm composter. She then plopped down on the couch and reached for me with her slender fingers.

Though Punyaaloka was slammed during holiday season, it was still too early for the dinner crowd. Taking a break from bartending, I was sitting on a stool, munching on a piece of papadum when part of the wafer crumbled in my hand onto the dark green marble.

"You still getting crumbs everywhere, honey," a voice rang out behind me. "Your poor mother having to clean that high-chair."

When I turned around, I saw the black woman that I once had a conversation with about bioethics, and later had reason to believe was entangled in some way with the affairs at Cellectech. She was wearing the same multicolored headwrap as before, and when she sat down next to me I had a chance to steal a glance at what I thought was a prosthetic left eye.

"I have something that might be of interest to you."

"Yeah, what's that?"

"A secret, baby."

"You've a secret for me?"

"The secret spice that gives the chutney here its zing. It's not amchur powder or minced red ants... or even Aleppo pepper as I thought. It's a rare spice that comes from Socotra. The Jewel of Arabia. It's from a plant species that's... what's the word... endemic to the island. The name, Socotra means paradise in Sanskrit. That's how I figured it out."

While listening to her, I glanced down at a text message from Zonnie. She was telling me that the Blue Star Kachina, Saquasohum, had just removed its mask in front of the crowd of tourists in the ceremonial plaza on the Hopi reservation in Arizona. The message ended by saying that this was the final sign of the beginning of the new world. Hooray! she added with a smiley emoji.

"There he is," I uttered as Jag walked in. "Only one hour late for work. Not bad. Not bad, at all."

"There's something from one of those yellow fellows in your office," he said, looking dejected by having to show up for work.

"All right, well you'd better get started making the syrup for those Starflowers. And don't forget the ice cubes with the borage flowers in them."

I excused myself and headed to the office to see what the courier brought.

When I opened the folder, I saw a scan of a sonogram that showed fetal development during the first trimester. I couldn't make out details of the blurry image, and the name, dates and other information printed on it had been redacted with a black marker, but under the image, someone had scrawled:

The Godling

I slid the sonogram back into the envelope and examined its cover for a return address. Seeing that it was blank, I went to question Jag in the private party room.

"There was no courier, was there. Where'd you get this?" I waved the folder in his face.

"It was geocached. The link to a website was, but its been taken down. I wasn't supposed to tell anyone, but I thought you should know about it."

"Look me straight in the eye, Jag. Did you take that piece of fruit?"

"No, like I kept telling you. No."

This time I believed him. I had been played by all of them, Jag excluded. They didn't need the last piece – they had the other one all along. No wonder Aaloka didn't care about it. All they needed was to distract me for a while so I couldn't get in the way of their work. The plan worked perfectly.

I went into the room where the main bar was to confront Josephina, or whatever her real name was, but saw that she had left. I hurried to the front door, hoping to catch her. When I stepped outside, it was raining hard. Ducking back inside, I grabbed an umbrella from the stand. It was a black one. Clicking the hand-spring, it snapped open. When I rushed into the parking lot, I spotted her getting into a passenger van with a to-go bag. As I ran towards it, I was blocked by the valets attending to arriving guests. Making my way through the maze, I banged on one of the beaded side windows of the van. When it rolled halfway down, I saw Zyla with her head raised, looking straight ahead. For the first time I could remember, she wasn't dressed like a sci-fi queen in a form-fitting silver ensemble. Instead, she was wearing an indigo V-neck maternity blouse.

She was pregnant.

As the van moved forward, while maintaining a dignified silence, she rolled the window up.

I was surprised that she didn't bother to wink.

ABOUT THE AUTHOR

The Paragon Junk is the second novel by **Blair MacKenzie Blake**, with his first one entitled *The Othering* (together being part of a projected trilogy). He is also the author of *Ijynx* (a collection of occult prose-poems), *The Wickedest Books In The World – Confessions Of An Aleister Crowley Bibliophile* (issued in three impressions), *The Curious Diary Entries Of Verity Pennington* (a short story), and is one of the co-authors of *Remember The Future*. He has contributed essays to ten volumes of the anthology *Darklore*, as well as to numerous esoteric-themed magazines, including *The CoSM Journal, Sub Rosa, Silkmilk* and *Dagobert's Revenge*. For over 21 years, BMB has been the writer/content manager for www.toolband.com and www.dannycarey.com. He currently resides in Las Vegas, NV.